W9-DGN-996

"IT'S TRULY EXTRAORDINARY," HE SAID . . .

"Who would believe it? 'Jewish girl risks all for German soldier,' Tell me, Patty Bergen—" his voice became soft, but with a trace of hoarseness—"why are you doing this for me?"

It wasn't complicated. Why didn't he know? There was really only one word for it. A simple little word that in itself is reason enough . . .

SUMMER OF MY GERMAN SOLDIER

Bette Greene's award-winning novel
The story of a very special friendship

"Courageous and compelling!"

—Publishers Weekly

Summer
of My
German Soldier

Bette Greene

BANTAM BOOKS
TORONTO · NEW YORK · LONDON · SYDNEY

*This low-priced Bantam Book
has been completely reset in a type face
designed for easy reading, and was printed
from new plates. It contains the complete
text of the orignial hard-cover edition.*
NOT ONE WORD HAS BEEN OMITTED.

RL 5, IL age 11 and up

SUMMER OF MY GERMAN SOLDIER
*A Bantam Book / published by arrangement with
The Dial Press*

PRINTING HISTORY
*Dial edition published October 1973
2nd printing . . . March 1974*

Bantam edition / November 1974

2nd printing . . . . . June 1975   9th printing . . . January 1979
3rd printing . . . October 1975   10th printing . . . August 1979
4th printing . . September 1976   11th printing . December 1979
5th printing . . . . August 1978   12th printing . . . . . May 1980
6th printing . . September 1978   13th printing . November 1980
7th printing . . September 1978   14th printing . . . . . May 1981
8th printing . . . October 1978   15th printing . . . October 1982
8th printing . . . October 1978   16th printing . . . April 1984

*Starfire and accompanying logo of a stylized star
are trademarks of Bantam Books, Inc.*

*Cover photos courtesy of Highgate Pictures—A Division of
Learning Corporation of America.*

All rights reserved.
Copyright © 1973 by Bette Greene
*This book may not be reproduced in whole or in part, by
mimeograph or any other means, without permission.
For information address: Dial Books for Young Readers,
a Division of E. P. Dutton, Inc.,
2 Park Avenue, New York, N.Y. 10016.*

ISBN 0-553-24565-1

Published simultaneously in the United States and Canada

Bantam Books are published by Bantam Books, Inc. Its trademark, consisting of the words "Bantam Books" and the por-
trayal of a rooster, is Registered in U.S. Patent and Trademark
Office and in other countries. Marca Registrada. Bantam
Books, Inc., 666 Fifth Avenue, New York, New York 10103.

PRINTED IN THE UNITED STATES OF AMERICA

H   24 23 22 21 20 19 18 17 16

For
Ann Sternberg
&
Donald S. Greene, M.D.
My Superstars

1

WHEN I SAW the crowd gathering at the train station, I worried what President Roosevelt would think. I just hope he doesn't get the idea that Jenkinsville, Arkansas, can't be trusted with a military secret because, truth of the matter is, we're as patriotic as anybody.

In front of the station house five or six Boy Scouts in full uniform circled their leader, Jimmy Wells, who was wearing the same expression Dane Clark wore as the Marine sergeant in *Infamy at Pearl Harbor*. "This is the situation, guys," Jimmy said. "The sheriff told me it's the Army's job to get the Nazis off the train and into the prison camp, but I figger they'll be mighty glad to have us Scouts on hand. And if any of those rats try to make a getaway"—he slapped the leather-encased Scout ax strapped to his waist—"we know what to do."

I looked around for a friendly group to join. Mary Wren was holding onto the arm of Reverend Benn's wife as though that was going to provide her with the Lord's own protection. There are plenty of jokes going around about our town's telephone operator. People say Mary is so generous that she'll give you the gossip right off her tongue.

Then I saw old Chester, the colored porter from my father's store, closing his eyes against the brilliant June sun.

I walked over. "Hey, Chester, don't you think this is the most exciting thing that has ever happened to our town?"

His eyes jerked open. "I'm going back to the stock room right now, Miss Patty. Ain't been gone more'n two, maybe three minutes."

"Don't go on account of me, Chester. I won't tell my father. Honest." Chester smiled wide enough to show his gold tooth. "I've never in my whole life seen a German, I mean, in person. Have you?"

"I seen some foreigners once, but they was fortune-telling gypsies."

I looked over to where Sheriff Cauldwell, Mr. George C. Henkins, the president of the Jenkinsville Rotary Club, and Mr. Quentin Blakey, editor of the *Rice County Gazette,* were standing on the gray-white gravel. "I wonder what the sheriff is saying about all this," I said, heading toward them.

Mr. Blakey's head was pitched back to look into the sun-and-leather face of the sheriff. "I said, 'Captain, I know you're only doing your job as a public information officer, but I'll never understand why I'm not supposed to write about what everybody here already knows about.'"

"That's telling him, Quent," said the sheriff, looking amused.

"More to it than that," said Mr. Blakey. "Captain wouldn't tell me how many POW camps there are or where they're located, but after a while he forgot about security—told me that up in Boston they got a bunch of Italian prisoners who do nothing but clean up after the elephants in Franklin Park."

Sheriff Cauldwell leaned his big head back and laughed the laugh of the healthy. "Captain wasn't talking security, he was talking crap."

From down the tracks, a whistle. Jimmy Wells ran over to one of the rails, dropped to his knees, and pressed his ear against it. His features were molded

2

into Dane Clark's odds-are-against-us-but-we-can-do-it expression as he announced, "She's a-coming!"

All talking stopped and the small clusters of people began merging into one single mass. Even Chester, the only Negro, was now standing in arm-touching contact with whites.

Then amid hissing, steamy clouds of white, the train braked, screeched, and finally came to a halt.

From the crowd a woman's voice—it may have been Reverend Benn's wife—asked, "Well, where are they?"

Jimmy Wells pointed to the last passenger car. "There!"

Everyone hurried toward the end of the train in time to see two GIs with their side arms still strapped in their holsters step quickly from the car. Then came the Germans. The crowd moved back slightly, leaving a one-person-wide path between themselves and the train.

The prisoners were unhandcuffed, unchained young men carrying regulation Army duffel bags. They wore fresh blue denim pants and matching shirts, and if it hadn't been for the black "POW" stenciled across their shirt backs you could easily have mistaken them for an ordinary crew from the Arkansas Public Works Department sent out to repair a stretch of highway. I tried to read their faces for brutality, terror, humiliation—something. But the only thing I sensed was a kind of relief at finally having arrived at their destination.

"Nazis!" A woman's voice shouted. And this time I knew for sure that it was Mrs. Benn.

A blond prisoner who was stepping off the train at that moment stopped short then smiled and waved. It was as though he believed, or wanted to believe, that Mrs. Benn's call was nothing more than a friendly American greeting.

3

I raised my hand, but before I completed a full wave Mary Wren pressed it down, shaking her head.

"I'm sorry, but I didn't think it would be polite—I guess I just forgot," I said, wondering if I was going to be served up as the main course for Mary Wren's gossip of the day.

The last two prisoners stepped off the train—there were fifteen or sixteen, maybe twenty in all. After them came two more American guards, one a sergeant. As the procession walked down the gravel slope to the waiting Army truck Jimmy Wells tapped on the sleeve of the American sergeant. "You mean this is all the Jerries we're gonna get?"

"Don't worry, son," said the sergeant. "We're gonna keep you folks well supplied. Most of them have already been transported here by truck caravan."

The prisoners and then the GIs climbed aboard the canvas-covered vehicle. At the highway it made a right turn and, shifting gears noisily, disappeared from sight.

And so I had seen it; all there was to see. Yet I felt a nagging disappointment as though something were missing. In the movies war criminals being hustled off to prison would be dramatic. Their ravaged faces would tell a story of defeat, disgrace, and downfall. But in real life it didn't seem all that important. Not really a big deal. My stomach growled, reminding me that it must be nearing lunchtime. I followed the railroad embankment toward home, walking sometimes between the tracks and sometimes only on one track, balancing like a tightrope walker.

I passed everybody's back yard: the Rhodes's, the Reeves's, the Benns', their laundry blowing on the line. The reverend wears striped boxer-style shorts, and the Mrs. has very heavy bosoms. Her bras look like a *D* cup to me.

Parallel to our Victory Garden I ran down the embankment past the lettuce, sweet corn, and tomatoes. The government says that until victory is won every-

4

body with a bit of land should grow their own food. Now, I know my father's patriotic all right, but he's not doing exactly what the government asked us to do. A colored man, Grover, is the one who did the planting.

I could see Ruth on the back porch, squeezing the clothes through the wringer. She is the color of hot chocolate before the marshmallow bleeds in. Sometimes I hear my mother telling her to lose weight. "It's not healthy to be fat." But she isn't actually fat; it's just that she has to wear large sizes. I mean, it wouldn't be Ruth if she were like my mother. And another thing, a little extra weight keeps a person warm inside.

"Hey, Ruth!" She looked up from her wash. "Ruth, know where I was? With the Germans going to the prison camp!"

She gave me her have-you-been-up-to-some-devil-ment look.

"I didn't do a single thing wrong!" I said, wondering if my wave would count against me. I decided that it wouldn't. "This is still my week to be good and sweet. I haven't forgotten."

Her face opened wide enough to catch the sunshine. "I'm mighty pleased to hear it. 'Cause before this week is through, your mamma and daddy gonna recognize your natural sweetness and give you some back, and then you is gonna return even more and—"

"Maybe so," I interrupted her, and she went back to putting bed sheets through the wringer, understanding that I didn't want to talk about them anymore.

"There was this sergeant guarding the prisoners—you should have seen his medals. I'm going to pray for Robert tonight, that he comes home with lots of medals—more than Jimmy Wells."

"Jimmy Wells?" Ruth repeated the name as though she hadn't heard right. "Jimmy Wells ain't no soldier!"

"No, but he must have about every medal that the Boy Scouts know how to give."

5

"Well, I don't care nothing about no wars and no medals, I jest cares about my boy coming back safe."

I wanted to tell her she had to care, how important it was for us to win this war. Put an end to Nazism forever! But I could see that Ruth's heart was too troubled to enter into that kind of discussion, so I just said again I'd remember Robert in my prayers.

A slow smile spread across her face and I found myself smiling too. See, I congratulated myself, I don't always do everything wrong.

"Go bring Sharon in from the sandpile," said Ruth. "I'll fix us up some good ole wienies and beans for lunch."

"Oh, I don't think I want any."

"Don't you go telling me what you don't be wanting, Miss Skin-and-Bones."

"Am not! As a matter of fact, if you haven't noticed, I'm really quite formidable." I exposed teeth, squinted eyes, and fashioned claws out of my hands. "Terribly and ferociously formidable!"

"That today's word?" asked Ruth.

"Yes. Isn't it grand? It means 'exciting fear or dread.' Like it?"

"I likes it right well," said Ruth thoughtfully. "But I think one of my best favorites is one of them from last month. 'Cause one night after I got home and fixed up some supper for Claude and me and cleaned up my kitchen, I got to noticing my shelf paper was getting a mite yellow so I says I better take care of it right now. Claude says leave it for another time 'cause it's pretty near to seven o'clock and I bees needing my rest. And I says Claude, you is right, but trouble is you done married a fastidious wife. A real *fastidious* wife."

My sister was sitting straight up in the sandpile, shoveling sand over her legs. Sharon's not yet six— exactly five years and ten months. But whatever she does seems to have, at least to her, a kind of purpose.

6

"Hey, Sharon," I called, "where are your legs?"

She giggled like she knew something I didn't. "Under the sand, silly."

"Are you absolutely sure? 'Cause once I had a friend named John Paul Jones, and John Paul put both legs under a lot of sand and when he went to pull them out—no legs. All those hungry little sand bugs had eaten them right off."

Sharon lifted her legs straight into the air. She seemed enormously pleased. "Well, I've still got mine. See?"

In the center of the square, breakfast-room table a bunch of back-yard roses lounged in a flowered glass that had once held pimento cheese. Ruth carried in steaming plates of wienies and beans and some cut-up tomatoes, lettuce, and radishes from our Victory Garden. I found my appetite.

Ruth gave Sharon a nod. "Your time to be asking the Lord's Blessing."

Immediately, without thinking, I said my own silent prayer: Please, dear God, don't let my father come in now. Amen.

Sharon clasped her hands tight. "We sure do thank you, dear Lord, for all the food we're going to eat up. Amen."

"Amen, Lord," echoed Ruth.

I heard myself sigh. I think maybe I worry too much. After all, it's just plumb silly to think of him walking in on us right in the middle of our prayers. But what could happen is that Sharon might just mention it. "Christian prayers in my house!" The nerve at his temple would pulsate. Shouts of "God damn you," directed at me and maybe at Ruth.

It's not that he's against praying or anything. Before the gasoline rationing I used to go to Jewish Sunday school at the Beth Zion Synagogue in Memphis, so I know that Jews pray too. My father asked those people down at the Ration Board for some extra stamps, but Mr. Raymond Hubbard said that he thought eighty miles round trip was a long ways to go praying and he couldn't in good conscience consider it a priority item.

"I made up some Jell-O for you," said Ruth, eyeing my empty plate.

"Uhhh, no thanks. I'm all filled up."

"I made it jest the way you like it." Her voice had softened. "It's got bananas and nuts and cut-up bits of marshmellers."

"I'll have a little. Did you, really and truly, make it especially for me?"

"Only this morning I asks myself what would Patty specially like for dessert. Then I tells myself the answer. And now you have your answer too." Ruth leaned back her head to let out a chuckle that was a full octave and a half down from middle *C.*

My sister took up the laugh. And her top-of-the-octave laugh struck me funny, and then everything was. That's the way it is with Ruth, Sharon, and me. It isn't that our jokes are all that great; it's like Ruth says, "We keep our jubilee in easy reach." Why can't it be that way with my mother and father? "Show them your natural sweetness," Ruth reminds me, " 'cause ants ain't the only thing sweetness attracts."

I looked out the window at the summer green and wished for winter white. An Alaskan blizzard with wild winds hurling ice darts onto head-high drifts. For four days and four nights the two of them have been isolated in the store. The power is down, the oil pipes have burst, and there is no food and no water.

Ruth pleads with me not to try to reach them. "You ain't gonna save them; you is only going to kill yourself dead!"

"Fill the thermos with hot soup," I tell her.

Seven times I think I can't go on. The drifts too high, my feet and face beyond any feeling. But I do go on and on and on, and finally I make it. I feed them soup and tuna-fish sandwiches, and when they regain their strength, they tell me how much they love me—how much they have always loved me.

"What you expecting to see out that window?" asked Ruth. "The Second Coming of the Lord?"

Never would I want her to suspect me of dreaming of a miracle. "I was just thinking I might take a walk down to the store. See what's cooking."

She didn't look exactly thrilled by my idea.

"Isn't it you who's always reminding me to be sweet? Now what could be more thoughtful than bringing them up-to-the-minute war news?" They would like that too. Doesn't my father listen to the five-minute news with his neck jutting out towards the radio? And when H.V. Kaltenborn comes on I swear if his nose isn't just about touching the cloth-covered speaker.

Ruth dropped her head into the U between her thumb and her first finger. "I expect you spent the morning advising President Roosevelt on where to send his armies. That where you got your up-to-the-second war news?"

"If you don't think a hundred ferocious Nazi prisoners arriving at the Jenkinsville depot is war news then I don't know what is."

On Ruth's face was the dawning of a smile. "Got some sweetness to go with your up-to-the-second news?"

I stood up. "Maybe you oughta spend a little time telling my father and mother to serve some sweetness to me."

"Reckon they'd listen?"

"Guess not."

Ruth nodded her agreement. "Could you tell this old lady why you is always talking about your father when all the other young girls be talking about their daddies?"

9

"Well, daddies act one way and fathers act another. And anyway, I don't happen to be a young girl. I've been a teenager already for two years."

She laughed. "Oh, Honey Babe, how can you be a teenager when you is only twelve?"

" 'Cause I've been one since I was ten. Not many people know this, Ruth, but teenage actually starts when you get two numbers to your age. See?"

I could tell that it hadn't convinced her. "Don't you see, ten is in reality tenteen. Now people don't generally go around calling it tenteen cause it sounds too much like the chewing gum, but that's the only reason."

The smile that Ruth had been holding in suddenly broke through. "Honey, you jest all the time go round making up rules to suit yourself. I got myself two big numbers to my age and I shore ain't no teenager."

"Well, I can explain that. When you have two numbers to your age, you're either teenage or after teenage. And you just happen to be after teenage, understand?"

"I think I'm beginning to see the light and I do 'preciate the kind explanation, little Miss Genius."

"Make fun of me and I'll stop talking to you."

"Can't good friends kid each other a little? Make each other smile?"

"I guess so. I've got to go to the store now."

"Hold up a pretty minute, Patty. I want you to do me a mighty big favor only you can do."

I tried to hide my pleasure that somebody needed a favor only I could do.

"I want you to take off them faded old shorts and put on one of them nice pretty dresses of yours."

Sounds of my mother! "For God's sake, why do I have to get all dressed up to go to the store? I'm coming right back."

"Pride, Patty Babe, you gotta have pride."

Pride. Maybe that's it, what Ruth has. What makes her different. Keeps her from looking down at her shoes

10

when talking with white people. Then it is all a lie what they say about her. Ruth isn't one bit uppity. Merely prideful.

"Is that why you wear a Sunday dress to walk back and forth to work?"

"That's right," she said, looking pleased that I had caught on so quickly. "It's the pride. It's me shouting out to the world that one of God's creatures is walking on by. You think God would like it if we went and used the Good Book for a doorstop?"

I shook my head No.

"Well, now, you think he bees liking it one bit better if one of his creatures be going round in dirty, worn-out clothes? You understands that, Patty?"

"I guess so."

As I crossed Main Street, the heels of my sandals made slight half-moon impressions in the hot asphalt pavement and I remembered what I'd heard said about heat at noon. "Hot by noon; Hades by afternoon." It was one reason why almost nobody was about. But then the farm folks never come in unless it's Saturday, and the town ladies were home fixing a noonday meal for their families. My father says most weekdays you can shoot a cannon down Main Street and not hit a single living soul.

Truth of the matter is, you'd probably need two cannons 'cause the business section of Jenkinsville is T-shaped. Main Street running up and down and Front Street running crossways. Most of the really important things like our store, the Rice County National Bank, the post office, the picture show, the Sav-Mor Market, and the Victory Cafe are on Main. I passed by the Victory and read the sign painted in neat red lettering at the bottom of the plate-glass window: PLATE LUNCH 25¢. Meat & 3 Vegs.

The smell of fried ham had taken command of the

11

air, so it was impossible to know exactly which three vegetables the Victory was serving.

And there, stuck between the Victory Cafe and the Sav-Mor Market, was our store—best in town. I liked the sign; it's been freshly painted. Big, bold, black letters with a dash of red for emphasis:

BERGEN'S DEPARTMENT STORE
Quality Goods for the Whole Family
Shoes, Clothing, Hardware, & Variety

Standing at the piece-goods counter with my father was a salesman, probably from Memphis or Little Rock, who was removing samples of men's dress shoes from a fitted black case. My father took a package of Tums from his freshly pressed suit coat, and as he popped one into his mouth he nodded at the salesman. "Give me the usual run of sizes in the brogue. Black only."

I wondered if I had time to give my father the news of the prisoners. I mean, if I talked fast. Better to test the water first. "Hello," I said, taking a step forward.

He dropped the Tums back into his pocket. "What are you doing here?"

The salesman smiled at my father. "This your daughter, Harry?"

My father's head moved slightly.

The salesman gave me a full smile. "Well, well, what's your name, sweetheart?"

"Patricia Ann Bergen, sir."

"That's a pretty name for a pretty girl. Here I have something for you." He pulled out a package of Juicy Fruit gum. The wrapper showed the soil of having lived in his pockets for a while.

"Well, thank you anyway, but you see I have this cavity," I lied.

"Oh, that's all right," he said as though he hadn't heard me. "You don't have to chew it now. Take it home."

12

I took the gum, thanking him as I backed away. I eased my disappointment by telling myself how smart I was to save my story for a more appropriate time.

I looked around for my mother. She was sitting on one of the three cushioned chairs in the shoe department with Gussie Fields, who had been clerking here since even before her husband died.

"Hello," I said, remembering to smile.

My mother said, "Hello," and Mrs. Fields said something about how pretty my dress was.

"She's only wearing that dress because Ruth told her to," my mother said.

"Ruth did *not* tell me to wear this dress," I said, hating the idea of being anybody's robot. Even Ruth's.

"What's Ruth doing?" she asked.

"Washing the clothes." I anticipated the next question so I just supplied the answer. "Sharon is playing in the sandpile."

"Did Ruth give you both lunch?"

"Yes, ma'am."

Mrs. Fields smiled her adult-to-child smile. "How are you enjoying your school vacation? As much as my niece, Donna Ann?"

I wondered how I could honestly answer the question. First I'd have to decide how much I was enjoying the summer—not all that much—then find out exactly how much Donna Ann Rhodes was enjoying it before trying to make an accurate comparison. Mrs. Fields' smile began to fade. Maybe she just wanted me to say something pleasant. "Yes, ma'am," I answered.

"When I was a girl," said my mother, turning toward Mrs. Fields, "I used to drive my mother crazy with my clothes. If my dress wasn't new or if it had the slightest little wrinkle in it I'd cry and throw myself across my bed."

"You were just particular how you looked," said Mrs. Fields.

"I wish Patricia would be more particular," Mother

13

said with sudden force. "Would you just look at that hair?"

"I don't have a comb," I answered.

Reaching into the side pocket of her dress, she produced a small red one. "Here. Go look in the mirror and do a good job. You know, Gussie, you'd expect two sisters to be something alike, but Patricia doesn't care how she looks while Sharon is just like me."

Didn't Mother know I was still standing here? Couldn't she, at the very least, do me the courtesy of talking behind my back? I walked over to the three-way mirror in the dress department, but Mother's voice followed. "Why, before we take the girls to Memphis Sharon has to try on a dozen dresses. And that one? Puts on the first thing her hand touches. She just doesn't care."

I took in my reflection: "Oh, mirror, mirror on the wall, who's the homeliest of them all?"

"Wait till she gets a boyfriend," Mrs. Fields was saying. "She'll spend all her time fixing herself up."

"I wish I was sure of that! Some children just seem to be born with things others aren't. Now, take Sharon, she was never a moment's trouble."

If there were no mirrors or mothers I probably never would know how ugly I am. But it was all there, plain as my reflection in the glass. Skinny bones, skinny face, feet too big, and nose too long. In the mirror I could also see my mother's profile: a high cool forehead and a slender nose that stopped where a nice nose ought to. A lot like Sharon's. And there were the lofty cheekbones that gave mother's face form, symmetry, and on occasion, great beauty. Sometimes I think God lavished so much beauty on her outsides that when he got around to her insides there just wasn't much of anything left over.

When I returned with the comb my mother pulled a stray hair from its teeth before sliding it back into her pocket. "Wonder if Ellie Mae would have time for me?" she said.

Walking to the wall phone, she fluffed her hair into place as she gave the crank a couple of turns. "Mary, please ring up M'Lady Beauty Parlor in Wynne City. . . . No, I don't have the number," she said, resting her arm on the Rice County telephone directory.

"Mother, did you hear about the POWs?" I asked. "A bunch of them just came in by train."

"I don't know why they don't keep them over in Europe where they belong. It's dangerous having those criminals a mile from town." Her head shifted back to the speaker. "Hello, is this Ellie Mae? . . . Do you know who this is? . . . Well, Ellie Mae, I can be in Wynne City in about fifteen minutes. Do you think you could take me right away? . . . Just a wash and set and one of your nice color rinses. . . . Oh, fine, see you in a few minutes."

Actually, and I've told her this, her hair looks its very best just before she goes to the beauty parlor. By the time they finish with her it's tight and unreal, like the hair on a department store manikin.

I watched her tear off a strip of adding-machine tape and write, "$5 Pearl," before exchanging her scribbled note for a fresh five-dollar bill.

As my mother carefully applied her make-up in front of the three-way mirror, Mrs. Burton Benn came into the store looking as though she was on an important mission. A step away from my mother she halted. "Mrs. Bergen," she said, in the same tone that she must use when calling her Sunday-school class together, "I have something to say."

My mother smiled. "What can I do for you today, Mrs. Benn?"

"It's about your Nigra!" said Mrs. Benn.

"Ruth?" answered my mother as though she weren't completely sure of the name.

"Yes, Ruth! After supper last night the Reverend told me that I ought to leave the dishes and get right over to the Sav-Mor Market, take advantage of the marked down hamburg. *Well,*" she said, making the word sound important. "Your Ruth, that uppity Nigra, sees me making a bee-line for the meat counter and she practically breaks out in a run to get there first. She tells Gene, 'Give me the rest of that hamburg.' " Mrs. Benn's voice sounded like a white woman trying to imitate a colored one. "Now, you just tell me what's a darky gonna do with two pounds of hamburg? All she wanted was to keep me from getting any and that's the truth!"

"Oh," said my mother, sounding genuinely grieved. "She's probably eaten it by now."

"I don't *want* that meat!"

"What do you want?" asked my mother, confused.

"To teach her a lesson. I want you to fire her!"

I watched my mother gently shake her head No. She's getting ready to tell off Mrs. Benn, I thought. She's going to tell her how good and kind Ruth is— how much we love her, Sharon and me. "I just can't fire Ruth," she apologized. "She's the best cook and house cleaner we've ever had."

In the shoe department my father sat alone, his lean body half-hidden behind the open pages of the afternoon *Memphis Press Scimitar.*

"I came here specially to tell you," I began, wishing that Ruth could hear all my sweetness, "about the Nazis that came into Jenkinsville on the eleven thirty train."

He turned from the paper. "What about them?"

I felt like an actress who finally gets her big chance, but just at the moment the spotlights expose her she remembers that she has neglected to learn her lines. "Well," I said, "there was a whole bunch of them. They were about as big and mean-looking as anybody could be."

His eyes went back to the *Press Scimitar.*

"Well, aren't you interested in the really exciting thing that happened?"

"What happened?"

Some people say that God strikes down a liar—Boom! I decided to risk it. "One of the prisoners tried to escape."

A wrinkle of genuine interest came slicing between his neat black eyebrows. "You mean, after they got off the train?"

"Yes, sir. As soon as he stepped off the train, I noticed that his head started moving around, so right away I became suspicious. I guess the guard noticed it too because he came right up behind him and said, 'Make one move and I'll blow your brains out.' Just like that. 'I'll blow your brains out.'"

"Is that all?"

"Yes, sir, that's all."

"Then let me read my paper in peace."

If you follow Main past Front Street, the road continues even though the pavement ends. I stood at the corner looking down the narrow dirt road towards Nigger Bottoms, wishing to be black for a while so that I could enter into the other Jenkinsville. By the side of the road two women stood. Nearby, a scrawny rooster chased a large speckled hen. The bigger of the women pointed to the hysterical hen before leaning her head close to the ear of her friend. Suddenly their heads fell back and the high notes of their laughter carried all the way up to Front Street.

The thought came to me that even from a distance people dislike being watched. I moved on down Front Street to Mr. Matthew Hawkes's run-down drugstore. People say the aspirin old Matty sells has been on the shelf so long that it gives more headaches than it could ever take away.

Next to Hawkes's drugstore is Cook Brothers' Furniture and Appliances. Then comes a secondhand-clothing store which never had a sign saying what its name is. After that is Mr. J.G. Jackson's cotton gin

17

office, and the office and printing press of Mr. Quentin Blakey's *Rice County Gazette*.

And right next to the *Gazette*'s office is something interesting. I mean, you wouldn't exactly think it was interesting because there's nothing there now besides a vacant building with a Coca-Cola advertisement and a sign that says THE CHU LEE GROCERY CO. Well, Mr. Lee—everybody called him "the Chink"—was the first merchant to open every morning and the very last to close. Maybe that was because of him and Mrs. Lee living in the back of the store, so convenient and all.

What happened I don't exactly understand. One day he was doing business just like always, and the next day without so much as a going-out-of-business sale he had taken his groceries and left. I guess it happens; people get sick or find better opportunities elsewhere.

But why would there be this hole, bigger than a football, right through the plate-glass window? At first I thought maybe the moving men hadn't been careful when they were carting things out, but when I looked inside the empty store there was all this glass lying around the floor, so the window just had to be broken from the outside.

I would have forgotten all about it except for what I happened to hear Mr. J.G. Jackson say to my father. "Our boys at Pearl Harbor would have got a lot of laughs at the farewell party we gave the Chink." Then Mr. Jackson laughed and my father gave a weak laugh, too, as though his heart wasn't really in it but still he wanted to keep the respect of so important a man as Mr. J.G. Jackson.

Later, when I asked my father what Mr. Jackson meant by that, he told me that I was never in my life to mention it again. All I know is that if Mr. Lee had been Japanese, then it might have made more sense. Anyway, there's probably a simple logical explanation. It couldn't be what I think.

2

IT WAS TEN O'CLOCK Sunday morning when my father came back from doing his bookwork at the store and asked, just as nice as you please, if we were all ready to go to Memphis. Like he didn't mind at all. My mother dearly loves "to go home" again. And Sharon likes playing with our little cousins, Diane and Jerry. Me? Sometimes Grandpa and I discuss the important things that are happening in the world. We both, for example, think President Roosevelt is a very great man. I talk a lot with Grandma too, but she's always asking me questions: Am I gaining any weight?—not really. How am I doing at school?—I make a lot of *C*s. Then she gets around to the hardest question of all: Do I have a lot of friends?—I guess so.

But even with the questions Grandma and Grandpa are nice, so I've never understood exactly why my father disliked them so much.

I think the problem may have started when he married my mother, and Grandpa didn't give him a job in his real estate business, S. Fried & Sons. Now, my father is always saying that he'd rather starve than have to work for Grandpa and his brothers-in-law, but I think he resented it all the same. Because the company is big enough not only for Grandpa and his two sons but for two of Grandpa's nephews and even the outsider, Bernard Kaplan, who runs the insurance end of things.

Considering the trouble my father had with his own parents, it's really sad that he doesn't have in-laws he can love. Even now, he never ever mentions his own mother. I don't remember Grandma Bergen as being mean, but I was only about Sharon's age when she died, so I don't know for sure. About the only sure thing I remember is her hair, which was auburn like mine. And I'm not the only one who's noticed that. Uncle Max, my father's oldest brother, says my hair, my eyes, and even "my way" remind him of her.

Uncle Max also told me that on a poor working-class street like Hamel Street, in South Memphis, the Bergens were considered the poorest of the poor. Grandma Bergen's dresses were washed so many times that the threads were almost countable. And poor Grandpa Bergen, a cobbler, died of a heart attack at forty-two when he was only seven dollars short of saving enough for a stitching machine. With one of those machines he was sure he could repair enough shoes to support his family.

Which gets to another point. Since the Bergens were so poor, I think my father would still be a ticket seller at Union Station if it hadn't been for Grandpa and Grandma Fried's lending him the money to go into business. So wouldn't you expect him to be all choked up with gratitude? Well, he's not! Maybe it's because he hates favors—not so much to give as to take them. "I don't like to be obligated," is the way he puts it. It's as though, in his own heart, he believes that he could never have made it without them. And he hates having needed them. But that doesn't make a lot of sense.

"Lock the doors," my father ordered as he backed the car down the driveway. At the First Baptist Church corner I touched his shoulder and pointed towards the glass-enclosed sign in the churchyard. "Hey, did you see that? It says, 'Sin now—pay later.' I didn't know they charged for that, did you?" I started up a laugh, but when nobody joined in, it made a hollow sound.

20

"O.K.," he said, "don't bother me when I'm driving."

Suddenly Sharon jumped off the back seat and touched my father's shoulder at the very spot I had touched. "There's a bee on you!" she shouted. "April fools!"

From deep within his throat my father chuckled, while Mother turned around to give Sharon a love pinch on her cheek. "Are you the bad girl that fooled your daddy?" she asked.

Sharon reached out to touch the neck of Mother's lavender dress. "There's a bee on you. April fools!" She squealed with delight.

Mother pretended horror. "Get that bee away!" she said, swatting at the neck of her dress.

After a few more of Sharon's April-fool bees, Mother seemed to tire of the game. "Can't you do something?" she asked me. "Amuse Sharon. Tell her the story of the 'Three Little Pigs.'"

"I don't know if I remember that story," I lied. "But the story of 'Cinderella' and her wicked stepmother is still fresh in my mind."

At the end of the story when Cinderella marries the world's handsomest prince at the world's fanciest wedding Sharon sighed, looking every bit as happy as the bride and a whole lot sleepier. She curled up in the corner, and with just a touch of a smile on her lips, fell asleep.

"So, if we take the men's underwear to the back of the store," Mother was saying, "we could use the front counter for an impulse item."

"Men's underwear is a big seller. We sold more than six thousand dollars' worth last year."

"But, Harry, we'd sell every bit as much," she argued, "because men come in specially to buy it. But with women's blouses it's different. A woman sees something pretty and she just ups and buys it spur of the moment."

21

"Well," said my father as though he didn't want to give in too quickly, "don't go moving things tomorrow; we've got a lot of merchandise waiting to be checked in."

When we reached the two-lane Harrihan Bridge that connects West Memphis, Arkansas, to Memphis, Tennessee, I looked down at the bluey-brown Mississippi. They say the river's current is strong and very few people have ever been able to swim across, although not a year goes by that somebody doesn't drown in the attempt. This may sound crazy because the only time I ever go swimming is a couple of times in early summer when Edna Louise Jackson's mother takes a bunch of us to the public pool in Wynne City, but I could swim it. The secret is in absolutely refusing to let the river beat you down. If I had to, I'd measure my progress in inches. One more inch I've swum—one less inch to swim. Once you know the secret, then nobody's river can bring you down.

On Riverside Drive, "Memphis's front door," my father dropped his speed down to between thirty and thirty-five miles per hour.

My mother was resting her head against the seat, her eyes closed as though she were dozing. She was wearing her healthy-looking black hair in my favorite way—brushed back so that her widow's peak shone like an extra added attraction above her high forehead. And hers wasn't an everyday pretty face. The shape of the nose, the cut of the chin, but it was more than that—more than its parts. My mother's face was an artist's vision of sensitivity, intelligence, and love. And so it had to be a big lie what they say about beauty being only skin deep. For if it weren't really there why would it show?

The problem must be me. I've never been what she wanted, never done what she asked. Always making my own little changes and additions. Why do I do it? Why can't I be better? More obedient? More loving?

I leaned over, placing my lips against hers. Those lips suddenly tightened. And there I stood, still bending over her. Ugly, naked, and alone.

She opened her eyes. "I wish you wouldn't bother me when I'm trying to sleep."

"Sorry," I answered, letting my head fall against the window of the back seat.

"I've been meaning to tell you," she said after a short period of quiet. "If Grandmother tries to give you money you just tell her you don't need anything."

"But I do need something," I answered, wondering if she could understand.

She didn't answer. She put her head back against the seat and closed her eyes again.

"If I were a rich grandmother with plenty of money," I said, "I would enjoy giving things to my grandchildren." I touched her shoulder. "Could you please tell me why it's all right for you to take things from Grandma—the mink coat, for example."

Her eyes shot open. "That was my birthday present."

At least I had her attention. "Well, then what about all that new porch furniture? That wasn't anybody's birthday present."

"That was an anniversary present—for being married to your daddy for fourteen years."

That wasn't a present, I thought, more a reward. I couldn't, at the moment, decide which one deserved the reward. Neither. Both. The only thing I could think to say was, "Oh." Until a few moments later I thought of something else. "What if Grandma has money for Sharon. Is that O.K.?"

"Sharon's little," she answered.

My father followed Jackson Avenue eastward until he came to the old stone gates of Hein Park, mostly hidden now by a pair of weeping willows. Grandpa had told me of last winter's ice storm, and how the elms and maples had been damaged. Only the willows

23

remained intact. "Bending," he had said, "beats breaking."

Hein Park was the greenest and most elegant residential area in the whole city. It had narrow, leafy roads which wound past fine old homes set back on limey green grass.

I nudged Sharon. "Hey, sleepyhead, wake up." She looked at me reproachfully, like Cinderella being disturbed while waltzing with the prince. "Come on, we're almost there." Her expression didn't change for the better, but she did manage to lift her chin as I retied the ribbon bow at her neck.

And there it was—my grandparents' house. A twelve-room Victorian painted the whitest white with windows large enough to welcome in the sun, each with its green-and-white-striped awning sloping down like a circus tent. It would have been nice growing up in that house.

Before we reached the front steps Grandpa was already at the door. He turned to shout over his shoulder, "Mamma, they're here! Pearl and Harry."

Grandpa has every bit as much hair today as he did in the wedding picture that sits on his bedroom bureau. Now, forty years later, it has changed color, and so has his expression. Then it was—resolute. Yes, resolute. And now it's just gentle.

His freshly shaved face carried the aroma of Old Spice. "My oldest grandchild—already a young lady," he said, hugging and kissing me.

From the kitchen, the warm, sweet smell of cooking—of roast turkey and carrot *tsimmes*.

"How are you, Boss-man?" my father asked, without shaking hands. "Tell me when you poor folks here in Hein Park are going to be able to afford some sidewalks." It was his favorite joke.

Grandpa said, "Soon as my rich son-in-law lends me the money," which happened to be his favorite answer.

24

Grandma came from the kitchen, wiping her hands on her flowery apron. Through the years Grandma has put on weight and now her face, while not exactly a perfect circle, is all the same quite round. Last time we were visiting, Grandpa said that he married a 90-pound girl and now he's got a 180-pound woman. Twice what he bargained for. That was about the only time I ever saw her mad. She insisted that she didn't weigh an ounce over 165.

Grandma hugged and kissed us all, with the exception of my father who hurriedly brushed past her on his way to the big chair with the matching ottoman.

Then she started worrying whether or not we were hungry. Uncle Ben and Uncle Irv weren't coming for another hour and a half, about two o'clock. "Pearl, wouldn't you like a nice bowl of soup now? Maybe Harry and the children would like a little something to hold them."

"Oh, Mother, I hope you didn't cook one of your big starchy dinners. You know I have to watch my weight."

"Watch your weight at your own house. Here, when my children and grandchildren come to visit, I cook."

Mother agreed to a cup of coffee, and my father, after finding out that it was chicken soup with matzo balls, his favorite, relented.

"I saw your brother, Max," Grandpa said to my father. "He doesn't go to many of the brotherhood meetings. He's a nice fellow, your brother."

"Good as gold," my father agreed. "And if you ever want the world to know something, just tell him. Worst blabbermouth in town."

Grandpa let his lips pout forward as if the thought were new and surprising. "I should worry about that? I'm too old for women. I pay my bills. I never hurt anybody. People with dark secrets should worry about Max. Me? I'm not going to worry."

25

Actually, Uncle Max wasn't really so much of a blabbermouth as he was a rememberer. There wasn't much that he forgot about people, especially about his family. I think that's why my father always seems funny—a little tense—around him. Maybe he enjoys remembering what my father enjoys forgetting.

Like the time last Yom Kippur when we were all standing around outside the Beth Zion Synagogue and one of Uncle Max's remembrances made my father so angry that he called him, "A damn liar," right to his face. He was telling what a hot temper my father had had when he was a boy. How he sometimes became uncontrollably mad at one of his brothers, usually Arnie. More than once, according to Uncle Max, Grandfather Bergen had to sit on his son's bed late at night, repeating, "You will not be violent. You will not be violent!"

Grandpa sat down next to me on the gold brocade sofa. "You been writing any more letters to the editor of the *Commercial Appeal?*" he asked, patting my arm.

"Oh, no, sir, not any more. I only wrote that one because of that stupid man who wrote that the war was all President Roosevelt's fault."

"Such an intelligent letter," said Grandpa, adjusting his eyeglasses. "Most people twice your age wouldn't have written so well."

I turned my head to see what my father thought of that. But he was too deep into *Look* magazine's story about a soldier's farewell to hear. And my mother was only interested in her fingernails, which she was filing with a well-used emery board. For a moment I thought I might come right out and ask her if she had liked my letter too, but I didn't. I didn't want to give her the impression that her opinion was all that important to me.

The dining room table was set for fourteen with a fine damask cloth, sterling-silver flatware, and real crystal glasses, two for each setting. Grandma always served

Mogen David and I couldn't remember a time when I was too young for my own wine glass. I could always tell how grown-up Grandma considered me by how much wine she poured. When I was Sharon's age only the bottom of the glass was covered, but when I was ten it was at the halfway mark. Last Chanukah, and I'm not exaggerating, it was three-quarters.

At our house we have damask cloths, crystal, and sterling too, but I can't remember my mother ever using them. Anyway, I know she's never cooked a dinner like Grandma. Now, Ruth is a very good cook too, but it's not the same. It's still like eating somebody else's food, while Grandma's is like finally coming home.

On the gas stove were two restaurant-sized pots, one filled with simmering golden soup and the other had kasha with noodle bows. Grandma opened the door of the oven, slid out the rack, and basted the turkey with a large metal spoon. She wiped her hands on a kitchen towel before looking me over. "My grandchildren are growing up," she said, sighing. "And when do I see you? Why don't you like visiting your grandmother?"

"But I do!"

"I ask your mother why she never brings you on the train with her, she says you're too busy with all your friends."

"My mother told you that?" I asked, not believing.

"Your mother always tells me that," she answered.

"Well, she's telling a lie."

Grandma looked at me and then she nodded her head as if she knew just what to do about it. "Listen, next week we'll plan a day; you take the eight o'clock morning train and we'll spend the whole day together. I'll buy you clothes—anything you want. We'll have lunch together. You like the top of the Hotel Peabody, the Skyway?"

"I just love it!" I said. "I've never been there but

sometimes I listen to WREC; they broadcast the dinner music right from the Skyway. I've always wanted to go there. Will Mother go too?"

"Well," said Grandma, thinking it over. Suddenly she shook her head No. "Let her stay home. She'll only tell me you don't need a thing and somehow we'll end up shopping for her."

"I can't wait," I said, feeling as though she had slipped into my team's colors. Backtracking, I tried to remember exactly what it was Grandma had said about buying me anything I wanted. Did that mean only clothes?

"Is there something wrong?"

"Oh, no, ma'am," I said, knowing it was those two vertical think-lines that sometimes invite themselves to my forehead that prompted her question. "It's just that I was wondering if—I mean, if I don't buy but one dress and if it's not too expensive do you think it might be all right if I bought a book? You see, we don't have a library in town except for the one at school and that's closed for the summer."

Suddenly she held up her index finger. "Wait!" she ordered, leaving the room in a rush. When she returned, she was folding a ten-dollar bill in half. "Take this," she said, "and buy some nice books and when you finish reading them, I'll give you money to buy more."

Stepping backward I clasped my hands behind my back. I tried to remember why I wasn't supposed to take the money. "Well, thanks anyway but—"

She pulled my arm from behind my back and systematically opened my fingers one by one to place the bill in my palm. "Buy what makes you happy," said Grandma.

"But my mother said—"

"Your mother!" A deep crease appeared on one side of her mouth. "This is not for your mother to know!"

28

Grandma poured my mother's coffee and set it down on the kitchen table along with a cup of matzo-ball soup for Sharon. Then she took a large blue crockery bowl and carefully ladled in the steaming broth before dropping in two fat matzo balls. At the kitchen door she called out, "Soup's ready." My father came at once, sat down, and finished off his soup while Sharon was still blowing on maybe the second or third spoonful.

My mother set her coffee cup down and asked, "How is it, Harry?"

"Not bad," he said, accepting his second bowl.

When I heard car doors slamming I looked at the kitchen clock—ten minutes after two. My little cousins, Diane and Jerry, were the first to run in. As I kissed Uncle Irv I saw that everybody else had found somebody to kiss. Uncle Ben called my mother "Sis" and asked, "How's everything?"

Then I heard Aunt Dorothy laughing her high-pitched laugh. "Don't kiss me, Harry. I might swoon."

"Come here, you beautiful thing, and kiss a real man," said my father, "and you'll never go back to that husband of yours."

Now it so happens Aunt Dorothy is no beautiful thing. Frankly speaking, she has buck teeth and good-sized pits on her cheeks, left over from her acne years. And her figure is fatless, though certainly not faultless. Sort of muscle and bone under tightly stretched skin, probably because of all the golf she plays. Two or three years ago her picture was in the *Commercial Appeal* when she won the Ridgeway Country Club's women's golf championship.

My father led Aunt Dorothy to the window side of the living room and began whispering in her ear. Suddenly her head fell back and she laughed like a woman laughs who wants to please a man. "Oh, Harry, you're a real card," she said.

29

It has always seemed strange to me, but women like my father. Of course, he's forever giving them attention, telling them what a big deal they are, so beautiful and all. My Uncle Max told me that my father was the only one of the five Bergen boys who was a genuine "ladies' man," spending his pay on clothes and girls. I thought he was just fooling me, but later I asked Aunt Rose which one of her brothers was the most popular with the girls, and right off the bat she answered, "Your daddy. The girls were crazy about him." But he can be very nice to other people. I've noticed that.

When we all sat down at the dining room table, each place had its own small plate of chopped liver resting on a leaf of lettuce. Grandpa stood and raised his wine glass. I reached for mine, and for the first time it was completely full. Just as full as Grandpa's or Uncle Ben's and if I'm not mistaken it was slightly fuller than my mother's.

At the moment of absolute quiet, Grandpa spoke. "We pray that we'll all be together for many, many years to come. And that Hitler and his Nazis should be finished—*Kaput!* And our dear President Roosevelt should be given a long life and much wisdom. *L'chayim!*"

"*L'chayim,*" we repeated, bringing our glasses to our lips.

The talk centered on war news. The fate of the Jews, the capture of General Wainright, and the Russian offensive on the Kalinin Front. My father gave dire warnings about the Russians—how it would be better if they were fighting against us. That way we could destroy both Hitler and Stalin at the same time. Two birds with one stone.

"Why do we always talk war, war, war?" my mother finally asked. "Why don't we ever talk about happy things like clothes or parties? Something nice?"

Aunt Dorothy nodded in agreement. "Ben, tell

30

your sister about the insurance meeting in New York that the company is sending us all to."

"Irv and I want to take in all the sights," said Uncle Ben. "But all the girls can talk about is shopping and plays. Plays and shopping!"

My mother turned her gaze from Uncle Ben to my grandfather. "You're sending them on a vacation but not me?"

Grandpa shook his head. "I'm not sending them any place—the company is."

"Papa, you *are* the company!" said my mother, not hiding the anger in her voice. "And you've always done that, given everything to your precious boys. Don't I count for anything? Don't I deserve something nice too?"

My grandma's chin lifted as though it had been struck by an uppercut. "That's foolish talk, Pearl. Foolish! The difference between you and your brothers is that they always liked whatever they were given, but you, Pearl, never liked anything once it was yours."

It was early evening when we drove across the Harrihan Bridge, entering the neon strip of highways known as West Memphis, Arkansas.

I leaned back into my dark corner of the car, patted my skirt pocket, and felt reassured by the folded square of paper. Grandma's ten-dollar bill. On the seat next to me was a whole bag of her freshly made cheese and onion *knishes*. I breathed in deep. It was as though I had just left home and was now going to where I lived.

31

3

WALKING BACK DOWN Main Street with the bank bag heavy with rolls of dimes, quarters, and halves, I began wondering what I could do with the rest of this Monday. If only I lived in Wynne City, there'd be no problem. The public pool is filled with kids, more kids than chlorine; the school library is open even when school isn't; and the Capitol Theater has a matinee practically every afternoon.

A drab-olive truck, canvas-covered from top to sides, passed. I recognized it as the Army truck that had picked up the prisoners from the train station. It turned and angle-parked in front of our store.

Two men in Army uniform and wearing guns in polished leather holsters jumped from the cab. One of the soldiers, quite muscular despite a prominent belly, called to the back of the truck, "All right, out! Everybody out."

And out they came: young men. Two, three, four. Not much older than boys. Five, six, seven. Wearing their matched sets of blue denims. Eight, nine, and ten. As they walked towards the entrance of the store the backs of their shirts revealed for all the world to see the stenciled black letters: POW.

They were, with one exception, blond- or brown-haired and wore pleasant enough expressions. Didn't they know they were losing the war? That they were at this moment entering a Jewish store?

As I followed the last prisoner inside, I watched my father approach the guard with the corporal's stripes. "Something I can do for you boys today?"

"Yes, sir, Mr. Bergen. These prisoners been spending more time passing out in Mr. Jackson's field than they do picking cotton. So Mr. Jackson gave them two dollars apiece and the commandant said it was all right to bring them here for field hats." He pointed toward the one black-haired prisoner who was moving away from the herd. "Reiker there speaks American. He'll talk for them."

"Tell the boys to come over to the hat department," my father said as though he didn't hate them. As if he had never said, "Every German oughta be taken out and tortured to death."

When the nine prisoners were gathered around the counter the corporal shouted, "Reiker!" Reiker didn't look quite so tall or strong as the others. His eyes, specked with green, sought communication with my father. "The men wish to purchase straw field hats to protect themselves from your formidable Arkansas sun."

My father remained impassive. "Here are some styles in men's straws. These are the best quality at one dollar and seventy-nine cents. They will last you for years."

Last you for years? I checked out my father's face to see if he was making a joke at their expense. But it was empty of expression.

The Germans began trying on the hats, smiling as though they were on a holiday. Reiker had pushed out from the center huddle and was exploring the broader limits of the store.

One very blond prisoner turned to my father. *"Der Spiegel?"*

33

My father shook his head. "I don't know what you're talking about."

"*Wo ist der Spiegel?*" said a second prisoner.

Again my father shook his head. "I don't understand your talk!"

Voices called for Reiker, and at his approach the men parted like the Red Sea for the Israelites. Again the word "*Spiegel.*" Reiker turned to my father. "They'd like to see themselves. Have you a mirror?"

Reiker used English cleanly, easily, and with more precision than anyone I know from around these parts. And he didn't sound the least bit like a German. It was as though he had spent his life learning to speak English the way the English do.

Again Reiker left the others to walk with brisk steps across the store.

The corporal was involved in selecting off-duty socks for himself while the other guard leaned heavily against a counter and rolled himself a cigarette. Neither seemed concerned as Reiker headed unobserved towards the door. He could be gone before they even got their guns out of their holsters. Terrified that the guards' casualness was only a cover for the sharpest-shooting soldiers in anybody's army, I closed my eyes and prayed that he would make it all the way to freedom.

But I heard no door opening, no feet running, and no gun firing. By sheer force of will I opened my eyes to see Reiker calmly examining the pencils at the stationery counter.

Stationery was one of the many departments seen to by Sister Parker. But Sister Parker was busy waiting on a lady customer, and lady customers take half of forever to make up their minds. Who was going to wait on Reiker? I wanted to, but I couldn't. I didn't even have a comb. Why, in God's name, didn't I carry a purse with a fresh handkerchief and a comb like Edna Louise? I ran my fingers through my hair and patted it into place.

34

I took a few hurried steps and stopped short. Reiker may not wish to be disturbed, anyway not by me. The skin-and-bones girl. But I can wait on him if I want to, it's my father's store. Who does he think he is, some old Nazi?

Pushed on by adrenalin, I was at his side. "Could I help you, please?" My voice came out phony. Imitation Joan Crawford.

Reiker looked up and smiled. "Yes, please. I don't know the word for it—" Above those eyes with their specks of green were dark masculine eyebrows. "Pocket pencil sharpeners? They're quite small and work on the razor principle."

"Well," I said, reaching towards the opposite end of the counter to pick up a little red sharpener, "we sell a lot of these dime ones to the school children."

"Yes," he said. "Exactly right." He was looking at me like he saw me—like he liked what he saw.

"What color would you like?" I asked, not really thinking about pencil sharpeners. "They come in red, yellow, and green."

"I'll take the one you chose," said Reiker. He placed six yellow pencils and three stenographic pads on the counter. "And you did not tell me," he said, "what you call these pocket pencil sharpeners."

He was so nice. How could he have been one of those—those brutal, black-booted Nazis? "Well, I don't think they actually call them much of anything, but if they were to call them by their right name they'd probably call them pocket pencil sharpeners."

Reiker laughed and for a moment, this moment, we were friends. And now I knew something more. He wasn't a bad man.

"Could I ask you something?" I asked, impressed by my own nerve. His face registered the kind of flat openness that comes when you haven't the slightest idea what to expect. "Well, I was wondering how—where you learned to speak such good English?"

He seemed relieved. "No great credit to me." He showed fine, white teeth. "My mother was born in Manchester, in England, and my father was educated in London."

"Gee, that's something," I said, immediately regretting my "gee." "Being born in one country," I went on, "and then having to go clear over to another to get educated."

"Keep in mind the relative smallness of European countries. It's like being born in Arkansas and going to a university in, say, Tennessee."

"Oh," I answered, still feeling the grandeur of it. "What did he study in England?"

"History. He's an historian."

"I never met an historian. What do they do? Teach?"

"What is your name?" he asked, quietly.

"Well, my real name is Patricia Ann Bergen," I said, grateful that I was able to remember. "Mostly, though, my friends call me Patty."

"And my real name is Frederick Anton Reiker, and when I had friends they always called me Anton. So I hope you will too, Patty."

"O.K.," I said, feeling too shy to speak his name.

"Back to your questions." He sounded very businesslike. "My father is a professor at the University of Göttingen in Germany. Before the war he wrote two books and a great many articles, but not any more. Now nobody is allowed to write." Anton sighed as though he had just run out of energy.

"And did you teach too?" I asked, wanting to know everything there was to know about him.

Anton moved his head from side to side. "Before I became a cotton picker I was a private in the German Army and before that a medical student."

"Someday when the war is over," I heard the sound of conviction in my voice, "you'll go back to school, become a doctor."

36

Anton shrugged. "Someday—perhaps." Then with a grin calculated to banish heaviness he said, "I believe it's here in the cotton fields of Arkansas that I'm destined to find fame and fortune." My smile joined his.

"Yes," I agreed. "You and Mr. Eli Whitney."

"Eli Whitney?" Anton repeated. "Should I know him?"

I searched his face for fraud. Surely a man as smart as he would know what every third-grader knows. "Well, Eli Whitney invented the cotton gin; it sucks all the seeds out of cotton like a giant vacuum cleaner."

"Clever of Mr. Whitney. Perhaps even genius. What is genius, anyway, if it isn't the ability to give an adequate response to a great challenge?"

"I don't know" I said thoughtfully. "I'll have to think about that."

"I hope you do, Patty. Next time we meet you can tell me your conclusions."

A distant voice intruded upon us. "All right, boys, the truck is leaving. Let's go."

Anton took a dollar bill from a cocoa-brown wallet made of the smoothest calfskin. A fine wallet, better even than our very best ones and they sell for five dollars. I counted back the change.

"Good-bye, Patty."

"Good-bye, Anton. I hope you'll be all right."

As he turned to go, my eyes closed. I found myself carrying on a silent conversation with God. Oh, God, would it be at all possible for Frederick Anton Reiker to become my friend? I understand that it's not an easy request, but I would be so grateful that I'd never bother you for another thing. But if this is something you can't arrange, then could you please keep him safe so that he can return to his own country and become a doctor? Thank you, dear God.

"Patty!" Anton's voice. I opened my eyes. He was pointing to some object behind the glass-enclosed jewelry counter. "Sell me this pin. The round one in back that looks like diamonds."

I followed his pointing finger. It was big and gaudy, nothing that Anton would in a million years buy. "Not this one?" I asked, expecting to be embarrassed by so obvious a mistake.

"Exactly right!" he practically shouted, as he took the pin tagged a dollar, dropped the money into my hand, and went off grinning a different, more jaunty kind of grin.

4

SISTER PARKER HELD the canvas bank bag aloft. "Patty, you know anything about this? Found it lying on the stationery counter."

"Oh! Yes, thanks. Change from the bank."

"Don't you know any better than to leave a bag of money lying around?"

"I was waiting on a customer and I forgot. Uh, don't mention it, please, to my mother or father."

Sister shook her head. "I've got better things to do than tattle."

I found my mother between dress racks with one of those heavy, colorless country women who all look alike until you focus in on the one thing that gives them their uniqueness. Sometimes it's the forehead that gives a faint suggestion of things noble. Once, I remember, it was long polished hair of deepest auburn. And another time it was the eyes. Large blue-green eyes that seemed to have come from the sockets of some jungle cat.

I lifted the bank bag to eye level. "Here's your change, Mother."

"Go put it in the big register. Where have you been so long?"

"Well, I just finished waiting on one of the prisoners and before that I stopped to talk with Edna Louise's mother—she was in the bank too."

"I didn't know," said my mother, "that you and

Mrs. Jackson had anything in common." She made an adjustment of the three-way mirror, presumably to give the customer a better view of her large economy-size behind.

I felt angry enough to burn my mother in her own insult, but open anger was not the tool I needed. "Know what Mrs. Jackson said to me? She said, 'Patty, it's always a deep and abiding pleasure talking with you.' Then she asked me, know what she asked me?" I could see that Mother wasn't going to bite, so I went right on. " 'Patty,' Mrs. Jackson said, 'just tell me where in this wide world did you acquire those nice, polite manners?' "

Mother glanced at me, shivering as if from a sudden chill. "Can't you do anything about that hair?" Then she turned back to her customer with a smile. "Now that fabric is what we call a bemberg sheer. It's lightweight, easy to care for, and very cool and comfortable. And I do believe that rose is your color, don't you think so? Do you know how much you'd have to pay for that dress in Memphis?" Mother apparently assumed that Mrs. Country Woman didn't know the answer, so she supplied it. "Ten ninety-five and not a penny less. But we only have a few left, and I'm closing them out at only five ninety-five."

Mother is what you might call a prize saleslady. I mean, she has an answer for everything. If there were silver-dollar-sized holes running across the backside of that dress Mother would be talking about how fine it is for ventilation, or maybe even that it was a definite aid for irregularity.

Now, customers expect salesladies to praise the merchandise, that's only natural. But I don't believe you should outright lie. God would consider that sinful even for a saleslady. But then, what would God think about the lies I tell—"Where in this wide world did you acquire those nice, polite manners?"

I punched the No Sale key on the register and

placed the rolls of change into their appropriate bins. I watched my mother still smiling her gracious smile as she set a pink leftover Easter bonnet on the woman's head. "Now doesn't that just make the outfit?"

Mrs. Country Woman shook her head. "No, ma'am, I don't want no hat today."

"That's perfectly all right," Mother said, soothingly. "I just wanted you to see the big difference the hat makes."

The woman pushed a loose straggle of hair beneath the bonnet and gave herself a front-view inspection. I thought I saw her smile. Yes, she had found something in her reflection to admire. She would buy the hat too; my mother would see to that.

But I didn't want to think about leftover bonnets or even my mother's ability as a saleslady. I only wanted to think about him. My friend, Anton. "The next time we meet," he had said. Anton Reiker. Mr. Frederick Anton Reiker.

Across the store, in Notions, Sister Parker was customerless, but far from idle. What is it I've heard Ruth say about idle hands and the devil? Sister Parker has no worries on that score. Her left hand held a couple of bottles of lotion while the right hand gave them a dusting with a big wad of cheesecloth.

Maybe it would be O.K. to talk to her about him, but not exactly straight off. First I'd talk about the prisoners in general. Later I might just mention that Anton didn't seem too bad—for a German. But I would approach with caution. Her kid brother, James Earl, will probably be sent to fight the Germans just as soon as he finishes up his basic training.

I stood by her side and tried to come up with a good opening. "Hey, that was pretty interesting, wasn't it? All those Germans coming in here buying things."

Sister Parker's hands didn't stop for a single moment. "I don't see much interesting about a bunch of Nazis." Her answers, like her hands, moved quickly. It

41

was as though she kept them on the topmost part of her brain for easy access.

"Well, I think it's interesting," I countered. "Gives you a chance to see the enemy close-up."

"I guess," said Sister, unconvinced.

"I wonder why they decided to build a prison camp right outside of Jenkinsville?"

"Well, we have as much empty space around us as anybody else." She sounded pleased with her logic.

"But they have even more empty space in Texas," I said. "Thousands of miles of empty space."

She sighed. Boredom or anger? I don't actually mean to be rude, but I am. My father says I ask a lot of questions and then go around contradicting every answer.

"You're probably right," I said, trying to make amends. "But I wonder who decided that Jenkinsville, Arkansas, would be a good place?"

"The President."

"Oh, not the President! He's much too busy for—" There I go again, contradicting. "Well, I guess it could be that way. Maybe he did have a little free time one day and said, 'Eleanor, I've been thinking about where we could build the new prisoner-of-war camp. In the Arkansas Delta there's a little town called Jenkinsville that would be just perfect. There are fields of cotton needing picking, plenty of open space, and no big city nearby where a prisoner could hide. Yes, Eleanor, Jenkinsville would be ideal.' "

"I guess it could have been decided like that," she said.

I continued to stand there watching the notions counter grow cleaner and more organized. Inside I felt a rising sense of discomfort. I just had to speak of him, of Anton.

I said, "I'll tell you something interesting." Sister glanced at me and I took it to be a go-ahead. "I sold one of the prisoners some pencils and things. He spoke

42

the most perfect English I've ever heard and he was really very polite. I mean, for a German he wasn't half bad."

Sister looked at me more carefully, her hands motionless. Something a little scary about those now-unmoving hands. "I saw you with him. Smiling and laughing. Did you like him?"

Betrayed! By whom? Anton? No, by myself. By my ugly, stupid self. Always having to talk, always having to tell people things.

Not one tear is going to come out of my eye. Strike back. "Sister, if you really want to you can tell everybody in town that lie. I really don't care." Make it good. Make it very, very good. "And I don't know if I should tell you the truth because I'm not certain you deserve it, but I'll tell you anyway. That prisoner was telling me that he hated Hitler more than anybody in this whole world because it was Hitler who had his mother and father killed—and his sister Nancy. And he told me that every night he prayed only one prayer, that God should allow the Americans to win the war."

The cheesecloth flew back into action. "Well, how was I to *know* he told you that?"

"You could have asked," I said, listening to the sounds of injury in my voice. "All you really had to do was ask."

Outside the store the sun had positioned itself in the dead center of the sky. As I walked down the only residential block in town it followed my steps, evaporating my energies. Soon there would be a real (just like the city) street sign on this corner. At the moment, though, nobody knew just what the sign would read. The town ladies, mostly from the missionary society, were holding out for Silk Stocking Street. "Elegant," they said. While Mayor Crawford called it, "A damn silly name."

Actually, there didn't seem to be much need either

for a street name or a sign. Everybody knows where everybody else lives. And if you're worrying about a stranger coming into town, well, all he'd have to do is ask. People in this town are friendly and that's the truth.

Set back against freshly mowed grass and twin dogwoods the Jackson house was the only two-story in town. I pressed the doorbell, which activated a series of chimes. Always at this point I'd get to feeling foolish. It was too grand a way to announce my arrival. I tried to tell myself that Edna Louise would be glad to see me especially if she didn't have any other visitors. After all, any company is better than no company, isn't it?

When the heavy, arch-shaped door opened, Edna Louise looked neither pleasantly nor unpleasantly surprised. She didn't look any way at all except in sort of neutral gear. Her freshly ironed pink dress was tied behind in an abundant bow, and her blond hair fell as always in obedient waves. She looked as though she were going to have tea with the Roosevelts, but Edna Louise always looked like that.

"I didn't know you were coming over," she said in the same tone she would say, "I didn't know the bank closes at four thirty."

While her greeting didn't sound especially hospitable, she did push open the screen door.

Now Edna Louise Jackson is not only the daughter of the richest man in town but she also has the reputation of being a little "boy crazy" so she'll understand why I like Anton.

Over heavy mauve carpeting, she led me through the orderly stillness of the living room. With its lemony polish anointing the proper mahogany furniture, the living room was the saved room in the house. Saved for something sometime when it would be taken out and used.

In the cleanliness-is-next-to-Godliness kitchen, background organ music gave drama to the words of a radio announcer, ". . . The story that asks the question

44

—Can this girl from a mining town in the West find happiness as the wife of a wealthy and titled Englishman?"

I sat down next to her at the kitchen table. "Do you follow *Our Gal Sunday?*" I asked. "It's probably my favorite soap opera."

"I like Sunday and Lord Henry, but I hate Elaine. She tells Lord Henry the most awful lies about Sunday."

"I know."

"Well, why don't they get her out of the story?"

"Because they need Elaine to make the story interesting," I said, surprised that the smartest girl in Miss Hooten's class hadn't figured that out for herself.

"But she's so bad!" protested Edna Louise.

"Without Elaine, Sunday and Lord Henry wouldn't be doing anything but holding hands and strolling through their mansion. What's interesting about that?"

"Nothing," admitted Edna Louise. "Sometimes you have good ideas," she added.

"Oh, well," I said, "I guess I like to notice things like that." With my confidence boosted I decided to tell her about him. "Today I met somebody that I like."

"A boy?"

"Yes. No! He's a man."

"How old is he?"

"Maybe twenty, twenty-one or -two, like that."

"And your mother's going to let you go out with him?"

"Uh, no, I guess not. But he can't go out anyway —he's a German from the prison camp."

"A German prisoner!" repeated Edna Louise. "That's almost as bad as going out with a nigger!"

Repelled by the comparison, I shouted, "It isn't!"

"It is too. God is on America's side and anybody who's against us is on the devil's side, and that's the truth."

"The truth is that he's a very good person," I said with full conviction. "And someday we're going to meet

45

again." Then, hitting upon a way to punish Edna Louise, I added, "And anyway, I have to go home now."

As she adjusted the volume on the radio she called out, "Bye."

5

On Thursday morning I boarded the eight forty-five train to Memphis.

At the Skyway, on top of the Hotel Peabody, Grandma and I were seated at a white-clothed table next to the wall of clear glass. As I pointed out the buildings on the bluff, the barges on the Mississippi, Grandma seemed pleased. "I told the maître d' to make certain my granddaughter has the best possible view."

During lunch Grandma spoke of her fears for her two sisters and their families in Hitler-occupied Luxembourg. They hadn't written Grandma, not in months. "Toby's husband, Aaron, is the finest doctor in the country—he treats the Grand Duchess Charlotte." She pressed her handkerchief to her nose. "I know they're all right."

I told her what I had read about mail sometimes being destroyed during wartime. "They're probably worried about you," I said.

Grandma fingered the diamond and platinum bar pin at her neck before looking up cheerfully to ask if I was ready for dessert. When I considered the price of my lunch, one dollar and forty-five cents, I said I was all filled up. But Grandma said, "Nonsense," as she ordered tea for two and persuaded me to try a long chocolate pastry with a French name. And that by itself cost thirty cents!

Later we walked arm-in-arm down busy Main Street, in and out of stores—Goldsmith's, Levy's, and Lowenstein's. Grandma bought me two pairs of shoes and two wool skirts with matching sweaters.

"Next time," she said, "we're going to shop for dress-up clothes."

When she took me to Union Station, I told her it was the best time I'd had all summer and that next Thursday she wouldn't have to spend even a cent on me. "I just want to be with you," I told her.

"Oh, Patricia darling, next Thursday is no good," she said, letting her face show a regret that I mistrusted. "Grandpa and I are leaving the following Friday for Hot Springs."

She went on talking about how sorry she was and that when she returned in August—but I had stopped listening. Why should I care? She's had her children; she doesn't want any more.

"Don't worry about it, Grandmother," I said more shocked by the chill in my voice than the actual words. "It's really not all that important."

I found an unoccupied double seat and stared out the filth-encrusted window until the train began to pull out from the station yard. And not until then did I cry.

The next day I wondered why I had acted so silly, and I wrote Grandma, thanking her for all the nice clothes and "for the beautiful day that we had together."

But outside of that day—that one day—the summer was hot, dry, and endless. Edna Louise, Juanita Henkins, Mary Sue Joiner, and Donna Rhodes had hopped aboard a bus that had taken them away from this flat and fried bit of earth that was Jenkinsville to the Baptist Training Camp up in the Ozarks. During the day they swim, hike, and learn how much Jesus loves them. At night they sit around the campfire roasting marshmallows and singing about how much Jesus loves them.

I asked my mother if I could go if I promised

(cross my heart) not to sing those songs and only to pretend to listen when they talked about Him. "After all," I pleaded, "Jesus isn't contagious." But she said, "No. It's only for Baptists."

So after they went away, the little good in the summer just wasn't there anymore. Ruth was preoccupied with her work and thoughts of Robert, and even Sharon didn't really have time for me. She and Sue Ellen spent practically the whole day, every day, getting in and out of a water-filled galvanized tin tub which was set beneath the chinaberry tree.

There was nobody to talk to and nothing to do. The school library was closed. I had finished reading the books bought with Grandma's ten dollars, and my father made it very clear that he didn't want to catch me hanging around the store.

A few times I rode my bike out to the prison camp. There was always the chance of maybe seeing him. My friend, Anton. Mr. Frederick Anton Reiker. Only thing I ever saw, though, was cattle-wire fencing strung high on Y-shaped poles which squared off a huge, open area. Back a distance towards the center of the treeless compound there were ten or more long whitewashed barracks sitting on their own patches of grass. Not many people were about during the day, although sometimes I did see a prisoner or two walking. But it was never Anton.

Outside of biking, the only other thing I liked doing was fixing up my hide-out. Actually, the hide-out isn't so much a hide-out as it is a forgotten place. It is a perfectly ordinary over-the-garage servants' quarters—one big room, a little kitchen, and bathroom—located halfway between our house and the railroad tracks. But it has been closed up for the ten years that our family has lived in the six-room frame house out front.

There are two important things that make the place secret enough to be called a hide-out. A long time ago my father pulled up the horizontal stair boards to keep hobos from finding a home. I like it that way because no grownup would balance himself on the brace boards to climb up like I do. The second secret point is that the stairs leading up to the hide-out are located inside the garage, so from our house it's impossible to be seen climbing up or down the stairs.

From the hide-out's back window I watched a slow freight rumble noisily down the tracks towards Little Rock. I opened *Webster's Collegiate* to the *F*s. Time to get going on my ambition. It's not the only one I have, but it's the only one I work at. Someday I'm going to know the meaning of every word in the English language.

I let my finger run down the page of the dictionary until it stopped at the first word that wasn't completely familiar: "Fragile." Lots of times boxes of glassware and things come shipped to the store marked: *Fragile! Handle with care.* But it must have more of a meaning than that. I copied the definition into my notebook: "Easily broken or destroyed; frail; delicate." My word of the day.

A few minutes later I climbed down the steps' skeleton and went into the house where I found Ruth leaning over the tub giving Sharon her bath. Up to her belly button in bubbles, it was plain to see that Sharon was in one of her giggly moods.

"Do you know why the little moron—" she interrupted herself with an attack of giggles. Again she began, only to act as though she had been breathing laughing gas.

It was becoming tiresome. "Ruth, you tell me the joke," I said.

Sharon straightened up. "No, let me! Do you know why the little moron took his loaf of bread to the street corner? 'Cause—'cause the little moron wanted to wait to get some jam." Hiccup-like laughter engulfed her and I joined in. Mostly because I had never before heard anybody louse up a moron joke.

I hung around watching while Ruth got Sharon all dolled up in her Shirley Temple dress and Mary Jane shoes for Sue Ellen's sixth birthday party. One thing, and it's not because she's my sister, but Sharon happens to be very pretty. Everybody says that with her black hair and dark eyes she looks just like Mother, while I look like—No, I don't think I look at all like him!

Outside, the two o'clock sun right away showed us that he was far from fragile. "We'll walk slow," said Ruth, "so as not to anger him up."

On the sidewalk in front of the birthday house Ruth adjusted Sharon's pink hair ribbon. "Now don't let me hear no bad reports come back on you, you hear me, girl?"

Sharon nodded, turning to go. "Hold up now!" called Ruth. "Remember what it is you is going to say to Sue Ellen and her mother 'fore taking your leave?"

"I had a very good time at your party and—and ah—" She looked into Ruth's face for the answer.

"And I thank you kindly for inviting me," supplied Ruth.

Sharon smiled. "And I thank you kindly for inviting me," she repeated. And without even a good-bye wave she skipped off into the birthday house.

As Ruth and I walked slowly back, I tried to talk to her, but she wasn't in too much of a mood.

"Ruth—why are you mad at me?"

"Mad at you? Oh, Patty Babe, I ain't mad at nobody about nothing. Sometimes when a person be thinking about one thing it don't mean they is mad about another thing. It don't mean nothing but that they is too busy for normal conversation."

Then it was Robert. Laughing, light-skinned Robert over there fighting in some faraway foxhole. God, would you please remember to keep Robert safe from harm? Please, God, 'cause he's all Ruth has. Amen.

"Want to know who is the strongest man I ever knew in all my whole life. Robert is. I bet he could

51

beat up six Germans and outshoot a dozen of them. Honest he could!"

A slow smile spread across her lips. But her eyes—Ruth's eyes had this gloss and they weren't smiling.

"Oh, Robert's going to be O.K., you'll see. And you know what? Robert's going to help win the war."

"Honey, I don't care about no war. I jest cares about my boy."

"You have to!" I felt embarrassed by the conviction rushing through my voice. "You're supposed to care! Don't you know the Germans will take everything you've got, and then they'll take you into the field and kill you? Don't you know that?"

Ruth laughed. At me? Let her. Let her laugh her fool head off. She's not my mother.

From a deep well between her bosoms Ruth brought out a white handkerchief with printed flowery borders and dabbed at her eyes. "Oh, Honey Babe, I got nothing in this here world worth taking, and no German or nobody else is gonna kill me till the good Lord is willing."

"If you believe that," I said, trying to frame the words, "then why can't you believe it's also true for Robert? No German can kill him unless God wills it."

There was no answer, nothing except the sound of shoes against blacktop. But then her arm dropped across my shoulders, bringing me to her in a sudden hugging motion. "Unless God Himself wills it," I heard her say.

I followed Ruth into the kitchen where a headless hen, its blood already drying on its body feathers, lay on the rubber drainboard. "Sit and talk a spell," she said.

I glanced again at the grotesque bird. "I'll see you when you finish with her," I said, backing away.

Out at curbside even the neat row of houses, mostly bungalows with screened-in side porches, seemed peopleless. Not a soul was about. I pictured the ladies of the houses, sitting with saucerless cups of coffee, their eyes fixed on the kitchen radio as they lived through Mary Noble's trials as a backstage wife, Helen Trent's over-thirty-five search for romance, and poverty-reared Our Gal Sunday's efforts to keep up with the local nobility.

I didn't want to grow up to spend my days like that, but I didn't want to spend my growing-up days like this either. Sitting alone on a curb trying to think of something to do.

If I had a horse as black as the night I'd go galloping off in search of her. Go, Evol, Go! North toward the Ozarks and never come back.

People would ask, "What a peculiar name, and what does it mean?" And I'd lie to them, saying it was short for "evolution." Evolution like in Darwin's theory.

But someday it would happen. I'd find her and she'd understand right away that Evol has more power spelled in reverse. And that would be the sign between us. She would be my real mother and now at last I could go home.

A car passed. Chrome hubcaps mirrored the sun's rays. I began collecting those gray-white stones that were within lazy reach. Improve your aim. Hit the hubcap. Win a prize.

From some distance away, I heard a boy's thin voice calling me. He was short-cutting across our yard, walking as though he wore springs on his feet, up-and-down Freddy Dowd.

The last time I saw Freddy, a week ago, we were playing marbles on the sidewalk and my best agate was at stake. Suddenly he appeared from inside our house, my father. "You get yourself in this house this minute!" As soon as I closed the front door, he was standing there, telling me that he didn't ever want to catch me playing with that Dowd boy, not ever again. I didn't understand why.

"But why can't I? He's very nice."

"Are you questioning me?" my father demanded. "Are you contradicting me?"

I told him that I wasn't, and after a while he cooled off and went back to the store. The crisis was over.

But later when I looked outside my bedroom window I saw Freddy was still there waiting for me. So I called down that I couldn't come out anymore, not today, because it was getting close to suppertime; and Freddy nodded before slowly loping away. Later, though, I thought about it, wondering if he could have heard. Feelings are fragile too.

Freddy said, " 'Lo," and sat down next to me. "Hey, whatcha doing?"

"Ohhhh, I'm playing Hit the Hubcap, it's a wonderful game I just invented. I'm having a wonderful time."

"Hey, lemme play."

"O.K., but first you have to gather up the ammunition." I held up a smooth, gray pebble. "Ten for you and ten for me."

Freddy wandered barefoot over assorted road gravel, searching out only the small quality stones he knew I would like. In winter Freddy wore denim overalls with a checkety shirt of faded red flannel, but now he was dressed in his summer attire—the same worn denims without the shirt.

He counted out the stones in a one-for-you and a one-for-me fashion and then sat down on the curb to play the wonderful game. When no car came along, we played Hit the Oilcan.

"Hey! Hey! There's a car a-coming!" shouted Freddy.

I called out last-minute instructions: "Dead center of the hubcap is bull's eye. Hundred points."

Achoo-ey, Achoo-ey. From the sound of its motor it was a tired old thing that used sneezes as a means of power. The car moved slowly into firing range. Then small stones pinged against metal. A single stone re-

volved around and around the hubcap before firing upward against—crack! *The Window!*

From inside the car a family of faces turned to
stare vacantly, like they had all experienced sudden,
violent slaps across their faces.

I ran. Oh, God, now what have I done? I ran
through our yard, behind our house, and to the field
beyond. I ran until my heart warned that it was ready
to explode. And then deep in the field I fell down and
let the tall grass bury me.

After a while my heart slowed down. Nobody was
hurt. It wasn't exactly the crime of the century or anything. Just an accident that I caused, but an accident I
could make right. Yes, if only I could find them again.
I remembered their car. The sickly sound of it. The
lackluster blackness of it. And there, sitting atop the
hood, a silver swan with V-spread wings. I could find
that car again. At this very minute it was probably
parked in front of some Main Street store.

Ruth would loan me the money to pay those folks
for a new window, I knew she would. I pictured the
scene between the car's owner and me—"I want you to
know that it was an accident, and I only hope you can
find it in your heart to forgive me." The old farmer
would slowly nod his head, taking it all in, before saying
that I was a fine, honest girl. Maybe we would even
shake hands before saying good-bye.

I got to my feet. Sticking to the front of my damp
polo shirt was a layer of field dust and down my knee
ran a single rail of dry, red blood. I couldn't remember
hurting my knee. As I walked through the field I could
hear Ruth singing: "I looked over Jordan and what did
I see-e?"

She didn't just sing from her neck up like other
folks I know.

"Coming for to car-ry me home. . . ."

Her songs always seemed to come from a deeper,
quieter place than that.

55

I swallowed down the sadness in my throat before going into the kitchen. She sat there at the white metal table shelling a small mountain of peas. Through squinting eyes she gave me a questioning look.

"Honey Babe, you is jest too pitiful-looking for the cat to drag in. You been fighting with Freddy? Now you tell Ruth."

"We didn't fight," I said dully. "I never in my whole life had a fight with Freddy, and that's a terrible thing to say, besides. You sound exactly like my father. Just 'cause Freddy's poor and doesn't dress up you think he's not as good as anybody else. Well, he is, and it says so right in the Constitution of the United States of America: 'All men are created equal.' "

Ruth shook her head. "I asks you if you had a fight and you gives me a history lesson. A person can shore learn a lot of things around here."

I sat down next to her at the kitchen table, but not one more word did she say. It wasn't supposed to happen like that. Gently, even against my will, Ruth was supposed to squeeze the information from me.

I realized it wouldn't happen that way, so I just spilled it out. For a long while Ruth didn't say anything. Then she sighed and asked, "Them folks, did you know them? Was they white folks or colored?"

"I don't remember knowing them, but they were white folks from the country."

Somewhere on her forehead a line deepened, and I knew it wasn't so good that they were white. Ruth pulled down a brown simulated-alligator bag from the top of the refrigerator. "Did those folks know you is Mr. Bergen's girl?"

"No—I don't know. Maybe they did," I said, remembering running towards the rear of our house. Not very smart.

She pushed aside a black eyeglass case and a Bible about the size of an open palm to bring out a red zippered change purse with the printed words, "Souvenir of Detroit, Michigan." Inside the change purse some coins jangled, but all the paper money was pressed neatly into one small square. She opened the three one-dollar bills to their full size. Carefully she refolded them before placing the money in my hand.

"Now you ask the man how much a window costs 'fore you go giving him all your money."

She would do all this for me? There between her neck and shoulders was the warm cove where a head could lie and rest. And there I would be home. Home safe.

Ruth's eyes met mine. Could she know? Could she possibly know? There's nothing to know! I'm not a baby and she's not my mother. I ran out of the back door, letting the screen make a slamming noise.

As I walked toward downtown I noticed a breeze pushing a few elm leaves around without doing much more than promising to cool things off. Still, my thoughts began to tidy themselves up and I felt better. After all, wasn't Ruth on my side? And wasn't I even now going out to right a wrong?

It was then that I saw a green Chevy roaring down the street towards me. My father! For a moment I thought I was going to take off behind one of the houses or maybe hide behind the shoulder-high hedges that separated front yards from public walks. But I didn't. Didn't run. Didn't hide. Didn't anything.

The car passed me and then came backing up to a jerky stop. The door was opened and hurled shut. His face was frozen a bluish whitish color, like all the red blood had iced over. With long strides he came toward me. My back pressed against the hedge.

"Let me tell you what happened. Please!"

It was just noise to him. A mask cannot really hear. He kept coming toward me. I propelled myself backward, falling into and finally through the tight little

57

branches. From across the protecting hedge he commanded, "Come here this instant!" At his temple a vein was pulsating like a neon sign.

"Please give me a chance to explain. It was an accident," I said. "I was aiming at the hubcaps."

He pointed a single quivering finger at me. "If you don't come here this instant I'll give you a beating you're never going to forget."

Did that mean if I came willingly he wouldn't hurt me? His face showed no sign of a thaw. Then I felt the warming spirit of Ruth. "The Lord gonna protect all His children." Fingers crossed, I stepped through the opening in the hedge to stand soldier-straight before my father.

"Closer!"

Only one foot advanced before a hand tore across my face, sending me into total blackness. But then against the blackness came a brilliant explosion of Fourth-of-July stars. Red, yellow, blue, and then green. I never knew those stars were real; I had always thought they were only in comic books. The pain was almost tolerable when a second blow crashed against my cheek, continuing down with deflection force to my shoulder.

Using my arm as a shield, I looked up. I saw the hate that gnarled and snarled his face like a dog gone rabid. He's going to find out someday I can hate too— "Ahhhh!"

Knees came unbuckled. I gave myself to the sidewalk. Between blows I knew I could withstand anything he could give out, but once they came, I knew I couldn't.

Hands that were in the throes of a fit worked to unfasten his belt buckle. Rolling over, I hugged the hedges. He bent low to send the black leather flying.

"Ahhhheeeeehh!" My God! Legs—on fire? After the first flash of piercing pain subsided, my hate roared up strong enough to keep the tears away.

"I'll teach you to throw rocks at people!" he shouted, whipping the belt backwards through space.

"Nooo—ohhhh! Please!" I begged. Can't stand more—can't.

I heard the leather sing as it raced against the air—my eyes clamped closed.

And then they came, ugly and unexpected, those violent little cries that seem to have a life of their own. Short yelps of injury mingled with anger and defeat.

A car-door opened and slammed shut. A motor gunned as though for a quick getaway and then roared off.

6

WHEN SATURDAY CAME I was glad. Most country folks stop working about noontime, and by one o'clock Main Street starts jamming up with muddy pickup trucks filled with yellow-haired children.

And there'll be lots of colored folks in town with their kids too, only difference is they'll be all scrubbed and shiny-shoed like it was Sunday. Another thing that's different about them, and I do a lot of listening in on other people's conversations so I know, is how they speak to one another. So respectful and everything. It's as though they try to give each other the respect that the rest of the world holds back.

I mean, if you'll notice how the poor white people talk to one another, mostly they don't even bother to call each other by name. But the colored are different, always remembering to give each other the title of Mr. Somebody or Miz Somebody except, and Ruth told me this, when they go to the same church and then it's Brother Somebody or Sister Somebody.

Saturday has always been my favorite day because my father hires extra salesladies, and he never says a word when I pitch in to help. Working makes me feel useful for a change, and I get to talk with an awful lot of people. If you really, really listen, you can learn things. Sometimes you can learn things people don't even know they're teaching. Like the preacher's wife,

Mrs. Benn, who only last Saturday was talking about the greed of some people, always wanting things. And then in the very next breath complaining how the First Baptist doesn't pay her husband enough so she can buy clothes or hire a Nigra.

From the corner closet, which I share with Sharon, I took out my light-blue middy dress. It happens to be my favorite and not only because I picked it out myself but because it has no sashes, no lace, and it isn't pink. Within twenty strokes of the brush my hair came alive. And it's just the right color hair too—not flashy red or dull brown, but auburn. Alive auburn.

Standing in front of the Victory Cafe, Mr. Blakey was talking to Mr. Jackson. Mr. Henkins pulled his black Oldsmobile into a narrow space, and before he was completely out of the car he called, "Hey, did y'all hear the news?"

"Sure did," said Mr. Blakey. "Heard it on the radio not five minutes ago. Isn't that something? Imagine the FBI catching those eight dirty Nazis 'fore they could do a nickel's worth of damage."

"Know whether they sunk the U-boats?" asked Mr. Jackson. "Sure hope they blew them to smithereens."

"The radio didn't say," said Mr. Henkins. "But they caught all them saboteurs and that's the important thing to remember."

Mr. Jackson became aware of my presence, so I just said, "Hello," while I brushed some imaginary dust from the skirt of my middy before walking into the store. I straightened the story out in a logical sequence so I could tell it in a businesslike way to my father.

He was leaning against the register, taking a long draw from a cigarette.

I walked over. "I came to give you some important news."

"What news?" He blew out smoke along with the question.

"The news of the landing in the middle of the night of the German U-boats. Right here on the American coastline." I was encouraged by his head which jutted forward as though he wanted to get closer to the source of information. "Now, the Germans thought they could land saboteurs and nobody would know, but the FBI, through very secret information, found out about the scheme and captured them, all eight of them!"

"Where did you hear that?"

"It's the big news. It was on the radio not five minutes ago." Snapping on the shelf radio, he gave me a look while waiting for the tubes to warm. I tried to figure out just what the glance meant: I'm too young and/or stupid to comprehend a news bulletin; I'm deliberately lying to him; or maybe I'm just having a childhood fantasy.

Finally the radio came on, and right away I recognized the voice of Lorenzo Jones apologizing to his wife, Belle, for buying fishing gear with money from the cookie jar. My father moved the dial—religious music. And again—a commercial for Pepto-Bismol.

"Just wait till the twelve o'clock news," I said, already backing away. "You'll hear about it then."

My mother was busy taking ladies' sandals from their boxes and placing them on a table where a boldly written sign stated: SPECIAL! ONLY $1.98. She worked hard in the store, you have to give her credit for that. And not just in selling or straightening up counters the way the other salesladies do but in thinking up ways "to turn a profit on the new and to get our money out of the old." She was especially good at that because I think she likes the store better than anything else.

Mr. Blakey came into the store, throwing my father a wave. "Harry, didya hear the news? About the Nazi saboteurs? They were planning on dynamiting the Alcoa Plant in Alcoa, Tennessee. FBI caught them with their pants down. Carrying one hundred and fifty thousand bucks in bribe money."

"Yeah, I heard," answered my father. "Patricia told me all about it."

"Patricia told me all about it" echoed in my brain. I had done something nice for my father, and he was pleased with me and he might never again question my honesty. And maybe I had even won the right to work in the store when it wasn't Saturday.

Suddenly I felt greedy; I wanted my mother to be pleased with me too. "Hey, Mother," I said. "Did you hear about the saboteurs the FBI caught?"

She stopped her work to see if I looked decent enough. "Did you and Sharon have lunch?"

I must have passed inspection. "Yes, ma'am."

She went back to unboxing the shoes. "What did y'all eat?"

"Oh, we had some—some—Oh, I know. Leftover meat loaf, and corn on the cob, and some of those store-bought cookies you bought for dessert."

"What're Sharon and Ruth doing?"

"Well, Sharon went to Sue Ellen's, and Ruth is taking all the dishes out of the cabinet. Are we gonna get busy today?"

"No. Why don't you run along—go play with Edna Louise instead of hanging around the store."

Without her even trying, she could get me mad. "Because, like I've told you before, Edna Louise and Juanita Henkins and just about everybody I know have gone off to Baptist Training Camp. And I wasn't planning to hang around; I was planning to wait on customers." I thought of a few other things to tell her too. Things like if she doesn't really want me then I'll go along. She'd be sorry to lose such a good clerk on a busy Saturday. But I didn't say it because I don't think she'd care one bit if I left. Actually, I believe she'd prefer it.

I'll tell her what a good saleslady I am. "Hey, Mother, you want to know something? Last Saturday I sold twenty-five dollars' worth of clothes and stuff to just one customer! Did you know that?" Liar. My best sale was barely eighteen bucks. Damn it, Conscience, go away.

Mother stopped her work to look again at me. Probably she had no idea that I was capable of making such a big sale. "I wonder," she said, more to herself than to me, "if Miz Reeves has time for you today."

Miz Reeves? Miz Reeves from the beauty parlor! "Oh, no! My hair looks fine just the way it is, and I washed it myself only two days ago."

She started walking towards the telephone as though she hadn't heard a word I said. "Let's see if she can take you now."

I ran slightly ahead of her. "Mother, would you please for once in your life listen to me? My hair is the best thing about me. People are always telling me how lucky I am having such naturally wavy hair. And you *know* Mrs. Reeves can't set hair. All she ever does is to make those tight, little-old-lady curlicues."

She picked up the receiver and gave it a crank.

I pressed it down again. "Listen to me! Everybody makes jokes about Mrs. Reeves. They say she only thinks she can set hair because she fixes up the lady customers at the Spencer Funeral Parlor and none of them ever made a complaint. And that's the truth!"

She looked at me, not liking what she saw. "Well," she said, "I'm very sorry you don't think Miz Reeves is good enough for you. You ought to be ashamed of yourself. A girl your age going around looking like you do."

I guess what she really was trying to tell me was that it shouldn't have happened to her. A beautiful woman—everybody says she's beautiful—has an ugly baby girl. Me. A wave of shame flooded over me followed by another wave of full-grown anger. Shame and anger, anger and shame mingled together, taking on something beyond the power of both.

"You listen to me!" My voice was pitched high. "I absolutely will not go and you can't make me. And another thing, if Mrs. Reeves is so good then why do you have to drive all the way to Wynne City to have your hair done? Can you answer me that? And one more thing," I said, looking her straight in the eye, "I don't even like you!"

She pushed my hand away, releasing the hook, and within moments she was smiling her saleslady smile into the mouth of the phone. "Hello, Miz Reeves, how you getting along on such a hot day? . . . Well, you drink yourself a cold glass of iced tea and that'll perk you right up. Miz Reeves, you know who this is, don't you? . . . Yes, that's right. I was just wondering if you could possibly give Patricia a permanent wave right now? . . . Oh, fine. I'll send her over. Bye-bye for now."

A permanent. She did say a permanent. For months and months, a frizzledy freak. Mother walked away, not bothering even to glance at me. From across the store I heard her voice soaring above the other noises. "And you'd think she'd been ashamed of herself going around like that. A girl of her age. And poor Miz Reeves just sitting there waiting for her too."

"Let's just see if she refuses me!" answered my father, coming closer.

Mrs. Fields and her customer, Mayor Crawford's wife, didn't even pretend to be interested in house shoes anymore.

"Har-ry, now don't you hit her!" My good old mother was pleading for me. "She's nervous enough from you as it is."

"Don't you tell me I make her nervous. That's a God damn lie and you know it!"

Mrs. Crawford, what would she think of us? Her pinched little face tilted a bit to the right while her dark owl eyes stared.

Then there he was, standing over me. He just

looked down without saying anything. Was he waiting for something? I will not beg or cry—and he won't even be completely certain that I'm afraid.

He looked at his watch. "I'm going to give you exactly two minutes to get yourself over to Miz Reeves's or else you'll get a licking like you never had before in your life. Understand?"

Nod Yes.

"You answer me!"

"Yes, sir."

The most direct route to the door was straight past my father. I wouldn't give him the satisfaction of walking around him. But carefully. There! My arm whispered past his sleeve. When I finally reached the door my breathing came back.

Out on the sidewalk my thoughts jostled and bumped each other fighting to be heard. Break a leg or an arm. Catch a cold or a train. Hide in the hide-out above the garage or under the railroad trestle at the edge of Nigger Bottoms.

Mrs. Reeves's house sat on the corner of Silk Stocking and Main. Its dull brown paint had been flaking and peeling for as long as I could remember. A front screened-in porch sagged toward the center and dusty wooden steps had been waiting a long time for the good, honest feel of a broom. For a while I just stood there, trying to remember the names of men who died fighting for their liberty.

Then, from within the house, a phone rang. My father! I took the three front steps with a single leap, pushed open the screen door, allowing it to slam closed.

"Oh, howdy, Clara," said Mrs. Reeves into the receiver. "How are you a-managing on such a day? The temperature is near about ninety-six degrees, and wouldn't you know it, I'm giving a permanent wave today. . . . The Bergen girl. . . . No, Patty, the oldest one." She laughed a conspirator's laugh into the receiver. "I reckon I can't hardly say you is wrong. Well now, Clara, I'll ring you a little later on. You try and stay cool, you heah?"

She placed the phone back on the hook and turned to greet me. "Ooh-whee, it's too hot for the niggers today. Ain't it awful?"

I sat down in the red plastic chair in front of the washbasin without answering. She droned on, not seeming to notice that I wasn't talking.

Her sharp little fingernails scoured into my scalp. I wondered if her other customers ever objected to those nails, but then I remembered that the kind of customers Mrs. Reeves was used to working on were long past objecting.

"You tender-headed, Patty?"

"No—ma'am."

"You finding much to do with all your friends gone off to camp?"

"Yes, ma'am."

"Miz Henkins told me that Juanita was having the time of her sweet life. Just a-swimming, and horseback riding, and making the prettiest handicrafts that you'd ever want to see."

"Well," I told her. "My father and mother probably might take Sharon and me to Overton Park."

"How come your daddy didn't let you go off to camp with all your friends?" She really wanted to know. Wanted some new little something to spread around about my father. Once I happened to overhear Edna Louise's mother talking about my father—"He's a peculiar man. Even for a Jew he's peculiar."

Mrs. Reeves's lips were sucked together in anticipation of my answer, and I wondered if it were possible that she lived on a diet of persimmons.

"Well, Miz Reeves, I don't know if I should tell you this or not, but—" I wasn't sure myself just where this was going to lead—"somebody told me that they have more mosquiters and black moccasin snakes at that camp than almost any other place in the whole United States of America."

"That so?" she said, impressed as all get-out. "Well, I sure didn't know that—"

I guess she was busy thinking about mosquitoes and snakes because things got quiet. I drifted into myself. Hold me here, old lady, if you must. Imprison me and disfigure me, but my thoughts are all my own.

"You want me to give you a nice cream rinse?" I opened my eyes to stare into her withered face. "It'll give your hair a real nice luster."

"No, thanks."

"I'll call your mother at the store and ask her, it only costs a quarter."

"I don't want it!"

By eleven the heat from the permanent-wave machine was sending steady runs of perspiration down my forehead. And when she finally cut the current at a quarter to one the only dry area on my middy dress was near the hem.

A few minutes later I knew that my hair had come out exactly as I had feared. A hundred frizzledy-fried ringlets obstinately refusing to flow into one another, refusing to do anything but remain separate and individual wire coils of scorched hair.

7

I WATCHED THE late afternoon sun play with rectangles of light against the blue walls of the hide-out. The two rooms and bath had undergone a real clean-up, fix-up. And with the single exception of Ruth's dyeing that worn chenille bedspread a cherry red, I had done it all myself. Not even Ruth could have made the wood floor of the living room or the linoleum in the kitchen and bath any cleaner or shinier.

A couple of times I was close to asking her to come see how I had fixed it up, but I never did. Partly it had to do with the problem of the missing steps. The other part was that I liked to think Ruth didn't know about the secret place. If she did, it wouldn't be so much of a secret anymore.

At the hide-out's back window, the one overlooking our Victory Garden and the railroad tracks beyond, a desk made from two sawhorses and an abandoned board held all my best books. I sat down, letting my hand prop up my head, and feeling the hair that Ruth had taken scissors against when I had come home from Mrs. Reeves. At least the worst of it had been cut away. "Messing up something beautiful," she had said when first seeing me in my frizzled state.

Soon my mother and father would be home and Ruth would be on the back porch calling me in for supper.

Then from outside the window some movement caught my eye. A man with dark hair, denim shirt and pants, running below the railroad embankment. Soon the five twenty to Memphis would be coming down those tracks, stopping at the Jenkinsville station only if there was a passenger wanting to get on or off.

But this man, and even from this distance there was something familiar about him, was running away from the depot. Maybe some poor fellow hoping to jump aboard at that point where the train slows before rounding the curve.

Then it struck me who he looked like. But it couldn't be—he's at the camp. It had to be him! Just like I prayed. God went and sent Anton to me.

The train blew a long whistle. In a single leap I took the steps. I won't lose you, Anton. Not now. I ran through the field faster than I was capable of running.

I could see the black-stenciled *P* on the back of his shirt. I called out, "Anton!" But my voice was canceled by the great engine. Cupping my hands around my mouth, I tried again. "Hey! Anton!"

Still he didn't hear. But just before the train approached, he stopped and hid against the grassy embankment. I ran my labored run, waving my arms like an overburdened windmill.

"Anton!" His head swung around. He looked at me and then up the embankment, and for part of an instant I knew he was about to bolt across those tracks to his death.

"Anton, it's me—it's Patty!"

His face registered shock and then pleasure. An open palm reached out, waiting for me while overhead the train sounded like a thousand snare drums beating in four-quarter time. Our hands touched; I didn't let go till the train passed.

Directly in front of my father Ruth set down the platter of freshly fried chicken along with a skier's mountain of mashed potatoes. On the second trip from the kitchen she carried a basket of hot biscuits and a bowl of mustard greens. I wished that Anton could join the feast, invisible to everyone but me.

My father was saying, "I told him I might not be your biggest account, but I'm not your smallest. Not by a long shot, and when I order six dozen I want seventy-two pairs."

"You should have kept the six dozen you ordered," said my mother. "We're running low on men's dress shoes."

"Don't you tell me what I should've done—not when I can get all the shoes I want at B.J. Walker's."

My mother blotted her lips with a paper napkin. "Oh, sure, you can cut off your nose to spite your face if you want to, but B.J. Walker or any other jobber is going to charge you another fifteen per cent. Then where will your profit be?"

He jumped to his feet, sending the chair to the floor with a crash. "Don't you dare contradict me! Think you're gonna treat me the way your God damn mother treats her husband?"

"Now, Harry, I don't know why you're getting so excited." Her face was a study in martyred innocence.

The insides of my stomach began swirling around. Did I overeat? I looked at my plate. With the exception of a hole that I had excavated in the potatoes, nothing had been touched.

"You know, God damn it. You know! And I hope to hell you croak on it!" His lips were pressed into a thin blue line and his hands were trembling with a rage beyond his ability to control.

"I don't know!" screamed my mother. "And I don't know why you're so mean and miserable."

My head began its circular rotation, matching in r.p.m.'s that of my stomach. Suddenly it came to me—I had a race to win. I reached the toilet bowl in time to

71

see the mashed potatoes turned green gushing from my mouth, splashing down to the water below.

Since seven thirty I had been listening to the sleep sounds of Sharon. Sometimes I think she's the wisest of us all. She isn't tactless like our mother or nervous like our father and she certainly doesn't always go rushing into trouble like me. I thought about all the trouble I could get into over Anton. My father would beat me, and if other people found out they'd never speak to me again unless it was to call me bad names.

Why did I have to see Anton running to catch that train? Twelve hundred people in this town and it had to be me. Why can't I be more like my sister? Sweet and nice and neat and with enough good sense to stay out of trouble.

Once I figured out that the only thing that Sharon didn't have was enough words. But I could teach her. All kinds. Thin ones like *ego* and *ode*. Fat ones like *harmonic* and *palatable*. And I'd teach her some beautiful ones like *rendezvous* and *dementia praecox*. Maybe (just for variety) throw in some ugly ones like *grief* and *degrade*. And when Sharon knew enough words she could teach me all those things she was born knowing.

At exactly nine thirty the yellow ribbon of light from underneath my parents' door went off. And less than ten minutes later the hard, grating snores of my father carried from the bedroom across the hall.

I put on my house shoes and robe before tiptoeing to the kitchen. He must be starving. In the fridge I found a bowl of leftover chicken that would make the beginnings of a great feast for Anton and me. How about mashed potatoes served cold? I placed everything into one of those brown grocery sacks Ruth is always saving, threw in some biscuits, tomatoes, and apples, and turned the door latch.

"Who's in the kitchen?" my father called out.

"It's nobody, just me."

"Get something and get back to bed."

I unpacked the bag in the darkness and found my way back to my room. Then from a distance a train whistle sounded.

8

I WAITED TILL I heard my father's car accelerate out of the driveway before getting out of bed.

"Well, if it ain't the Sleeping Beauty!" said Ruth. "Morning to you, Miss Beauty."

I yawned a smile and then yawned again as I dropped into my chair at the table.

"How about a nice hot bowl of oatmeal?"

I nodded a Yes and then, thinking of Anton, asked, "Could I please have a couple of hard-boiled eggs too? And leave the shells on."

Spotting the *Memphis Commercial Appeal* on the table, I saw the biggest, blackest headline I'd seen since Pearl Harbor.

FBI SEIZES 8 NAZI SABOTEURS
LANDED BY U-BOATS ON FLA. & N.Y.
COASTS TO BLOW UP WAR PLANTS

**Explosives Hidden by Nazis on Fla. Beach
Plan Against Alcoa Plant in Tenn.
Carried $150,000 Bribe Money**

Two groups of saboteurs, highly trained by direction of the German High Command at a special school for sabotage near Berlin, were seized by the FBI. The men, all English-speak-

74

ing, were carrying cases of powerful explosives and $150,000 bribe money.

Under cover of night one submarine released its saboteurs at Amagansett, Long Island.

In possession of the men was a list of special industrial plants they were to sabotage. Sabotage of department stores during their rush hours was also planned, to create panic and to break the morale of the American citizens.

The eight captured saboteurs are thought to be part of a larger underground network already operating within this country. The FBI has rounded up 27 men and 2 women from the New York–New Jersey area. Director J. Edgar Hoover says that many more arrests are imminent.

In Washington, Attorney General Francis Biddle said, "The Nazi invaders will be dealt with swiftly and thoroughly. The Justice Department will try the men for treason."

Articles of War proclaim, "Any person acting as a spy in wartime shall suffer death."

I felt my heart striking against the inner wall of my chest. I'm no spy! I'm not giving information to the Germans. But then again I suppose the Justice Department wouldn't stand up and applaud me for hiding a Nazi? He's not a Nazi! A technicality. A captured German soldier is close enough.

I turned to the inside pages in search of "Li'l Abner" while consoling myself that after darkness came Anton had probably hitched a ride on a freight train.

Opposite the comics there was a smiling soldier from Wynne City with a row of colored ribbons on his chest. He wore his hat at a slight angle to show the world he wasn't afraid.

S/Sgt. Clarence C. "Red" Robbins, son of Mrs. Mary G. Robbins, of 18 School St. in Wynne City, Arkansas, died on June 26 from injuries received at Corregidor.

"It wasn't Anton's fault!"

Ruth brought in a bowl of oatmeal and a glass of milk. "It wasn't whose fault?"

"Nothing. Just something I read in the funnies."

She went back into the kitchen wearing a look of disbelief, and I went back to Red Robbins.

S/Sgt. Robbins was a member of the 1941 graduating class of Wynne City High School where he was voted "Mr. Personality." He earned his letter playing football.

His commanding officer, Capt. Simpson B. Graves, wrote in a letter to Mrs. Robbins: "Your son was a brave soldier and a splendid patriot."

A brave soldier and a splendid patriot. They were stirring words all right. When you help your country you're a patriot. But if you help the enemy then you're a— Fear pierced the calm of my stomach.

Ruth stood over me, hands on hips. "What you gonna do, girl? Eat it or meditate on it?"

I looked into her face deep below the surface of her eyes where the wisdom is stored. There are answers there all right. Good sturdy answers fashioned by Ruth to fit Ruth. Nothing there in my size.

"I don't know, Ruth," I said. "I just don't know."

By eight thirty the vacuum cleaner was roaring in the living room and the kitchen was all mine. I filled the paper bag with the best pieces of fried chicken, the mashed potatoes, two apples, hard-boiled eggs, and hot coffee tightly sealed in a Mason jar.

Outside the sun was beginning to warm itself for another sizzler of a day, and from the sandbox side of the house shrill sounds of Sharon and Sue Ellen made everything seem like always. I prayed to God that the hide-out would be empty too like always.

Inside the garage I strained my ears for sounds overhead. The creak of a chair? A footstep? But there was nothing. Then I remembered that the very last thing I had heard last night was the whistle of a train. He must have been on that train.

I stuck the sack between my teeth and started the climb up the stair braces. He has to be there. He wouldn't leave without so much as a good-bye. "Anton —it's me. Anton!"

Suddenly the door at the top of the landing swung open and a hand reached down to pull me up and in. "Don't shout my name!" Without touching the shade he bent to look out the window. "Don't you know better than that?"

"I'm sorry. I was afraid you'd gone."

"Well, I'm still here." Anton's frown began to melt into a smile showing a perfect set of white teeth. "And I am happy to see you." He smelled of soap and water, but his face showed the very beginning of a beard.

"I wanted to come back last night," I apologized. "But it wasn't safe. You knew I'd be back, didn't you?"

"Yes, I think so," he said, letting his eyes settle upon me. I turned my head away. I'm not much to look at.

As I ripped open the sack, spreading it flat against the desk like a tablecloth, I felt his eyes still watching me. "I'm sorry about not having a cloth, and I know I should've warmed the potatoes, but—"

"Please!" He lifted an open palm. "It looks good enough to eat." Anton pulled out the desk chair for me. Then, motioning towards the chicken, he asked, "White meat or dark?"

"Oh, no, it's all for you. I'm really not hungry."

Gray eyes flecked with green looked up from the food. "Then we'll wait until you are."

I tried to calculate how long it had been since Anton had eaten. "I'll have something if you want me to."

Anton didn't let a hungry stomach interfere with his hunger for talk. Sometimes maybe a minute or more would pass before a bite of chicken was eaten. And when he spoke his face moved, matching the humor or intensity of his story. He talked about his parents' home three blocks from the University of Göttingen, a home of gables and gazebos where every Sunday afternoon at three, tea was served to professors, students, and long-time family friends.

Anton described his father, University of Göttingen history professor Erikson Karl Reiker, as being "a truly civilized man" for whom the war started back in the early thirties.

The president of the university had summoned him to his office. "Professor Reiker, these unfortunate statements, these jokes, that you are making about the new regime must cease! Did you actually tell your students that Chancellor Hitler sleeps with a Raggedy Ann doll?"

"No, Herr President, I did not. What I actually said was that I *suspect* Chancellor Hitler sleeps with a Raggedy Ann doll."

The president would not be put off. "Listen to me well, my friend. I will not jeopardize this university so that you may demonstrate your wit. If one, just one more of these treasonous remarks comes back to me, then you will give me no choice but to inform the authorities. These are dangerous times and one cannot make such statements and survive."

Anton took a swallow of coffee from the Mason jar. "Late that very night, something—I don't know what—woke me. I followed the light downstairs to my father's study, where I found him sitting, his head resting on his desk.

"He said that he was O.K. and nothing was wrong, but then he began speaking of his grandfather who had once been president of the university. Pointing to the books in mahogany cases that ran the breadth of the room, he said that some of these books were written because Grandfather believed that a president's job was

78

to encourage scholarship. But our current president, he said, would be as comfortable burning libraries as building them."

For moments Anton just stared down at the bony remains of chicken. Then, abruptly, his forehead wrinkled along his hair line as he said, "It wasn't long after that, in the early summer of 1933, when students and S.S. men stormed through the university burning books."

"I wish people would have stood up to Hitler," I said.

"Some people did, but not many. My father chose acquiescence and life rather than resistance and death. Not a very admirable choice, but a very human one."

Anton went silent and I placed a red apple in his hand. "Tell me about your mother," I said. "Do you have sisters and brothers? And, if you don't mind telling me, how did you escape from the prison camp?"

He smiled. "You're a funny one, Patty Bergen. I'll answer your questions—then I'll ask one of my own. Yes?"

I nodded Yes.

Anton leaned back in the canvas lawn chair.

"My mother's minor virtues are limitless," he said as though he was warming up to the subject. "She sings on key, calls flowers by their generic names, and looks like she was born knowing how to pour tea from a silver service. And of her major virtues there are at least two—her warmth and her great sense of fun. She has special ability to find adventure on a trip to the greengrocer. But primarily there is her warmth." He paused to brush away a smile. "I remember once, I must have been all of seven, running home from school, expecting her undivided attention. Instead the house was empty. There was a light on in the kitchen, pots of food simmering on back burners, and I knew she hadn't gone far or for long. And yet there I stood, brimming over with the most inconsolable disappointment."

Anton stopped for a moment, pressed his lips together before confiding, "It's funny, but I might feel something of that today. Now to your question—sisters or brothers? One sister, Hannah, three years younger whom I never had time for." He shook his head. "I'd like another chance."

"You will have one!" I said, totally convinced. "Just as soon as the war is over you can go back to Göttingen, start again. Will you return to medical school?"

"How did you know that?"

"You told me. Remember? The first time we met."

"I'm going to remember that you store information the way squirrels store nuts. Yes?"

"Only if I'm interested," I said. "Well, are you going back?"

"I'm only concerned with now. And from now on I must be free." Anton breathed deeply as though the air outside barbed wire was different somehow.

"But can't you get hurt escaping?" I asked. "And wouldn't you have been free sooner or later anyway? Wars don't last forever."

A crease, like an exclamation mark, sliced Anton's forehead. "What do you know about sooner or later? Is a moment only a moment when you're in pain? For twenty-seven months I've been mostly bored to death and occasionally scared to death." Anton flung his hand out as though giving an emphatic good-bye to all of that. "Well, enough!"

Scared. Anton was a coward! "Our American soldiers aren't scared, do you think?"

"I think it's not in the best masculine tradition to admit it."

"How—I mean, why do you?"

Anton winked. "Because it's just another emotion."

"Sometimes I cry," I said, feeling exceptionally brave admitting it.

"And so do I." Anton began laughing as though he was having a good time.

"I'm glad you're here," I said. "I want you to stay safe."

"I will. There's no reason why the Americans should bother with one missing prisoner. An ordinary foot soldier." He adjusted his gold ring, the surface of which had some sort of a crest. "Also, I'm lucky. Twice I've been so close to exploding bombs that only a miracle could have saved me. And so I've had a couple of miracles."

He took a quick look out the hide-out's front and back windows. "But suppose I am recaptured. What will the Americans do? Deposit me in the nearest POW camp where I'll have to wait till the end of the war. But in the meantime this day, this month, this year belongs to me."

Anton began carefully polishing his apple. "What was the last question?"

"I was wondering how you managed to escape?"

"The actual mechanics of the escape are not important," he said. "The pertinent point is that I was able to create a—a kind of climate that permitted the escape. Specifically, my deception was believed because it was built on a foundation of truth. Hitler taught me that."

I heard him say it. "Hitler taught you?"

Anton smiled. "I learned it by analyzing his techniques. Hitler's first layer is an undeniable truth, such as: The German worker is poor. The second layer is divided equally between flattery and truth: The German worker deserves to be prosperous. The third layer is fabrication: The Jews and the Communists have stolen what is rightfully yours."

"Well, I can see how it helped him, but I don't see how it worked for you."

"Because I had a rock-bottom truth of my own," he said, striking his chest with his index finger. "My excellent English. I let it be known that I had had an

English governess. And this gave me the advantage of being considered wealthy. But I didn't have a good workable plan that would capitalize on my believed riches until I saw that pin with the glass diamonds— the one you sold me."

"Yes! I couldn't for the life of me figure out why you wanted it. So gaudy and not at all like something you'd like."

"I loved it!" protested Anton. "Because those glass diamonds were going to make me a free man. One of the guards was a simple fellow with financial problems. One day I told him my father would pay five thousand dollars to the person who could get me out of prison. The guard looked too surprised to answer. But eight days later he followed me into the latrine and asked, 'What's the deal?' 'Five perfect diamonds, each diamond having been appraised in excess of one thousand dollars, will be given to the person who drives me out beyond those gates,' I told him. So he did, and I paid him with a dollar's worth of glass jewelry."

"I'm glad you made it," I said, "but that guard— he could get into an awful lot of trouble."

"I don't feel guilty." His hand rubbed across the slight indentation in his chin. "His concern was for reward; mine was for survival. But, on the other hand, I wouldn't wish to implicate him."

I nodded. "Now I'm ready to answer your question."

His teeth pressed together, giving new strength to the line of his jaw. "I'm certain you appreciate the seriousness of what you have done, aiding an escaped prisoner of war. I was wondering why you were taking these risks on my behalf. Because of your German ancestry? Perhaps your father is secretly sympathetic to the Nazi cause?"

"That's not true! My father's parents came from Russia and my mother's from Luxembourg."

Anton looked alarmed. "I'm sorry. It's just that Bergen is such a good German name."

"It's also a good Jewish name," I said, pleased by the clean symmetry of my response.

His mouth came open. "Jewish?" An index finger pointed toward me. "You're Jewish?"

I thought he knew. I guess I thought everybody knew. Does he think I tricked him? My wonderful Anton was going to change to mean. As I nodded Yes, my breathing came to a halt while my eyes clamped shut.

Suddenly, strong baritone laughter flooded the room. Both eyes popped open and I saw him standing there, shaking his head from side to side.

"It's truly extraordinary," he said. "Who would believe it? 'Jewish girl risks all for German soldier.' Tell me, Patty Bergen—" his voice became soft, but with a trace of hoarseness—"why are you doing this for me?"

It wasn't complicated. Why didn't he know? There was really only one word for it. A simple little word that in itself is reason enough.

"The reason I'm doing this for you," I started off, "is only that I wouldn't want anything bad to happen to you."

Anton turned his face from me and nodded as though he understood. Outside, a blue-gray cloud cruised like a pirate ship between sun and earth, sending the room from sunshine into shadows.

9

ON MAIN STREET, something was different—too many people hanging around for an ordinary weekday better than an hour before noontime. And it wasn't the usual little groups of farmers slow-talking about too many bugs and too little rain. There were quick movements of their hands and high excitement in their voices. "And I'll tell you this—them people would sooner espionage you than look at you."

There were also late-model cars licensed "Arkansas—Land of Opportunity," but with a combination of letters and numbers that marked them as having come from places other than here.

Everywhere this strong current of excitement and pleasure, only slightly disguised, that at long last something pretty big had happened right here in Jenkinsville.

I stood in front of our store, watching the editor of the *Gazette* holding informal court for six of Jenkinsville's leading citizens. Mr. Blakey looked up as a shiny black sedan passed slowly down Main Street. He studied the two business-suited occupants before reporting, "FBI agents from the Little Rock bureau. Those fellers gonna find out this was no ordinary escape. No, sir!"

"Then you figger the POW was fixin' to join up with them eight saboteurs?" asked Mr. Jackson.

"I didn't say that," answered Mr. Blakey. "Still, something's mighty fishy. Harold himself told me that the Nazi was seen sitting on his bunk at five o'clock; at five fifteen he was reported missing; and at five seventeen those Dobermans couldn't find a scent worth picking up."

"What about the train, the five fifteen to Memphis?" asked Mr. Henkins.

Mr. Blakey nodded. "Gone through with a fine tooth. Why, that train was held up for better'n thirty minutes in Ebow." He shook his head. "No, sir, I'm telling you this was no ordinary escape."

Mr. Jackson said, "Quent, why don't you quit saying what it ain't and tell us what you think it is."

Mr. Blakey swallowed down some excess saliva. "If you want my opinion, I will say this—Reiker had to have help. All right, if he had help where did he get it from?" Mr. Blakey was like a champion fighter readying his knockout punch. "Not from inside the camp, I'll wager, 'cause them guards are good clean Americans."

The crescent of men tightened around Blakey. "If you fellers will recall," he continued, "a couple of weeks ago there was this troop train that derailed in California. Before that an Army Air Corps plane up and explodes over New Jersey. And yesterday, the very same day that Reiker escapes, four Nazi saboteurs are landed on the Florida coast while four more land on Long Island. And you want to know what I think? I'm gonna spell it out for you. I sincerely believe that there's a Nazi underground working in this country, and for all anybody knows, it could be working right here among us."

Inside the store I saw that the only activity was over by the hardware. Three farmers were lined up in front of a counter.

My father called for Chester. The black man in his gray porter's jacket came running from the back storeroom. "Yes, sir, Mr. Harry?"

"Chester, go bring up all the twelve-gauge shotgun shells we've got."

"Yes, sir, Mr. Harry."

Two men wearing striped ties and business suits came in the door and headed directly towards my father. I followed them.

"Mr. Bergen?" asked the older of the men as he flipped open a small leather case.

"Yes, sir, I'm Harry Bergen." My father came from behind the counter to shake hands with both men. "What can I do for the FBI today?"

"I'm John Pierce. This is my partner, Phil McFee. We're here investigating the escape of the prisoner from the POW camp." Pierce handed my father a black-and-white glossy photograph. "Do you have any recollections of this man?"

"Once," said my father, "some POWs were brought in here to buy things, but I didn't pay much attention to what those rats looked like."

Pierce pointed to the photograph. "Look carefully, Mr. Bergen. Reiker may have been acting as interpreter for the others."

"Oh, you know, there was one." My father nodded his head up and down. "He was a kinda smart aleck, that one. Tried to joke with me, but I told him right off I wasn't interested in making jokes with Germans."

Pierce struck the picture with his index finger. "Is that the man who tried to joke with you?"

"Well, he might be the one. I'll tell you fellows the truth, I didn't pay much attention to what he looked like. There was one thing I remember. Don't know if it'll help you boys much."

"What?" asked Pierce.

"He talked in a funny way, pretending to be a Harvard boy instead of a convict."

"And there's nothing else?"

"No, sir. I sure wish I could be more helpful to you and Mr. Hoover 'cause he's one of the two greatest living Americans. The other one's General MacArthur."

McFee, who looked as though he hadn't gotten comfortably settled into his twenties yet, allowed his chest to swell to enormous proportions. "Thank you, sir. I appreciate your saying that."

Pierce crossed the store to show the picture to my mother and Gussie Fields, who shook their heads in unison. Then Sister Parker was asked to take a look. She said No and was about to return the photo when she gave a second, more thoughtful appraisal. "You know, he looks a little something like the man Mr. Bergen's girl waited on." Sister Parker turned to find me only a step behind. She held Anton's picture aloft. "Patty, isn't this that German you were talking and laughing with?"

The eyes of the FBI were upon me. I asked, "Is it all right if I look?"

The older agent took the picture from Sister Parker's hand and gave it to me. As a precaution against the shakes, I let my hand rest against the top of the counter. "Well, this might be the same prisoner I waited on. It looks like it could be him only I don't remember his hair being so dark."

"Why didn't you say something before now?" asked McFee. "You've been following us since we entered the store."

"I have a right to be in this store if I want to. It's my father's store."

"You were laughing with him," pressed McFee. "Did he say something funny?"

"No."

McFee's face came in close. "Then why did you laugh?"

"I laughed because—because—" The dam that kept my tears back sprang a leak. "Because he didn't know what to call a pocket pencil sharpener." I hid my eyes in my hands, letting the sobs come at will, regulating their own intensity and volume. Sister Parker put her arm around me, giving me little now, now pats to my shoulder.

My father's voice approached. "What's the matter? What's happened?"

McFee shrugged. "We were merely asking her a few questions and—"

"They made her nervous," interrupted Sister. "Both of them questioning Patty like she went and took that German out of prison."

"Do you realize what you did?" asked my father, grabbing my wrist away from my face. It vibrated wildly like the agitator from some old washing machine. "Look at that child's hand! She's highly nervous and I don't appreciate one bit your upsetting her. I'm going to call the FBI and ask them to give me an explanation for this."

Pierce held his head like he was holding onto a headache. "Now, Mr. Bergen, please—"

"Don't you please me!" said my father. "I want to tell you both something. I'm a Jew and I'd rather help a mad dog escape from the pound than to help a Nazi. Come to my house! Search it from top to bottom, attic, garage, everything!"

"Are you finished talking?" asked Pierce in a voice that just missed being a shout. "Allow me to say this. There is not the slightest suspicion against either you or your daughter. I apologize for my partner who's new with the bureau and sometimes gets carried away. But now that he understands the situation, I'm certain that he'll want to apologize to both you and your daughter. Don't you, McFee?"

"Sure, I'm sorry. I didn't know the girl was a nervous wreck."

"Go wait in the car," barked Pierce. He turned his attention to my father. "I'm going to have to ask you a favor. The escape of the prisoner Reiker may pose a threat to the very security of this nation, and it is considered essential that he be quickly apprehended. We're working night and day to do just that. Now, with that in mind, Mr. Bergen, I'm asking you to please let me talk with your daughter. It's just possible that she might provide some useful thread of information."

I wiped away the last of the tears and said, "I'll tell you anything I can." Just as long as the information is worthless.

Mr. Pierce smiled. "Fine. Fine. As you may have heard, we're fighting the Germans because they're bad, and if one of them gets loose it's very, very important to catch him. The reason we have to catch him is so he can't hurt children and other people. You understand that, don't you?"

"Perfectly."

"That's fine," he said, taking out a yellow pencil scarred by teeth marks. Mr. Pierce jotted down a few words on a stenographic pad as I told my story. He asked me to tell it one more time, adding anything that came to mind. The second time, I remembered the color of the pocket pencil sharpener—it was red.

The agent removed the pencil from between his teeth to inquire whether I had noticed if there was much money in the prisoner's wallet. I didn't remember seeing a lot of money. The agent wanted to know if I was absolutely certain that the only thing the prisoner bought was the sharpener, paper, and pencils.

I thought about the pin with the circle of glass diamonds. "There was something else," I said. "Now that I think of it. The prisoner carried a large tan sack. He must've bought a straw field hat like the rest of the prisoners. Yes! I think he did."

"Would you say," asked Pierce, lowering his voice, "that there was anything peculiar in his behavior?"

"Yes, there was something out of the ordinary about him."

"What was it?"

"Politeness," I said, aware of beginning to enjoy the interview. "He was very polite."

The FBI man muttered a thanks as he walked with weighted steps out of the store.

Across the store, Quentin Blakey and his crescent of men came in to catch the twelve o'clock news: "The FBI has rounded up an additional fifteen spies," said the announcer's voice. "These spies were preparing to help the eight U-boat saboteurs once they established themselves on the mainland. FBI director J. Edgar Hoover said in Washington today that the spies had enough money and weapons to carry out a two-year reign of terror. At two o'clock this afternoon, Director Hoover will give a full report to the President. In Arkansas a prisoner of war escapes," continued the announcer. "That's us!" said Mr. Blakey. "Throughout the country, law enforcement agencies are searching for a German prisoner of war. Frederick Anton Reiker, five feet ten inches, one hundred sixty-five pounds, vanished yesterday from a prison camp near Jenkinsville, Arkansas. The twenty-two-year-old former Nazi soldier is dark-haired, speaks flawless English, and should be considered extremely dangerous. The weather for Little Rock and vicinity is—"

My father clicked off the radio. "Serves them right for coddling those Nazis. Our boys sure don't get that good a treatment when they're taken prisoner."

The president of the Rotary Club nodded. "The trouble with this country is that it's too Christian. The Bible admonishes us to turn the other cheek, but we forget that it also tells us to take a tooth for a tooth, and an eye for an eye."

"I'll tell you something, George," said my father. "I don't think they oughta take prisoners. Not live ones, anyway." There was a chorus of appreciative male laughter.

One of the men suddenly gave George Henkins an alerting poke to the ribs, "Would you looky what's a-coming in the door."

She was young, wearing a tailored dress of sea green, with shoulder-length hair that bounced in rhythm with her walk. But as she came up to the male quartet, they all appeared disappointed. For what looked like dazzling beauty at a distance was at close range only a trim figure and freshly laundered hair.

"Excuse me, gentlemen, I'm Charlene Madlee of the *Commercial Appeal,* and I'm looking for Sheriff Cauldwell. They told me you might know where I could find him."

"I haven't seen Harold since morning," said Mr. Blakey. "You fellows know where he might be?"

The town sign painter, Blister, shook his head. "I reckon with all the 'citement, he's busier'n a hound dog during hunting season."

I followed the lady reporter out to the sidewalk and offered to show her to Sheriff Cauldwell's office. As we drove together down Main toward Front Street I noticed an occasional cluster of men on the sidewalk. Then it struck me. Where were all the womenfolk? Didn't any of the town ladies have bread to buy or an electric bill to pay? It reminded me of a movie I saw: The town men were stationed with guns behind every buckboard, waiting for the Comanches to attack, while all the women and children were holed up in the saloon.

The sun, when did it pull its disappearing act? The complexion of the day had changed to unrelieved grayness.

"There's the jailhouse," I said, pointing to the dirty stucco bungalow with the rippled tin roof that squatted on an open grassy space between Dr. Benson's drugstore and the Rice County National Bank. "The sheriff's office is right inside, but I doubt if he's around today."

She made a skillful entry into something less than a full parking space. "I'll be right back," she said, which I took as an invitation to stick around.

I thought about Anton, alone and getting hungrier. Just as I decided that I'd better hurry back to him with news and food, the reporter returned. "Would you know how to get to the prison camp?"

She followed my directions through the center of

town and then turned right onto Highway 64. "My name is Charlene Madlee," she said, pulling a cigarette from a puffy beige pocketbook. "And I think it's very sweet of you to guide me around."

"Oh, that's O.K.," I said. "I think it must be very interesting being a reporter. How do you become one?"

Charlene smiled. I could tell she liked my question. "What's your name?"

"Patty Bergen."

"Well, Patty, you need to decide whether you have the aptitude—the ability—for it. A good reporter has to have enough curiosity to kill a dozen cats and a love for words. Does that sound like you, Patty?"

"Yes, it does, Miss Madlee, really."

"Call me Charlene."

"O.K., Charlene. Well, I'm very curious and that's one of the things that upsets my father. He says that all I do is ask questions. And I do like words, I use them all the time," I said, stumbling over my enthusiasm. I laughed and so did Charlene. "What I meant to say is that, well, you'll probably think this is strange, but I read dictionaries."

"Really?"

"I keep reading until I find a word I don't know and then I write down the word and its meaning. I got all the way through *Webster's Elementary Dictionary* two years ago and now I'm working my way through *Webster's Collegiate*."

Charlene turned her eyes from the road to look at me. "How did you become interested in dictionary reading?"

"Well, it's all mixed up with curiosity. When I read a book, I want to understand precisely what it is the writer is saying, not just almost but precisely. And it's the same when people are talking to you. Like a moment ago you used the word 'aptitude,' and because you didn't think I understood, you substituted the word 'ability.' But you didn't actually mean ability. We both know that I don't have the ability to be a reporter today, but I just might have the aptitude."

"That's very well put," said Charlene admiringly. "I'll bet you're a real whiz in school."

"No, I'm not."

"And you're modest too?"

"No, it's the truth. I'm not at all good in school. Mostly I make Cs—sometimes worse."

At McDonald's dairy barn, we left the blacktop to turn right on a dusty side road. Farther in the distance those familiar Y-shaped posts connected a network of barbed wire which squared off the compound. Charlene brought the car to a sudden stop in front of the gate, where two rifle-carrying soldiers marched sentry duty. A third soldier stepped out of a guard house and threw Charlene a salute. "Where are you going, ma'am?"

"I'm Charlene Madlee, a reporter for the *Memphis Commercial Appeal,* and I want to see your warden."

The soldier asked us to wait while he phoned the commandant's office. Within a couple of minutes he returned, shaking his head. "I'm real sorry, ma'am, the commandant cannot see reporters today."

Charlene opened the car door, "You get that commandant back on the phone. I want to speak with him." The soldier's obey reflex had been made strong by constant use. Without hesitation he returned to the telephone. "It's all yours, ma'am," he said, extending the black receiver to Charlene.

"Commandant? This is Charlene Madlee of the *Memphis Commercial Appeal.* Commandant, I have information that suggests that the security of this prison is lax and . . . Of course. Yes, I understand that. . . . No, I know it isn't fair, and that's the reason I drove the forty miles from Memphis just to get your side of the story. . . . First barrack on the left. Thank you."

Charlene shook her head in disbelief. "The commandant just fell for the oldest newspaper trick in the world."

The first barrack on the left was indistinguishable from all the others spread around the compound, with their painted white walls. We came to a stop directly in front of a sign which stated: RESERVED FOR GENERAL STAFF.

A soldier wearing two chevrons on his sleeve approached. "You're the reporter?"

As we followed a few steps behind him, Charlene handed me some sheets of yellow paper and a thick, eraserless pencil. "You really want to be a reporter, then we'll let this be your first assignment. Write down everything that you consider pertinent to the fact that a prisoner has escaped."

The name on the door read: MAJOR ROBERT E. L. WROPER, COMMANDING. I wrote that down. He rose from his desk as we entered. "Yes, happy to see you. Please come right in, Miss Maudlee."

"Madlee," corrected Charlene as she shook his extended hand. She introduced me as her friend, Patty Bergen, "who has the aptitude to become a good reporter."

"Major, what I came here to find out," said Charlene, "is how was it possible for a prisoner to escape this camp?"

He pushed some imaginary strands of hair across a hairless dome. "We're real proud of our security system here, Miss Madlee. We follow the same master plan for security as eighty similar camps across this country —the alarm system, the many security checks, the K-9 Corps of trained Dobermans. Even the exact amount of voltage per square foot of area is written out. And I'm here to see that the orders are carried out according to the master plan." Major Wroper unrolled a blueprint of the camp.

While my writing hand was cramping from the race to get it all down, Charlene seemed to be working at a more leisurely pace. I began to worry that maybe I was doing it all wrong.

94

Charlene lit her own cigarette with a small gold lighter and blew smoke in the general direction of the officer. "Then, Major Wroper, how is it possible that a prisoner did, in fact, escape?"

"That has not as yet been fully determined. We are not in charge of the investigation, that comes under the jurisdiction of the FBI. But you should know that nothing is 100 per cent foolproof. There's been no prison built that somebody hasn't escaped from."

Major Wroper's statement seemed persuasive. I looked at Charlene to see if she too was impressed. She leaned back in her chair, stretching her legs forward. "But, Major, is it usual to escape without even leaving a clue?"

His eyelids lowered. "Who told you that nonsense?"

"Oh, then there were clues?" Charlene's voice was positively sunny.

"As I've tried to indicate to you, the FBI is in charge of the investigation and—"

"Is it true," interrupted Charlene, "that the dogs were unable to pick up a scent anywhere? Not even from the prisoner's own bed?"

"Young lady, I'd like to cooperate with the press, but I will have to ask you not to write anything that would make us look foolish. I can't have shame brought down on the heads of the loyal men in my command."

Charlene lifted an eyebrow. "Let me assure you, Major, that it is not my intention to bring ridicule upon you or your men. All I want is the information so that I can bring back a story that will make my editor happy."

The officer sighed like a great weariness had overtaken him. "Very well." He picked up an index card and read, "The escapee's name is Frederick Anton Reiker. Serial number GL 1877. Rank: Private, German Army. Height: 5 ft. 10½ inches. Weight: 165 pounds. Age: 22. Born: Göttingen, Germany. Prison

Record: Co-operative. Health: In May Reiker was hospitalized in the prison infirmary for appendicitis." He pitched the card across his desk. "At exactly four fifty yesterday afternoon the prisoners of Barrack 314, having eaten their evening meal, filed out of mess hall. A few minutes later Reiker was sitting on his bunk with another prisoner named Blinkoff. Reiker was reading his palm. At five seventeen roll call Reiker was reported missing.

"A general alarm was sounded and the camp dogs were immediately taken to Reiker's bunk, but they were unable to get his scent. This was due without doubt to the fact that Reiker had had three other prisoners sitting on his bed for palm readings. The dogs were hopelessly confused. A search was made for Reiker's clothing and personal effects, but nothing was located."

Major Wroper rotated his swivel chair toward the window. His eyes seemed to scan the grounds for the prisoner who, like a pair of reading glasses, would turn out to be only temporarily misplaced.

It was Charlene who broke the spell. "Major, did Frederick Reiker escape prison to join forces with the eight saboteurs?"

"I have no reason to believe that."

"What I would like to do now, with your permission, is to speak with some of the people who knew Reiker."

"Oh. Yes, indeed," he said, pressing a button. The door opened and the corporal appeared as quickly as a genie. Major Wroper explained Charlene's request and told the soldier to offer, "all assistance."

We followed the corporal into the outer office where he began making phone calls. A clock gave the time at five minutes till two. If only I could get some word to Anton. Let him know. He must be hungry and worried.

The corporal hit the receiver back onto the hook.

96

"I'm sorry. It looks like everybody's out on work detail."

"Then take me over to your infirmary," said Charlene.

Inside the infirmary, the smell was all soap and Lysol. The corporal led us past a ward with two dozen white-sheeted beds, but only five or six patients. At the end of the hall he opened the door where a sign read: CAPT. GERALD S. ROBINSON.

A crew-cut soldier with a single chevron sat in a cluttered outer office two-finger typing. Captain Robinson, a small fastidious man, stood up behind a large untidy desk when we entered. "Interesting," he said, giving Charlene a smile. "The FBI hasn't yet been around to interview me and I may have known Anton Reiker as well as any American in this camp."

"Lucky I found you, Doctor, or should I call you by your military title?"

"Oh, you probably should, but don't."

"Dr. Robinson, would you say that the escapee was a tough kind of a prisoner?"

He selected a pipe with a curved stem from a rack of six. "I'd say so, but not in the conventional sense. It seems to me that Reiker has a toughness of mind. In medicine when a person is in constant contact with a disease and yet is able to resist catching it himself, then he would be considered to have great resiliency or, in street parlance, toughness." The doctor looked at Charlene. "Do you know what I'm talking about?"

"Yes!" I said with a suddenness that surprised me. "His mind was strong and clear, and he didn't believe what the Nazis wanted him to believe!"

"More or less," said the doctor.

"Then in your opinion," said Charlene, "he didn't escape for the purpose of joining forces with the eight U-boat saboteurs?"

"Oh, I suspect he wanted his freedom and nothing more."

"But, Dr. Robinson, isn't it a distinct possibility that Reiker was merely faking an attitude that he could later use to advantage?"

He took a long puff from his pipe. "It is possible, but I doubt it. Some of our prisoners, mostly former members of the S.S., are truly fanatical men. They're arrogant and they don't care who knows it. Reiker wasn't cut from that mold. He was a scholar, interested in books and ideas. And, perhaps more important, he was a loner."

"This is very interesting, but could you give me a concrete example of something that the prisoner said or did that gives you this impression?"

Dr. Robinson leaned deep into his chair. "I can't honestly remember specifically anything that he said, only—"

Charlene's body pitched forward. "Only what?"

"It was only that he seemed like a decent man."

Before the prison gate stood the same obedient sentry. His eyes swept over the blue sedan before calling, "Proceed, ma'am," as Charlene blasted off, leaving behind a trail of raised dust.

Charlene didn't say anything, and I was grateful for the chance to remember the doctor's words. It was then that I experienced the last of my fear taking flight. Nestling down in its place came exultation. At this moment on a dusty back road within smelling distance of McDonald's dairy barn I felt the greatest joy I had ever known.

10

CHARLENE IDLED THE MOTOR in front of the store. "Nice having you with me today. Would you like me to send you an autographed copy of the story?"

"Yes, thanks very much."

"And if I can ever help you in any way—"

"Well, maybe I could write you a letter?" Why would she want to hear from me? "You wouldn't have to answer, well, I mean, unless you have the time."

"Tell you what, next time you're planning a visit to your grandparents, write me. I'll show you around the paper; it should be very interesting for a girl who has the aptitude to become a reporter."

A reporter? Was it true that just a couple of hours ago I thought about becoming a reporter? Then the word journalist had had a ring to it, but now it's gone. A journalist's life might be fun but fun, like champagne bubbles, can't completely fill you up. Anyway there was something else I'd rather do with my life.

I wanted to run the two blocks home but I remembered Anton's advice to do what I've always done and to go where I've always gone. "Be visible," he had said, "highly visible." I walked visibly into the store. He might like a couple of Hershey bars for dessert.

My father's voice caught me. "What are you doing wandering around? I want you to go right home and stay there. There's a criminal loose!"

"Yes, sir, I know. It is all right if I fool around the yard?"

"Well, stay in the yard where Ruth can keep an eye on you. And, under no circumstances, go farther than the garage."

"Oh no, sir, no farther."

The tub water was only lukewarm against my foot as it gushed from the "hot" faucet, and after a minute it became uncomfortably cool. As I dried myself I wondered if I would ever trade this body of sharp, thin lines for something more gentle, more womanly. "Ruth," I called out from the bathroom, "do you have something for me to eat? I'm starved!"

"Since when you begin asking for food? And taking baths without being told?"

"Since always," I said, buttoning up a fresh white shirt.

Ruth shook her head. "When God went and parted the Red Sea for the Israelites that was a miracle too."

The brown paper bag felt heavy between my teeth as I climbed up the stair ribs. A scent of salami liberally seasoned with pepper and garlic assaulted my nose and started up a series of small sneezes. As I sneezed only an arm's length from the door, I became frightened that he would be frightened. But before I could call his name, his hand reached down and touched mine.

"*Gesundheit!*" he said, and smiled as though I was somebody special.

"I brought you lunch and some fresh clothes," I said, surprised at my matter-of-fact tone.

As Anton measured the Palm Beach trousers against his waist I reached back into the sack and touched cardboard. The box was cocoa-brown, and the cover came embossed with three golden acorns, the symbol of Oak Hall, the finest men's store in all of Memphis. Inside was the shirt, the Father's Day present. Not the Father's Day of a few weeks ago, but of a year before that.

I remember how important it had seemed then to give something special, something of value. At first my mother and I went to Goldsmith's, Memphis' largest store, and we found this perfectly nice sport shirt that she tried to talk me into buying. "And you'll have two whole dollars left over from your birthday money to buy something nice for yourself," she told me. When I said I wanted to walk over to Oak Hall to see their shirts, she got all worked up. "It's just plain stupid to pay two dollars more for a label. You got so much money you can throw it away? Don't you know labels are worn inside the collar where nobody can see them?"

But because my determination outdetermined her determination, she told me to go by myself. I was to meet her back in Goldsmith's in exactly one hour on the fourth floor, better dresses. One whole hour of my very own. Freedom, freedom. I felt happy and practically grown-up. So I took the scenic side trip up in the elevator to the seventh floor book department.

Over a table, a sign decorated with a painted Teddy bear said CHILDREN'S BOOKS. Some were books that I had long ago passed through. *A Treasury of Mother Goose* and Beatrix Potter's *The Tale of Peter Rabbit*. Then there were the Bobbsey Twins and *Winnie-the-Pooh*. On the next table were stacks of the Hardy Boys and good old Nancy Drew. Her father is a hot-shot lawyer, but it takes Nancy to solve all the mysteries.

It was in the adult section that I found the books I wanted to take home. *The Best Stories of Guy de Maupassant* and another collection by O. Henry. Goldsmith's had some good books, beautiful books, and five dollars would buy two or three.

When I glanced up I saw a saleslady starting towards me, and I knew if she just said, "May I help you?" I'd buy de Maupassant and O. Henry. But instead I turned and half-walking, half-running made it back into the elevator with integrity and five dollars still intact.

Inconspicuously printed on the store window in gold Gothic letters were the words, OAK HALL SINCE 1887 and just underneath, three golden acorns. Inside the heavy brass door a middle-aged manikin posed majestically with riding stick. He wore a deep-blue shirt with a Paisley ascot at his neck.

A carefully attired salesman who, like the acorns, must have been with Oak Hall since 1887, took out stacks of size fifteen sport shirts from behind a sliding glass door. Many of the shirts were marked five and six dollars and some cost as much as ten dollars. One was the exact shirt worn by the manikin. The buttons were pearl, but dyed in perfect matching blue. My hand glided across the fabric, which had the smoothness of marble. The label read, FINE EGYPTIAN COTTON. It was a shirt for presidents and premiers, princes and polo players.

It took only a few minutes' wait for the initials "H.B." to be ironed onto the pocket. But it was only by the greatest amount of self-control that I was able to check my impulse to present the shirt to my father that very night. Actually I did cheat, but only a little, when I told him that I had bought him a perfectly wonderful Father's Day gift.

When Sunday finally arrived I felt the way I used to feel about Christmas. My imagination had played the scene over so many times. I knew that he would be pleased with my gift. He'd say it was the finest shirt he'd ever owned. And then the focus would shift from gift to giver and I would rest there in his arms like a long-lost daughter come home.

The reality wasn't like that. He opened the box, said "Thanks," and then, replacing the cover, he tossed it casually out of sight. But it's what happened next—what I did next—that even now makes me feel the painful pinch of shame. I brought the shirt back to him. "Look, it has your initials, H.B.," I said. "And see the buttons, genuine pearl dyed to perfectly match the fabric which is very special too. Comes all the way from Egypt."

With a sudden half swing of his hand, he pushed both me and the shirt out of his way. "I *said*, 'Thank you,' " he said, edging each word with finely controlled irritation.

Anton asked me to excuse him while he went into the bathroom to change into the pants. It was then that I handed him the cocoa-colored box. "A shirt. You'll need a shirt." I turned my head away. Maybe it isn't such a great shirt. Maybe he won't like it either. But I turned my head back just in time to see his face change from surprise to pleasure. His hand stroked the blueness and his fingers even stopped momentarily to examine a button.

"Thanks," he said, touching my cheek with his hand.

Then he was gone and the room seemed emptier than it had ever before been. Probably it was just that before Anton the room had grown accustomed to its loneliness.

Anton came back, filling it up. His eyes looked blue now, very blue, like the shirt he wore. During our lunch I told him about all the excitement in town, and about my visit to the prison camp. He seemed confused by it all, especially about my interrogation by the FBI.

"Why is there such interest in me? An ordinary soldier."

"Only because they think you're a threat to our national security."

"Me?"

103

"Because of the German saboteurs from the U-boats the FBI captured. They think you escaped to join up with them."

"U-boats were here, Patty?"

"They just stopped long enough to let off the saboteurs."

"And they think I—"

"Yes."

"It was the timing. It was the worst possible timing!"

"But you're safe here, Anton. You can stay here till the end of the war! Nobody knows about this place and I can bring you food and books to read and anything else that you want—tell me what you want!"

Anton raised his eyes to look at me without raising his head. "A bit of your courage, P.B."

"P.B." he called me, and my initials took on a strength and beauty that never before was there. And now that I had of my own free will broken faith with my father and my country, I felt like a good and worthy person.

Anton laughed, keeping it well within his throat. "After the war when I'm with my family again I'll tell them about you. How an American Jewess protected me."

I searched through his words for even a slight implication that when he was with his family again I'd be there too. But I couldn't find it. I was close to coming right out with it—asking him, begging if that would help, to let me go where he goes.

Then my hand brushed across my hair and I felt the forgotten—the tizzledly, frizzledy handiwork of Mrs. Reeves. The moment went sour.

"Tell me," he said, showing a perfect set of teeth like an advertisement for toothpaste. "Why have you suddenly taken the vows of silence?"

A knot of anger rose up. Anger towards Mrs.

Reeves who uglified me, towards Anton who pretended not to notice, but mostly against myself for believing that a prince could love a plowgirl.

"If I talked less would you talk more?" he asked, still showing off his teeth. Show-off!

"No! It's only because—because I don't feel like any more talking. You want coffee? I'll bring you coffee." As I reached for the door, I saw his hand reach out towards me. But I closed the door firmly between us.

I found myself in front of the house and sat down on the steps, out of view of the garage. The carousel inside my brain began its revolutions: He's nice to me only because I'm useful. He's nice to me only because he likes me. He's handsome. I'm homely. Love is blind and beauty, skin deep. He's laughing at me—with me. With me. Why did I have to find him? How could I endure losing him?

My head dropped forward and rested in the dark hollow of my hands. Remember what they say? My father, mother, the clerks in the store, and the salesmen with heavy sample cases from Memphis, St. Louis, and Little Rock: "You only get what you pay for."

From somewhere a voice called my name. My eyes remained closed. At any moment he'll sit down next to me, and after a little quietness he will ask me to go away with him. "You really want me to go with you?" He'll nod his head, and I'll say, "Yes, Anton, yes."

"Looky here!" said the voice close up. "I got me some salt pork for crawdading."

Freddy Dowd! "I don't want to catch any crawdads, Freddy. I might have a headache." How do you tell a boy who never has anything more to brag about than a piece of salt pork that you want him to go away? Poor Freddy, so thin, like he never quite gets enough to eat.

He sat down next to me. "Salt pork is what them crawdads would rather eat than anything in this here world."

"Have you ever tasted crawdad, Freddy?"

He laughed, showing jagged areas where his teeth had darkened and decayed. "Crawdads ain't for eatin', they'se for catchin'."

"Did you know that crawdads are in the same family as lobsters and crabs? The crustacean family, and only people who are very, very rich can ever afford to taste them."

He looked at me like I was telling him the stars are stuck to the heavens with little bits of cellophane tape. "I'm a-gonna ask my daddy," he said after an interval.

Freddy is getting very close to being twelve years old, and he still believes that being a grown-up man is the same as knowing things. Daddy Dowd is a big, slow-moving, slow-speaking man who delivers milk, but drinks something else. Poor Freddy, you're not going to find many answers there.

O.K., so Freddy is simple. There are worse things than that. There's hypocrisy, for example, pretending to like somebody just so they can keep you safe from the FBI. And with Freddy a person can feel comfortable because from his miserable perch he's not likely to be laughing at anybody. Sometimes I feel Freddy and I are related. Well, not exactly related as much as we share something that makes us both outcasts.

Part of our outcastness has to do with simple geography. He is a country boy who because of some accident of his daddy's job lives right here in town. And my geography problem is in being a Jewish girl where it's a really peculiar thing to be. Even when I went to Jewish Sunday school in Memphis the geography thing was still there. I would come in on a cold Sunday morning wearing short-sleeved, short-legged

106

union suits under my sash-tied dresses, while the other girls looked as though they were born into this world wearing matching sweater and skirt outfits.

It struck me that neither of us had said anything for a while. I looked over at Freddy who was busily picking at a piece of scab. How like Freddy to sit quiet and amuse himself when I don't feel like talking. One thing you can say about him is that he's appreciative. He's just happy having someone to sit with.

Leaving downtown was the familiar roar of a car motor. (Did all Chevys sound angry?) It must be six o'clock. Moments later I watched my father steer a wide turn in front of the house and gun the car up the gravel driveway.

"Oh, Harry, leave her alone!" cried my mother through the open car window.

Me? What did I—oh, God, it's Freddy! Where do I keep my mind?

"Go, Freddy!" I whispered. "Go home!"

The car door slammed shut. My father's face was a pasty white. "How dare you disobey me!"

"Please let me explain something to you." My hands automatically reached out in a gesture that looked futile even to me.

My mother stationed herself between us. "Now, Harry. Harry, leave her alone. Please!" With one hand, he gave her a strong push that sent her staggering backward across the grass.

"God damn you!" he shouted at me. "You'll obey me if it kills you!"

My legs were carrying me in reverse toward the rear of the house. "Let me at least tell you what happened. I was sitting there and he just came over a moment ago and sat down. I swear to God that's the truth!"

His feet came faster and I moved to keep space between us. The sounds of Ruth's kitchen radio tuned

107

into the gospel station poured out the open window. "Op-pressed so hard they could not stand. Let my people go . . ."

We were deep into back-yard territory and my eye caught sight of the garage hide-out. God! Don't let him see this. I tried to maneuver back toward the front of the house, but my arm was caught with an explosion of pain.

"Awllll!" My arm felt as if it was pulled out of its socket. Then the barrage. "Noooo-ohhh." The ground reached up and laid me down. Oh, God, can't you help?

Everything was quiet. Was it all over? It seemed too quick to satisfy him. I forced my eyes open. He was standing over me, the brown of his suit in perfect outline against the white of the garage. His breath was coming in quick, heavy gasps and I began to hope that his exhaustion would cut short the agony.

Metal clicked against metal. A leather belt rushed through fabric loops. As the belt whipped backward, I saw Anton with raised fists racing toward my father's unsuspecting back.

"Nooo!" I shouted. "Go way! Go way!"

The belt came down. "Ohhhh-nonono!"

Anton, his hands outstretched before him, froze. His face was like I had never seen it, dazed with horror. Then he clapped his hands to his eyes and backed towards the garage.

11

"SHE HAS TO BE taking it home with her; I can't think of any other explanation. That kosher salami cost one dollar and ten cents." My mother repeated the price a second time for added emphasis.

I pulled the top sheet over my head to block out the early morning sounds from the kitchen and rolled over a now very warm ice bag and remembered. In another few minutes they would be leaving for the store. Only then would I get out of bed. Just as soon as my mother downs her second cup of coffee and my father finishes his corn flakes. As long as I can remember it has been corn flakes and nothing but corn flakes. He's got the same loyalty towards cars. "I'll buy any kinda car as long as it's a Chevrolet." And cigarettes too. He's never had a cigarette in his mouth that wasn't a Lucky Strike.

"So you'd better talk to her, Harry."

"Talk to who?"

"To Ruth!" Her voice hit a shrill note. "I want to know what's happening to the salami and chicken and all the other food that's been disappearing around here lately."

"Well, how do you know she's taking it home? I don't know what you're talking about. But she'll be coming any minute now, and if you want to fire her it's fine with me. Something about that woman I never liked."

I didn't want to speak to them, but I didn't want them to suspect either. I yelled out, "I'm sorry about the salami 'cause I ate most of it myself. And about the leftover chicken, Sharon and Sue Ellen ate the last of it."

"Now you see that!" he told her. "Don't ever talk to me again about missing food."

I'll have to say this for him, he's always generous about food, even when we eat in restaurants. Like that Sunday in Memphis not too long ago when we ate at Britlings' and I ordered the chopped sirloin steak and he said, "That's nothing but a hamburger. Wouldn't you like to have a real steak?" My mother didn't like the idea of ordering "an expensive steak that will just go to waste." But my father told her to mind her own business, and that as long as he lived I could eat anything I wanted.

The phrase, "as long as he lived" sounded like a vague prophecy, and I became sorrowful that he might die now that he was being good to me. I became so sorrowful, in fact, that it was Mother's prediction that was soon fulfilled. An expensive steak went to waste.

The familiar sounds of a spiritual—Ruth was passing below my window on her way to the back door. "Morning, folks," she called. "Well, I heard the weatherman say we're gonna get us a little rain by afternoon, enough to cool things off." My mother agreed that a little shower would be very nice. "Is that piece of toast all you've had to eat?" asked Ruth. "That's no kinda breakfast, Miz Bergen. I could make you some hurry-up griddle cakes."

"Griddle cakes are fattening. Besides I have to leave now."

A couple of minutes later the car backed out of the garage, the motor gunned for the two-block trip, and they were gone.

Ruth came into my room, bent over and picked up the flowery chenille bedspread that had fallen to the floor, and asked, "Are you feeling all right?"

I remembered who had brought me the ice bag and aspirins for my head and the ointment for my legs. "I don't know. I guess I am."

From the other twin bed came a long, low, early morning sound as Sharon flopped over to a better dreaming position.

"Come on into the kitchen," whispered Ruth as she tip-toed out of the room.

The marshmallow slowly began to bleed its whiteness over the steaming cup of chocolate. On the shelf of the breakfast room's built-in cabinet our one surviving goldfish, Goldilocks, began her vigorous after-breakfast swim.

"How come that fish got sense enough to eat her breakfast and you don't?" asked Ruth as she sat down at the table.

I ignored the buttered toast and scrambled egg, but took a long drink of the now lukewarm chocolate. "Don't know except maybe Goldilocks has a better cook than I do."

"Must be the truth," Ruth smiled, showing her left-of-center, solid-gold tooth. "You know what you needs, Honey? One of them fancy Frenchmen who cooks up a fine dinner and jest 'fore serving it, he sets it all afire."

We sat for a while in silence, Ruth taking small now-and-then sips of coffee while I sat stirring my chocolate and watching Goldilocks. Ruth's spoon made an attention getting noise and I saw that those brown eyes were upon me.

"I want you to tell Ruth the truth about something. You hear me talking, girl?" I nodded Yes.

"You tell me who is the man."

"Man?"

"Honey Babe, you can tell Ruth. The man that ran out from the garage. The man that wanted to save you from your daddy."

"That man—the man—the—" My voice was still in some kind of working order even if my brain did just up and die.

How can those eyes that rest so lightly see so deeply? And from them there is nothing in this world to fear. "The man is my friend," I said at last.

"You got him hid up in them rooms over the garage?"

"Yes."

Ruth sighed like she sometimes does before tackling a really big job. "He's not the one the law's after? Not the one from the prison camp?"

"Yes."

Her forehead crinkled up like a washboard. "You telling me, Yes, he's not the one?"

"No, Ruth, I'm telling you Yes. Yes, he's the one."

Ruth's head moved back and forth in a No direction. "Oh, Lord, why are you sending us more, Lord? Don't this child and me have burden enough?"

I stood up and felt this sensation of lightness, near weightlessness, like somebody had just bent down, picked up, and carried away all my trouble. My arm fell across Ruth's shoulder. "Everything'll be all right, honest it will." Beneath my arm, there was no movement, no feeling of life. I squeezed Ruth's shoulder and a hearable breath rushed through her nostrils. "You know how you're all the time helping me because you're my friend? Well, Anton's my friend and I have to help him, you know? Don't you know?"

"I don't know what it is I know," she said in a weighted voice.

In the pantry there was plenty of peanut butter,

but the jar of strawberry jam was only fingernail high. I turned on the gas burner under the aluminum percolator. I began to worry that maybe prison camp food was better than this, but at least the loaf of white bread was yesterday fresh.

Ruth followed me into the kitchen. "Honey, them peanut butter and jelly sandwiches ain't no kinda breakfast for no kinda man." She looked up at the kitchen clock. "After I bring Sharon down to Sue Ellen's I'll fix up some hot griddle cakes with maple syrup and a fresh pot of coffee."

I threw my arms as far around Ruth's waist as they would go and tried to lift her up by the pure strength of my will.

"Oh, Ruth, you're good, good, good!"

"Now, girl, don't go 'specting no amount of praise to turn my mind about 'cause my mind ain't come to no clear thought yet. All I knows for sure is that I'm gonna fix up a proper breakfast for you and the man."

"O.K., thanks, but would you mind not calling him the man, 'cause he's my friend, Anton. Mr. Frederick Anton Reiker. You may not know this, but you and Anton are all the friends I've got."

Ruth nodded slowly. "I understands that, Honey."

That understanding made me want to tell her everything all at once. "Ruth, he talks to me and he tells me things because I'm his friend. Ruth, he likes me. He really and truly likes me."

"I knows that too."

My heart swelled up for if Ruth knows it, it must be the truth. "How do you know that? Tell me how you know!"

She gave my arm a couple of short pats before finding my eyes. "That man come a-rushing out from the safety of his hiding 'cause he couldn't stand your pain and anguish no better'n me. That man listens to the love in his heart. Like the Bible tells us, when a man will lay down his life for a friend, well, then there ain't no greater love in this here world than that."

Before I reached the landing I heard his footsteps, and then the door opened. I felt certain he was smiling a welcome, although I was looking past him into the familiar interior of the room much as I would look past the brilliance of the sun.

"How are you?" he asked, making it sound more like an inquiry than a greeting.

"Fine." Cowardliness kept me from looking at him. "Did you sleep O.K.? Were you too hot?" I asked.

"No."

The shortness of his answer frightened me. Maybe it's disgust for what he saw yesterday. My eyes shut in a feeble try at pushing away the memories.

"Sure you're all right?" His eyes were on the red raw stripes that crisscrossed my legs.

I moved quickly to the opposite side of the desk. "Oh, yes, thanks."

"About yesterday—"

"It's O.K."

"No," he said with a force I had never heard him use before. "It's not O.K.! Listen to me, P.B. What happened yesterday bothers me. Tell me if I was in any way responsible." Between his eyebrows there was a deep crease, a mark of concern—for me.

All that painful dabbing of layer after layer of face powder that I subjected my legs to may have been a mistake. Concern might be a little like love.

"It wasn't you," I said. "You weren't responsible."

"Then what? Please tell me what you did to deserve such a beating?"

How could I say in words what I couldn't really understand myself? Sometimes I think it's because I'm bad that my father wants to do the right thing by beating it out of me. And at other times I think he's beat-

114

ing out from my body all his own bad. My head began its confused revolutions.

"Come over to the window," I said finally, pointing toward the tracks. "See over there? The shack with the tin roof? There's a boy who lives there who my father told me I'm not to have anything to do with. Yesterday he saw Freddy sitting next to me on our front steps." I told Anton about sleepy Freddy who cuts grass in his spare time so he can make enough money to sleep during the Saturday matinee. Scholarly Freddy who has been in Miss Bailey's fourth grade for two years because he's finally found, "The one teacher I likes." Fearless Freddy, brave hunter of crawdads. And generous Freddy who once bought me the gift of not quite half of a melted mess of a Hershey bar.

"He sounds perfectly delightful," said Anton with a smile. "But why is your father so opposed to him?"

"Maybe it's because he's so poor, but I'm not sure."

He looked a little perplexed. "Why don't you inquire?"

"I can't inquire." My words had a harshness that I didn't intend. "In my father's vocabulary to ask why is to contradict him."

"I don't like him!" The words seemed to dash out. Then Anton caught my eyes as though asking permission.

"Oh, that's O.K.," I said pleased that Anton was taking my side. "I'll tell you something I've never told anyone before. If he weren't my father, I wouldn't even like him."

"But because he is, you do?"

"Oh, well, I guess I—" Then the image came. The image of his thin, rabid face. "I guess I don't too much. No, I don't like him." That was the first time I had even thought anything like that myself. Funny, but Edna Louise once told me, "Your daddy is so sweet." Probably because every time he sees her he says, "Edna

115

Louise, you sure do look pretty today." To Edna Louise he has to say nice things as if she weren't conceited enough.

"Do you have any idea where your father went—what he did immediately following the beating he gave you?"

"Not exactly, I could guess. He probably went into the house, smoked a Lucky Strike cigarette, washed his hands, and ate a perfectly enormous supper while he listened to the evening news."

"Not true. He stood watching the housekeeper help you into the house. Then he came into the garage and talked to himself. Over and over he kept repeating, 'Nobody loves me. In my whole life nobody has ever loved me.' "

"Anton, it must have been somebody else. That doesn't sound like my father."

"It *was* your father."

"I don't understand. Why? How could he be so mean and then worry that he isn't loved? It doesn't make sense."

Anton shook his head. "I met your father once; I interpreted for some of the prisoners who came into the store."

"I remember! You said the prisoners needed hats to protect themselves from our formidable Arkansas sun."

Anton smiled, and the smile made him look very young, more like a boy my age than a man. "How could you possibly remember that?"

"Easy. Nobody from around here says things like that. I also remember that he didn't think your remark was very amusing."

"I can believe that because—" Anton paused like he was trying to put some new thoughts into good running order before continuing—"because it seems to me that a man who is incapable of humor is capable of cruelty. If Hitler, for example, had had the ability—

116

the detachment—to observe the absurdity of his own behavior he would have laughed, and today there might not be a madman named Adolph Hitler."

Was he making a comparison between Hitler and my father? "Do you think my father is like that? Like Hitler?"

Anton looked thoughtful. "Cruelty is after all cruelty, and the difference between the two men may have more to do with their degrees of power than their degrees of cruelty. One man is able to affect millions and the other only a few. Would your father's cruelty cause him to crush weak neighboring states? Or would the *Führer's* cruelty cause him to beat his own daughter? Doesn't it seem to you that they both need to inflict pain?"

"I don't know."

Anton smiled. "I don't know either. But you see, the only questions I like to raise are those that are unanswerable. Trying to calculate the different degrees of cruelty is a lot like trying to calculate the different degrees of death."

I laughed, but I knew that tonight while our house slept I would stay awake trying to understand his words. "I'm so glad you're talking to me, teaching me." I heard my enthusiasm running over. "I want you to teach me everything you've learned."

Anton stood, executing a princely bow. "I'm at your service."

"I think I want to be intelligent even more than I want to be pretty."

"You're already intelligent and pretty."

"Me?"

"You. I come from a line of men who have a sure instinct for a woman's beauty. So, P.B., I speak as an expert when I tell you you're going to have it all."

"Well, why hasn't anyone else seen it? That I'm going to have—what you say?"

"They will. Because you are no common garden flower—you are unique."

"Oh."

"I think I'm going to enjoy being your teacher if you'll keep in mind that life produces no maestros, only students of varying degrees of ineptitude. Wait!" said Anton. He jumped from his chair to go rummaging through a GI regulation duffel bag. "Here it is!" He waved a book with a bruised, blue cover. "I checked it out of the prison library the same day I checked myself out. R.W. Emerson. Are you familiar with his work?"

I admitted that I wasn't while I wondered if escaping with a book could be called anything besides stealing. My father would never do anything like that.

Anton asked, "Is something wrong?"

"Uhhh, no. Well, I was wondering how you are going to return the book."

"Oh," he said thoughtfully. "You want to know if I am a thief?"

"Oh, no! I know you're not!"

"In this classroom we call things by their rightful name. I became a thief when I took that book. I couldn't very well pay for it, and I didn't want my brain to starve if I had to go into hiding."

I felt close to laughing. "You're very honest. I mean you don't lie, do you?"

Anton shook his head. "I try never to lie to myself, and I dislike lying to friends." He took a yellow pencil from his hip pocket and made two small check marks in R.W. Emerson's Table of Contents. "Read these essays," he said, like he felt pleased to be making a contribution to my education. "And tomorrow we can start mining the gold."

Then a voice from below us called up, "Come on folks! It's ready." Anton's face was caught in a moment of fear.

118

"It's all right," I whispered. "That's only Ruth, our housekeeper. She's made griddle cakes for us."

He looked at me. "Why did you—tell?"

He believed—he actually believed—that I would. "But I didn't! Honest! Ruth saw you run out of the garage last night; she saw how you wanted to protect me from my father."

Anton's hand rushed to his forehead. "I came running out of hiding to—My God, I did, didn't I?" His hand dropped to his side, and I could see he was smiling his wonderful glad-to-be-living smile. "After almost two years of being as inconspicuous a coward as possible I had no idea that I would voluntarily risk my life for anyone." He shook his head in disbelief. "But I'm glad I could. I'm glad I still could."

12

A PLAYFUL BREEZE brought a scent of roses into the breakfast room where it mingled with the purely kitchen aroma of coffee perking, griddle cakes rising, and bacon frying. The table was set for two with real cotton napkins, the newest of the everyday tablecloths, and our fancy dinnertime *made-in-Japan* china.

Ruth pointed to the chair where my father always sits, and Anton sat down. His appetite was healthy, and while we ate I heard Ruth singing in the kitchen: "Rinso white, Rinso white, happy little washday song."

She came into the breakfast room carrying the percolator and refilled the empty cups. Anton rose, pulling out a third chair. "Come join us." I watched Ruth's face for signs of embarrassment, for I was sure no white man had ever before offered her a chair. But if there was any, Ruth has better camouflage than the United States Army.

"Mr. Reiker, don't you worry none about me. I jest enjoys cooking for folks who enjoy eating." There it is! That's one of the things that Ruth does that makes the white ladies say she's uppity. All the other colored folks would have called him Mr. Anton, leaving the poor whites the privilege of calling him Mr. Reiker. But then, if Ruth played the piano I think she'd play only the cracks between the keys. She seems best suited for walking that thinnest of lines between respectfulness and subservience.

After a while Ruth brought in a cup of coffee and made herself comfortable in the chair that Anton had selected for her. Looking over at him, she chuckled. "Yes, sir, it is a pleasure to cook for folks who enjoys their food. They sure ain't no eaters in this house. Not Sharon and not—" she threw a nod over in my direction—"this child. She'd rather be sitting with me shelling peas than eating them. Mr. Bergen, he'd rather be left alone with his cigarettes, and Miz Bergen says she's gotta watch her girlish figure. Imagine that!" said Ruth. "A woman that bore two children wants a figure like some young girl's. I always tells her—a fruit-bearing tree knows better'n try to look like some young sapling."

Anton laughed. "You've been talking to my mother. Except she would have quoted the Bible, 'To every thing there is a season, and a time to every purpose under the heaven.' "

"A time to be born," supplied Ruth. "And a time to die."

Soon Ruth and Anton found a second point of agreement—that a good cook needs an appreciative eater or two. Then Ruth asked something a little surprising. It was something that she might have wondered out loud to me, but not to any other white person.

"How do they treat the colored folks there in Germany?"

"There aren't any."

Ruth's face slowly turned incredulous. "Then how do you folks keep your houses clean?"

I watched Anton laugh without making a sound. "The German housewife treats dirt as her mortal enemy. Anyway, our houses are fine; it's our politics and hearts that give us the trouble."

"It ain't only in your country, Mr. Reiker, no, sir! We've got plenty bad hearts right here in America.

When I was jest a girl I 'members my mamma saying, 'Things gonna be a lot better for my Ruth. My Ruth's smart and she's gonna grow up to be a teacher.' But my mamma was wrong. She didn't figger on them bad hearts. No, sir. And Mr. J.G. Jackson's daddy was one of them."

Ruth's eyes rolled downward to the sun-speckled linoleum floor. "He's gone on his reward now, Mr. Eugene Jackson. Well, back then he used to keep my mamma's savings for her in his office safe. Every Saturday for so many years my mamma would go into Mr. Jackson's office in the back of the cotton gin with fifty or seventy-five cents in her hand and tell him, 'Put this in the envelope, Mr. Jackson. Put this away, please, for my girl's education.' Well, when the time come for me to go away to teacher's school, there weren't but three dollars and twenty-five cents in that envelope."

Is it possible that the rich would steal from the poor? Why hadn't she ever told me that story before? After all, that was my friend Edna Louise's grandfather. "Ruth, how come you never told me before about what Mr. Jackson did to you?"

" 'Cause telling bad stories 'bout the dead ain't the best way to be spending time, and I ain't proud of myself even if I did jest tell it for purposes of illustration."

Then almost on signal we all began silently to watch the white dotted swiss curtains respond to the gentle change in the wind. The breakfast room was filled with lazy warmth, and I wondered if there was any better place to be than here. Here with my two favorite people getting to know each other.

Though after a while when you start to feel more the hardness of the chair than the softness of its cushion it would be good if just the two of us could get up and take a walk together down Main Street. I'd introduce him as my good friend, Anton. Anton Reiker.

And when he'd look back at me and smile everybody would see, plain as day, that this beautiful man really liked me.

Ruth's spoon sounded against the saucer beneath her cup. "When I had my boy, my Robert," she looked over at Anton. "He's 'bout your age now. I said, like my mamma before me said, 'Things gonna be different for my child 'cause I ain't gonna save no money in no white man's private safe, no, sir!' I put it all in the Rice County National Bank where Mr. John Rusk marked down every deposit in a little blue book. And so one fine day I saw my dream come true.

"On that day just before the sun come up Claude and me walked Robert down to the railroad station. And in his hand Robert was carrying all his things in a suitcase the church had given him the Sunday before. When they flagged down the Atlanta train, the one that was gonna take him to Morehouse College, I pulled out my handkerchief and Robert said, 'Don't you cry none, Ma. I leave here only a man, but I'm gonna come back to you a true minister of God.'

"And he would have been too 'cepting for the letter he got a few precious months later from Mr. Price Cook, the head man of the draft board. I went right down to Cook Brothers' Furniture and Appliances store and I 'plained to him how this is Robert's one chance in this world and I begged him to just let my boy finish up his schooling, let him become a true minister of the gospel. 'Ruth, I'm surprised at you,' he told me. 'You oughta know I can't do that. Why, this is your boy's country too and he's gotta do his share so this country will always belong to us Americans.'"

Funny, but Ruth never talked like that to me. Oh, sometimes she says just enough of something to let me know it is all a lie what the white folks keep saying. That lie they tell each other so often that they come to believe it's true: "I understands these niggers; they're happy and they don't know no better."

"Mr. Reiker." She called his name slowly, thought-fully. "You're a smart man. I was wondering, do you reckon that this here world is ever gonna amount to much?"

"Call me Anton. Well, I'm not exactly overburdened by excessive optimism. For centuries men have believed that religion is the answer." Ruth, as if by instinct, clutched the gold cross at her throat. "But I have seen the evil perpetrated by religious men. Did you know that before every battle Hitler calls upon God for victory?"

Anton paused to make sure his point had sunk in. "A lot of people today believe education can save the world. I used to believe that, but I became discouraged while watching the educated Germans express their enthusiasm for this war. To give you an example," he said, looking from Ruth to me, "would one of you ask me what is the oldest tradition of the proud University of Göttingen?"

"What is their oldest tradition?" I asked, feeling like a parrot.

"Dueling. The *landsmannschaft!*" He stopped short like he had just run into a snag. "I don't know if you have anything like this in your country or not. It's a secret society. The word means 'clan.' "

"We have the Klan, sure do," responded Ruth.

"Well, the *landsmannschaften* would challenge each other to a duel on any pretext," Anton continued. "Sometimes even the narrow sidewalk of Göttingen was disputed by students from opposing clans. It's called 'defending their honor.' "

"I think maybe good changes will come when our leaders are better and there aren't any more evil dictators," I said.

Anton nodded. "There are those who would agree with you. But leaders don't usually spring forth to impose their will upon a helpless people. They, like department stores, are in business to give people what they

124

think they want. So basically you always come back to people. How do you make better people?"

"I believes," said Ruth, "the Lord himself would be mighty interested in creating better people. But if the Lord already knows how to do it then I don't, so you jest tell me."

"Maybe psychiatry?" I offered. "I read in the *Readers' Digest* where lots of people are helped to be better by psychiatry."

Anton's lips pressed together. "Maybe. Maybe not."

"Why can't you believe it?" I challenged. "The *Readers' Digest* wouldn't say it if it wasn't so."

Anton grinned. He looked like a charter member of *Our Gang Comedy*. "Maybe you're right, but maybe, just maybe, we all have an enormous capacity for believing in anything that will provide us with a bit of comfort." Anton caught Ruth's eye. "Haven't you found this to be true?"

"I'll tell you the truth, Mr. Rei—Anton. Yes, sir, I've found this here a cold world, a mighty cold world, and a man and a woman, well, they needs a little comforting 'fore they freeze to death."

"I can't argue with that," said Anton heavily, as though conceding to Ruth.

"You don't believe in religion or education or psychiatry," I said, holding up three fingers. "Is there anything at all you do believe in?"

"Of course." Anton raised the coffee to his lips and when he replaced the cup, it was empty. "I believe that love is better than hate. And that there is more nobility in building a chicken coop than in destroying a cathedral."

Ruth nodded in affirmation. "Ain't it the truth."

Suddenly I heard the crunch of driveway gravel over the low hum of a car motor. Ruth clasped her heart. "Mr. Bergen! Lordy, it's him! Hide him, Patty, under your bed! Quick!"

As I led Anton to my bedroom I squeezed his hand so he'd know we would never betray him. Anton's hand left mine as he slid under the maple bed.

Out in the driveway a voice called Ruth's name. A woman's voice! I cautiously lifted one slant of the venetian blind to see Mrs. Henkins, little Sue Ellen's mother, protruding her beauty parlor coiffure out of the car window. "Is it O.K. to take Sharon to Wynne City with us? I have to buy Sue Ellen a pair of tap dancing shoes."

"Yes, Miz Henkins, I reckon it'll be O.K. What time you figgering on returning?"

I didn't hear Mrs. Henkins' answer, but the car backed down the driveway and took off in the direction of Wynne City.

In the breakfast room we three sat totally absorbed in watching agitated curtains being egged on by a suddenly gusty wind. It was as though we were all waiting for something to happen.

After a while, Anton spoke. "About what happened—I'm sorry. There's no reason why you both should have to take risks. Tonight when it's dark I'll go."

"I'll pack you up some food to take with you," said Ruth with unaccustomed speed. "And I have a couple of dollars and some change you can have."

Did she realize what she was saying? Did she understand that he meant to leave us for good? "We're not afraid of anything, really. And it's not safe for you to leave here. They're all looking for you, Anton. Tell him, Ruth. Tell him!"

But Ruth didn't say anything. She got up from her chair, letting her eyes sweep across the table as she picked up the empty coffee cups and carried them off to the kitchen.

13

FROM OVER AT the button factory the five o'clock whistle blew, which didn't mean a thing since quitting time wasn't for another hour. I leaned back against the front stoop and tried to come up with the logic behind a five o'clock whistle.

But two men were all that I could think of. If I ever had to sacrifice one for the other which one would it be? The one who had fed and sheltered me, or the one whom I had fed and sheltered?

Sharon came out the front door, clutching her Baby Jane doll by the hair. Sharon, pretty Sharon, if I had been born that pretty maybe they would like me as much as her. And she's going to be about as popular as Betty Grable. My father says that in a few years, "the boys will be swarming about, thick as flies."

She sat down. "My baby has a boo-boo." Sharon pointed to a dark smudge on the doll's forehead.

"Rock your baby in your arms," I told her, "and tell her that you love her."

Sharon swayed back and forth and in a small voice began to chant: "I love you, little baby, I love you little baby. I love you, love you, love you, little baby."

Six o'clock came before my thoughts had congealed into plans. My father's green Chevy pulled into the driveway and stopped inside the garage. How close were the two men now? In yards, feet, and inches, exactly how far above my father is Anton? Funny, but with just a little information from me my father could achieve an instant acceptance in this town. The kind that he has wanted all his life. And it would only take one phone call: "Hello? Sheriff Cauldwell? . . . Yes, this is Harry Bergen. I've got your Nazi . . . . Yes, he's hiding in the rooms above my garage. Now here's what I want you to do . . . ."

Mr. Harry Bergen, prominent local merchant. His picture would be in all the newspapers. The President, or J. Edgar Hoover at the very least, would pin a medal on him, and the Jenkinsville Rotarians would call him a hero.

And then one evening after all the commotion had died down, I'd be sitting alone on the screened-in porch. In the twilight he'd come out and without saying a word, he'd sit beside me on the metal glider. After a while he'd casually drop his arm around my shoulder and say, "I haven't been much of a father, have I?"

It would take me a couple of swallows before I could manage to say, "Oh, you've been all right, really."

We'd just sit there for a while longer not saying anything. Every once in a while, though, he'd give my arm a couple of gentle pats to show how much he appreciated my help in apprehending the dangerous Nazi. Then probably he'd remark what a hot night it was, and maybe we ought to take a walk to the drug store for a cold Dr Pepper. "Oh, I'd like that, Daddy, I really would."

From inside the house I heard Ruth calling us to supper. I stood up and wondered how to go about starting from the very beginning. All the bad things were in the past. This is now and I am his daughter and he will love me. They say Jesus lived a truly perfect life. If I tried, really tried, I too could be perfect, or at the very least, sweet like Sharon. As my hand reached out for the door, I saw Sharon's Baby Jane doll lying face

128

down beneath the rainspout. "And I love you, love you, love you, little baby."

I sat down at my place, but immediately jumped up and cheek-kissed both my mother and father before sitting down again. Look at him now. Be sweet. "Hey, that's an awfully nice tie you're wearing, is it from the store?" He said it was. A compliment about the store, maybe that would please him more. "That sign you put up over the shoe department—the large red one that says, SHOE DEPARTMENT. What a good idea! Is it good for business?"

His head was bent. "Eat your dinner and don't ask so many questions."

"But did you know that this doctor from Boston, I read it somewhere, said pleasant conversation is good for the digestive system?"

"And I told you to shut up and eat your dinner!" His anger ended my flirtation with perfection. If there were questions or confusion before, they weren't there anymore. I knew what I was going to do, and I knew why.

He lifted a fork overburdened with mashed potatoes, and I watched as the gravy started to roll down his chin. Across his mean, thin line of a mouth he smeared the paper napkin. It's not even a contest leaving you, dear Father. I know it will be difficult for you, deciding what to tell people, but will you miss *me*?

And what about you, Mother? Will I miss you? And do you love me? I only know for sure that we've never liked each other. Anyway it'll be easier loving you from a distance.

And Sharon. I'll love you no matter where I am. Sharon and Ruth, that's who I'll miss.

Ruth came out of the bathroom wearing her blue rayon walking-home dress, and at the bottom of the *V*-neck was the rhinestone pin in a flower design that I gave her last Mother's Day. In a brown grocery sack she carried the cotton house dress that always got a washing and an ironing every time it got a wearing.

"I'll walk you a-ways," I offered.

When we reached Nigger Bottoms, Ruth said that it was getting on towards seven and I'd best be turning back. "Well, before I go," I said, wondering what I was going to say next, "I want to wish you a nice evening and—and good-bye."

Ruth smiled and wished me a pleasant evening. Then her forehead wrinkled up and I expected that I was in for some kind of warning. "Now, Honey Babe, I don't want you nowhere near that garage, you understand? Anton's gonna be leaving after dark, and it won't do nobody no good if the law catches him here. No Jewish girl and no colored woman needs that kinda trouble."

I hated seeing her so heavy with cares. "Ruth, you oughtna worry. This doctor in Boston says that worrying makes you feel old before your time."

"This here doctor from Boston you're always talking about," she said. "Did he say what you're 'pose to do with your burdens? They got pills in Boston for that?"

When she gets sarcastic there's not much I can think to say to her. But I didn't want to leave her like that. I guess I didn't want to leave her at all. "Well, now," I said, grabbing her hand, "you be good now." What a stupid, idiotic, last good-bye thing to say. Even for me. "Well, Ruth," I said, trying again. "Good-bye."

As I turned I caught a look on her face of surprise or suspicion. I walked on, feeling a painful pinching against the hollow of my stomach. "Well, see you tomorrow," I called out, and without even turning to look I knew her doubts were being laid to rest.

I found my bedroom in quiet shadows. I was aware of the room like you are when you look, I mean

130

really look, at something for the first, or last, time. The twin maple beds with their matching yellow and blue chenille spreads, the linoleum with its pictures of the cat and the fiddle and the old lady in the shoe that had been a source of embarrassment for quite a few years now. I remember Edna Louise looking at that linoleum and saying, "I haven't liked Mother Goose in years."

The only thing that I really liked in my room was the desk my grandma had bought me. Inside was my simulated leather five-year diary. I wanted to record my life so I wouldn't forget anything, but then I discovered there wasn't much worth remembering.

For a while I tried to use my diary for self-improvement. I made three vertical columns down the page and marked the headings: DATE. CRITICISM. FROM WHOM. I thought if I could see them written down then correcting my shortcomings might not be all that difficult. I didn't have to wait long for my first entry. "5/15/41—7:35 A.M.: 'Get that hair out of your face.' —Mother. 5/15/41—7:45 A.M.: 'Even when you comb it, it doesn't look it. Can't you get that dirty hair out of your face?'—Mother."

Water began to drain noisily down the pipes. Sharon shrieked for a towel. Still time enough for packing. What did I need? Springy tennis shoes for jumping aboard slow-moving freight trains, polo shirts that never need ironing, blue jeans that save the legs from cockleburs, and a sweater for when the nights turn chilly. And, in case we go out together in some distant place, a dress.

In the bottom drawer of the kitchen cabinet Ruth stores dozens of neatly folded grocery sacks. I picked one for my suitcase and thought of Robert's suitcase, the one the whole church chipped in to buy him. How proud he must have felt—all those people wishing him well.

After the nine o'clock news was over, the big upright radio in the living room was snapped off, and

131

my mother and father began readying for bed. At nine thirty his breathing deepened into snores, and I guessed that my mother must be sleeping too. Sure she was. Haven't I heard him joke about it, "Pearl falls asleep on her way to the pillow."

The unhooked window screen pushed out with a sound so slight that I didn't bother to check to see if Sharon slept on. I dropped my paper bag to the ground and started to follow when I thought of something. I went over and stood for a moment by my sleeping sister.

Sharon lay curled on her side, just a small soft thing, her lips resting against her thumb. Already past the age when she needs to thumb-suck, but not yet ready to stop keeping it handy.

"Well, be good now," I said. "I sure hope you grow up nice." Sharon's reluctant eyes opened. She took hold of my hand and closed her eyes again. As I tried to loosen my hand she seemed to get a better grasp, like she didn't want me to go or maybe she didn't want me to go without her. "Want to come along?" I whispered. Groaning like her sleep was being disturbed, she released my hand and turned over.

Outside, the darkness was complete. I walked by the sandpile and the chinaberry tree whose strongest branch supported our chain swing. The seat had been cut from an old restaurant sign, and there was still the word, "EATS" painted in faded red letters.

Is this how it all ends? Leave everything you know, and all that comes to mind is trivia—sandpiles and chinaberries.

I left my sack at the foot of the garage steps and crawled my way up through the blackness. "Anton," I whispered. But behind the closed door, there was only silence. A feeling of loss swept over me. "Anton!" I cried, hitting the door with my fist. "It's me! Patty!"

Abruptly the door opened. "Quiet!" As he led me through the blackness I tried to find my voice. "I

132

thought, I thought you had gone," I said and then from somewhere came crying. Only after my tongue had tasted saltiness did I know its source.

Anton squeezed my hand.

"I'm sorry," I said. "I didn't know I was going to do that."

Anton brought my hand to the slightly moist inner corners of his own eyes. "Just wanted to point out that the biggest difference between us is that you cry more noisily than I."

I laughed, feeling grateful for the darkness which concealed my eyes.

"We both knew that I couldn't stay. It had to happen, P.B., you always knew that."

"No, I didn't!" I breathed in deep. "Anton—" I needed to say his name aloud again as though it were a magical incantation. "Anton, I won't even be that much trouble. What I'm trying to tell you is—" The hurdle felt too high for vaulting.

"P.B., I don't think—"

"Don't talk. Listen to me." It was my hurdle, and I had to clear it myself. "I don't think you oughta leave me, not now. I haven't learned all those things you were going to teach me—things about Emerson and—and— Oh, Anton, let me be with you, go where you go."

His thumb pressed against my palm. "You know what you are asking is impossible, but if you're saying that you love me—"

"Yes," I answered, wondering if it came out audibly. "Yes."

"Then know this, Patty, it's not completely one-sided. I love you too, and in my own way I'll miss you."

He opened the door, climbed quickly down, and offered up his hand to me.

Outside, the moon, almost full-grown now, threw soft illumination on his forehead and cheeks while

133

leaving the deeper recesses in shadows. Then it struck me that if someday I grow old and forgetful, forgetting even friends' names and faces, his face I could never forget.

He looked down at the luminous hands of his watch. "The train comes by about ten fifteen."

"Yes," I replied and then, thinking that my answer sounded curt, I added, "Yes, it does."

"Let me help you back into the house," he offered. "There's still time."

I began to feel jealous of time and trivia. Of last moments consumed in pass-the-salt type of comments. "No thanks. My bedroom window screen is unhooked and the water spigot is there, makes a good foothold."

"Well, I must say good-bye now."

"Oh, I almost forgot." I dug into the right-hand pocket of my jeans. "Here's some money—only four dollars and sixty-five cents. It's all Ruth and I had."

He took the money. "Thanks for this, for everything. And I have something for you too. It belonged to my father and his father and even his father before that." Anton looked down at his hand. Then warm metal encircled my finger. "This ring was made by Germany's most famous goldsmith for my great-grandfather when he was president of the university of Göttingen. The crest represents the office of the president."

A thing of value! He'd give it to me? "Maybe you'd better keep it, Anton. I mean, it has been in your family for so long." My tongue! I could bite it off. The ring had been mine for only a moment, and now I would lose that too.

"The greater the value, the greater the pleasure in giving it. The ring is yours, P.B." Then in the darkened silence, I heard him breathe in deeply. "Am I still your teacher?" Without pausing for an answer he continued, "Then I want you to learn this, our last, lesson. Even if you forget everything else I want you to always remember that you are a person of value, and you have

134

a friend who loved you enough to give you his most valued possession."

"I will, Anton. I'll remember."

I saw or felt it coming—my chin tilted up as my eyes closed. Then our lips touched, lingered together briefly before going their own separate ways. When I opened my eyes Anton was gone.

Time passed. I stood rigid and unmoving, wanting nothing new to happen to me. New time was nothing except a way to determine how long he had been gone. From under the weight of my foot I felt a chinaberry being pushed into the damp ground. My finger passed over the indented crest of the gold ring.

Then from down the distant tracks came the ten fifteen.

14

FOR A WHILE I carefully kept track of time without Anton. One day, one day and a third, five days, seventeen. Then abruptly I stopped counting. For one thing I didn't like the time being long or the distance great. And marking off time struck me as something like counting empty spaces—spaces you know can't ever be filled.

"Patricia Ann." A voice came intruding into my world. "Do you find the schoolyard more interesting than our little problems in fractions?"

A classroom of heads turned to stare at me. Quick, answer the question. About fractions, was I interested in them?

"Oh, yes, ma'am," I said, trying to put real conviction in my voice. "Yes, ma'am, I sure do."

Miss Hooten's head tilted slightly to the right while Edna Louise led the class in snickering. "Are you sassing me, Patricia Ann?"

"Oh, no, ma'am, I only meant that I do like fractions, and I apologize for looking out the window."

While Edna Louise attempted to revive the snickering, Miss Hooten's face gradually relaxed. "Boys and girls, you have just heard a proper apology, and I hope that the next time any of you are called down that you will be able to do as well. Hear me talking, Edna Louise?"

It had to be a dream. Who would dare call Edna Louise Jackson down?

Edna Louise let out a wail. "I don't know why you're picking on me. I wasn't looking out the window." Her index finger pointed at me. "Patty was!"

I found myself focusing on that finger aimed at destroying me. You would never have loved her, Anton. Never given her your ring. Pulling the yellow chain up from around my neck, my fingers passed across the heavy crested ring. "Oh, you're weak, Edna Louise," I whispered to the ring. "And you're no person of value either."

Juanita Henkins between, "Well, uhs," was trying to remember the principal crops of Brazil when the three-fifteen bell sounded. "Saved by the bell!" called out one of the boys. C.J. Peters I think it was.

By the time I had walked the block to the store I had come to a decision—a ring of such power and beauty has no business being hidden away beneath some dress front. It should be worn proudly for all the world to see.

In the store there was a small gathering of people. From their backsides I recognized Gussie Fields, Sister Parker, my father, a couple of women customers, and my mother. They were all the approving audience of a single performer, little Sharon, who was dancing and prancing around as she sang: "They're either too young or too old. They're either too dull or too grassy green."

When she finished, Sharon dropped her head and gave her fans an adorable little curtsy.

"Oh, Honey," cried Gussie Fields, "that's just wonderful." She gave her boss a congratulating pat on the shoulder. "I didn't know such talent ran in your family. Bet she takes after you."

My father laughed and then, finding a remaining Lucky in a flattened pack, he said, "Now, Gussie Mae, you're gonna think I'm crazy when I tell you this, but to my mind Sharon is every bit as good as Shirley

Temple. And remember, Sharon hasn't had anywhere near the training that Shirley Temple has!"

"Mr. Bergen," said the clerk, "you're not one little bit crazy. No, sir! I'll tell you the truth. When I saw that child sing and dance in Sue Dobbins's dance recital, well, I said to myself right then and there she's got that special something—that movie-star sparkle, I guess you'd call it."

"I've never in my life told this to anyone before," said my father, pausing to blow out a blue-gray puff of smoke. Was he about to make a confession to Gussie? He mustn't see I'm listening. I bent down to tie a shoe-lace before realizing that I was wearing my brown loafers. "But one night, I sat up till almost midnight," he said, "thinking that I oughta take Sharon, now don't laugh, right out to Hollywood. All they'd have to do is to see her sing one of her little songs or do one of her cute dances. Well, in my opinion, it would put Jenkinsville right on the map."

My sister a real name-in-lights movie star?

Sharon spotted me and came running over, pointing to her left elbow. "Look! It's skinned." What's she always bothering me for with her tiny scratches? Little big shot. My hand became a hard fist that wanted to ram itself into her pretty face.

In my meanest voice I said, "Why can't you just leave me alone?"

I ran to an out-of-sight place between counters stacked high with blue overalls and burrowed my head between two stacks of denims.

I felt something pressing into my chest bone—the ring! Pulling it up, I gave it a wet kiss before making a prayer-wish: "Oh, God, please don't ever let Anton find out that I was so hateful and mean. Help me to become a person of value."

Funny that I could forget about my ring. After all that's why I came into the store. I wanted a piece of tape to wrap around it.

138

Sister Parker dropped a jar of Royal Peach Hair-dressing into a tan sack, handed it to a colored woman, and rang twelve cents on the cash register.

I asked, "Want me to help you do something?"

"Well," she said, "you can staple the candy bags closed if you want to."

More than a hundred cellophane bags of orange slices, chocolate-covered peanuts, and peppermint discs lay on the counter waiting for the staple gun. As I stapled, Sister tore open a fresh fifty-pound box of my favorite chocolate-covered malt balls.

"That'll make up into lots of sacks," I said.

"I reckon."

"About how many, do you think?"

After a long pause Sister said, "A lot, I know that."

I stopped my stapling, got pencil and paper, and in less than a jiffy came up with the answer. "Now you give one ounce to each sack, so that fifty pounds will make up into eight hundred sacks."

Sister Parker didn't say anything, so I asked, "Isn't that interesting?"

"I guess. It's interesting enough for folks who have nothing better to do than to think."

"But, Sister," I protested, feeling like Anton was here borrowing my voice for his thoughts. "A person's got to think, otherwise that person's no better than a trained seal balancing a ball on his nose. If only that seal could think, he'd know he was making a thousand children laugh."

"What do you want me to think about?" asked Sister, sounding more tired than unfriendly. "Eight hundred bags of candy?"

"Maybe you could think about eight hundred people who are going to enjoy the candy you sacked. After all, work should have relevance," I said, borrowing one of Anton's words.

My ring was dazzling me with its closeness and

139

its power. Sister seemed receptive (another of his words), so I decided to slide into the subject like it was the most natural thing in the world. I extended my left hand. "Did you see my ring?"

Sister looked up. "Did your boyfriend give it to you?"

"Boyfriend?" I asked, confused. "Who are you talking about?"

"Well, I don't know," she said. "You oughta know who your boyfriend is."

"It's a real solid gold ring." I dropped the ring into Sister's hand. "Feel the weight?"

"Where did you get it?" She was really interested all right.

"Well, I'll tell you the truth," I said, interested myself to know what the truth was going to be. "It happened on Monday. Now, I know for sure it was a Monday 'cause that was the day school started, you remember?"

Sister nodded.

"Well, as I was walking home from school, it was only about noontime. School let out early that day, remember?"

Sister answered with only a "Hmmm."

Then it came to me—my vision of the truth. "Well, I saw this man walking down the road. He looked like an old man 'cause of his whiskers—white whiskers. He asked me if I lived nearby and if I could spare a piece of bread with maybe a bit of butter on it.

"I took the man home and he sat on the back doorstep, and while Ruth was busy vacuuming the living room I kept bringing him our best food. Well, after the man finished eating he thanked me and said that because I was obviously a person of value he was going to reward me with his most valued possession. And so he slipped that very ring on my finger."

Sister Parker's hands had forgotten their work and her eyes looked slightly larger than I remembered. I

140

felt powerful, like I finally had something somebody else wanted even if it was only the rest of the story. Well, I'd give her an ending—a great motion picture ending.

"But it was what happened next that was the most surprising thing of all. I mean—" I said, stalling. "It was what he said next."

"What did he say?"

"He told me that he wasn't really poor. He only pretended to be to find all the good people in the world. He said that he gives his wife—want to know her name?"

"All right."

"Agnes. He said that Agnes could buy this whole town and everything that's in it with just the money he gives her weekly."

Sister began shaking her head. "Now tell me another."

I felt annoyance rising in me. "I guess you also don't believe that Jesus walked on water. I mean you don't seem to believe in anything unless you see it happen. Haven't you any faith?"

"I have faith, plenty of it. But, well, why don't you tell me the rest."

"All right, it might be helpful to you. The man told me that because I was able to show such good faith towards a stranger I would be rewarded on my eighteenth birthday. No matter where I might be, my present would reach me on that day."

"And this ring," said Sister, holding it between her fingers, "is yours for a remembrance?"

"Mine for a remembrance," I said, thinking of Anton. "You know, it's my most valued possession."

"Hey, Mr. Bergen," called Sister Parker across the store. "Is this ring really solid gold?"

"What? What are you talking about?" He strode over in his save-the-nation gait. "Whose ring is this?"

Sister looked surprised. I held hands with myself

141

to keep them steady. "Why it's Patty's—I guess it is."

I didn't say anything; my brain felt like Jell-O left too long in the heat. Why did I have to tell anybody? Why can't I keep my stupid mouth shut? He examined the ring by squinting his right eye and then his left one. Suddenly he jerked away the tape.

"Twenty-four carat," he said slowly. "Whose ring is this?"

"Mine—"

"How did you get it? Where'd it come from?"

"Well— You know how we got out of school early on Monday 'cause it was the first day of school?"

"Get to the point!"

My last year's dress suddenly felt too small. "I'm trying to tell you if you'll please be patient."

"You better tell me in one hell of a hurry!"

I noticed that the stuff that the drug store had sold him for those tobacco stains on his teeth wasn't helping. "Well," I said, "I met this man who asked me to give him some food because he was very, very hungry. I told him to follow me home, and he did, and he sat on the back doorstep while I brought him—you want to know what I brought him?"

I didn't see how my father responded because my eyes were fixed on the SHOE DEPARTMENT sign at the back of the store. "Bread and butter and some slices of American cheese—and I think two oranges." I forced myself to look him in the face. "And so—that's what happened," I concluded.

"What *happened?*"

What does he want from me? It isn't like him to get excited about a little cheese and a couple of oranges for a starving man.

"Are you gonna tell me!" His mouth smelled like yesterday's ash tray. "Tell me who he was."

"A man, a hungry man. I told you."

"White or colored?"

It wasn't the food that bothered him, but what?

"White," I said, hoping this would give him some re-assurance. "He was white."

My father sucked in a deep breath. "How old was he?"

Where were we going? I searched Sister Parker's face for a clue, but the only thing I could see was interest and, maybe, fear. "He wasn't too young. He had whiskers that were turning gray; I guess he was at least forty."

"And this man, you gave him something too, didn't you?" My father's voice had become calm, almost confidential.

Then it came to me what this was all about. Sure. That must be it. I thought about the time I sneaked into the movies without paying and later when I told him about it, he made me go back with the money. He's a regular Abraham Lincoln. My confidence reappeared.

"Yes, sir," I said. "I sure did."

"What was it?"

Maybe he did care about the oranges, which might be kind of expensive, coming all the way from Florida. "I gave him what I told you. Bread and cheese and —and two little oranges that were overripe and about to go bad."

"What did he do to you?"

What does he want me to say? "The only thing he did was to thank me. He was very polite."

"You're lying, you dirty girl."

"No, sir, I'm telling the truth."

"Liar! He touched you. You let him put his hands on you, *filthy, fil-thy* girl!" As he raised his hand I clamped my eyes shut.

"Awww!" I fell backward against the magazine stand and slid down while a landslide of periodicals tumbled across my chest and legs.

As he walked away I spoke to his back. "And I don't love you. Nobody does!"

15

SISTER PARKER LED ME by the elbow toward the back of the store and then up the steps to the balcony. "You're gonna be all right," she said.

From below came my mother's voice. "What did she do? Why did you hit her? *Harry?*"

Sister guided me past large cartons of unopened merchandise and my father's polished pine desk to the brown studio couch. A couple of times a day my father whispers to my mother, "Watch out for things. I'm gonna go rest my eyes on the couch."

"Now lie down," said Sister. "I'll bring you a cold towel for your face." There? She wants me to lie down there where his head has rested?

"No, it's too soft. Here on the floor, where it's cool." Sister Parker stooped to place the couch's tired brown bolster under my head before turning to leave.

From downstairs I heard the rapid cranking of the phone. "Mary? Is the sheriff in his office? All right, then try his home. Hello? Sheriff Cauldwell? . . . This is Harry Bergen. I want you to come down to the store right now. . . . I don't know whether it is or not. Come over and find out." The receiver was slammed down.

"What did you call *him* for?" I heard my mother's voice go hysterical. "Harry, tell me what's wrong!"

"Nothing."

"Yes, something *is*."

144

"Damn you, woman, don't you go calling me a liar! Your mother may lead your old man around by the nose, but you're not gonna do it to me!"

Damn them! Damn them both! Must they let the whole world see them fight?

Where he hit me my face felt bruised and hot. My stomach, though, felt the worst. All the food I'd eaten, all the food I'd ever eaten, moaned and churned, growing putrid and decayed.

"Anton," my voice whispered, "why did you have to go and leave me?" Hiccupy sobs came to keep company with my body shakes. God, I wish I could shut up and sink deep and unnoticed into the ground. Die. Yes, die with the mark of his hand still across my face. Explain that to people, to the sheriff, to the judge.

Outside, a car made a sudden attention-getting stop, and within moments I recognized the guns-and-bullets voice. "What's up, Harry?"

My brain felt too bruised to even think about a plan. How long did I have? Not very. Remembering my source of strength, my right hand went rushing across left fingers. Then I remembered that I didn't have it anymore. I didn't have my ring!

Footsteps, like cannons, ascended the balcony stairs. Beat me! Kill me! Not one thing am I going to say till I get back my ring. "Remember," Anton had said to me, ". . . you have a friend who loved you enough to give you his most valued possession."

The footsteps stopped at my head and for a moment all was quiet. Then my father broke the silence. "Get yourself off that floor." As I rolled over on my stomach he spoke again. "The sheriff is here. There's a lot of things he wants to know. Do ya hear?" I stood up and looked him in the eye.

"Answer me!"

The words struck wounds that hadn't even begun to heal and the crying started anew.

"Go on downstairs. Let me talk to her, Harry," said the big voice.

"Talk to her," said my father. "Go on, but I'm gonna stay right here."

"Now, Patty, we've been knowing each other for quite a long spell now." The big voice was speaking softly. "And you're a smart girl, and I respect that. I want you to respect the fact that I'm a big old two-hundred-and-fifty-pound sheriff who'd never raise his hand against you."

"Ask the questions," demanded my father.

"Harry, which one of us is the sheriff of this here county? If you let me be the sheriff then I'm gonna let you be the merchant." Sheriff Cauldwell sat me down on the couch and he settled into my father's desk chair. "Patty, if some man did something to hurt you, you gotta tell me about it so I can stop him. So that he can never do it again to some other young girl. Now, you tell me, Patty, 'cause you ain't got a thing to be afraid of."

I looked past the sheriff's elbow to see if my father had disintegrated. He hadn't. "Sheriff Cauldwell, please, may I have my ring back now?"

"Why, shore you can. Harry, give her back her ring."

"I'm keeping it for evidence."

"You being the sheriff again, are you? Give Patty back her ring."

I heard the air rushing like a powerful vacuum through my father's nostrils. I prayed that if God wouldn't protect me, surely Sheriff Cauldwell would. One, two, three, four, five, six, seven, eight, nine, ten. I opened my eyes to see my ring pass from my father's fingers to the sheriff's and finally back into my waiting hand.

"Oh, thanks. Is it mine to keep? Is anybody going to take it away from me?"

Sheriff Cauldwell turned a steady gaze on my

father. "Anybody touches that ring gonna have to answer to me first. Now, you want to tell me where you got it?"

"Yes, sir. There was this man—he was kinda old 'cause his whiskers were white—and he told me that he hadn't eaten in quite a while. So I told him that if he would follow me home and sit on our back doorstep I'd bring him some food from our refrigerator. And so I did and so he gave me the ring."

The sheriff rubbed his chin. "Did anything else happen? I mean, did he hurt you in any way?"

"Oh, no, sir."

"Well, did he touch you anywhere on your body?"

"Oh, no, sir. Except—"

"Except what?" Something of the guns-and-bullets quality returned to his voice.

"Except when we touched hands to shake good-bye."

Sheriff Cauldwell released a low chuckle, shaking his head. "And that's all there was to it, huh? Where was your colored woman when you were feeding this man?"

"Well, she was in the house, cleaning the living room, I think. But she didn't know anything about his being there."

The sheriff was looking at me with his heavy, yet strong-jawed face, and I got to liking him, this man of power who didn't like to hurt. "And you're saying your colored woman was close enough that if you hollered she'd have heard you and come a-running?"

"Oh, yes, sir! She would have run so fast—Ruth wouldn't let anybody hurt me."

Sheriff Cauldwell let out a deep sigh. "Well, now, Harry, I'm gonna tell you; I'm real satisfied. You?"

"No, I'm not." My father's voice sounded stretched, like rubber bands, to the breaking point. "I'm a long way from being satisfied. Why'd he give her the ring, can you answer me that? Twenty-four carat gold?"

"I reckon I'm not above asking. Why did he give you the ring, Patty?"

"Well, I mean, you want to know the real reason?" I asked, waiting for my brain to send forth some kind of message.

"Yep," said Sheriff Cauldwell.

I rubbed the ring's indented crest across my lips and waited for its powers to surge forth. "Well, I suppose it's what he said to me after eating the food—" Then the reason came to me, dropping like a highly accurate weapon into my shooting hand. I turned and aimed it directly at my father. " 'Patty,' said the old man, 'I could go through this world proud and happy if only God had seen fit to give me a daughter exactly like you.' "

16

THE SUMMER OF my Anton was gone; fall was here and winter was coming. It felt like the right time to add up the gains and subtract the losses.

My losses were only one, only him. And yet that far outdistanced any gains. My fingers held his ring while my eyes explored, for an uncountable time, the mysteries of its princely crest.

There has been something to the good, I guess, because somehow it's different with my father. He sees me differently, maybe with more power. Yes, that's it! I tried to remember how it came to be and at what moment. I only knew that it was there, unmistakably there. The new ingredient wasn't love, it wasn't as good. It was, I guess, respect. Respect for a person who he's incapable of destroying.

I thought of last April when the tornado came roaring through town like the Missouri Pacific, taking with it the roof on Mr. McDonald's dairy barn. Tommy McDonald himself told me how all eleven of the milking cows were hurt except for the one which was outright killed. Only one animal, Esmeralda, a ten-year-old striped cat with one eye, survived intact.

And that's what he didn't know before. He knows that I'm an Esmeralda too for, whatever he may say or do, I'm going to survive pretty much intact. One gain.

Then there's my mother. Any gains there? Same

mother with the same little hit-the-victim-and-run comments. But now at least it's not my hair. She has a newer one: "How come Edna Louise has all the friends?" Just being in the same room with you, Mother, is like being feast for a thousand starving insects.

Tally it up: one loss, one gain, and one tie score.

From Anton's hide-out I watched a random leaf from a sturdy oak cut its family ties and float free on a small current of air.

Wish I were like that leaf. Someday, when the time is ripe, I'll soar away on my own air current. At eighteen the law says a person is no longer a child, and I'll have graduated from high school. Then there's the war bond, the one whole thousand-dollar war bond that Grandma and Grandpa Fried bought for me. Did they say for my college education? I don't remember. Well, what if they did? A person can do whatever she wants with her own money.

How far is it? And how much does it cost? A thousand dollars must be money enough, yes, of course, I can do it. But why didn't I think of it before? Suddenly I felt as though I had something to look forward to.

Something that I had once said to Sister Parker now seemed to carry the seeds of prophecy. That story I told about the ring and the man who promised me I would be rewarded on my eighteenth birthday. Could a made-up story carry a prophecy?

It was the most natural thing in the world. The war would be over by then, and surely for Anton I could grow at least a little beautiful. And Greyhound buses go to New York and boats to Germany and trains to Göttingen. Six more years isn't tomorrow—but it isn't forever either. I'd be eighteen and grown-up with gentle curves and long shiny hair. My hand felt some of the remaining brittle handiwork of Mrs. Reeves, and I remembered what Ruth is always saying, "Folks keep

150

forgetting that wishing don't make nothing so, but prayer sometimes do."

"Oh, Lord," I called out like he had suddenly grown hard of hearing, "please give me long beautiful hair for him to love, Amen." And then as an afterthought, "And a bosom." My hand struck across the flat terrain of my chest. "I want a bosom of my very own!" Then it hit me that what I had asked for might come under the heading of blasphemy, so I quickly added, "If it's not too much trouble. I mean if it's O.K. with you that I should have one—I mean two."

"Patty! Oh-de-ho-ho, Patty!" Ruth always had this way of making a call from the back porch sound like a little song. She was waiting for me with a put-upon look. "How come he's a-coming home this time a day? What does he want to see you fer?"

"Who's coming home? Who wants to see me?"

"Him. Your daddy."

"But I haven't done anything!" I looked into Ruth's face, but the only thing there was a reflection of my own confusion. "Did he sound mad?"

Ruth's face registered mild surprise. "No. Not any madder than usual."

Then tension gushed from my body like air from a punctured inner tube. "He just wants me to do something for him, don't you think?"

Ruth nodded in agreement. Now, whatever he wants done, you jest shake your head and tell him, 'Yes, sir.' You hear me talking to you, girl?"

I gave Ruth a half nod.

"And if you knows of a faster way, or a cheaper way, or even a nicer way, you jest keeps that information to yourself. He don't wanna hear nothing like that from you."

Annoyed, I answered, "I know all that." Yet, I was grateful for the reminder. I gave my ring a kiss for luck. "You don't suppose Sheriff Cauldwell told my father that he could take my ring away, do you?" Then I answered my own question. "The sheriff wouldn't do such a thing. Besides, this is the most valuable thing I own. It's like—like my Bible, know that?"

"It tells one of them same stories the Bible do, love thy neighbor."

I pulled the ring from my finger, dropping it into the pocket of Ruth's apron. "Well, nobody's going to take it from me, not as long as I live."

From the distance of two blocks I heard the motor of the car gun itself up like it was just beginning the journey of a thousand miles, all up mountain. I didn't want him to think he had me concerned, so I grabbed a copy of the *Readers' Digest* and belly-dived to the bed.

The front door opened and slammed shut. I heard the sound of his voice without catching his words. But Ruth's voice came through unmistakably clear: "In her room, I reckon."

As the door swung open my eyes continued keeping company with the *Readers' Digest*. A rattle from a throat sent my gaze towards the door. Two men. And my father too. What do they want? *Danger!*

One of the men took a step forward. "Well, young lady, I'm Mr. Pierce. Remember me?"

Yes, so that's who it is. "No sir," I lied.

"Well, I just stopped by to chat."

"You tell him everything he wants to know," said my father, "or so help me you're gonna wish you'd never been born."

"Lots of time I wish that," I said in a normal voice, surprised that my thoughts came out in hearable words.

"God damn you, girl," he said, his face fired with sudden redness. "Who in hell do you think you're talking to?"

Mr. Pierce looked shocked or frightened or both. "Now, Mr. Bergen, please. She's only a kid."

I watched my father's face change to a color that more closely resembled purple "A kid! Now, you listen

152

here, Mr. FBI"——he pointed a trembling finger at me——
"that's no little kid, never has been, 'cause when she
was born her brain was bigger than yours is now. Understand?"

Was it possible that he was actually giving me a
compliment?

Mr. Pierce's ears seemed to catch my father's color-
ing. "I fail to understand what insulting me has to do
with the matter at hand?"

"I wasn't insulting you, I was warning you. You just
be careful of that girl, she can make lies sound like the
truth and the truth sound like a pack of vile lies. But
no matter how she lies, she wouldn't spit on a Nazi if
his body was on fire."

Pierce nodded. "Let's get on with it. I'd like to ask
your daughter a few questions."

"So question. Question!"

Pierce took out a gold fountain pen from his breast
pocket and opened a stenographic pad to a clean page.
"Tell me," he said after a pause, "what grade are you
in?"

"Seventh," I said, relieved at the way the questions
began. I'd feel even more relief if I knew what this was
about.

"Who are your teachers?"

"Teachers? I only have one," I said. "Miss Hooten,
unless you—do you want to know who my study hall
teacher is?"

"All right," he answered.

All right he did or all right he didn't? I had the feeling I shouldn't make any mistakes. "Do you want me
to tell you?"

"Yes."

"Coach Rawlings," I said as Mr. Pierce wrote something in his pad. "But he's not my teacher or anything.
We can go to the library on Fridays and read or study,
and he just sits there and keeps the kids quiet." I knew
I was making too much of it.

153

Pierce looked up from his pad. "You have a lot of friends?"

"Well, I guess so," I answered, grateful my mother wasn't here to contradict.

"Name them," said Pierce.

"Well," I said, thinking of Anton and Ruth, "they're just kids."

"Who are they?"

"Well, there's Edna Louise Jackson, she's one of my friends." I wondered if Edna Louise would ever list me as one of her friends. "And Juanita Henkins, and I guess, Donna Rhodes. I guess those are my main friends."

"Anybody else?"

I thought of good-old-raggedy-old Freddy Dowd who couldn't be mentioned in my father's presence. "No, sir, that's about all."

Mr. Pierce looked down. "Patricia, did you within the last five months give food to some tramp, somebody that you'd never seen before?"

It was plain he'd been talking to the sheriff and now he wanted to find out if the tramp could be Anton. "Yes, sir, I sure did."

"Tell me about it."

"Well, sir, during the summer I met this man and he looked an awful lot like a tramp and he told me that he hadn't eaten in—I forgot how long. Is it important? Should I try to remember?"

"Just go on with the story," said Pierce.

"Anyway, he asked if I could spare him some food and I told him that I could. And so I did—give him some food from our fridge. Is that what you want to know?"

"What was his name?"

I shook my head. "He didn't tell me."

"What was he wearing?"

"Just some old clothes that weren't clean."

"What did he look like?"

"He didn't look like anything too special. He looked tired 'cause his eyes had this redness like he hadn't been getting enough sleep."

"About how old would you say he was?"

"Well—" I began conjuring up my original vision of the tramp, the one I had used for Sister Parker and Sheriff Cauldwell. "He wasn't too young, some of his whiskers were getting grey. He may even have been forty, as old as that."

"Anything of a special nature that you noticed about the tramp?"

"Well, if there was any one thing I guess I'd have to say it was his politeness. He thanked me for every bit of food that I brought him."

Then Pierce asked his height, but before I had finished telling him that he wasn't too tall the FBI man was off on another question. "Did he talk like people from these parts?"

"Well, sir—" As he deliberately speeded up his questions, I deliberately slowed down my answers. "I'm not sure that he did."

The other FBI man led my father from the room saying something that sounded like, but it couldn't be, "Show me your clothes."

"How did he talk different?"

"Well, for one thing, he had polite manners."

"You told me that. I want to know about his accent. Did he, for example, sound like a Southerner?"

"No, sir, I really don't think so."

Pierce picked up a briefcase at his feet. "Where do you think he came from?"

"New York," I said automatically before even deciding whether it could do any harm. How could that help the FBI? After all, Anton wasn't from New York. Still, I felt uneasy.

Pierce slipped a glossy black-and-white photograph

from his briefcase. "Is this the tramp?" he asked, placing the picture before me.

It was him. Anton! "Sir?"

"I asked you if this man was the tramp?"

"Well, sir—," I said, not really sure of what to say. I couldn't quite figure out if it would hurt or help Anton if the FBI believed he was the tramp.

"Surely, you know whether or not this was the tramp. You gave him food; he gave you his ring. Why aren't you wearing it?"

"I lost it."

Pierce struck the photograph with his finger. "Well, is it him?"

I held the photo close and then out to arm's length. Ideas crashed head-on into other ideas. One idea revived itself: Make Mr. Pierce believe that I want to help him. "Well, Mr. Pierce," I said, finding his eyes. "It sure doesn't look too much like him, although, it could be if he were wearing a disguise. Do you think he wore a disguise?"

He answered my question by asking rapid-fire questions of his own. How did the tramp look like the picture? How did he not look like it? Eyes? Hair? Same or different? How? Why? Moles? Birthmarks? Clothes? Where did the tramp say he was going? Where had he been?

My head began to fog up. "Did you give the tramp any clothes to wear?" How much longer can this go on? Will there be a point when there are no more questions left to ask? Stay calm. Important, staying calm and pretending to be helpful. After all, how can I hurt Anton? I don't know where he is. He never told me where he was going. Yet, in my mind's eye I always saw him in New York City walking down Fifth Avenue, maybe even wearing an ascot from some fancy store.

Suddenly, something blue was pulled from the briefcase. "Do you recognize this shirt?" asked Pierce.

It was the Father's Day present. Near the shoulder was a tear, but it was still the shirt because on the pocket remained the initials, H.B.

"Well, do you?"

Anton ought to know better than to leave it lying around for people to find. "I may have seen it before, but I'm not sure. One shirt looks pretty much like another to me."

"You've seen this shirt before. Your daddy told me you bought it for him." Pierce picked up Anton's picture and waved it before my eyes. "And then you gave it to this man. This prisoner of war."

"Sir?"

"You heard every word I said!" He shoved the garment into my hands. "Look at it and tell the truth."

The tear was not so much a tear as a hole, quarter-sized, with purple stains smeared around it and two thick blotches of stain below. It was exactly the color you would expect to see if you mixed the blue of the shirt with the color red.

"Blood?" I waited for Pierce's denial. "Looks a little like blood." In a moment he would explain that it was only catsup stains. As I waited I searched his face, which was firmly set.

"Blood? *Blood!*" I screamed. "Did you hurt him?"

Pierce's face unset, and I knew that good news was coming. I waited for him to tell me that it was nothing serious—a few scratches across his chest.

Pierce's lips parted. He allowed himself the smallest of smiles. "Is who hurt?"

"You know who! The shirt's person."

"What's his name?"

"Reiker!" I shouted. "Frederick Anton Reiker. Is he going to be all right?"

I heard a noise that sounded like the sweet breath of satisfaction. Pierce took out a yellow half sheet of paper from his briefcase and read:

FREDERICK ANTON REIKER WAS SHOT EARLY THIS
MORNING WHILE TRYING TO AVOID ARREST. HE
DIED AT 10:15 A.M. IN NEW YORK'S BELLEVUE
HOSPITAL.

What was Pierce saying? Making jokes? Then it
struck me that the agent wasn't laughing and wasn't going to, for what he said wasn't meant to be a joke. Yet,
it couldn't be true. His words came back to me—at
10:15 A.M. Frederick Anton Reiker died in New York's
Bellevue Hospital.

The alarm clock on the night table ticked out the
seconds. A cry like from a wounded animal scattered
the quiet for what seemed like all time.

Lunging suddenly up, my fingernails plowed red
rows into his freshly shaved face. "You killed him!" my
voice screamed. "You killed him—Ohhhhh!"

My neck was caught in the *V* of his arm, and I
wanted nothing so much as to breathe again. Releasing
his hold, Pierce wiped the blood from his cheeks. The
air that I greedily sucked into my lungs came rushing
out again, carrying with it a single word that I hurled
at him in a spray of spit.

"Murderer!"

17

As I LAY across my bed I pinched my forearm until the colors changed from white to pink and finally to a crescent of red. If this is nothing but a bad dream a little pain should scare it away. But I can see him still, his face contorted. Harder, pinch harder! The red crescent turned purple. But Anton's sprawled body was still there bleeding across the city sidewalk.

Pierce stood just outside my door talking on the hall phone. ". . . All right, yes, yes, I'll hold. Mr. Bergen, these calls aren't costing you anything. I've reversed the charges."

"Hurry it up. I've got to call my lawyer."

"I'm doing the best I can, Mr. Bergen. My instructions were to bring the girl into Little Rock. Since you'd rather I bring her into our Memphis bureau, I'm gonna have to get permission for that."

"Do what you can."

". . . Hello, Chief Gilford? John Pierce here. We got a virtual confession out of the girl. She knew he was a prisoner of war, and she sheltered him. McFee is out checking the abandoned rooms above the family garage. . . . All she says is that she did it and did it alone. Listen, Chief, I've run into a snag. The father wants her taken into Memphis, wants a certain Memphis lawyer to handle the case . . . . I don't know if he thought of that. Hold on, let me talk to him." Pierce held the receiver against his chest. "Uh, Mr. Bergen. Our bureau chief, Tom Gilford, says we can question her from the Memphis bureau, but that it would pose a problem you might not be aware of."

"What problem?"

"He says that any charges that might come out of the investigation would be processed through the Arkansas courts and that you would be better advised to have an Arkansas lawyer who knows the local courts."

"And I still want her taken into Memphis!" my father said.

My father walked into my bedroom and slumped into the maple rocker. I heard his young voice quiver, but not from rage. "I don't understand. How could you? A girl who is Jewish. You disgrace me, your own father. And for what? A Nazi. A God damn Nazi!" He brought a white handkerchief out of a back pocket and began blowing his nose.

At another time I might have felt his grief was mine. But now his was his and mine was my own and that was burden enough.

He jumped out of the rocker as though the cushion had suddenly been replaced by hot coals. "Tell me why," he shouted, his voice hollow.

"I can't tell you. You wouldn't understand."

"Tell me!" he screamed, but this time he seemed more vulnerable than violent.

"He was good to me."

My father looked as though I had just finished telling him the world's most incredible lie. "Are you going to tell me or do I have to knock it out of you?"

"I've already told you. He was kind to me."

"And I don't believe you. You let him put his hands on your body, didn't you?" His thin lips contorted into a sneer. "You—you filth!"

"That's a lie! Anton's a good man. A better man than you."

"God damn you!" The paleness left his face. "How

160

dare you compare me to that Nazi! Why you—you're no good. From the day you were born you've brought me nothing but misery."

Ruth rushed into the room, brushing past my father. "You've got no call talking to this child like that." She sat down beside me, giving the bed a bounce. "Mr. Bergen, now I only works here and I ain't 'pose to be telling you nothing, but some things needs saying. Lord knows that's the truth." Her arm spread over me like a great shield. "That man from the government didn't say Patty did bad. All I heard she do is let a tired man sleep where nobody else wanted to sleep and gave him food that came from nobody's mouth."

"And I want you to stop interfering in something that's none of your business."

The earth-colored yolks of Ruth's eyes rose to their highest point, leaving a splash of whitness below. "This here is the Lord's business, Mr. Bergen, and I'm trying to do the work He set out for me." Her hands were clasped and her eyes stayed heavenward. After a moment she nodded as though she understood her silent instructions. "God is our refuge and strength, and a help in troubles. Therefore will we not fear, though the earth be removed and the mountains be carried into the midst of the sea. . . . Be still, and know that I am God."

"Ruth, get yourself out of here."

"Listen to the Lord speakin' to you, Mr. Bergen."

Couldn't Ruth see she was wasting her time? "Leave him alone. He doesn't understand," I whispered.

"God almighty is crying out to you to bring forth your humanity. He wants you to quit your tormenting and put your faith in Him."

My father threw Ruth a look that could have split rock. "And now I'm telling you, you've pushed me past my endurance. I think a lot of Patty's meanness is your doing. This family doesn't need you anymore." He took

161

out his wallet and threw a five-dollar bill and three ones onto the bed. One of the singles rested for a moment at the side of the bed before fluttering to the floor. Neither Ruth nor my father made any effort to pick it up. "Now, I'm paying you for the week, but I don't want you here one second longer. Get your things and get out. Now!"

"Lord knows I needs this job, Mr. Bergen. Lord knows I needs the money, but—" Ruth's arm tightened around me. "This child needs me even more than I needs the work. Truth is she does."

"Don't send Ruth away! Please, don't do it." My arms couldn't complete the circle around her waist. "If you never in your life do another thing for me, don't send her away. She's all I have left."

"Take the money, Ruth," said my father in a voice marked by sudden calmness. "And then you tell those fat legs of yours to take you out of here."

18

PIERCE WALKED to the door of my room without entering. "All settled, Mr. Bergen. We're taking the girl into Memphis." Then he gave me a nod. "Better pack a few things."

"How long will she be gone?"

"Don't know, sir. She'd better take a few changes."

I got the smallest of the three suitcases out of the closet and began putting in some clothes like a robot who feels nothing. I wasn't even conscious anymore of wanting anything except maybe to be left alone, and I wasn't even strong on that. Living was too big a deal and dying too much trouble.

When I snapped the case closed the agent asked, "Ready to go?"

"Yes."

My father was shouting into the phone, ". . . Well, get Mr. Kishner out of conference. This is an emergency. Let the Hardwood Dealers of America wait! . . . . No, it's not about my business. I guess I oughta know what kind of a lawyer I need. . . . Less than an hour? Have Mr. Kishner call me back collect at number two five five, Jenkinsville, Arkansas. Got that? Number two five five."

"We're ready, Mr. Bergen," said Pierce.

"I can't leave. I want to be here when the lawyer calls."

"No problem. It's only a couple of blocks to our car. McFee, get the suitcase, will you?"

As I walked past my father I said, "Good-bye," but maybe he didn't hear. At any rate he didn't answer.

The sidewalk was too narrow for three, so Pierce and McFee walked a few steps behind me. Across the street Freddy Dowd looked up from his worm diggings. "Where you going? Someplace?"

"Memphis."

"Boy, oh, boy," he said, letting out his widest grin, "I sure wish I was you!"

I laughed inside. "There are better wishes to wish for, Freddy."

As we came close to my father's store I saw people milling in front. Too many people for a weekday unless today is dollar day. Suddenly, the FBI men were walking at my side. "Stay close to me," whispered Pierce. There were ten, more than that, at least fifteen people and all with fixed faces. They know about me. How could they have found out so soon? Then I spotted Jenkinsville's leading gossip merchant, Mary Wren, holding onto the arm of Reverend Benn's wife.

The agents maneuvered me away from the sidewalk and into the center of Main Street. The crowd followed. A glob of liquid hit me in the back of the neck and when I saw what my hand had wiped away I gagged.

Suddenly a woman's voice called, "Nazi! Nazi!" Other voices joined in. A man's voice, one that I had heard before, shouted, "Jew Nazi—Jew Nazi—Jew Nazi!"

When we reached the car, the mob blocked the doors. "You people are obstructing justice," said Pierce. "Please move back."

"Jew Nazi-lover!" screamed the minister's wife.

Tires screeched to a stop. A car door opened and

164

Sheriff Cauldwell shouted, "Get away from that car. What's the matter with you folks, anyway?"

People slowly moved away from the car, crowding into a huddle on the sidewalk. Sheriff Cauldwell opened the back door of the car for me, and then, whipping out a small black Bible from his shirt pocket, he pressed it into my hand. "Times when I was down this helped lift me up. God bless you."

"Thanks," I said, feeling the tears stinging at my eyes.

McFee drove in second gear all the way down Main Street before taking a right turn onto Highway 64. As we passed McDonald's dairy, I looked down the long dirt road leading to the prison camp. But I knew I wasn't going to find him there or any other place on God's earth.

I was already awake when the phone first rang downstairs at a quarter to eight. By nine there had already been three or four incoming calls. I wondered if they concerned me.

At nine thirty I knew I couldn't put it off any longer. I would go downstairs and face my grandparents. Last night it was pretty late when the agents brought me here, and Grandmother Fried said that I looked very tired and she took me straight to bed. This morning, though, it might be different. She might get around now to the questions she hadn't asked.

I saw her at the kitchen table, stirring a cup of coffee with one hand and holding the phone with the other. "You sure about Harry selling the store? Things blow over. People forget. . . . Pearl, I'll talk to Poppa. . . . Didn't I say I would? If Harry had been maybe a little nice to us all these years then I know Poppa would say, sure. Now, I don't know. . . ." My grandmother looked up as I entered the kitchen. "Pearl, I have to go now. Patty just woke up. . . . Yes, Pearl, I'll talk. I'll talk! Tonight, after supper. Good-bye."

165

"My father has to sell the store?"

"Maybe he does, maybe he doesn't. Who knows? My daughter always makes a *gontzeh tsimmes* out of everything."

"And my father wants to go to work for Grandfather?"

"Your mother wants it; only *Gott in Himmel* knows what your daddy wants."

Grandmother brought me a perfectly oval omelet. "I'm sorry to cause you all this trouble," I said.

"Trouble? An omelet is trouble?"

"Well, that and having to stay up to let me in last night."

"It's nice having you—" she said, patting my cheek—"even if it's because of this *mish-mosh*."

"*Mish-mosh?*"

"What else? Does a person have to ask for credentials before they can give food to a hungry man? Are you responsible because you gave nourishment to a bad man? The whole business is a *mishegoss*."

"I'm glad you're not angry with me."

"What is there to be angry about? I have messages for you. I'm going to drive you to Lawyer Kishner's office at quarter till eleven, and he's going to take you himself to the FBI. Also a friend called." She began searching through a pad of paper. "I wrote it down myself. Here! It's a Miss Charlene Madlee. She's coming by tonight to see you."

Mostly, I told the FBI everything they wanted to know, and I told it about a dozen times to four different agents. One question they seemed keen on asking was if anybody else knew. Sometimes they'd just ask, "Who else knew?" or "Why are you taking all the blame?" Things like that. But always I gave the same answer— "Nobody else knew. It was only me."

It was after four in the afternoon when the boss agent, Mr. Wilhelm, told one of the younger agents to

166

drive me back to my grandmother's. "I don't believe we'll be needing you anymore, Patty, but you'd better stay here in Memphis for a while. Things are unsettled in Jenkinsville."

"Unsettled?"

"Well, I understand your parents are being harassed."

"How?"

"Telephone calls, a store window broken, things like that."

"Why would they bother them? Can't you tell people that they had nothing to do with it? They didn't even know."

Mr. Wilhelm scratched his forehead like he was trying to come up with an answer for me. "When people's emotions are involved they don't want to listen."

At eight o'clock my grandmother opened the door for Charlene as I stood at the top of the stairs, waiting for my trembling to subside. Would she hate me?

"It was kind of you to let me come tonight, Mrs. Fried." If there was any hate in Charlene's voice I couldn't catch it.

"Our pleasure, Miss—"

"Madlee. Charlene Madlee."

"Yes, well, Miss Madlee, Patty needs all her friends now. You saw the evening paper?"

"Oh, yes, I read them as well as write for them."

"You write? For newspapers? You told me you were a friend of Patty's. Friends we need; reporters we don't."

"Believe me, Mrs. Fried, I am a friend. When we met during the summer, Patty told me that her grandparents lived in Hein Park. Also I came here tonight to bring you encouraging news."

As I walked down the stairs, Charlene gave me a real smile. Still my friend. My grandfather pulled out a dining room chair for Charlene. "My wife makes the best strudel in the world. Wait'll you taste!" He smacked his lips.

Charlene ate a forkful. "You know, Mrs. Fried, I think your husband is right. You do make the world's best strudel."

"It's wonderful," I said. "I remember reading somewhere that kissing doesn't last, but cookery does."

My grandfather jumped up from the host's chair to give Grandmother a noisy kiss on her cheek. "Does that answer your question, young lady?"

"Sam!"

We all laughed, then abruptly turned to Charlene as if hoping she might give us something of substance to laugh about.

"I talked today to Charles Hammett," said Charlene.

"He's the editor of the *Commercial Appeal?*" asked Grandfather.

"He's our publisher. Well, Mr. Hammett had lunch with a high official from the Justice Department, which would be the agency responsible for initiating legal actions in such cases as Patty's. The feeling is that the government would be very reluctant to prosecute a twelve-year-old under the Treason Act. Also he mentioned that our allies would consider us barbaric if we did such a thing."

Grandfather clapped his hands. "Thank God! I knew this American government was 100 per cent O.K. After all, what did my granddaughter do that's so terrible? She's only twelve, so she didn't act wisely, O.K. But she meant good, you have to admit that. And do you think for one minute that fellow, *aleva-sholem,* told Patty that he was an escaped prisoner? Also one other point, excuse me for bringing this up, Miss Madlee. I recognize that you aren't of our faith, but do you think that if we were Protestants there would be all this hullabaloo?"

"I'm certain there wouldn't, Mr. Fried. There's no question that this gave some people an excuse to parade their anti-Semitism. But all the interest isn't anti-Semitic. Some people may find love and brotherhood in the story. The Memphis bureau of United Press sent it over the international wires, which means that tonight people throughout the world will be reading about how a Jewish girl befriended a German boy."

"I pray to God," said Grandmother, "that when they read about Patty they'll feel a little closer to their brothers no matter what faith or nationality."

"I'm just glad it's over," said Grandfather.

Charlene looked confused. "I'm sorry if I implied that all charges against Patty will be dropped; I meant only the serious charges of treason. The man from the Justice Department felt that if there was a public outcry the state of Arkansas might wish to prosecute Patty on a lesser charge."

"But I'm not guilty of a lesser charge! They can call it treason, but they can't call it anything else."

"At best, Patty, all charges will be dropped," said Charlene. "But if the Arkansas politicians are pushed to move against you they could easily get you on, say, a delinquency charge. In that way the Federal Government is off the hook, and people will still feel that justice has been served."

Grandmother clasped her hand to her heart. "You don't think—it's not possible that they would send my granddaughter to jail?"

"It's only the slightest of possibilities," said Charlene slowly, as though she were choosing her words with inordinate care. "But there does still exist the chance that Patty might be sent to reform school."

19

O! Little town of Bethlehem,
How still we see thee lie!
Above thy deep and dreamless sleep,
The silent stars go—

The music from the car radio turned to static. "Too far from Jonesboro to get much reception," said Mr. Calvin Grimes.

"Guess so."

"Well," he said, snapping the radio off, "reckon that's it."

"Yes, sir, guess it is," I answered, trying to keep up my end of the conversation.

The sky was purply, deepening even as I watched, warning of the approach of darkness and maybe even of snow. Along the highway rows of never-been-painted tenant shacks glowed with the softness of kerosene lamps. Their windows without curtains gave quick exposures of tenant families, mostly colored, sitting around the supper table.

Then with sudden speed Mr. Grimes swerved from the right- to the left-hand lane to pass a poky tractor. "Feller should know enough," he said, "to have his lights on this time of day, wouldn't you think? Slow-moving vehicle like that."

"Yes, sir, he sure should," I said.

As the road turned off to the left, there was a definite rise from the flatness of the delta lands. Beginning in me was a matching feeling of ascent. Where have you been for such a long time, Hope? Remember the last time you came paying me a visit? Wait six years, you told me, only six years and I would have outside beauty—more even than my mother's—while inside I would grow beautiful like Ruth. And then I would find Anton again, and he would love me for everything I was, everything I had become.

Suddenly a chuckle started up in me and then a second and a third. Without moving my eyes from the side window I could tell Mr. Grimes had turned to look at me. "Girl, if you've got yourself a funny, why don't you share it?"

"Uh, no, sir, I don't actually know any jokes or anything like that, it was just that—Well, I was thinking of a friend of mine whom I liked being with so much because he could always make things fun. Know what I mean?"

"Reckon I do." Mr. Grimes measured out his words. "Them kind of folks always nice to have around."

"Not just big things," I explained because for some reason I really wanted him to understand, "but little things too. Things that lotsa folks wouldn't even find amusing."

"Girl, that's one of the Lord's blessings. Laughter and them that makes it. Like he gives it to some folks to be strong, others to be rich. Now, to me he gave a fine wife and four good boys. Them's blessings, girl. Everybody got to find the Lord's bounty and give thanks. You know your blessings? Counted them? Laid them aside and said your thanks?"

I thought of Ruth, Grandmother, and Grandfather. I thought of the frizzle that had finally grown out of

171

my hair. And then I thought of him, and I wondered if a blessing is still a blessing if it lasts for only a little while?

Then with my eyes quite open Anton's face came through. I closed my eyes to blot out all possible distractions. He was smiling that smile, I'd seen it before when he said to me, "Remember, P.B., remember when . . ." But I didn't hear the rest of his words. I was just too filled up with feelings of pleasure and privilege to think that in those short days together we had begun making memories.

"Ya gettin' hungry?" Mr. Grimes' dry voice popped my bubble of reverie. "There's a restaurant down the road jest past Lambert. We could stop there for hamburgers 'cause I'm not in a million years gonna make Bolton till after ten o'clock. I jest don't know whether one of them matrons would save you a bite of supper. Wouldn't bet my last nickel on it, tell you that fer sure."

In the distance a large red neon sign blinked:

SHANLEY'S GULF STATION
Good Food—Good Gas

Even a car-length away from Shanley's front door the smell of things fried—hamburgers, potatoes, and onions—was pretty powerful.

At the back of the restaurant a fancy jukebox changed from red to purple to blue as it blared forth, "Shuffle on down to Memphis Town. . . . Oh, shuffle on down to Memphis Town. Ain't got no money but I'll show you around."

I followed Mr. Grimes to the only empty booth, empty of people but not of their dishes. Ashes and cigarette butts filled the glass ash tray to capacity.

Our waitress, who was about sixteen and I guess you'd call her pretty, wore beaded Indian moccasins

172

but no stockings over her hairy legs. She dropped a menu wrapped in a cellophane folder on the table and left without bothering to clean up the mess. With the back of his arm Mr. Grimes swept the dirty dishes to the edge of the table. "I like it clean and neat when I eat," he said. "Seems like ever since the war, waitresses been going from bad to worse."

As he shook his head, I noticed deep lines which ran like chicken wire from the corners of his eyes clean out to his hairline. Mr. Grimes was far away from being young and, judging from the leanness of his body, he'd never been especially strong.

After we had eaten our hamburgers and french fries and drunk down our coffee, Mr. Grimes waved to the waitress. "What kinda pie you got?"

She gave her hair, which was the color of brown wrapping paper, a good scratching. "We're all out of apple." Nodding in the direction of the counter, she said, "Gave that feller the last piece."

"What kind have you got left?" asked Mr. Grimes, not bothering to keep the irritation out of his voice.

" 'Bout the only thing I know we got is some sugar doughnuts left over from the morning and some lemon meringue pie."

"I'll take a piece of that meringue," he said, and he looked over at me. "Ya wanna piece too?"

Behind the counter a penciled sign read: All Pies 12¢. "Well, uh, no, thank you. I guess I don't care for any pie today."

"Better get some," encouraged Mr. Grimes. "This might be your last decent meal for a while."

When I laid my fork down the pie plate had only a few pin-point-sized crumbs left on it. I wanted to send my fork after those too, but didn't want Mr. Grimes to think I was still a little hungry. I felt his eyes upon me and looked up.

"Oh, by the way," he said, "I don't think you

173

oughta go mentioning to anybody that we stopped off for a bite of supper 'cause jest strictly speakin', I ain't 'spose to stop nowhere with no prisoner."

Prisoner? Me? The judge never once used that word: "I hereby sentence Patricia Ann Bergen to be committed to the Arkansas Reformatory for Girls at Bolton, Arkansas, for a period of not more than six months nor less than four months." But if Mr. Grimes calls me a prisoner, I guess he ought to know. Funny, the word has no sting. But then nothing has much sting anymore.

He rubbed his fist back and forth across his chin. "So we'll jest keep this between you and me, O.K.?"

I didn't want him fearing for his job on my account. "Mr. Grimes, it was sure nice of you to stop so I could have something to eat, and I will never say anything to anybody. If I got you in trouble—Pow! God should strike me down dead."

His smile showed a vacancy between two front teeth. "Lord, girl, I sure don't want nothing like that happening to you."

I felt myself smiling back. He was really quite nice. "The whole thing is, and I thought about it quite a lot, it's not true what they said about me. In court they called me a person of no loyalties—a traitor. But it just couldn't be true 'cause it was my loyalties that got me into trouble in the first place, know what I mean?"

He nodded. "I read about it in the papers, how you helped out that German boy."

I was grateful he called him a boy; better than the others calling him Nazi or spy. "I wanted to help him because he wasn't a Nazi or a spy, and he wasn't even mean. Anton was the kindest, smartest man I've ever known. I wanted to tell that to the judge so he'd understand why I had to hide him. Why I had to help him stay free. But Mr. Kishner just kept shaking his head No."

174

Mr. Grimes was looking at me as though Anton couldn't be all those things I said he was. Why did I have to go spouting off to him? What made me think he would understand when nobody else could? "Don't you think," I asked, hearing the anger in my voice, "that a German can be good?"

"Oh, I reckon on St. Peter opening up them pearly gates for some Germans," he said. "Now, there ain't no need to go getting your dander up jest 'cause I don't understand who's this Mr. Kishner."

"I'm sorry. He's the man, the lawyer, my father hired to tell my side of the story in court. Only thing is he kept saying that the really important things were not pertinent to the case."

"Them lawyers are tricky fellers all right," said Mr. Grimes. "One time, oh, this was two or three years ago, I was taking a feller name of Cranston Hollis to the Cummins Prison Farm."

He waved his empty coffee cup in the air and Miss Beaded Moccasins filled both of our cups from a steaming pot. "Well, Mr. Cranston Hollis, he was one big man. President of a state savings bank in North Little Rock. Only thing was when the bank examiner came to look at the ledger he found that Mr. Hollis' bank was shy one hundred and eighty-five thousand dollars and that ain't even counting the change."

I said, "That's a lot."

"Ooh-whee, I'll say it is. More money than I'll make in all my working lifetime. Well, this Mr. Hollis, he was one smart man, told me eight people other than him worked in that bank. Six of them had more opportunity than he did to take the money. But his lawyer didn't even entertain the notion that he was defending an innocent man. So Mr. Hollis' advice to anyone who has to go up before the bar of justice is to beware of at least two people: the lawyer the state hires to convict you and the lawyer you hire to defend yourself."

It was easier for me to agree with poor Mr. Cranston Hollis now than before my experience with Mr. Kishner. But it wasn't exactly his fault. I mean, actually he didn't want to take my case in the first place. My father had especially wanted Mr. Kishner because he was known as a really big Memphis lawyer, and I know for a fact how proud the Beth Zion Synagogue is that he is one of them.

When my father first phoned him, Mr. Kishner said that it wasn't the kind of thing he wanted to get involved in, and besides since the case would be tried in the Arkansas courts, it would be much better to hire a local, non-Jewish attorney. Somebody who knew all the local judges and wouldn't be afraid to speak out.

After Mr. Kishner refused to take my case, my father placed another long distance call to Memphis. This time it was to Morris Frank, president of Beth Zion, who I think my father had met before. Mr. Frank said that he had known Harold Kishner for more than thirty years and if anybody could get him to take the case he could. And he did.

On the very next day Mr. Kishner's thin and unsmiling secretary led me into an office of dark wood, real leather chairs, and an oriental rug of such fire and density that it must have taken a hundred weavers all their lifetimes to complete. A window behind the great man gave a fine view of the Memphis skyline.

The lawyer sighed into the receiver, "Leo, why can't you keep in mind that we're treating it as a tax preference item?"

When he finally placed the receiver on the hook he nodded at me without smiling. I nodded back while forcing a smile. He got up from his chair. I edged forward in mine. Finally he said he was my lawyer, hired to be, and that he was going to see if he could help me.

He asked me to tell my story just as it happened, and as I did he scribbled notes on a long yellow pad. Every so often he would interrupt to ask a question or

176

clarify a point. A couple of times and in slightly different ways he asked if I were afraid of Anton, afraid that harm might come to either me or my family if I failed to obey.

Mr. Kishner's lips thinned when I shook my head. "I was never afraid."

Then he tried to get me to say I was too young to understand that Anton was an escaped prisoner. How could I not have understood that? I wanted to tell him that I had some pride left and that they could accuse me of being a traitor, but not of being stupid. But I kept quiet.

Finally Mr. Kishner replaced his fountain pen in his onyx desk set and rose, looking me over closely for the first time, and I knew that he would speak. "Young lady, you have embarrassed Jews everywhere. Because your loyalty is questionable, then every Jew's loyalty is in question." He sighed before adding, "I just wanted you to know."

Outside Shanley's Restaurant the air came up sharp and clean. "Cold enough for you?" asked Mr. Grimes.

"Oh, I don't mind," I said. A vision of snow on distant mountaintops came to me and I was close to asking if there were mountains at Bolton, but fear that he would say there was only flat land kept the question unasked. With the end of Anton, hope had taken to its sickbed, if not its deathbed.

I found a small bit of courage within, not enough for mountains, but maybe for a little snow. I decided to squander it. "Any chance we might get snow for Christmas?"

Mr. Grimes looked to the right and then the left, shifted into second, and entered the two-lane highway before speaking. "Weatherman on the radio said the Carolinas might get some, but I ain't never heard of snow taking no geography lessons. Back in '38 or '39—

'38 it was—we got almost an inch of snow for Christmas."

"I'd like that to happen again," I said as I brought my shoeless feet up beside me on the car seat. My head found a resting place in the bough of my arm. I felt myself going down, down to sleep.

Against my arm, tapping. "Wake up, girl. We're almost there."

"Wha—" I stifled my yawn inside the crook of my elbow.

"We're coming into Bolton, thought you'd like to see it. The school's east of town."

"Oh," I said, conscious of feeling nothing but sleepy.

Then, spanning the width of the street, strings of Christmas lights—red and blue, green and yellow. A lighted movie marquee announced, *The Five Sullivans* and Xmas cartoons.

"I saw that movie!" I said, coming alive. "All about five brothers, sailors on this ship that was sunk. Saddest thing I've ever seen. Try to see that movie if you get the chance."

"Nope," answered Mr. Grimes. "Don't have to spend my money for sadness. Plenty of that to be had for free."

Mr. Grimes followed the road through town, past two blocks of houses, a gas station, and then open land. Headlights picked up a black iron fence, and as the car swung through open gates I saw a sign with the Arkansas state seal. It read:

THE JASPER E. CONRAD
ARKANSAS REFORMATORY FOR GIRLS
BOLTON, ARKANSAS

The lights were on in the three-story building. In the darkness it looked no different from any other three-story brick. No! There was something different. The windows were covered, all covered, with diamond-shaped, heavy wire screening. At the Memphis Zoo they use the same kind of screening for the animals.

20

MY EYES OPENED. I measured the bleakness of the morning against the painted grayness of the walls and estimated the time to be six thirty. Ever since I had been here, and today marked the thirty-second morning, there had been this new ability of mine to awaken, fully awake, without stretching or yawning. Part of it was knowing that this thirty minutes before the wake-up bell was the only time that belonged to me.

All right, get to it, I told myself. This is finally going to be the morning when things come to me: My plans for a lifetime. I gave myself the usual instructions: Try new roads; check out all byways, explore every possibility. But my mind hadn't even finished its pep talk when the familiar vision intruded. "Go away," I said out loud, "I have to be practical." I couldn't risk everything on such a slim hope. It didn't make sense!

Think practical; think about living in Memphis with Grandmother and Grandfather. My father wouldn't hear of it. Didn't he tell the FBI that they had no right to take me to Grandma's that evening after they had finished questioning me?

Then think about going away to school, to some private place in New England where nobody would know me. My mother wouldn't let me. Even before the scandal I clipped an ad from the back pages of

The Ladies' Home Journal showing a girl about my age smiling at her horse, and underneath the picture it read, "Briar Cliff: an experience in living."

My mother only glanced at the ad before starting to laugh, "Where do you dream up such ideas?" she demanded. "Are you such a fancy girl you need such a fancy school?" No possibility there, none at all.

Well, I've heard about people working their way through school, and there are things I can do. I could take care of the horses. I'd love that, but even if that job were filled there are other things. Cooks need helpers, or maybe I could use the work experience that I'm getting here. As I brought my hands from beneath the blanket bleach attacked my nostrils. That smell may have been part of my imagination, but my red, chapped hands weren't. No, I don't want to work in anybody's laundry anywhere, anymore.

The vision was still there waiting for me, soft and appealing. I let it in. It's six years from now. I'm eighteen. The war is over. With my thousand-dollar war bond, I have money enough to take a train to New York and from there a ship to Germany. Another train ride and I'm in Göttingen. At the train station I change into my prettiest dress before dialing the number. No, not at the station, better at a hotel.

A woman answers and I ask, "Mrs. Reiker?"

"This is Mrs. Reiker," says the voice in elegant English.

"Mrs. Reiker," I say slowly, "I'm an American. My name is Patricia Bergen. I knew your son, Anton." There is only silence, so I stumble on. "We were friends back when he was a prisoner of war, in America."

"You knew Anton?" she asks, her voice hollow like it was traveling over great distance, or great sorrow.

I breathe in deeply before answering. "Yes, I knew Anton. We were friends. I tried to help him."

"You tried to help him? Where are you?" asks Mrs. Reiker, sounding suddenly energized.

181

I tell her that I'm right here in Göttingen and she asks, "Could you possibly have dinner with us tonight? And of course any traveling companions you have would be most welcome."

"Well, I don't actually have any traveling companions," I say.

"Then you must stay with us," she replies. "We have a large house. We could make you most comfortable."

My heart floated up like a helium ballon until the ringing of the wake-up bell punctured it. I cried out against the intrusion, wondering if there weren't some way to hold onto the vision. It seemed unfair. I had lost my chance to become a member of the family.

"Hey, Natz, you gonna get up? Scrambled egg day."

I pulled the covers down to look directly into the Raggedy Ann eyes of my roommate, Mavis McCall. "I'm getting up," I said, wiggling my feet to give the impression of forward movement. "Could you please stop calling me Natz?"

"Geez, whatta ya want me to call ya, Nazi or Spy like them others do?" Mavis managed to look as though I had just spit upon her grandmother's grave.

"Well, if it's all the same to you, you could call me Patty or even the name I was born with, Patricia." Mavis looked a long way from being convinced so I added, "I don't call you Thief, do I?"

In the cafeteria line Mavis stood in front of me as rigidly silent as the angel on the topmost point of the room's Christmas tree. "Don't they know that Christmas trees are supposed to be taken down as soon as Christmas is over?" I asked.

"Can't go 'bout taking a Christmas tree down on a Sunday!" she said, sounding shocked at my ignorance. "Wouldn't be right."

I was grateful that she was still talking to me. "No, guess not," I answered.

As Mavis wiped the last crumbs from her plate with a piece of white bread, I saw her eyes check my plate. "I haven't touched my eggs," I said, pushing my plate towards her and wondering why the eggs didn't taste as powdery to her as they did to me.

Mavis scraped them onto her plate, then paused with her fork directly over my mound of grits. Her eyes sought my permission. "I'm all finished eating," I said.

"You ain't much of an eater, is you?" she said and then added in lieu of thanks, "Patty."

After breakfast the day room, with its hard-backed chairs lined like soldiers against the wall, was empty. The girls had all gone over to the nondenominational services in the chapel. On my first Sunday here I had gone because the head matron, Miss Laud (secretly called "Miss Bald" due to the fact that pink skin was beginning to show through her hair) kept emphasizing that the services were absolutely nondenominational. Now maybe, and I'll give her the benefit of the doubt, the services are nondenominational for Baptists, Methodists, and Jehovah's Witnesses, but they are definitely not nondenominational for a Jewish girl. I say this because the minister spent just about his whole sermon talking about the method the Jews used when they killed Jesus.

The clock high above the doorway of the day room read ten till ten, yet the grayness of the morning hung on. On the side table sat the room's most valuable item, a mahogany radio with an arched top. Usually it was ablare with sad-sounding cowboys singing of girls they had loved and lost, but for the time being it sat quietly neglected.

I snapped the knob to the right and waited for the tubes to warm. I tried to find something good to listen to on a Sunday morning. Phil Baker and his *Sixty-four Dollar Question* wasn't till evening and so was *Baby Snooks*. Even Andre Kostelanetz and his orchestra wasn't till later.

183

"For God so loved the world, that he gave his only begotten Son, that—"

I moved the dial. This time to singing. "Where he leads me, I shall follow—"

And another turn of the dial. "Tell me why it is, dear friends," cried out a man's voice in apparent anguish, "that people will believe the promise of a bank. Give us your money, we'll keep it safe. And they'll believe the promise of a boss. Work for me, and I'll give you money. Then why is it that these same people have trouble believing in the greatest promise ever given to mankind? Jesus made that promise to you, and he made it to me. And this was his promise: Whosoever believeth in me shall be given life everlasting."

I snapped the knob to the left, and, except for the steady hissing of the radiator, the room was silent.

Back in my room the thick Sunday edition of the *Memphis Commercial Appeal*, a gift subscription from Charlene Madlee, lay on my bed. It was nice having a lady like that for a friend. And I liked having my very own newspaper subscription. I mean besides reading it, it was nice in another way too. It was the something good (instead of always the something bad) that set me apart. I wasn't like them, like the others, and the paper was proof of that.

After my trial Charlene Madlee was the only reporter (and the courtroom was filled with them) who came over to say she was sorry. And she was too! I caught a look on her face of genuine distress. On my second day at Bolton I received her first note. I read it so many times that it became engraved on my brain.

Patty,
I'm sending you a subscription to my paper
with the hope that you will enjoy reading it.
Keep smiling!

Charlene Madlee

And in each reading of Charlene's note I scoured her words for the gift of friendship. Sometimes, like an optical illusion, I found it, and other times I didn't.

Anyway I wrote Charlene back, thanking her and saying the thing I liked most to read were the stories that carried her by-line. That wasn't hard to say. People like honest compliments, I know that. It was what I said next that made me hesitate because it sounded presumptuous. "I still think I'd like to study to become some kind of reporter or writer someday." But she didn't think I was just a presumptuous kid, because she wrote me right back, a whole page.

Footsteps. Determined footsteps came echoing down the corridor. Miss Laud? What would she want me for? I'm not breaking any rules: no cigarettes, no shoes on the bed, door open. About the nondenominational services? But I've already explained that, how the services go against my beliefs. I won't go!

As the footsteps stopped at my door, fear took hold. I forced myself to look up at the full standing authority of Miss Evelyn Laud.

"You know a Nigra named Ruth Hughes?"

"Ma'am?"

"A Nigra named Ruth Hughes, says she's your nanny, that right?"

"Uh, yes, ma'am, that's right."

Miss Laud nodded.

"Well, go on down to the visitors' room and see her."

"Ma'am?" I asked, like one who has suddenly stopped understanding the English language.

"Well, go down and see her," repeated Miss Laud in tones loud enough for the deaf.

Through the open archway of the visitors' room I could see Ruth, her back towards me, looking out the mesh-covered window to the courtyard below. She was wearing a dress I had never seen before, deep

185

blue like the sky gets toward evening. It looked to be crepe and good enough not only for Sunday but for Easter Sunday as well. Strange, she didn't seem to hear my approach for her gaze never strayed from the window.

"Ruth?"

Like a spring suddenly released, she turned, her brown face showing a wide, welcoming smile. But it wasn't the smile that caught me quite as much as her eyes. They had this shine, a gloss that I remembered seeing once before, but I couldn't quite remember when.

Arms circled me, bringing me close. "Patty, Honey Babe, how you doing?" A fragrance of bath powder scented gardenia. "You doin' all right, Honey?" My head found its resting place next to her shoulder and I closed my eyes while I silently prayed for the world to go away. "Are they treating you all right here?"

I nodded my head Yes, but I didn't know for sure whether she got my message, so I said, "I guess they are. Yes." And there in the protection of her circle, I felt freshly born.

Ruth, still with an arm around my waist, led me to a wooden bench next to the radiator, but before we sat down she pushed me an arm's length away and gave me a careful looking over. "You shore ain't doin' no overeating hereabouts, are you?"

"On Sundays we have scrambled eggs for breakfast," I said, wondering if my answer fit the question.

"There's six other days need accounting for."

"Well, mostly they serve grits for breakfast."

Ruth looked angry. "You never would eat no grits."

"I eat them sometimes," I said, feeling that we should somehow be spending this time together on better things. "Tell me something. What's new in Jenkinsville?"

"Same old town it's always been, Honey. When

186

the Bible says that there ain't nothing new under the sun, I think they musta had Jenkinsville in mind," Ruth laughed, enjoying her own joke. When her face resettled she added, "Tell you this, I got myself a new job, keeps house for the colored schoolteacher, Miz Cora Mae Ford. You knows her?"

I said that I did while the feeling of betrayal swept over me.

Ruth went on. "She and her husband, Robert, he's got himself a good job too, drives one of them trucks for Dixie Transport. Well, they got themselves three of the cutest children. Now the baby, Michael Augustus, ain't even walking yet and I declare if he ain't 'bout the sweetest little thing I ever did see."

I told myself to forget it. Ruth didn't just up and desert me, remember that. She was fired. Fired! She has to make a living, get along as best as she can. And if she didn't care for me, would she have made this long trip just to see me?

"How did you ever manage to get here, Ruth?"

Her eyes grew wide and the gloss disappeared. It must have had something to do with how the light from the window struck her eyes. "Would you ever think that your old Ruth would come a-visiting in a big vehicle driven by a chauffeur?"

"Really? You're kidding me?"

She put a look of mock disgust on her face. "Well, if'n a Greyhound Bus ain't a big vehicle and if'n a uniformed driver ain't a chauffeur then I don't know much of nothing no more."

I felt the muscles about my mouth tugging upward into an unnatural or, at least, seldom-used position. "I'm really glad you came to see me. Must have been a long trip."

"No-o-o-o," said Ruth. "Wasn't too long 'cause I got to see me places I ain't never seed before. Heard about, but never seed. Places like Wynne City, Jones-

187

boro, Bolton, places like that." She suddenly jumped up and rushed across the room to a red-and-white-striped shopping bag.

Reaching low into the bag, she brought out a box whose lettering was clearly readable through the white tissue paper wrappings. "Ginger snaps. Thanks. You know they're my very favorites." I gave Ruth a quick hug. "I'm sorry I don't have anything for you this year, but I didn't get to do any Christmas shopping."

"Now that don't make no nevermind, Patty Babe, 'cause come next Christmas I'm gonna give you a list more'n six feet long. But right now I got you a little somethin' else." She reached into her shopping bag to bring out a yellow shoe box tied with red paper ribbon. I broke the string to find a whole family of fried chicken breasts, each one sitting on its very own pink paper napkin.

"Nothing there but the breasts," she said. "See, Ruth remembers."

And I saw too that Ruth had remembered her own rule about the proper frying of chicken. "Secret is," she used to say, "to fry it, and fry it done in corn meal." And while the chicken fried, there was something else she always did. She'd break an egg or two into a bowl of corn meal, throw in a chopped-up onion, and then she'd drop spoonfuls of the batter into the pan next to the chicken. Hush puppies. I don't think I ever in my life had fried chicken without them.

I pinched off a crispy piece of skin and placed it on my tongue. "Haven't had anything this good since I've been here."

"Miz Bergen, she been up visiting you?"

Ruth's question sounded vaguely disloyal, maybe because any true answer would be pointedly disloyal. "She's got a bad back. Says long trips make it worse. Have you seen her? Any of them?"

Her face brightened. "In the Sav-Mor Market a

188

couple of Fridays ago I heard this little voice a-calling, 'Ruth! Ruth!' and when I turns around sweet little Sharon comes a-rushing to my arms. 'Ruth,' she says to me, 'where you been so long?' " She shook her head like she was still short an answer. "Poor little thing, and her all the time asking, 'Where you been so long?' "

"You saw my mother too?"

"I surely did. She was nice to me too, said she was glad to see I was gettin' on all right. I 'members more'n fifteen years ago when your folks moved to Jenkinsville to open the store. Folks, white and colored, said Miz Bergen was the best lookin' woman to ever come to town, and I reckon she still is."

"She say anything, Ruth? I mean, did she mention me at all?"

Ruth looked surprised. "Why, shore she did, Honey. You her daughter, ain't you?"

"What did she say?"

"Why, she said 'bout what any mother would say."

I waited to see if Ruth was going to add anything more 'cause vagueness wasn't exactly her natural state. I watched while she looked down and began adjusting the gold band on her left hand.

"Ruth, I would very much appreciate your telling me the truth. The whole truth. Please!"

"Patty, Honey, I ain't never lied to you and I ain't gonna start lying now, but the truth be known, Miz Bergen didn't say too much. But I'll tell you everything I recollect. Well, let's see now," she said, warming up. "Told me she gets letters from you and how you always say you're getting along fine."

I nodded Yes.

"And she told me how she had just sent off a sweater to you through the mails."

"It's the one I'm wearing."

Ruth looked at the sweater and I hoped that I hadn't distracted her. Then she gave me a look like

189

she had turned a little shy. "And Miz Bergen said"—Ruth gave her wedding band a full turn—"she said I was the only one knows how to handle you."

Anger blazed within me. "That's all they ever think about—handling me, controlling me! Why can't they just let me be?"

I watched Ruth shake her head like she didn't quite know what to say anymore. But I felt like I just had to ask her the question I was always asking myself.

"Ruth, I want you to tell me something. You know me better than anybody else. What's really wrong with me?"

"Oh, Honey Babe!" Ruth shook her head like she was trying to shake my words from her ears. "There ain't nothing wrong with you—nothing a few years and a few pounds won't take care of."

"There's gotta be!" My voice was high enough for scaling mountains. "There's just gotta be something or I wouldn't always be getting into trouble, having people hate me."

"When you get older you're gonna see that sometimes it looks like most of the good folks done gone and acquired most of the troubles. Yes, siree! Even the Lord Jesus could've 'voided getting himself crucified if he could've learned to stay out of trouble." It sounded as though Ruth was pretty close to blasphemy, and I searched her face for a secret sign made only to God that she was just kidding. She gave me a squeeze. "Sometimes I shore wish you knew how to go pussyfooting around your pa and your ma, but then I says to myself, if Patty learned pussyfooting then it wouldn't hardly be Patty no more."

"Even if you don't know for 100 per cent positive sure," I encouraged, "there must be things that you suspect about me. And if I knew I'd begin working on ridding myself of them. Only first I've got to be sure what's wrong."

"Don't ask me to tell you something I don't know.

190

There ain't nothing bad about you, and that's the God's truth. I've cared for chillun white and I've cared for chillun black. I've loved every single one of them, but nary a one as much as you, Patty Babe. Nary a single one."

"You couldn't love me as much as you do Sharon."

"Don't you go telling me what I couldn't do! 'Cause I knows what I knows. And from that first day I walked into your house I loved you the most, and I loves you the most today."

"It's so hard to believe."

"Why, I ain't even the only one. He loved you. Anton did. With my own eyes I saw that man come rushing out of his hiding place to save you. And I saw his face, and I ain't never gonna forget what was written there. 'Cause it said: 'I'd give my own life to save her.' "

"Maybe that's true. He gave me his ring so I'd never forget that he loved me, and that I was a person of value. Only thing is I lost the ring, and then gradually I guess I lost its meaning."

Ruth snapped open her pocketbook. "Honey Babe, you didn't lose your ring. I heard you tell that to the man from the FBI and you musta told that story so many times, you come to believe it." She held up the ring. "You gave me this for safekeeping when I told you your pa was coming home to see you. Remember?"

I brought his ring to my lips, barely believing it. "He did love me," I said to Ruth. "And maybe one day my mother and father will too."

Ruth's eyes came level with mine and I could feel her resources rushing forward like front line soldiers to battle. "I ain't nevah 'fore cast me no 'spersions on other folks' folks," she said slowly, "but your folks ain't nevah gonna feel nothing good regarding you. And they ain't the number one best quality folks neither. They shore ain't. When I goes shoppin' and I sees the label stamped, 'Irregular' or 'Seconds,' then I knows

I won't have to pay so much for it. But you've got yourself some irregular seconds folks, and you've been paying more'n top dollar for them. So jest don't go a-wishing for what ain't nevah gonna be."

"But I always thought it was me. Because I was bad."

"You ain't bad!"

I kissed my ring again, and then gave Ruth the strongest squeeze I could manage. "Nothing has changed, but I feel different. Good. Like a good person! And that was what all the whispering was about!"

"What whispering you talkin' bout?"

"Every so often, there's this whispering going on inside me. And whispering's always so soft I could never make it out before."

"Was it God a-speakin' to you?" asked Ruth, her eyes wide.

I never thought about it being God. What would God be wasting his time with a twelve-year-old for? "I don't think," I said, "that God would whisper, do you?"

Ruth pressed her lips together. "The ways of the Lord are filled with wonder and mystery."

"Well, just the same, it didn't sound like God. I think, actually, it was truth. Truth growing inside like a baby, and for a long time it was just too little, too weak to say anything. But day by day it gains strength."

"And to what use is you gonna put this truth?"

"Well, maybe, I don't know right at this moment, but I do know that in spite of everything I did and everything people say about me I don't feel bad, not anymore. I'm not bad, and right now that seems important."

Ruth drew me to her and I could tell that she understood too.

21

TOGETHER WE WATCHED an icy rain make slapping sounds against the window. After a while Ruth said something, something about her galoshes which I didn't quite hear, probably because I had become too deeply encased in comfort. With my eyes closed, feeling the warmth of Ruth against me, I could believe in so many things. Ruth had never been fired; I had never been found out; and Anton had never been killed. He was waiting for me now, alive in the hide-out, and when night came, we'd go away. Morocco or Mexico. Somewhere, anywhere, together.

"And I was halfways out the door when I said to myself, ain't no guarantees about no weather so I went right back and got 'em."

"Good idea," I said. "I'm glad you remembered."

We fell into quiet again, and it was comfortable. Then Ruth began humming and soon she found the words, "Nobody knows the troubles I've seen. Glory hallelujah."

"I don't want to go home again," I said with a suddenness that surprised even me.

"Well, you ain't got nowhere else for going. You's too old for 'dopting and too young for marrying."

"Even so—"

She looked me full in the face. "Even so what? What you planning on doing, girl?"

"I ain't—I'm not planning on anything 'cause I can't think of anything to plan on! I just don't want to look back. If they didn't like me before all this happened, they're sure not going to love me now. So what I was thinking was I might get a job. Go somewhere."

"So you thought you'd up and run away and find yourself a job, that what you thought, girl?" I recognized her I-ain't-gonna-listen-to-none-of-your-nonsense voice. "Well, now I'm right glad you told me 'cause ole Ruth can tell you something. I keeps a clean house, minds the chillun, and cooks the evening supper, and for doing all these things it takes me six workdays to earn seven dollars and fifty cents. Now how many of those things can you do? And how much you reckon you'd be earning for doing them?"

"There are other jobs."

"There's plenty more jobs. They got judges, doctors, and sheriffs. Which one you qualified for, girl?"

"There has to be something."

"There is something. Now, you listen hard 'cause Ruth gonna tell you jest like I'd tell my own child, which you is! You is goin' back home and finishing up with your high school education. Nevah you mind what folks say, most folks don't know what they is saying nohow. Then you tells your daddy that you wants to go way to college to be somethin'. And you bees somethin'! A teacher or a nurse, don't matter what you takes a notion to being as long as it's something."

"I know the something I'd like to be," I said, pausing just long enough to build interest. "A reporter. I already have my first assignment and my *nom de plume* too."

"Your what?"

"Nom de plume. Pen name. What do you think of Antonia Alexander?"

"Antonia Alexander," repeated Ruth, like she was tasting the words. "Mighty fancy."

I was pleased that its elegance hadn't escaped her.

"I got the Antonia from Anton, and I picked Alexander because of the alliteration, both names starting with the same letter."

"What is you fixin' to write?"

"An article about the conditions at the Bolton Reformatory for the *Memphis Commercial Appeal*." I checked Ruth's face to see if she was as impressed as I was. "Charlene Madlee said if it was good, they'd run the story in their Arkansas edition."

"I'se glad, Honey Babe. You shore is gonna be somethin'." Ruth gave a sigh filled with pride for my future accomplishments. "And then you won't have to go home ever again, less'n you want to."

"I guess sometime I'll have to come home again to see you."

I heard the footsteps first and then the rattling of keys.

Mis Laud appeared in the archway. "Visiting time is over. Separate and leave immediately."

"Not yet, Miss Laud, please. Ruth just now got here."

"She has been here for thirty minutes. Her time is up. Leave immediately."

I knew I was going to beg. "Miss Laud, please, she came so far. She's the only visitor I've had since I've been here, and she's the only one I'm gonna get, I know." The cracks sounded in my voice.

"Miss Laud, if you'd kindly be so kind—" Ruth knew what to say. She'd listen to Ruth—"as to give us a few more minutes to say our last minute things, that'd help make the parting less hurtful."

Miss Laud's eyes jumped, all the time jumping from Ruth to me and back again. Something about them I saw for the first time. There was the palest circle of blue surrounding pupils the size of points on an ice pick. Miss Laud raised a trembling finger and pointed it toward me. "That's why you're in trouble. Not happy getting what others got, are you?" She shook her head.

"Trouble is you're a greedy, spoiled girl. Don't like anything we try to give you, do you? Don't like our religion, don't like our laundry, and you don't think our food is worth eating. You told that to one of the girls, didn't you? Tell the truth!"

She waited for me to answer her charges, but the only answer I gave was a direct stare.

She wet her lips with her tongue. "Truth is you only like Nigras and Nazis!"

"Miss Laud!" said Ruth in as loud a voice as I'd ever heard her use. "Leave the child alone! I'se goin' now. See me goin'?"

I threw my arms around Ruth's neck. "Take me with you. Find a way to take me with you!"

"Shush, Honey Babe, shush now."

"Don't leave me here, Ruth! Please, please don't leave me alone."

"Honey Babe, you know better'n to ask Ruth to do what she jest ain't got the power to do." Ruth patted my cheeks as she wiped away the wetness. "Everything gonna be all right," she whispered. "One fine day, you is gonna wake up and your heart gonna rise up singing, everything gonna be all right."

"Wallace!" shouted Miss Laud. "Wallace, Rogers! Here! Come here!"

I hung onto Ruth with all my might; she was my life raft and without her the icy waters were waiting to pull me under.

Footsteps raced across linoleum. As Matron Wallace and Matron Rogers came through the archway Ruth raised her hand as though she were stopping traffic. "You leave this child be! Now, I'm a-telling you, jest *leave* this child be!"

The traffic stopped short. The matrons looked as though their very breath had been sucked out of them.

"Jest seems like," said Ruth under her breath, yet loud enough for hearing, "some white folks ain't nevah learned how to be decent."

And with her arm around my waist and her strength supporting my weakness she led me through the archway and into the center hall. "Go on back to your room, Patty Babe," she whispered. "Go on back."

The three matrons had followed us at a respectful distance, but Miss Laud's distance was the most respectful of all. Suddenly, Ruth whirled on her. "Miss Laud, the red shopping bag in the waiting room. Patty's Christmas. Would you fetch it, please?"

The head matron looked confused. She turned to Matron Wallace. "Well, get it, Wallace! Don't just stand there. Go get the bag!" Then Miss Laud started up the flight of stairs followed closely by Miss Rogers.

As soon as Miss Wallace dropped the bag at Ruth's feet she took the stairs, two at a time. And it was just Ruth and me.

"I reckon they is gonna give us our good-bye time, after all," said Ruth.

I tried to sound all put back together. "Well, Ruth, I sure do appreciate your visit."

She gave me some gentle pats on the back. "And you be strong and don't let them folks get you down 'cause better times a-coming for you. I feels it in my bones."

"Do you really? You really and truly think so?"

"I shore enough do."

Yet Ruth's face was filled with the deepest kind of sadness.

"And for you, Ruth, are better times coming for you too?"

"Mostly things don't get no better for old colored ladies."

"Oh, but I want them to be. I want everything to be good for you. Everything!"

She turned her head. "Good-bye, Honey Babe." She released her hold on me and where her arms had been turned cold. It felt as though something inside me were being torn away. I watched her walk with careful steps back to the bench where she had left her belongings. And watching her, she seemed older and more fragile than I had remembered.

Suddenly I had to give her something, something like the world! I quickly indexed the valuables from my upstairs room—the blue Schaeffer pen and pencil set (a birthday present from my grandparents), a collection of the short stories of Guy de Maupassant, and *Webster's Collegiate Dictionary*. Nothing there for Ruth. She moved slowly towards the door, buttoning her gray coat.

"I don't have anything to give you," I said. "I have nothing at all to give you."

"You got love to give, Honey Babe, ain't nothing better'n that."

"Just the same, I wish I could—say, how about taking back some of the chicken breasts to eat on the bus?"

She clicked open her simulated alligator pocketbook, giving me a view of the inside. "I got me a tunafish sandwich and a hard-boiled egg, and I reckon that's plenty for me. Thank you kindly." Then Ruth reached out, patted my cheek, and with aging steps moved towards the door.

I watched her. It was like watching my very own life raft floating away towards the open sea. And yet somewhere in my mind's eye I thought I could see the faintest outline of land. Then it came to me that maybe that's the only thing life rafts are supposed to do. Taking the shipwrecked, not exactly to the land, but only in view of land. The final mile being theirs alone to swim.

As Ruth pulled open the heavy front door my heart felt as though it was spilling over with so many things I wanted to say, but I didn't have the words for a single one of them. For a moment I thought I was about to call out, "Good-bye," but I didn't. The door closed. And the moment and Ruth were gone.

198

For moments or minutes I stood there. Not really moving. Barely managing to tread water. Was it possible for a beginning swimmer to actually make it to shore? It might take me my whole lifetime to find out.

ABOUT THE AUTHOR

BETTE GREENE grew up in a small Arkansas town and in Memphis, Tennessee. She studied in Paris and in New York, where she was a student of Martha Foley's at Columbia University. She has published short stories and newspaper and magazine articles. Her other novels include the sequel *Morning Is a Long Time Coming; Philip Hall Likes Me, I Reckon Maybe* and *Get on Out of Here, Philip Hall*. Mrs. Greene now lives in Brookline, Massachusetts, with her husband and two children.

TEENAGERS FACE LIFE AND LOVE

Choose books filled with fun and adventure, discovery and disenchantment, failure and conquest, triumph and tragedy, life and love.

☐	23556	**I WILL MAKE YOU DISAPPEAR** Carol Beach York	$2.25
☐	23916	**BELLES ON THEIR TOES** Frank Gilbreth Jr. and Ernestine Gilbreth Carey	$2.25
☐	13921	**WITH A FACE LIKE MINE . . .** Sharon L. Berman	$2.25
☐	23796	**CHRISTOPHER** Richard Koff	$2.25
☐	23844	**THE KISSIMMEE KID** Vera and Bill Cleaver	$2.25
☐	23370	**EMILY OF NEW MOON** Lucy Maud Montgomery	$3.50
☐	22540	**THE GIRL WHO WANTED A BOY** Paul Zindel	$2.25
☐	24143	**DADDY LONG LEGS** Jean Webster	$2.25
☐	20910	**IN OUR HOUSE SCOTT IS MY BROTHER** C. S. Adler	$1.95
☐	23618	**HIGH AND OUTSIDE** Linnea A. Due	$2.25
☐	24392	**HAUNTED** Judith St. George	$2.25
☐	20646	**THE LATE GREAT ME** Sandra Scoppettone	$2.25
☐	23680	**CHLORIS AND THE WEIRDOS** Kin Platt	$2.25
☐	23004	**GENTLEHANDS** M. E. Kerr	$2.25
☐	20474	**WHERE THE RED FERN GROWS** Wilson Rawls	$2.50
☐	20170	**CONFESSIONS OF A TEENAGE BABOON** Paul Zindel	$2.25
☐	14687	**SUMMER OF MY GERMAN SOLDIER** Bette Greene	$2.25

<u>**Prices and availability subject to change without notice.**</u>

Buy them at your local bookstore or use this handy coupon for ordering:

Bantam Books, Inc., Dept. EDN, 414 East Golf Road, Des Plaines, Ill. 60016

Please send me the books I have checked above. I am enclosing $_____ (please add $1.25 to cover postage and handling). Send check or money order —no cash or C.O.D.'s please.

Mr/Mrs/Miss_____

Address_____

City_____ State/Zip_____

EDN—4/84

Please allow four to six weeks for delivery. This offer expires 10/84.

SPECIAL
MONEY SAVING
OFFER

Now you can have an up-to-date listing of Bantam's hundreds of titles plus take advantage of our unique and exciting bonus book offer. A special offer which gives you the opportunity to purchase a Bantam book for only 50¢. Here's how!

By ordering any five books at the regular price per order, you can also choose any other single book listed (up to a $4.95 value) for just 50¢. Some restrictions do apply, but for further details why not send for Bantam's listing of titles today!

Just send us your name and address plus 50¢ to defray the postage and handling costs.

THEY ARE TALKING ABOUT
MAI ZETTERLING'S "DOCTOR GLAS"—

"It covers the problems of man's repressed sexuality
. . . for those who cherish thoughtful, intimate works.
Rare talent."

—*Cue* Magazine

"A first-rate equivalent of a Dostoevskian novel . . ."
—*Newsday*

"Captures people within a time, their inter-relationships
and conflicts, blending them into daydreams and night-
mares and giving them ultimate and overwhelming uni-
versality. (There is) a lyricism of tone and a throbbing
humanism that will not leave you untouched."

—Judith Crist
New York Magazine

"Arresting. You follow it with intense attention. Amaz-
ingly effective."

—*N.Y. Post*

READ THE SEXUALLY EXPLOSIVE NOVEL ON
WHICH THIS POWERFUL FILM WAS BASED!
Doctor Glas, by Hjalmar Söderberg

DOCTOR GLAS

Hjalmar Söderberg

Translated by
Paul Britten Austin

AWARD BOOKS
NEW YORK   TANDEM BOOKS
LONDON

First Award printing 1969

First published by Little Brown and Company, New York

Translation © MCMLXIII by Paul Britten Austin

Library of Congress Catalog Card No. 64-15046

AWARD BOOKS are Published by
Universal Publishing and Distributing Corporation
235 East 45th Street, New York, N. Y. 10017

TANDEM BOOKS are published by
Universal-Tandem Publishing Company Ltd.
14 Gloucester Road, London SW 7, England

Manufactured in the United States of America

PUBLISHER'S NOTE

Doctor Glas by Hjalmar Söderberg was first published in Sweden in 1905 and has since attained the status of a contemporary classic. Although Söderberg (1869–1941) was the author of other novels, plays, and many short stories, *Doctor Glas* remains his masterpiece, the book in which his celebrated prose style reached its height.

Hjalmar Söderberg, son of a civil servant in Stockholm, studied for a short time at Uppsala and then entered the civil service, which he soon abandoned to become a professional journalist on a Stockholm daily, *Svenska Dagbladet*. He then lived as a free-lance writer and devoted himself to a full-time literary career. After his first marriage ended in divorce, he married a Danish woman and lived the later part of his life in Copenhagen. In his younger days he took a prominent part in intellectual debates in Sweden, and in the 1930's he drew attention and admiration by his articles attacking Fascist and Nazi thought. The German occupation of Denmark in 1940 caused him to be less outspoken, and he died unmolested by the enemy.

Although the character of Doctor Glas has been judged to be in the nature of a self-portrait, the story —with its protest against ecclesiastical complacency and its sympathy with ethical murder—is pure fiction. The moral questions posed were debated in Sweden for decades, and the author was himself drawn into the controversies which raged over his work. To American readers today the novel will seem no less contemporary. The English writer William Sansom has written: "When the book first came to me, I got again that marvellous rare feeling, after the first page or two, of being quite certain I was in the hands of a master, knowing that I could trust this book entirely—knowing that this intelligent and beautiful writer would make me both sit up startled by various excitements and at the same time lie back with wonderful relief to know I was securely protected against the second-rate . . . In most of its writing and much of the frankness of its thought, it might have been written tomorrow . . . That this is a work of art and a masterpiece is to my mind unassailable."

I've never known such a summer. A sultry heat-wave since mid-May. All day a thick cloud of dust hangs unmoving over streets and market-places.

Only as evening falls do one's spirits revive a trifle. I am just back from my evening stroll, which I take almost daily after visiting my patients, and they aren't many now in the summertime. From the east comes a steady cool breeze. The heat-wave lifts and drifting slowly off turns to a long veil of red, away to westward. No clatter, now, of workmen's carts; only, from time to time, a cab or tram clanging its bell. My footsteps take me slowly down the street. Now and then I fall in with an acquaintance and for a while we stand chatting at a street corner. But why, of all people, must I keep running into the Rev. Gregorius? I never see that man without remembering an anecdote I once heard told of Schopenhauer. One evening the austere philosopher was sitting, alone as usual, in a corner of his café, when the door opens and in comes a person of disagreeable mien. His features distorted with disgust and horror Schopenhauer gives him one look, leaps up, and begins thumping him over the head with his stick. All this, merely on account of his appearance!

Well I'm not Schopenhauer. When I saw the parson coming towards me in the distance across the Vasa Bridge I halted abruptly and, turning, leaned my arms on the parapet to admire the view. Grey houses on Helgeand Island. The crumbling wooden architecture of the old Nordic-style bath-house, reflected in The Stream, in whose flowing waters the grand old willows trail their leaves. I

5

hoped the clergyman hadn't seen me, or wouldn't recognise
my rear-view. Indeed, I'd almost forgotten him, when suddenly I realised he was standing beside me, his arms like
mine resting on the parapet and his head cocked a little
to one side—exactly the same pose as twenty years ago,
in Jacob's Church, when I used to sit in the family pew
beside my late lamented mother, and first saw that odious
physiognomy, like a nasty fungus, hop up in the pulpit
and heard him strike up with his Abba Father. Same
greyish pudgy face; same dirty yellow side-whiskers, now
greying slightly, perhaps: and that same unfathomably
mean look behind the spectacles. Impossible to escape!
I'm his doctor now, as I am many others'. And sometimes he comes to me with his aches and pains.—Well,
well . . . good evening, Vicar, And how are you?—Not
too good; in fact not at all well. My heart's bad, thumps
irregularly, sometimes stops at nights, so it seems to me.
—Glad to hear it, I thought. For all I care you can die,
you old rascal, and rid me of the sight of you. Besides,
you've got a pretty young wife, whom you're probably
plaguing the life out of, and when you die she'll remarry
and get herself a much better husband. But aloud I said:
Really? Really? That so? Perhaps you'd better come and
see me one of these days. We'll look into the matter. But
there was a lot more than this he wanted to talk about.
Important things: It's quite simply unnatural, this heat.
And: It's stupid, building great big parliament buildings
on that little island. And: My wife isn't really well, either,
if it comes to that.

In the end he cleared off, and I went on my way. Entering the Old Town, along Storkyrkobrinken, I strayed
among its narrow alleys. A close evening atmosphere
among the cramped passages and between the houses:
and along the walls strange shadows. Shadows never seen
in our quarters.

Mrs Gregorius, yes! That was a queer visit she paid me the other day. She came to my surgery hour. I noticed clearly when she arrived, but although she had come in good time she waited until the last, letting others who had come after her see me first. At last she came in. Blushed and stammered. Finally blurted out something about having a sore throat. Well, it was better now.—I'll come back tomorrow, she said. Just now I'm in such a hurry. . . .

So far she hasn't come back.

Emerging from the alleyways, I walked down Skeppsbron Quay. Over Skeppsholmen Island the moon hovered, lemon yellow in the blue twilight. But my quiet and peaceful mood was gone. Meeting the parson had spoilt it. That there should be such people in the world! Who hasn't heard the old conundrum, so often debated when two or three poor devils are sitting round a café table: If, by pressing a button in the wall, or by a mere act of will, you could murder a Chinese mandarin and inherit his riches—would you do it? This problem I've never bothered my head to find an answer to, perhaps because I've never known the cruel misery of being really and truly poor. But if, by pressing a button in the wall, I could kill that clergyman, I do believe I should do it.

As I went on homewards through the pale unnatural twilight the heat seemed as oppressive as at high noon; and the red dust-clouds which lay in strata beyond Kungsholmen's factory chimneys, turning to darkness, resembled slumbering disasters. With long slow steps I went down past Klara Church, hat in hand, sweat breaking out on my forehead. Not even beneath the great trees in the churchyard was the air cool. Yet almost every bench had its whispering couple; and some, with drunken eyes, sat in each other's laps, kissing.

* * *

Now I sit at my open window, writing—for whom? Not for any friend or mistress. Scarcely for myself, even. I do not read today what I wrote yesterday; nor shall I read this tomorrow. I write simply so my hand can move, my thoughts move of their own accord. I write to kill a sleepless hour. Why can't I sleep? After all, I've committed no crime.

* * *

What I set down on these pages isn't a confession. To whom should I confess? Nor do I tell the whole truth about myself, only what it pleases me to relate, but nothing that isn't true. Anyway, I can't exorcise my soul's wretchedness—if it is wretched—by telling lies.

* * *

Outside, the great blue night hangs over the churchyard and its trees. Such silence now reigns in the town that sighings and whisperings among the shadows down there reach up to me in my eyrie. And, once, an impudent laugh pierces the darkness. I feel as if at this moment no one in the world is lonelier than I—I, Tyko Gabriel Glas, doctor of medicine, who at times help others, but have never been able to help myself, and who, at past thirty years of age, have never been near a woman.

* * *

June 14

What a profession! How can it have come about that, out of all possible trades, I should have chosen the one which suits me least? A doctor must be one of two things: either a philanthropist, or else avid for honours. True, I once thought I was both.

Again a poor woman was here, weeping and begging

me to help her, a woman I've known for years. Married to a minor official, four thousand crowns a year or so, with three children. In the first three years the babies came, one after another. Since then, for five years, perhaps six, she has been spared. Has regained a little health, strength, youth. She has had time to put her home in order, recuperate a little after all her troubles. Bread, of course, has been short. But they seem to have managed somehow.—And now, all of a sudden, here it is again.

She could hardly speak for tears.

I replied, of course, with my usual lesson. Known by rote, I always recite it on such occasions: My duty as a doctor. Respect for life, even the frailest.

I was serious, immovable. In the end she had to go away; ashamed, bewildered, helpless.

I made a note of the case. The eighteenth in my practice. And I'm not a gynæcologist.

I shall never forget the first. A young girl, twenty-two or so; a big, dark-haired, rather vulgar young beauty, the sort, you could see at a glance, which must have filled the earth in Luther's day, if he was right when he wrote: It is as impossible for a woman to live without a man, as for a man to bite off his own nose. Thick middle-class blood. Father a wealthy businessman. I was the family doctor, so she came to me. She was distraught, out of her wits; but not particularly shy.

—Save me, she begged, save me. I replied with duty, etc., but that was clearly something she did not understand. I explained to her how the Law does not connive at any jiggery-pokery in such cases.—A glance of non-comprehension. The Law? I advised her to confide in her mother: She'll talk to Papa, and there'll be a wedding.— Oh, no, my fiancé hasn't a penny, and Father would never forgive me. They weren't engaged, of course; she used the word 'fiancé' because she could find no other, and 'lover' is a novelist's word, foul in the mouth.——Save me! Haven't you any mercy? I don't know what I'll do! I'll throw myself into the harbour!

I became rather impatient. Indeed, she did not inspire me with any very merciful feelings. These things always arrange themselves, where there is money. Only pride has to suffer a little. She sniffed, blew her nose, talked wildly and in the end threw herself on the floor, kicking and screaming.

Well, in the end it all turned out, of course, as I expected. Her father, a crude blighter, smacked her face once or twice, married her off double-quick to her partner in crime, and packed them off abroad on a honeymoon.

Such cases never worry me. But I was truly sorry for this poor little woman today. So much suffering and misery, for so little pleasure.

Respect for human life—what is it in my mouth but low hypocrisy? What else can it ever be on the lips of anyone who has ever whiled away an idle hour in thought? Human life, it swarms around us on every hand. And as for the lives of faraway, unseen people, no one has ever cared a fig for them. Everyone shows this by his actions, except perhaps a few more than usually idiotic philanthropists. All governments and parliaments on earth proclaim it.

And duty! An admirable screen to creep behind when we wish to avoid doing what ought to be done.

Besides, no one can risk his all, social position, respectability, future, everything, merely to help strangers he is indifferent to. Rely on their silence? That would be childish. Some woman friend gets into the same fix, a word is whispered as to where help is to be found; and soon you're a marked man. No, best stick to duty, even if

it is nothing but a piece of painted scenery, like Potem-
kin's villages. I am only afraid I recite my duty-formula
so often that in the end I shall come to believe it. Potem-
kin only deceived his empress; how much more dispica-
ble to deceive oneself.

*   *   *

Position, respectability, future. As if I were not ready,
any day or moment, to stow these packages aboard the
first ship to come sailing by laden with action.

*   *   *

Again I sit at my window. The blue night is awake beneath me; under the trees, rustlings and whisperings.

Yesterday, while taking my evening stroll, my eye fell
on a married couple. I recognised her at once. It is not so
many years since I danced with her at a ball, and I
haven't forgotten how, every time I saw her, she pre-
sented me with a sleepless night. But of that she knew
nothing. She was not yet a woman. She was a virgin. She
was a living dream; man's dream of woman.

Now she goes walking down the street on her husband's arm. More expensively dressed than before, but
vulgarly, more the bourgeoise. In her gaze is something
extinguished, worn. Yet at the same time it is a contented
wifely look, as if she were carrying her stomach before
her on a silver-plated salver.

No, I don't understand it. Why must it be like this,
why must it always be like this? Why must love be the
troll's gold that on the morrow turns to withered leaves,
filth, or beery indulgence? Does not all that side of our
culture not directly designed to still hunger, or defend us
against our enemies, spring from mankind's longing for
love? Our love of beauty knows no other source. All art,
all poetry, all music has drunk at it. The most insipid

modern historical painting, every bit as much as Raphael's madonnas and Steinlen's little Parisian working girls; 'The Angel of Death' as the Song of Songs; and *Das Buch der Lieder,* the Chorale and the Viennese waltz, yes, every plaster ornament on this dreary house I live in, every figure on the wallpaper, the form of the china vase over there, the pattern on my scarf, everything made to delight or embellish—no matter whether successful or unsuccessful—springs from this origin, albeit often by the longest and most circuitous of routes. Nor is this a brainwave of mine, born of the night, but something proven a hundred times over.

But that source's name isn't love. It's the dream of love.

And then, on the other side, everything to do with this dream's fulfilment, instinctual satisfaction, and all that follows therefrom. To our deepest instincts it appears as something ugly, indecent. This can't be proved. It's only a feeling; *my* feeling, and, I believe, everybody's. People always treat each other's love affairs as something low or comic, often not even making exception for their own. And the consequences . . . A pregnant woman is a frightful object. A new-born child is loathsome. A deathbed rarely makes so horrible an impression as childbirth, that terrible symphony of screams and filth and blood.

But first and last, the act itself. I shall never forget as a child under the great chestnut trees in the schoolyard hearing a schoolmate explain 'what happens'. I refused to believe it. Several more boys had to come over, laughing at my stupidity, and confirm it. Even then I hardly believed them, but ran away, beside myself with fury. Had Father and Mother done that? And would I do the same, when I grew up? Was there no escape?

Always I had felt a profound scorn for the bad boys

who scribbled dirty words on walls and hoardings. But at that moment it seemed to me as if God Himself had scribbled something filthy across the blue spring sky; and I believe it was then I first began to wonder whether God really existed.

Even today I've hardly recovered from my astonishment. Why must the life of our species be preserved and our longing stilled by means of an organ we use several times a day as a drain for impurities; why couldn't it be done by means of some act composed of dignity and beauty, as well as of the highest voluptuousness? An action which could be carried out in church, before the eyes of all, just as well as in darkness and solitude? Or in a temple of roses, in the eye of the sun, to the chanting of choirs and a dance of wedding guests?

* * *

How long have I been pacing my room? I don't know.

Out there it's becoming lighter, the church cock gleams to the eastward, and the sparrows twitter, shrill and hungry.

Strange, how a shudder always passes through the air just before sunrise.

* * *

June 18

Today it has been a little cooler, and for the first time in more than a month I went riding.

What a morning! I had gone to bed early and slept soundly all night. I never sleep without dreaming, but last night's dreams were blue and light. I rode out towards Haga, round the echo temple, past the copper pavilions. Dew and spiders' webs on all the bushes and shrubs, and a great sighing among the trees. Deva was in highest spir-

its, the earth danced on beneath us, young and fresh as
on creation's first Sunday morning. I came to a little inn;
having been there often when out for my rides last spring,
I recognised it, dismounted, and drained a glass of ale at
a gulp. Taking hold of the brown-eyed girl by her waist, I
swung her around me; kissed her hair; and rode off.

As the song says.

*　　*　　*

June 19

So, Mrs Gregorius. And that was her business! Rather
unusual, I must admit.

This time she came late, the surgery hour was over,
and she was left alone in my waiting-room.

She came in to me, very pale, said 'Good morning' and
found herself standing there in the middle of the room. I
waved her to a chair, but she just stood where she was.

—I was fooling you last time, she said, I'm not ill; I'm
perfectly well. It was something completely different I
wanted to talk to you about, Doctor. I just couldn't get it
out, then.

Down in the street a brewer's dray went rumbling by. I
went over and shut the window, and in the sudden silence
I heard her say, in low quick tones, but the words trembling a little, as if on the brink of tears:

—I've conceived such a horrible loathing for my husband.

I stood with my back to the stove, in the corner. I
bowed my head, to indicate I had understood.

—Not as a human being, she went on. He's always
kind and good to me; he has never said a hard word to
me. But he awakens in me such a horrible distaste.

She drew a deep breath.

—I don't know how to express myself. What I thought

of asking you is something so unusual. And perhaps it is at variance with what you consider to be right. I don't know what you think of such matters, Doctor. But there's something about you that inspires me with confidence and I don't know anyone else I can confide in in this matter, no one in the whole world who could help me. Doctor, couldn't you talk to my husband? Couldn't you tell him I'm suffering from some disease, some infection of the womb, and that he must give up his rights, at least for a while?

Rights. I passed my hand over my forehead. Every time I hear the word used in that sense, I see red. God in heaven, what has happened to people's brains, that they should have made rights and duties out of it!

It was immediately clear to me that I must come to the rescue here, if I could. But just then I couldn't find anything to say, I wanted her to go on talking. Possbily, too, my sympathy for her was not unmixed with a dose of pure simple curiosity.

—Mrs Gregorius, I said. Forgive me for asking, but how long have you been married?

—Six years.

—And what you call your husband's rights, have they always seemed as difficult to you as they do now?

She blushed a little.

—It's always been difficult, she said. But recently it has become unbearable. I can't stand it any longer, I don't know what will become of me.

—But, I observed, the Vicar isn't a young man any longer. It surprises me that at his age he càn . . . bother you so much. How old is he, in point of fact?

—Fifty-six, I think—no, maybe fifty-seven. But he looks older, of course.

—But tell me, Mrs Gregorius—haven't you ever spoken to him about this, yourself? Told him what suffering it is for you, asked him in a simple friendly way to excuse you?

—Yes, I did ask him once. But he answered with a homily. He said we could not know whether God meant to give us a child, even though we haven't had one so far; and that it would therefore be a very big sin if we ceased doing what God wished us to do in order to get a child. . . . And perhaps he's right. But it's so hard for me.

It was more than I could do to suppress a smile. What a hardened old sinner!

She saw me smile, and, I believe, misunderstood it. For a moment she stood there silent, as if gathering her thoughts; then she began speaking again, in a low, trembling voice, while her blush spread higher and redder over her complexion.

—No, she said. You'll have to know the whole story. Perhaps you've already guessed it, you see right through me. I'm asking you to play the fool for my sake. Well then, at least I must be straightforward with you. Judge me as you will. I'm an unfaithful wife. I belong to another man. And that's why it has become so terribly hard for me.

She avoided my glance as she said this. But I,—only now, for the first time, did I really see her. For the first time I saw a woman was standing in my room, a woman whose heart was full of desire and misery, in the flower of her womanhood, perfumed with love, yet blushing with shame that this perfume should be so strong and noticeable.

I felt myself turn pale.

She looked up and met my glance. I don't know what she thought she read in it; but unable to stand any longer, she sank down on a chair, shaken with weeping. Perhaps she thought I was taking the whole matter quite frivolously; or was indifferent and hard, and that she had perhaps exposed herself to a strange man all to no purpose.

I went over to her, took her hand, patted it slowly: There, there, don't cry, don't cry any more now. I'll help you. I promise.

—Thank you, thank you. . . .

She kissed my hand, wetting it with her tears. Another sob. Then a smile shone through her weeping.

I had to smile, too.

—But you were foolish to tell me the last bit, I said. Not because you need be in the least afraid I shall abuse your confidence; but such matters have to be kept secret. Always, without exception, as long as possible! And naturally I should have helped you, anyway.

She answered: —I *wanted* to tell you! I wanted someone I respect and look up to to know about it and yet not despise me.

Then came a long story. Once, about a year ago, she had heard a conversation between me and her husband, the vicar—he was ill and I was visiting him. Our discussion had turned to prostitution. She remembered everything I had said and now she repeated it to me—something quite simple and ordinary, about these poor girls being human beings, too, and so they ought to be treated as human beings, etc. But she had never heard anyone talk like that before. From that day on she had looked up to me; and that was why she had plucked up courage to come and confide in me.

All this I had totally forgotten. . . . But 'what is lost in the snow comes up in the thaw'.

Well, I promised to talk to her husband that very same day; and she left. But she forgot her gloves and parasol. Coming back to fetch them, she disappeared again, radiant, happy, dizzy with joy, like a child that has got its own way and looks forward to some great pleasure.

* * *

I went there in the afternoon. She had prepared him, as had been agreed. In a room apart I had a conversation with him. He was even greyer in the face than usual.

—Yes, he said, my wife has already told me how things are. I can't say how sorry I am for her. We had both so deeply hoped and longed for a little child. But I'll have nothing to do with separate bedrooms,—I must make that quite clear. After all, it's so unusual in our circles, it would only lead to gossip. And besides, I'm an old man.

He gave a hollow cough.

—Yes, I said. Of course. I don't doubt that you put your wife's health before everything else, Vicar. And in any case we have good hopes, of course, of getting her well again.

—I pray to God we shall, he replied. But how long do you think it may take, Doctor?

—That's hard to say. But half a year's absolute abstinence will certainly be necessary. Then we shall see. . . .

He has a couple of dirty brown spots on his face; they turned even darker and stood out even more clearly, now, against his colourless complexion. It was as if his eyes had shrunk.

* * *

He has been married once before; a pity she died, that first wife! In his study hangs a portrait of her, enlarged from a charcoal sketch; a simple-minded, grumbling, pious, sensual type of lass, not wholly unlike the good Catharine of Bora.

She certainly must have suited him. Pity she died!

* * *

June 21

Who's the lucky man? This question I've been asking myself ever since the day before yesterday.

Odd, that I should so soon get to know the answer. And that it should turn out to be a young man with whom I am acquainted, if only slightly. It's Klas Recke.

Well, well. He's certainly quite another creature from the Rev. Gregorius.

I met them only a little while ago, as I was taking my evening stroll at random through the streets in the warm rose-tinted twilight. I was thinking of her, the little woman. I think of her often. I walked into a deserted side-street—and there, suddenly, I saw them coming towards me. They were just coming out of a doorway. Hastily, to hide my face, I pulled out my handkerchief and blew my nose. It was hardly necessary. He, I am sure, scarcely knows me by sight; and she, blind with happiness, did not see me.

June 22

I sit reading the page I wrote yesterday evening, reading it over and over again, and saying to myself: so that's the way of it, old chap, you've become a pimp, have you?

Nonsense. I've freed her from something horrible. I felt it just had to be done.

What else she does with herself is her own business.

June 23

Midsummer Eve. Light, blue night. From childhood and youth do I not remember you as the lightest, giddiest, airiest of all nights of the year. Why, then, are you now so oppressive, anxious?

I sit at my window, passing my life in review and trying to find a reason why it should have fallen into a

furrow so unlike all the others', so far from the highway.
Let me think.

Just now as I crossed the churchyard I saw again one
of those scenes of which letters to the newspapers are in
the habit of saying they 'defy description'. Obviously an
instinct that can compel these wretched people to flout all
convention in a churchyard must be an immensely strong
and powerful one. It drives frivolous men into all sorts of
mad pranks, and forces honest intelligent men to subject
themselves to every sort of tribulation and sacrifice. As
for women, it drives them to surmount those feelings of
modesty which the education of generation upon generation of young girls had been designed to awaken and de-
velop, and causes them to suffer terrible bodily torments
and often plunge into deepest misery.

Only me it has so far not driven to anything. How
can this be possible? Not until late did my senses awaken
and by then my will was already a man's. As a child I
was very ambitious, becoming early accustomed to self-
control and to distinguish between what was my inner-
most constant will and transient wishes, the moment's desire. I learned to hearken to the one voice, and despise
the other. Since then I have noticed how unusual this is
among human beings, more unusual, perhaps, than talent
and genius, therefore it sometimes seems to me as though
I really ought to have become something unusual, signifi-
cant. Wasn't I a shining light at school? Always youngest
in my class, a student at fifteen, didn't I take my student
exam at fifteen and my M.A. at twenty-three? But there I
stopped. No special studies followed, no doctor's dispu-
tation. There were those who would have been willing
enough to lend me money, almost any amount of it; but I
was tired. I felt no desire to specialise further. All I
wanted was to earn my daily bread. My schoolboy ambition to get high marks, satisfied, had withered away but,

oddly enough, no grown man's ambition took its place. This, I fancy, must have been because it was just then I began to think. Up to then I hadn't had the time.

During all those years other instincts had lain half-asleep; they had been enough, certainly, to stir up vague dreams and desires, as in a young girl; but not mighty, imperious, as in other young men. And even if from time to time I lay awake at nights, indulging myself in hot fantasies, yet it always seemed to me unthinkable that I should find satisfaction with the women my comrades visited, women they had sometimes pointed out to me on the streets, but who to me appeared merely disgusting. This must also have been one reason why my imagination grew so solitarily, almost out of touch with my schoolfellows'. Therefore when they talked of such things I at first understood nothing; and, understanding nothing, became accustomed not to listen. In this way I remained 'pure', not even making the acquaintance of boyhood sins; scarce knowing what they were. I had no religious faith to sustain me, yet I made up my own dreams of love, oh yes, very beautiful dreams, and one day, I was sure, they would come true. But I had no desire to sully my white student cap or sell my birthright for a mess of pottage.

My dreams of love—once they seemed to me so close, so very close, to realisation! Midsummer night, strange pale night, always you revive that memory which in truth is all I have and which alone remains when everything else sinks away and turns to dusty nothingness. And yet what happened then was so insignificant! I was staying at my uncle's country place during the midsummer holidays. There was youth, and dancing, and games. Among the young people was a girl. I had already met her a few times at family parties, but until then I had not thought much about her. But now when I saw her there, something a schoolmate had once said about her at a party came into my mind: That girl certainly has an eye to you, she's been looking at you the whole evening! Now I recalled this, and although I did not exactly believe it, yet it made me observe her more closely than I might otherwise have done. I noticed, too, that she looked at me from time to time. She was, perhaps, no more beautiful than many another; but she was in the full bloom of her twenty years and over her young breasts she wore a thin white blouse. We danced together a few times round the maypole. Towards midnight we all went up on to a knoll to look out over the wide countryside where a midsummer bonfire was to be lit, our intention being to stay until sunrise. The path led through the forest, between tall straight pines; we went two by two, and I was walking beside her. She stumbled over a root in the shadowy forest and I gave her my hand, and a thrill of pleasure passed through me as I felt her little soft, firm, warm hand in mine. So I went on holding it, even where the path was smooth and easy.

What did we talk about? I don't know, not a word has remained in my memory, all I remember is that a secret current of silent and determined devotion flowed through her voice and all her words, as if this action of walking together with me hand in hand through the forest was something she had long dreamed of and hoped for. We came to the hilltop. The other youngsters, having arrived before us, had already lit the bonfire, and we gathered in groups and scattered couples. Above us the sky hung vast and light and blue; below us lay the creeks and sounds and the deep wide channels, shining like ice as they stretched away into the distance. Still I held her hand in mine, and I believe I also plucked up courage to stroke it slowly. I stole glances at her and saw how her skin seemed to glow in the night's pallor and how her eyes were full of tears, though she wasn't crying, and her breath came quiet and even. Silent, we sat there together. But inside me it was as if I was singing a song, an old song which came to mind, I don't know how:

> *There burns a flame, he burns so clear,*
> *like a thousand wreaths of fire.*
> *Shall I enter that flame with my dearest dear,*
> *and dance with my heart's desire?*

A long while we sat there. Some of the others got up and went off homeward, and I heard someone say: There are some big clouds to the eastward, we shan't see the sunrise. The crowd on the hilltop thinned out, but we two sat on and on, until we were left alone. I looked at her a long while and she met my gaze. Then I took her head between my hands and kissed her, a light innocent kiss. At the same moment someone called her. She gave a little start, tore herself free, and ran away, running on light feet, downwards through the forest.

When I caught up with her she was already with the others and all I could do was silently squeeze her hand, and she pressed mine in response. Down there in the field they were still dancing round the maypole, country girls and farmhands all mixed up with the young gentry, as the custom is on this one night of the year. Again I took her into the dance, a wild and dizzy dance; already it was broad daylight but was the midsummer witchery still in the air; the whole earth danced under us and the other couples flew past, now high above us, now far beneath; everything went up and down, and round and round. So at last we escaped out of the swirling confusion of dancers and, not daring to look at one another, crept away without a word behind a hedge of lilac. There I kissed her again. But now it was something else, her head lay back on my arm, she closed her eyes, and her mouth became a living thing under my kiss. I pressed my hand against her breasts, and I felt her hand lay itself on mine —perhaps she meant to defend herself, or remove my hand, but in fact she only pressed it harder to her breast. Meanwhile a radiance came over her face, faint at first, then stronger, and at last like a violent flash; she opened her eyes, but was forced to close them again, blinded; and when at last we had kissed our long kiss to its end, we stood cheek to cheek, staring amazed straight into the sun which had burst out of the cloud-layers to the east.

I never saw her again. That was ten years ago, ten years ago tonight, and even today when I think of it I feel sick and mad.

We made no tryst next day; it did not occur to us. Her parents lived at a place nearby and we took it for granted we should meet and be together next day, every day, all our lives. But next day it rained and the day passed without my seeing her. And in the evening I had to go into town. A few days later I read in a newspaper she was dead. Drowned while bathing, she and another girl— Yes, it's ten years now, since all that happened.

At first I was in despair. But I must really have quite a strong nature. I worked on, just as I had done before, and took my exam in the autumn. But I suffered too. At nights I always saw her before me. Saw the white body lying among weeds and slime, rising and falling on the water. The eyes were wide open, and open, too, the mouth I kissed. Then people came in a boat with a grapnel. The grapnel fastened its claw in her breast, the same young girlish breast my hand had touched so recently.

A long while was to pass after this before I again felt I was a man or that there were such creatures as women in the world. But by then I was hardened. Once, at least, I had felt a spark from the great golden flame, and I was less than ever inclined to put up with mere dross. Others may be less exigent on that score, that's their business; and I don't know whether the whole question is of much importance. Yet I felt it was important to me, even so. It would surely be naïve to think a man's will could not regulate these trifles, if only the will existed. Dear Martin Luther, worthy fount of all the Rev. Gregorius' doctrines, what a sinner in the flesh you must have been, and so much nonsense you talked when you came to this chapter! Even so, you were more honest than all your present-day disciples, a fact which shall be held to your credit.

So year followed year, and life passed me by. I saw many women who rekindled my longings, but just these particular women never noticed me. It was as if I did not exist for them.

Why was that?

I think I understand now. A woman in love has just that magic spell about her walk, her complexion, her whole being, which alone can hold me in thrall. And it was always such women who awakened my desires. But naturally, being in love with other men, they did not see me. Instead, there were others who looked at me; after all, I was a qualified doctor of youthful years and with the makings of a good practice. Therefore I was regarded as an excellent match. Indeed, I became the object of a good deal of obtrusive attention. But it was always love's labour lost.

Yes, the years went, and life passed me by. I labour in my calling. People come to me with their maladies, all sorts, and I apply what remedies I can. Some get well, others die, most drag on with their aches and pains. I perform no miracles; one or another whom I have been unable to help has afterwards turned away from me to quacks and notorious charlatans, and got well again. But I think I regard myself as a careful and conscientious doctor. Soon I see myself becoming the typical family doctor, he of the great experience and the calm look that inspires confidence. Perhaps people would not have so much confidence in me if they knew how badly I sleep at nights.

Midsummer night, pale blue night, once you were so light and airy and intoxicating, why do you lie now like anxiety on my breast?

June 28

On my evening stroll yesterday I walked past the Grand Hotel. Klas Recke was sitting at a table on the pavement, alone with his whisky. I went on a few steps, turned, and sat down at a nearby table to observe him. Either he did not see me, or did not wish to. The little woman has naturally told him of her visit to me and its happy outcome—presumably he is grateful for the latter, but perhaps it disturbs him a little to know that there is someone else in the secret too. He sat motionless, looking out over the water, smoking a very long slender cigar.

A newsboy went by; I bought an *Aftonblad* to use as camouflage, observing him over the edge of its page. And the same thought passed through my mind as when I first saw him, many years ago: why has that man got just the face I ought to have had? That is more or less how I would look, if I could re-make myself. I who in those days suffered such torments because I felt as ugly as the devil. Now I don't care.

Hardly ever have I seen a more handsome man. Cold pale grey eyes, but in a frame that makes them dreamy and deep. Perfectly straight and level eyebrows reaching far back toward the temples; a white marble brow, hair dark and rich. But in the lower half of the face the mouth is the only perfectly beautiful feature; otherwise there are small queer features, an irregular nose, a complexion dark and as it were scorched, in a word everything necessary to save him from that sort of flawless beauty which mostly only awakens ridicule.

What does the man look like inside? Of that I know almost nothing. All I know is, he passes for a very clever fellow, seen from the ordinary careerist point of view. I seem to recall having seen him more often in the company of the head of the department where he works, than among his contemporaries.

As I watched him sitting there, motionless, his gaze fixed on abstraction, not touching his glass, and his cigar slowly dying, a hundred thoughts came into my head. A hundred old dreams and fantasies broke out afresh as I thought of the life that is his, and compared it with my own. Often and often have I said to myself: *Desire* is of all things the most delightful, and the only one which in some small degree can gild this miserable life of ours; but the satisfaction of desire can't be much to write home about, judging at least by all these consuls and consuls-general who deny themselves nothing in that line of country and who, even so, have never aroused in me the least qualm of jealousy. But when I see such a man as Recke over there, then, very deep down inside me, I feel bitterly envious. For him that problem which poisoned my youth and which, far though I am advanced in manhood's years, still weighs me down, has solved itself. True, so it has also for most other people, but the solution to the problem causes me no envy, only disgust. Otherwise it would have solved itself for me too. But to him love has seemed from the outset a natural birthright; never has he stood trying to choose between hunger and rotten meat. Nor, I fancy, has he ever had much time for thinking, never had time to let reflection drip its poison into his wine. He is happy. And I envy him.

And with a shiver I thought, too, of her; of Helga Gregorius. Through the twilight I saw that look of hers, quenched in happiness. Yes, these two belong together, it's natural selection. Gregorius! Why must she trail that name and that creature after her through life? It's meaningless.

Night began to fall, a red sunset glow lit up the soot-streaked façade of the Royal Palace, across the water. People passed along the pavement; I listened to their voices. Thin gangling Yankees, with their drawling slang. The nasal tones of little fat Jewish businessmen. An ordinary middle-class folk, a Saturday contentment in their voices. One or another nodded to me; and I nodded back. One or another raised his hat; I raised mine. Some acquaintances sat down at a table quite close to me,—it was Martin Birck and Markel, and a third gentleman I've met some time or other, but whose name I've forgotten or perhaps never known—he's very bald and every time I've met him before it's always been indoors. That was why I didn't recognise him until he took off his hat to greet me. Recke nodded to Markel, whom he knows, and soon afterwards got up to go. Then he passed near my table, saluted me with extreme politeness, if a little distantly. We were on Christian-name terms at Uppsala. But he has forgotten that.

As soon as Recke was out of earshot the company at the table began to discuss him, and I heard the bald gentleman, turning to Markel, ask:

—So you know that chap Recke, he's said to be a fellow with a future—ambitious, they say?

MARKEL:—Yes, ambitious. . . . If I say he's ambitious it's mostly for the sake of our close friendship; otherwise one would be putting the matter more correctly if one said he wants to get on in life. Ambition is something so rare. We've got into the habit of calling someone ambitious if he wants to become a minister of state. Minister of state—what's that? A petty wholesaler's income and hardly enough power to be able to help one's own relatives, much less impose one's ideas, if one has any. I don't mean to say I wouldn't mind being a minister myself, it's certainly a better job than the one I've got—only it shouldn't be called ambition. It's something else. In the days when I was ambitious I worked out a very pretty little plan for conquering the whole earth and rearranging things as they ought to be; and when, in the end, everything became so good it almost began to be boring, then I was going to stuff my pockets with as much money as I could lay hands on and creep away, vanish in some cosmopolis and sit at a corner café and drink absinth and enjoy seeing how everything went to the devil as soon as I wasn't on the scene any more. . . . But, anyhow, I like Klas Recke. He's good-looking and he has an unusual talent for arranging things pleasantly for himself in this vale of woe.

Markel, yes! By and large he is what he has always been. Nowadays he's a correspondent for a big newspaper, writing articles in the mood indignant, articles that are intended to be read seriously and which sometimes really deserve to be. A bit unshaven and shaggy in the mornings, maybe, but always elegant by evening and with a good humour that lights up with the street lamps. Beside him, Birck sat with absent eyes, wearing a big raincoat in all this heat; he wrapped it round him with a frozen gesture.

Markel turned to me and asked me if I would care to join this select circle of dipsomaniacs. I thanked him, but replied that I was shortly going home. And such was my intention, although in reality I felt no longing for my solitary room, and sat on a long while more, listening to the music from Strömparterren as it penetrated clear and loud through the dusky silence of the town and looking across to where the Palace mirrored its blind staring windows in the waters of The Stream—a stream which just then was no stream, but lay glassy as a forest pool. And I looked at a little blue star which stood shivering over Rosenbad. I listened, too, to the conversation at the neighbouring table. They were talking of women and love, the question being: what is the cardinal condition for a man to enjoy himself thoroughly with a woman?

The bald gentleman said: That she's sixteen, dark-haired, slim, and has hot blood.

MARKEL, with a dreamy expression: That she's fat and plump.

BIRCK: That she's fond of me.

July 2

No, things are beginning to become too horrible. Today, about ten in the morning, Mrs Gergorius stood in my room again. She looked pale and wretched, and her eyes were wide as they stared at me—What's the matter, I asked. What has happened—has something happened?

She answered in a low voice.

—Last night he raped me. As good as raped me.

I sat in my chair at the desk, my fingers playing with a pen and a piece of paper, as if about to write out a prescription. She sat in the corner of the sofa.—Poor child, I said, as if to myself. I couldn't find anything else to say.

She said:

—I'm made to be trampled on.

We fell silent a moment. Then she began to talk. He had woken her up in the middle of the night. Unable to sleep, he had begged and pleaded. Wept. Said his salvation was at stake. Didn't know what grievous sins he might commit if she did not give in to his wishes. It was her duty to do so; and duty came before health. God would help them. God would anyway give her back her health.

I sat dumbfounded.

—Is he a hypocrite, then? I asked, at length.

—I don't know. No, I don't think so. But he has got into the habit of using God for everything under the sun, as suits him best. They always do it, I know so many clergymen. I hate them. But he isn't a hypocrite; on the contrary, he has always thought it self-evident his religion is the right one, and so he tends to regard those who reject it as swindlers, wicked people who are intentionally telling lies in order to bring others to perdition.

She spoke calmly, but with a little tremble in her voice. In a way, what she said surprised me. Up to now I hadn't realised that this little feminine creature ever did any thinking, or that she was able so clearly, and as it were from the outside, to weigh up such a man as she was speaking of, even though she must surely feel a deadly hatred for him, a deep disgust. I felt that disgust, that hatred, in every tremulous word she uttered; and as she told her tale to the end, it infected me, too. She had wanted to get up, get dressed, go out into the streets all night, till morning came. But he held her fast. He was strong. Wouldn't let her go. . . .

I felt myself burn, my temples were beating in my head, inside me I heard a voice, so clear I was almost afraid I was thinking aloud, a voice whispering between its teeth: Beware, priest! I've promised this little woman, this feminine flower with the silken hair, over there, that I shall protect her against you. Beware, your life is in my hands. And before you want to go there I both can and will send you to paradise! You don't know me. My conscience bears not the least resemblance to yours. I am my own judge. I belong to a species of human being you do not even suspect exists!

Could she really be sitting there, listening to my thoughts? A little shiver ran through me as I suddenly heard her say:

—I could murder that man.

—My dear Mrs Gregorius, I said with a faint smile. Naturally that's only a manner of speaking. But it's one that shouldn't be used, even as such.

It had been on the tip of my tongue to say: least of all as such!

—But tell me, I went on in almost the same breath, and to change the subject. Tell me how it really came about that you married Mr Gregorius? Pressure from your parents; or perhaps a little infatuation at confirmation time?

She shuddered as if chilled.

—No, nothing like that, she said. It all happened in such a strange way, it was nothing you could guess at or understand of your own accord. Naturally, I was never in love with him, never in the least. Not even the usual girlish calf-love for the clergyman who confirmed me—nothing at all! But I'll try to explain. I'll tell you the whole story.

She settled deeper into the sofa. Hunched up like a little girl, and gazing beyond me and into abstraction, she began to speak:

—As a child and in my early youth I was so happy. When I think of that time it all seems like a fairy-story. Everyone liked me and I was fond of everyone. Then I came to that age . . . you know. But at first it made no difference. I was still perfectly happy, yes, happier than before—up to my twentieth year. A young girl, too, has her sensuality, as you understand; but in her earliest youth it's only a source of happiness to her. The blood sang in my ears, and I sang too—I was always singing as I went about my chores in the home, and when I walked down the street I used to hum under my breath. And I was always in love. I had grown up in a very religious home; but I didn't think it a terrible sin to be kissed. When I was in love with some young man and he kissed me, I just let it happen. I knew there was something else, too, which you had to look out for and which was a terrible sin, but it was all so dim and faraway to me, and I wasn't tempted. No, not at all. I didn't even understand that it could tempt anyone, I thought it was just something you had to submit to when you were married and wanted children, certainly nothing that could have any meaning in itself. But when I was twenty I fell deeply in love with a man.

He was good-looking and kind and sensitive—at least, so I thought then, and whenever I think of him I still believe it. Yes, he must be—later he married a girlhood friend of mine, and he has made her very happy. It was summer when we first met, out in the country. We kissed. One day he took me deep into the forest. There he tried to seduce me, and he came close to succeeding. Oh, if only he had succeeded, if only I hadn't run away—how different everything could have been now! Then I might have married him, perhaps—at least I shouldn't have married the man who is my husband today. Perhaps I would have had little children and a home, a real home; and should never have needed to become a faithless wife. —But I was wild with fear and shame. I squirmed out of his arms and ran away, ran for my life.

A terrible time followed. I didn't want to see him any more, dared not. He sent me flowers, wrote letter after letter, begging me to forgive him. But I thought he was a scoundrel. I left his letters unanswered and, as for his flowers, I threw them out of the window.—But I thought of him constantly. And now it was no longer only kisses I thought about; now I knew what temptation was. Although nothing had happened, I felt as if some change had occurred in me. I imagined others could see it written on me. No one can understand how I suffered. In the autumn, when we had moved back into town, I was out walking on my own one evening in the twilight. The wind whined round the corners of the houses, and now and then a raindrop fell. I entered the street where I knew he lived, and walked past his house. Seeing a light burning in his window, I stopped, and in the lamplight saw his head bowed over a book. It attracted me like a magnet. I thought how nice it would be to be in there with him. I crept in through the doorway and was already halfway up the stairs—but then I turned back.

If he had written to me in those days I should have answered. But he had tired of writing without ever getting any reply, and so we never met again—not for many years. And by then, of course, everything was quite different.

I've told you already, haven't I, that I was very religiously brought up. Now I sank wholly into religion. I began training to be a nurse, but had to give it up because my health had begun to fail. So I came home again, did odd jobs about the house as before, and dreamed and had longings and prayed to God to free me from my dreams and my longings. I felt things were unbearable as they were, and that there must be a change. Then one day I heard from Father that the Rev. Gregorius had asked for my hand in marriage. I was utterly astounded. He had never made me any advances, never given me the least intimation. He was an old friend of the family. Mother admired him. And Father, I think, was a bit scared of him. I went to my room and cried. In some special way I had always felt there was something repulsive about him; I believe it must have been this which made me decide to say yes. No one forced me. No one argued me into it. But I believed it was God's will. Hadn't I always been taught to believe that God's will was always that which most contradicted our own? Hadn't I lain awake, only last evening, praying to God for freedom and peace? Now I believed He had heard my prayers—in His own way. I thought I saw His will shining clearly before my eyes. Beside that man, so I fancied, my longings would be extinguished and the desire die away. In this way, I thought, God had arranged things for me. And I was sure he must be a good and fine man, since he was a clergyman.

Well, it all turned out quite differently. He wasn't able to kill my dreams. He could only besmirch them. Instead, little by little, he killed my faith. This is the only thing I have to thank him for, because I certainly don't want it back again. Faith—when I think of it now, it seems merely queer. Everything one longed for, everything delightful to think about, was sin. A man's embraces were sin, if one longed for them and really wanted them; but if one found them ugly and repulsive, a scourge, a torment, something disgusting—then it was sin *not* to desire them! Tell me, Doctor Glas, isn't that queer?

She had grown hot from talking. I nodded to her over my glasses:

—Yes, it's queer.

—Or tell me, do you believe my love now is sin? It isn't only happiness. Perhaps, even more, it's anxiety. But do you think it's sin? If it is sin, then everything in me is sin, since I can't find anything in myself that is better or more valuable.—But perhaps you're surprised at me, sitting here and talking to you about all this. After all, I have someone else I can talk to. But when we meet our time is so short, and he talks to me so little—she blushed suddenly—so little about the things I think of most.

I sat quiet and silent with my head in my hand, observing her through half-closed eyes as she sat there in the corner of my sofa, rosy-hued under her rich yellow hair. The Maiden Silkencheek. I thought: if she had these feelings for me, there wouldn't be time for talk either. And I thought: When she next begins to speak I'll go over to her and close her mouth with a kiss. But now she sat silent. The door to my big waiting room was ajar, and I heard my housekeeper's footsteps in the corridor.

I broke the silence.

—But tell me, Mrs Gregorius, haven't you ever considered divorce? You're not tied to your husband by any economic necessity—your father left a fortune, you were his only child, and your mother's still alive, in good circumstances. Isn't that so?

—Ah, Doctor Glas, you don't know him. Divorce—a clergyman! He'd never agree to it, never! Whatever I did, whatever happened. He would sooner 'forgive' me seventy times over, rehabilitate me, everything imaginable. . . . He'd even be capable of holding prayers for me in church.—No, I'm made to be trampled on.

I got up:

—Well, my dear Mrs Gregorius, what do you want me to do now? I can't see any way out any more.

At a loss, she shook her head.

—I don't know. I don't know anything any more. But I think he's coming to see you today about his heart. He mentioned it yesterday. Couldn't you speak to him, just once more? Of course without letting him suspect I've been here today and spoken to you about this?

—Well—we'll see.

She left.

When she had gone, I took up a medical journal to distract my thoughts. But it was no use. I kept on seeing her before me, telling me her life-story and how it came about that she had got into such an impossible situation.

Whose fault was it? Was it the fault of that man who had tried to seduce her in the forest, one summer's day? Alas, what is a man's business with a woman in this world of ours, if not to seduce her, whether in the forest or in the bridal bed, and then help and support her in all that follows? Whose fault was it, then—was it the clergyman's? After all he had only desired her, as thousands of men have desired thousands of women, desired her quite honourably into the bargain, as they call it in their queer jargon—and she, without, knowing or understanding anything, merely influenced by the strange confusion of ideas in which she had grown up, had consented. When she married that creature she was not awake, she did it in her sleep. And in dreams of course the oddest things occur, though they seem completely natural and ordinary—in dreams. But when one is awake and remembers what one has dreamt, one is astounded, and either laughs out loud or else shivers with fear. Now she has woken up! And her parents, who, after all, ought to have known what marriage is but gave their consent even so, and perhaps were even delighted and flattered—were they awake? And the clergyman himself: did he have the least sense of how unnatural, how grossly indecent his behaviour was?

Never have I had so strong a feeling that morality is a merry-go-round, a spinning top. I knew this before, of course; but I had always imagined its phases must be centuries or aeons—now they seemed to me to be minutes or seconds. There was a flickering before my eyes. And inside me, my only guide in this witches' dance, I heard again a voice whisper between its teeth: Have a care, priest!

*   *   *

Quite correct. He came to my surgery hour. Inside me as I opened the door and saw him sitting out there in the waiting-room, I felt a sudden secret merriment. There was only one patient before him, an old woman who wanted her prescription renewed—then it was his turn. Spreading out the tails of his coat he sat down with ponderous dignity in the same corner of the sofa as his wife had sat hunched up in a few hours before.

As usual, he began by talking a lot of drivel. The communion question was what he now entertained me with. As for his heart trouble, that only came out in passing, in parenthesis, and I received the impression that he had really come to hear my opinion as a doctor on the question (at present being debated by all the newspapers by way of relief from the Great Lake Monster), as to whether Holy Communion constitutes a danger to people's health. I haven't followed this discussion, though now and then I've seen some article on the matter in a newspaper and half-read it. But I was far from being well-informed on the subject, and instead it was the clergyman who had to expound the situation to me. What is to be done to prevent infection at the communion table? That was the question. The Vicar very much regretted it had ever been raised. But now it had been raised, and so it must be answered. Various solutions could be envisaged. Perhaps the simplest would be if each church acquired a number of small beakers which the verger could clean at the altar after every group of communicants—but this would be expensive, and perhaps it might even be impossible for poor country parishes to acquire a sufficient number of silver cups.

I remarked casually that in our time, when interest in religion is steadily on the increase and masses of silver cups are bought up for every bicycle race, it should not prove impossible to get hold of identical cups for religious purposes. For the rest, I do not remember a single word about silver appearing in the institution of Holy Communion; but this reflection I kept to myself.—Further, the Vicar went on, the possibility had been considered of every communicant bringing his own cup or glass. But how would it look if the rich brought along artistically embellished silver cups and the poor, maybe, a brandy glass?

For my part I thought it would look rather picturesque; but I held my peace and let him continue.—Then, he went on, there was a clergyman of the modern, freethinking variety who had suggested that Our Saviour's blood could be swallowed in capsules.—At first I wondered if I had heard him aright. In capsules, like castor oil?—Yes, in capsules. Finally one of the Court Chaplains had constructed a communion cup of an entirely new sort, patented it and formed a limited company. The Vicar described the invention for me in detail. It seemed to be designed along more or less the same lines as a conjurer's glasses and bottles. Well, the Rev. Gregorius, for his part, is orthodox. He is nothing of a free-thinker. These innovations, one and all, fill him with profound misgivings. But so, too, do germs. So what's to be done?

As I heard him utter this word, a light dawned. Instantly, I recognised the tone of voice. Once before I recalled hearing him speak of germs; and now it was at once clear to me he was suffering from the disease known as bacillophobia. In his eyes, evidently, germs lie mysteriously beyond the pale equally of religion and our system of conventions. This, of course, is because they are so new. His religion is old, almost nineteen hundred years old, and as for our system of social conventions, it dates at very least from the beginning of the nineteenth century, from German philosophy and the fall of Napoleon. But germs, assailing him in his old age, have taken him completely off his guard. According to his way of seeing things it has not been until this lattermost age that they

have begun their nasty activities, certainly it has never occurred to him that, as far as we can judge, there must
also have been masses of germs in the simple earthenware
pot which passed round the Table at the Last Supper in
Gethsemane.

Impossible to decide, whether he's more fool or fox.

I turned my back on him and let him talk, meanwhile
arranging something in my instrument cupboard. Casually, I asked him to take off his coat and waistcoat; as
for the communion question, without more ado I decided
my vote should go to the capsule method.

—I admit, I said, at first glance this idea did seem a bit
objectionable, even to me; though I certainly cannot
boast any warm religiosity. But, on closer reflexion, all
objections must be waived. Surely, the essence of the
communion does not lie in the bread and wine, nor even
in the church plate, but in faith. And true faith obviously
cannot let itself be influenced by such outward things as
silver cups and gelatine pills. . . .

With these last words I put my stethoscope to his
chest, asked him to be quiet a moment, and listened. It
was nothing remarkable I heard, in there. Only the slight
irregularity of the heart movements which is so usual in
an elderly man who is in the habit of eating more for dinner than he needs, and then rolling himself up for a
snooze on the sofa. One day it can lead to a stroke. One
can never be sure of course; and it is by no means inevi-
table. Not even a particularly threatening possibility.

But my mind was made up. This was going to be a serious consultation. I listened, much longer than necessary.
Moved the tube. Tapped. Listened again. I noticed how it
pained him, having to sit silent, passive, under all this—
he's used to talking incessantly, in church, in company, in
his home. He has indeed, a distinct talent for it. And this
little talent, it must have been, which first attracted him

to his calling. My examination frightened him a bit—
probably he would have preferred to run on awhile about
his communion pills, and then, with a sudden glance at his
watch, make a dash for the door. But now I had him on
my sofa. And I wasn't letting him slip away. Silently, I
listened. And the longer I listened, the more troublesome
his heart became.

—Is it serious? he asked, at length.

I did not answer immediately. Instead, I took a few
paces across the floor. A plan was fermenting in my
mind. In itself, it was quite a simple little plan. Even so,
unpractised as I am in intrigue, I hesitated. And if I did
so, it was also for the good reason that my whole plan
was based on his stupidity and ignorance—but . . . was
he stupid enough? Did I dare? Or was it too crude? Perhaps he saw through me?

I broke off my promenade. For a couple of seconds I
threw him my very sharpest doctor's glance. The greyish
white, podgy face lay in its sheepish pious folds. But his
eyes eluded me. His spectacles reflected only my window,
its curtains, and my rubber plant. I decided to be bold.
Sheep or fox—I thought—even a fox is much more stupid than a human being. With him there was decidedly no
risk in playing the charlatan awhile—he liked charlatan
tricks, so much was obvious: my pensive promenade to
and fro across the floor and my long silence after his
questions had already impressed him, softened him up.

—Queer, I mumbled at last, as if to myself.

And again I approached him with the stethoscope.

—Forgive me. But I must listen just a little while
longer. I must be quite sure I'm not making a mistake.

—Well, I said, at length. To judge from what I hear
today, that's not a strong heart you've got, Vicar. But
somehow or other I can't think it's all that bad in the or-

dinary way of things. I fancy it has its special reasons for giving trouble today!

Hurriedly, not quite successfully, he tried to re-form his face into a question-mark. I saw at once his bad conscience had comprehended me. His lips worked as if about to speak, ask me, perhaps, what I meant. But, not managing it, he merely coughed. Certainly, he would have preferred to avoid any closer explanations—but I was not letting him escape me.

—Let us be honest with one another, Mr Gregorius, I began.

At this opening he jumped with fright.

—You have certainly not forgotten the conversation we had a couple of weeks ago, about your wife's health. It is not my intention to put any awkward questions, as to how you've kept the agreement then reached. I will merely say, Vicar, that had I known then how your heart was, I could have adduced even stronger reasons for the advice I then permitted myself to give you. For your wife, it's a question of her health, over a longer or shorter period. For you, it can easily be a question of your life.

He looked horrible as I spoke—a sort of colour came into his face, but nothing reddish, only green and mauve. I had to turn away, he was so dreadfully ugly to look at. I went over to the open window to get a breath of fresh air; but it was almost more oppressive outdoors than in.

I went on:

—My prescription is clear and simple: it reads 'separate bedrooms'. I remember you don't like it, but that can't be helped. For it isn't only ultimate satisfaction which, in this case, involves a grave risk; it's also important to avoid everything which can whet or excite your desires.—Yes, yes, I know what you're going to say; that you're an old man, and a clergyman to boot; but after all, I am a doctor, and I've the right to speak openly to a patient. And I don't think I'm exceeding the bounds of what is reasonable if I point out that the constant propinquity of a young woman, particularly at nights, must have much the same effect on a clergyman as on any other mortal man. I've studied at Uppsala. I knew many theologians there. And I did not exactly gain the impression that theological studies were more efficient than others as a fire insurance for young bodies against this sort of outbreak. As for age—well, how old are you, sir?—fifty-seven; it's a critical age. At your age desire is much the same as it ever was,—but satisfaction brings in its revenges. Well, it's true there are many ways of looking at life, and various ways of evaluating it; and if it was an old rake I was speaking to I should naturally be prepared to hear from him an answer logical enough, seen from his point of view: To the devil with all that! There's no sense in forsaking the thing which gives life its value, merely in order to retain life itself. But of course I know such a way of reasoning is wholly foreign to your way of thinking, Vicar. My duty as a doctor in this case is to warn and enlighten—this is all I can do, and I am certain, now you know how serious it is, nothing more will prove needful. I find it hard to believe it would be to your taste to drop dead like the late-lamented King Frederick I or, more recently, M. Félix Faure. . . .

I avoided looking at him as I spoke. But when I had made an end, I saw he was sitting there with his hand over his eyes, and that his lips were moving. And I guessed, rather than heard: Our Father, which art in Heaven, hallowed be Thy name . . . lead us not into temptation, but deliver us from evil. . . .

I sat down at my desk, adding as I handed him the prescription:

—And staying in town all through this hot summer isn't good for you, either. A visit to the waters would do

you a world of good. Porla; or Ronneby. But in that case,
of course, you must go alone.

July 5

Summer Sunday. Everything stiflingly close and dusty,
and only the poorer sort of people stirring abroad. And
the poor, alas, are not congenial.

About four I went and sat down on board a little
steamer to have dinner at Djurgårdsbrunn. My housekeeper had gone to a funeral. Afterwards she was to
drink coffee out in the open air. The dead person was no
relative or friend of hers, but for that class of woman a
funeral is always a great pleasure and I hadn't the heart
to refuse my permission. This meant that I, too, must
dine out. As a matter of fact, acquaintances had invited
me to their villa in the archipelago; but I did not feel like
it. I have no particular liking for acquaintances or villas
in the archipelago. Least of all for the archipelago. A
mincemeat landscape, all chopped up. Little islands, little
waterways, little rocky knolls and wretched little trees. A
pale and poverty-stricken landscape, cold colours, mostly
grey and blue, and yet not poor enough to have the grandeur of true desolation. When I hear people praise the archipelago's natural beauties I always suspect them of having quite other things in mind and on closer examination
this suspicion is always confirmed. One person thinks of
the fresh air and fine bathing, another of his sailing boat,
a third of the perch-fishing, yet for them all this falls
under the rubric of natural beauty. The other day I was
talking to a young girl who was in love with the archipelago but, as our conversation proceeded, it transpired that
in point of fact she was thinking of sunsets; possibly also
of a student. She forgot that the sun sets everywhere and
that students are mobile. I do not believe I am wholly in-
sensitive to natural beauty, but for that I must go further

afield, to Lake Vättern or Skåne, or else to the sea. But I rarely have time, and within a radius of twenty or thirty miles of Stockholm I have never seen a landscape to compare with Stockholm itself—with Djurgården or Haga or the pavement overlooking the Stream, outside The Grand. This is why I mostly stay in town, summer and winter. I do this the more willingly, having the solitary person's constant desire to see people around me—*nota bene,* people I do not know and so do not have to speak to.

So I arrived at Djurgårdsbrunn and found a table by the glass wall in the long pavilion. The waiter hurried forward with the menu and discreetly spread a clean white napkin over the remains of gravy and Batty's mustard left by an earlier party. The next moment, handing me the wine list, he disclosed by his hasty 'Chablis'? a memory containing, it may be, depths of knowledge immeasurable as many a professor's. No regular winebibber, it is true that when dining out I never drink any other wine but Chablis. And he was an old hand who knew his man. His first youthful frenzies he had stilled balancing punch trays at Berns, afterwards with the seriousness of riper years fulfilling the more involved duties of dining-room waiter at Rydberg and Hamburger Börs. Who knows what transient rejection at destiny's hands was now responsible for him—hair thinning and evening dress a trifle frayed—labouring at his calling in this somewhat humbler place? The years had lent him an air of belonging wherever there is a smell of food and bottles to be uncorked. I was pleased to see him, and we exchanged a glance of secret understanding.

I looked round at the clientèle. At the next table sat the pleasant young man I usually buy my cigars from. He was treating his girl friend, a tasty little shop assistant with sharp mousey eyes. A little further away sat an actor

with his wife and children, wiping his mouth with sacer-
dotal gravity. And, in a corner, a solitary old eccentric
whom I must have seen in the streets and cafés these
twenty years, sharing his dinner with his dog. The dog,
too, was old and his fur had gone a little grey.

The Chablis had come and I was sitting enjoying the
play of sunbeams in the light wine in my glass when,
quite close at hand, I heard a woman's voice that seemed
familiar. I looked up. A family had just come in. Husband. Wife. And a little four- or five-year-old boy, a very
pretty lad, but stupidly—indeed ridiculously—dressed up
in a pale blue velvet blouse and lace collar. It was the
wife who did the talking and it was her voice which had
sounded so familiar.—We'll sit over there,—no, not
there,—that's in the sun—no, there we won't have any
view—where's the head waiter?

All at once I recognised her. It was the same young
woman who had once writhed weeping on the floor of my
room, begging and pleading with me to help her—to free
her of the child she was expecting. Afterwards she had
got married to the oaf she had so desired, and had her
child—a bit too quickly, but that makes no odds, now. So
here we have the *corpus delictii*; in velvet blouse and lace
collar. Well, my little lady, and what do you say now—
wasn't I right? The scandal passed over; but your little
boy is left to you, and you have the pleasure of him. . . .

Yet, I wonder whether it really is that child? No, it
can't be. The lad is four, at most five, and it's at least
seven or eight years since that old story. It was at the
very beginning of my practice. What can have happened
to the first child? Perhaps it has come to grief in some
way. Well, that's of no importance—they seem to have
repaired the damage afterwards.

Anyway I don't much care for this family. On closer
inspection I see the wife is young and still quite beautiful,

but she has put on a good deal of weight and her complexion is almost too blooming. I suspect her of passing her mornings sitting in cake-shops, drinking stout to her pastries and gossiping with women friends. And the master of the household is a counter-jumper Don Juan. From his appearance and manner, I should judge him faithless as a cock. Furthermore, they both have that habit of scolding the waiter in advance for the negligence they expect of him: a habit which makes me feel sick. In a word, scum.

I washed down my mixed impressions with a deep draught of the light acidulous wine, and gazed out through the great wide sliding windows. Out there, rich and quiet, the landscape lay warm in the evening sun. The canal mirrored the greenery on its banks and the blue of the sky. Quietly, lightly, a couple of canoes, paddled by men in striped blue sweaters, slid in under the bridge and vanished, bicyclists spun over the bridge and scattered over the roads, and in the grass beneath the big trees people were sitting in groups, enjoying the shade and the beautiful day. While over my table fluttered two yellow butterflies.

And while I sat like that, letting my gaze sink into the summer greenery out there, my thoughts idled into a fantasy with which I divert myself at times. I have a little money saved up, ten thousand crowns or a little more, in good securities. In five or six years or so I shall perhaps have saved enough to be able to build myself a house out in the country. But where shall I build it? It has to be by the sea. It must be on an open coast, without islands or skerries. I want an open horizon, and I want to *hear* the sea. And I want the sea to lie to westward. The sun must set in it.

But there is one more thing, as important as the sea; I want to have a wealth of greenery and great sighing trees.

No pines or spruces. Well, pines are acceptable, providing they are tall and straight and strong and have succeeded in becoming what they are intended to be; but the jagged contour of a spruce forest against the sky causes me an inexplicable sadness. Furthermore, in the country as in the town, it sometimes rains and a spruce forest in rainy weather makes me feel ill and depressed. No, it must be an Arcadian meadow, sloping gently towards the beach, with clumps of big leafy umbrageous trees, a vaulting of greenery, above my head.

But, alas, the coastal scenery is not like that; it is mean and raw. The sea-breezes make the trees knotty, small, dwarfish. I shall never set eyes on the coast where I wish to build and live.

And then, building a house; this, too, is an endless business. It takes a couple of years before it's ready. Probably, during that time, you go and die. Then it takes two or three more years before it's in order, and then there's a wait of about another fifty years or so before a house becomes really agreeable to live in.

A wife, too, should really be part of the scheme. But that isn't always plain sailing, either. I find it so difficult to stomach the idea of someone looking at me while I'm asleep. A child's sleep is beautiful, a young woman's too; but hardly a man's. It's said that a hero's slumber by his camp-fire, his head pillowed on his knapsack, is lovely to behold; and this is possible, for he is so weary and sleeps so sound. But what can my face look like when my thoughts are in a coma? I should scarcely enjoy seeing it myself, if I could—still less should anybody else.

No. The dream of happiness does not exist that does not bite its own tail.

I often wonder, too, what character I should prefer for myself had I never read a book or seen a work of art. In that event perhaps it would not even occur to me to choose—perhaps the archipelago, with its rocks, would do for me. All my thoughts and dreams about Nature are most probably based on impressions drawn from poetry and art. From art I have acquired my longing to wander at ease in the ancient Florentine's flowery meadows and nod on Homer's seas and bend the knee in Böcklin's sacred grove. Alas, what would my own poor eyes see of this world, left to themselves without all these hundreds and thousands of teachers and friends among those who have sung and thought and seen on behalf of all the rest of us? Often in my youth I have thought: To have been there! To have had the chance! To be allowed to give, for once, and not always receive. It's so dreary, always moving on alone, with a soul barren of fruit, at one's wits' end to know what to do to feel that one is something, means something, or to have a little respect for oneself. Probably it's a most happy state of affairs that most people are so undemanding in this respect. I have not been undemanding, and long it has pained me; though I believe the worst is over now.

I could hardly have become a poet—I see nothing which others haven't seen already and given form to. Of course I know a few authors and artists; queer creatures, in my view. There's nothing they have a will to; or, if there is, then they do the opposite. They are just ears and eyes and hands. Yet I envy them. Not that I would exchange my will for their visions, but I should very much like to have their eyes and ears into the bargain. Sometimes when I see one of them sitting silent, absentminded, staring into emptiness, I think to myself: perhaps at this very moment he sees something no one has seen before and which he will shortly oblige a thousand others to see, myself among them. What the youngest among them produce I certainly do not understand—as yet—but I also know and foresee that, once they are recognised and known, I, too, will understand and admire them. It is the same as with new modern clothes, furniture, everything else; only those who have become rigid, dried up, who long ago are finished and done with, can resist them. And the poets themselves, are they really the legislators of the age? God knows, but they hardly look like it to me. Rather I should say they are the instruments the age plays upon, aeolian harps the wind sings in. And what am I? Not even that. I have no eyes of my own. I can hardly see the drinkers and the radishes on the table, over there, with my own eyes; I see them with Strindberg's and think of a supper he ate in his youth at Stallmästaregården. And when the canoeists flew past on the canal, just now, in their striped vests, it seemed to me for a moment as if the shade of Maupassant fled on before them.

And now, as I sit at my open window, writing this by a flickering candle—I detest touching oil-lamps and my housekeeper is sleeping too soundly after her funeral coffee and cakes for me to have the heart to wake her— now, as the candleflame flutters in the draught and my shadow shivers and flutters like the flame on the wallpaper, as if trying to come to life—now I think of Hans Andersen and his tale of the shadow. And it seems to me I am the shadow who wished to become a man.

July 6

I must make a note of the dream I had last night.

I stood at the Rev. Gregorius's bedside; he was ill. The upper part of his body was bared and I was listening to his heart. The bed stood in his study; a harmonium stood in one corner and someone was playing on it. No hymn tune, hardly a melody. A door was open; it worried me, but I could not bring myself to have it closed.

—Is it serious? asked the clergyman.

—No, I replied, it's not serious; but it's dangerous.

I meant that what I was thinking of was dangerous to myself. And in my dream I thought I had expressed myself with profundity and elegance.

—But for safety's sake, I added, we may as well send to the chemist's for some communion pills.

—Must I be operated on? asked the clergyman.

I nodded.

—It looks like it. Your heart is no use at all, it's too old. We'll have to take it out. But don't worry, it's a perfectly safe operation, it can be done with an ordinary paper-knife.

This seemed to me quite a simple scientific truth, and it so happened I had a paper-knife in my hand.

—We'll just lay this handkerchief over your face.

The clergyman groaned aloud under the handkerchief. But instead of operating I swiftly pressed a button in the wall.

I took away the handkerchief. He was dead. I felt his hand; it was stone cold. I looked at my watch.

—He's been dead for at least two hours, I said to myself.

Mrs Gregorius got up from the organ, where she had been sitting and playing and came up to me. Her look seemed worried and sorrowful and she handed me a posy of dark flowers. It was only then I saw she was smiling ambiguously, and that she was naked.

I held out my arms to her and wanted to draw her to me, but she eluded me, and instantly Klas Recke was standing in the open doorway.

—Doctor Glas, he said, in my capacity of temporary departmental chief I declare you under arrest!

—It's too late now, I told him. Don't you see anything?

I pointed to the window. A red flash burst in through both the windows of the room; suddenly it was broad daylight, and a woman's voice that seemed to come from another room whined and whimpered: The world's on fire, the world's on fire!

And I woke up.

The morning sun was shining straight into the room. Last night when I came home I'd forgotten to draw down the blind.

Odd. These last days I haven't been thinking about the ugly parson and his beautiful wife at all. Haven't *wanted* to think about them.

And Gregorius has anyway gone to Porla.

* * *

I do not write down all my thoughts here.

I seldom write down a thought the first time it comes to me. I wait and see if it recurs.

July 7

It's raining, and I'm sitting thinking about unpleasant things.

Why did I say 'no' to Hans Fahlén that time last autumn, when he came and asked to borrow fifty crowns? True, I hardly knew him. But next week he cut his throat.

And why didn't I learn Greek when I was at school? It makes me feel almost ill with annoyance. After all, I studied it for four years. Was it perhaps because my father had forced me to study it instead of English that I persevered in learning nothing? How can one be so brutishly stupid! Didn't I learn everything else, including that nonsense called logic. Yet I studied Greek for four years, but know no Greek.

And it can't possibly have been my teacher's fault, for he afterwards became a Minister of State.

I should like to dig out my school books again and see

whether I can learn anything now; perhaps it is not too late.

* * *

I wonder what it feels like to have a crime on one's conscience.

* * *

I wonder whether Christina won't soon have dinner ready.

* * *

The wind shakes the trees in the churchyard, and the rain chatters in the roof gutters. A poor devil with a bottle in his pocket has sought shelter under the church roof, in a corner of a buttress. He stands propped against the red church wall, his gaze straying blue and pious among the driving clouds. The rain drips from the two lean trees by Bellman's grave. Across this corner of the churchyard, a little to one side, stands a house of ill fame; a girl in her petticoat pads over to a window and draws down the blind.

But down among the graves the vicar of the parish picks his cautious way through the mud in galoshes, stalking under his umbrella, and now he creeps in through the little door into the vestry.

* * *

By the way, why do the clergy always go into church by a back door?

July 9

It's still raining. Days like these are kin with all the secret poison in my soul.

Just now, on my way home from visiting patients, I exchanged greetings at a street corner with a man I do not like to meet. He insulted me once—deeply, politely, and in such circumstances that I see no chance of repaying him.

Such things I do not like. They touch my health.

*   *   *

I sit at my desk, opening one drawer after another and looking at old papers and things. A little yellowed newspaper clipping falls into my hands.

> *Is there a life after this?* by H. Cremer theol. dr. Price: 50 öre.

> *John Bunyan's Revelations* A survey of the life to come, Heaven's splendour and the horrors of Hell. Price: 75 öre.

☞   MAN'S OWN STRENGTH   ☜

> The right way to distinction and riches by S. Smiles, Price: 3.50 eleg. bnd. in cl. w. glt 1. 4.25

Why have I hidden this old advertisement? I remember cutting it out when I was fourteen, the year my father's fortune went up in smoke. Saving up my little pocket money I bought Mr. Smiles' book, albeit without gold lettering. As soon as I had read it I sold it to a secondhand bookseller; it was too exaggeratedly stupid.

But I still have the advertisement. It is also more valuable.

And here is an old photograph: the country place we owned for a few years. Mariebo, it was called, after my mother.

The photograph is yellowed and faded, and a mist seems to hang over the white house and the spruce forest behind it. Yes, that is just how it looked there, on grey and rainy days.

Somehow I never really enjoyed myself there. Father beat me so during the summers. They say I was a fractious child at such times as I did not have school and lessons.

Once he beat me unjustly. This is almost one of my happiest childhood memories. Naturally, it hurt my skin; but it did my soul good. When I went down to the lake afterwards it was blowing half a gale and the foam was whipped up into my face. I'm not sure I have ever felt myself so deliciously flooded with noble feelings as I was then. I forgave my father; he was so quick-tempered; and he was also very much worried about his business.

It was harder to forgive him all those times when he beat me justly; I'm not sure I've forgiven him, even now. Like that time when, in spite of strictest prohibitions, I'd bitten my nails again. How he hit me! And for hours afterwards I wandered about in pouring rain in that wretched spruce forest, and cried and swore.

There was never really anything peaceful about my father. He was rarely cheerful, and when he wasn't, could not abide the cheerfulness of others. But he liked parties; he was of the company of melancholy wastrels. He was rich, and died poor. To this day I do not know whether he was completely honest; after all, he was involved in such big transactions. How I pondered, as a child, some words I once heard him let fall in jest to one of his business acquaintances: "Well, my dear Joseph, it isn't so easy to be honest when one is earning such big money as we are. . . ." But he was strict and hard and had perfectly clear and definite ideas about duty, where others were concerned. For oneself one can always find circumstances that alter cases.

But the worst thing was that I always felt for him such

a strong physical revulsion. How it tormented me when, as a little boy, I had to bathe with him and he wanted to teach me to swim. I slithered like an eel out of his hands, again and again thought I was going to drown and was almost as scared of death as I was of coming in contact with his naked body. Certainly he cannot have suspected how acutely this purely physical revulsion increased my pain when he beat me. And much later on, travelling in his company or for some other chance reason, it was a torment whenever I had to sleep in the same room with him.

Yet I was fond of him, even so. Perhaps mostly because he was so proud of my brains. And also because he was always so well-dressed. For a while I hated him, too, because he was unkind to my mother. But then she took ill and died. And then I noticed he mourned her more than I could, with my fifteen years, and so of course I couldn't hate him any longer.

Now they are both gone. And gone are they all—all those who walked and stood among the furniture in my childhood's home. Well, not all, but all those I cared for. My brother Ernst, who was so strong and so stupid and so kind, my help and protector in all the adventurous happenings of a schoolboy's life—gone. He went away to Australia, and no one knows whether he's alive or dead. And my beautiful cousin, Alice, who used to stand so pale and upright by the piano and sing with sleepwalker's eyes and in a voice that shimmered and burned, sang so that I was shaken with shivering in a corner of the great glassed-in verandah, sang as I shall never hear anyone else sing again. What became of her? Married to poverty, with a smalltown schoolteacher, already old and ill and worn-out. I fell into a sudden convulsion of weeping when I met her last Christmas in her mother's home, and she was affected, and we both wept. . . . And her sister

Anna with the hot cheeks she who had the same fever in
the dance as her sister had in song, she ran away from
her scoundrelly husband, with another scoundrel, and was
abandoned. Now, so they say, she lives off her body in
Chicago. And their father, the kind good-looking, witty
Uncle Ulrik, whom they always said I resembled, although I resembled him in an ugly way, he was swept
away in the same crash that overthrew my father, dying,
like him, in poverty. . . . What plague was it that tore
them all away, within a few short years, into the grave or
a shadowy life of misery, all, all, even most of those
friends who thronged our rooms in festal days gone by.

God knows what it was. But they are all gone.

And Mariebo; if I'm not mistaken, it's called Sofielund,
now.

July 10

At my writing-desk.

It occurs to me to press the spring which opens the little secret drawer. Of course I know what lies there: just a
little round box with some pills in it. I don't want to have
them lying about in my medicine cupboard, some confusion might arise one day, and that wouldn't be a good
thing. I made them up myself, a number of years ago,
and they contain a little potassium cyanide. At the particular moment when I made them up I was not thinking of
taking my own life. But I was of the opinion that a wise
man should always be ready.

If you take a little potassium cyanide in a glass of wine
or suchlike, death follows instantly. The glass slips from
your hand and falls to the floor; it is clear to one and all
there has been a suicide. That is not always desirable. If,
on the other hand, you take one of my pills and then
drink a glass of water, a minute or two will elapse before
the pill has time to dissolve and take effect. You have

time to put the glass back quietly on the tray, sit down in a comfortable chair and unfold your *Aftonbladet*. Suddenly, you collapse. The doctor reports a stroke. Naturally, if there is an autopsy, the poison will be detected. But where there are no suspicious or particularly interesting circumstances from the medical point of view there is no obduction. And no such circumstances can be said to exist if someone has a stroke while reading *Aftonbladet* over his after-dinner cigar.

Therefore I am consoled to know that these flour-coated balls, resembling smallshot, are lying there, awaiting a day they may be needed. Within them slumbers a force, evil and hateful in itself, mankind's and all living things' enemy from the beginning. Only to be released when it becomes the one passionately desired liberator from a worse.

What was I most thinking of, when I made up those little black pills for myself? Suicide from unhappy love— that's something I've never been able to conceive. From poverty, rather. Of all so-called outward calamities poverty certainly takes the deepest inward toll. But it appears not to threaten me. Personally I regard myself as among the better-off, and sociologists would place me among the wealthy. What I was thinking of was illness. I have seen so much . . . cancer, blindness, paralysis. How many unfortunates have I not seen to whom I would not have felt the least compunction in administering one of these pills, if, in me as in other decent people, self-interest and respect for the law had not spoken louder than mercy. Instead, how much useless, hopelessly ruined human wreckage have I not helped to preserve in the course of my duties—not even blushing to take payment. But such is the custom; and in matters that do not affect us deeply or personally it is perhaps right we should. And why should I make a martyr of myself for a view which sooner or later must become the view of all civilised people, but which today is still criminal?

The day will come, must come, when the right to die is recognised as far more important and inalienable a human right than the right to drop a voting ticket into a ballot box. And when that time is ripe, every incurably sick person—and every 'criminal' also—shall have the right to the doctor's help, if he wishes to be set free.

There was something beautiful, grand about that cup of poison the Athenians, once believing his life was dangerous to the State, allowed the doctor to administer to Socrates. Our time, if it were to judge him in the same light, would have dragged him up on to a mean scaffold and slaughtered him with an axe.

*   *   *

Good-night, evil power. Sleep well in your little round box. Sleep till I need you. For me you shall have no untimely awakening. Today it's raining, but perhaps tomorrow the sun will shine. And not until that day dawns when even the sunshine seems pest-ridden and diseased shall I wake you, in order myself to sleep.

July 11

At my writing-desk, one grey rainy day.

In one of the little drawers I have just found a piece of paper on which some words were written in my own handwriting, as it looked some years ago—for everyone's handwriting changes ceaselessly, the tiniest little bit every year, unnoticed perhaps to oneself but as inevitably and surely as one's face, stance, movements, soul.

The words were: "Nothing so reduces and drags down a human being as the consciousness of not being loved."

When did I write that? Is it some reflection of my own, or a quotation I jotted down?

Don't remember.

*　　*　　*

I can understand the ambitious. I only have to sit in a corner of the Opera and hear the coronation march in *The Prophet* to feel a hot, if transient, longing to rule over humanity and have myself crowned in an old cathedral.

But it must be during my lifetime; the rest, for all I care, may be silence. Never have I understood those who go chasing after an immortal name. Humanity's memory is unjust and has its lapses, and we have forgotten our oldest and greatest benefactor. Who invented the cart? Pascal invented the wheelbarrow and Fulton the locomotive, but who invented the wheeled vehicle? No one knows. In return, history has preserved the name of King Xerxes' personal coachman: Patiramfes, son of Otanes. He drove the carriage of the great king. As for that blockhead who set fire to the Temple of Diana of Ephesus so that people should not forget his name, he certainly succeeded in his enterprise. You can look him up in Brockhaus.

*　　*　　*

We want to be loved; failing that, admired; failing that, feared; failing that, hated and despised. At all costs we want to stir up some sort of feeling in others. Our soul abhors a vacuum. At all costs it longs for contact.

July 13

I have grey days and black moments. I am not happy. Even so, I know no one with whom I would change places; my heart shrinks at the thought of being this or that person among my acquaintance. No, I don't want to be any one else.

In early youth I suffered much from not having good

looks and, in my burning desire for good looks, thought myself a monster of ugliness. Now, of course, I know I look very much like everyone else. Not exactly a source of rejoicing, this, either.

I am not particularly fond of myself, neither shell nor entrails. But I don't want to be anyone else.

July 14

Blessed sun, who hast the strength to seek us out, even down to the graves under the trees. . . .

Well, that was just now; now it's dark. I've come home from my evening walk. The town lay stretched out as if in a bath of roses, and over the southern heights hung a light rosy mist.

Awhile I sat alone at a table on the pavements outside The Grand and drank a little lemon cordial; just then Miss Martens came walking by. I got up and saluted her, and to my surprise she stopped, held out her hand and said a few words before going on her way, something about her mother's illness and the lovely evening. While she was speaking she blushed slightly, as if what she was doing was unusual and open to misinterpretation.

I at least did not misinterpret her. Many times I have noticed how soft and friendly, unaffected by all formality, her way is with almost everyone; and this has always pleased me.

But even so—how radiant she was! Is she in love with someone?

Her family was one of the many who suffered from my father's crash. Of recent years the old colonel's wife has been in bad health and she often uses my services. I have never wanted to accept any fee, and of course they understand why.

She rides, too; I have seen her several times recently during my morning rides, in fact as recently as yesterday.

With a merry 'Good morning' she rode past me at top speed, then in the distance I saw her slow down at a curve in the road, and falling to a walk, ride on a long way with slackened reins, as if in a dream. . . . But I . . . I kept to my steady pace. In this way we rode past one another several times within a short space of time.

* * *

She isn't exactly beautiful, but there's something about her in some peculiar way close to what for many years, and up to quite recently, was my dream of woman. Such things can't be explained. Once, after a great deal of trouble—it must be two or three years ago now—I managed to get myself invited to the home of a family I knew she was friendly with, merely in order to meet her. And, indeed, she did turn up; but on that occasion she scarcely noticed me and we didn't exchange many words.

And now: I recognise her well enough. She is the same as she was then. It is myself I don't recognise.

July 17

No, sometimes life shows a face altogether too vile. Only a moment ago I came home from a night call. I was woken by the telephone ringing, took a name and address —it was quite close by—and a hint of what the trouble was: a child had suddenly fallen seriously ill, probably with the croup, at the home of so-and-so, a wholesaler. A cloud of drunken nightbirds and whores swarming about my coat-tails, I hurried through the streets. It was the fourth floor of a house in a side-street. The name I'd just heard on the telephone, and which I now saw on the front door, seemed familiar; although I could not place it. The wife received me in dressinggown and petticoat,—it was the lady from Djurgårdsbrunn, the same I remembered from that time years ago. So, I thought, it's the pretty little boy! I was shown through a narrow dining-room and an idiotic hallway, illuminated, just then, by a greasy kitchen lamp placed in the corner of a whatnot; and so into a bedroom. Evidently the master wasn't at home. "It's our eldest boy who is ill," the wife explained. She led me over to a little bed. In it lay, not the pretty little lad, but another, a monster. Enormous ape-like cheekbones, a flattened cranium, little evil stupid eyes. It was obvious at first glance: an idiot.

So—this was her first-born! It was him she was carrying under her heart, that time. This was the seed she begged me on her knees to free her from; and I answered with duty. Life, I don't understand you!

And now death at last wished to take pity on him and on them, take him away from the life he should never have entered. But it's not to be. There is nothing they long for so much as to be quit of him. Yet their cowardly hearts impel them, even so, to send for me, the doctor, to drive away kind merciful death and keep this monster alive. And I, no less a coward, do 'my duty'—do it now, as I did then.

All these thoughts, of course, did not immediately pass through my head as I stood there, wide awake in that strange room, beside a sickbed. I merely followed my calling, thought nothing—stayed as long as was necessary, did what had to be done; and left. In the hall I met the husband and father, who had just come home, somewhat under the influence.

And the ape-boy is going to live—perhaps for many years yet. The loathsome brutish face with its evil stupid eyes pursues me, even into my room. I sit reading in them the whole story.

He has been given those very eyes the world looked at his mother with, when she was big with him. And with those same eyes the world fooled her into looking at what she had done.

And now, here's the fruit—a lovely fruit!

The brutal father who hit her, the mother whose head was full of what friends and relatives would say, the servants who looked askance at her, giggling and rejoicing in their hearts at this confirmation that their 'betters' are no better than their inferiors, aunts and uncles who became stiff with idiotic indignation and half-witted morality, the clergyman who made short work of his sermon at the humiliating wedding, a little embarrassed, perhaps rightly, at having to exhort the contracting parties on our Lord's behalf to do what so blatantly was already done—all, all contributed their mite, all had their little part in what ensued. Not even the doctor was missing—the doctor, that was me.

Couldn't I have helped her that time when, in her hour of utmost need and despair, she went down on her bended knees in this room? Instead, I replied with duty, in which I did not believe.

But neither could I know, or guess. . . .

Her case, at least, was one of those where I was sure of myself. Even if I did not believe in 'duty'—did not believe it to be the supremely binding law it gives itself out as being—yet it was perfectly clear to me that in this case the right, the prudent thing to do was what others call their duty. And I did not hesitate to do it.

Life, I don't understand you.

* * *

"When a child is born deformed, it is drowned."

(Seneca)

* * *

Every idiot at the Eugenia Home costs more in annual

upkeep than a healthy young labourer earns in annual income.

The African heat has come back. All the afternoon it lies motionless over the town like a cloud of golden smoke. Not until dusk does it get cooler, bringing relief.

Almost every evening I sit for a while on the pavement outside. The Grand, sipping light lemonade through a straw. I'm fond of the hour when the lamps begin to gleam in the curves along the quayside. It's the best hour of my day. Usually I sit there alone; but yesterday I sat with Birck and Markel.

—I praise God, said Markel, that they've begun to light the street lamps again. I don't know myself in the darkness of these lampless summer nights we've been wandering about in so long. Although I know this arrangement has been made exclusively for reasons of economy, a perfectly respectable motive, that is, I cannot help thinking it has, even so, a certain vulgar flavour of being arranged to suit the tastes of tourists. 'Land of the Midnight Sun'—to the devil!

—Yes, Birck agreed, they could at least content themselves with putting out the lights for two or three nights around midsummer, when it really is almost daylight. Out in the country these twilight summer nights of ours are quite magical, but here they don't belong at all. Street lights are a proper ingredient of a town. I've never felt the happiness and pride of being a townsman so keenly as in my childhood when I came into town of an autumn evening and saw the lamps alight round the quays. Now, I thought to myself, now those poor wretches out there in the country have got to stay indoors if they don't want to stump about in darkness and filth.

—Though it's true, he added, in the country there's

quite another sort of starry sky from what we have here. Here, in competition with the gas-lamps, the stars succumb. And that's a pity.

—The stars, said Markel, simply aren't up to lighting our footsteps as we wander about in the night. It's sad to see how they've lost all practical importance. Once they regulated our whole life; and to open an ordinary penny-halfpenny almanack one would think they still did. It would be difficult to find a more striking instance of the toughness of tradition than the fact that the most popular almanacks are full of detailed information on matters which no living person any longer cares a fig for. All these astronomical signs which the poorest peasant had some idea of two hundred years ago and studied diligently, believing his whole well-being depended on them, —today they're unknown, incomprehensible, to most educated people. If the Academy of Science had any sense of humour it could amuse itself by shuffling the Crab, the Lion and the Virgin in its almanack, like lottery tickets in a hat, and the public wouldn't be any the wiser. The starry sky today has sunk to a purely decorative rôle.

He sipped his whisky, and went on:

—No, the stars can't congratulate themselves on enjoying at all the same popularity they once had. As long as one's fate was believed to hang on them, they were feared, but also loved and worshipped. And as children, of course, we all liked them. We imagined they were pretty little lights God lit up in the evening to amuse us. We thought it was us they were winking at. But now we know rather more about them they're only a constant, painful, insulting reminder of our own insignificance. One evening, maybe, one takes a stroll down Drottninggatan. One thinks thoughts, grandiose, yes, even epoch-making thoughts; thoughts no human being, one feels, has ever had the strength or courage to think in this world before.

Admittedly, somewhere deep down in our unconscious, lurks the experience of many years, whispering that, without a shadow of doubt, tomorrow morning we shall either have forgotten these same thoughts or else have no eye for their grandiosity, their epoch-making qualities. It's all one. As long as our thought-orgy lasts, nothing takes away an iota from our happiness. But one only has to look up by chance and see some tiny star sitting motionless between a couple of tin chimneys, shining and winking, to realise that one may as well forget them at once. Or else you go walking along, looking down into the gutter, wondering whether you're really right to drink yourself to death, or whether, perhaps, there isn't some better way of passing the time. Suddenly—and this really happened to me the other night—one stops, and gazes at a little sparkling point, down there in the gutter. A moment of reflection—and one realises it's a star that's mirrored there. To be precise it was Deneb, in the Swan. And at once it becomes obvious how absurdly unimportant the whole question is.

—Well, I permitted myself to remark, you can really call that looking at drunkenness from the angle of eternity. But it's hardly natural to us, while sober; and the method is hardly suited, anyway, to daily use. If the star Deneb were to hit on the idea of looking at itself *sub specie asternitatis* it would realise perhaps how altogether insignificant it is, and not take the trouble to shine any more. As things are, however, there it sits, for some while now, faithful at its post, and shines very prettily, doubtless mirroring itself not only in the oceans of planets unknown, whose sun it is, but even, now and then, in a gutter on our dark little earth. Follow its example, my dear chap! That's to say: generally speaking, and by and large—not only where the gutter is concerned.

—Markel, observed Birck, greatly overestimates the

range of his thinking, if he imagines he can consider even the least and weakest of his whiskies and sodas from the angle of eternity. It simply isn't within his power. He'd never come out alive. I seem to remember reading somewhere or other that to do this is God's exclusive prerogative. And that, no doubt, is why He has ceased to exist. . . . The recipe must have been too strong, even for Him.

Markel didn't reply. He looked serious and sad. At least, so it seemed to me, from what I could see of his face there in the darkness, under the great red-striped awning; and as he struck a match to relight his cigar, which had gone out, it suddenly seemed to me he'd grown old. He'll die between forty and fifty, I thought to myself. For the rest, he's well over forty.

Suddenly Birck, who was sitting in such a way that he could look out over the pavement towards the town, said:

—Look, there's Mrs Gregorius coming along. The woman who's married to that disgusting clergyman. God alone knows how she happened to get caught by him. Seeing those two together makes one turn one's head away. The simplest neighbourly consideration requires it.

—Is the Vicar with her? I asked.

—No. She's alone. . . .

Of course. The parson was still at Porla.

—I think she looks like a blonde Delilah, said Birck.

MARKEL: Then let's hope she has a proper understanding for her rôle in life and puts enormous horns on the Nazarite of the Lord.

BIRCK: I should hardly think so. Naturally, she's religious. Nothing else could explain that marriage.

MARKEL: On the contrary, according to my simple notions it would be incomprehensible if, after a suitable period of marriage with the Rev. Gregorius, she had the tiniest inkling of religion left in her—and anyway, she can't possibly be more religious than Madame de Maintenon. The true faith is an invaluable help in all life's predicaments and has never hindered the traffic.

Our talk fell silent as she went by in the direction of the Museum and Skeppsholmen. She was wearing a simple black dress. She walked neither slow nor fast, looked neither right nor left.

Yes, her walk. . . . Involuntarily, as she went by, I had to close my eyes. She has the walk of someone going to her fate. She went with her head lowered a little, so that the nape of her neck shone white under the fair hair. Did she smile? I can't say. But suddenly I chanced to recall my dream of the other night. The sort of smile she wore then, in that horrible dream. I have never seen her smile it in reality; and never wish to.

When I looked up again I saw Klas Recke going by in the same direction. As he passed us he nodded to Birck and Markel; perhaps also to me, it was hard to say. Markel waved to him to come and sit with us, but he passed on, pretending not to notice. He was following in her footsteps. And I thought I saw a strong hand holding them both, the same invisible string, drawing both of them in the same direction. And I asked myself: Where was the way leading, for her, for him? But what's that to me! The way she is going she would have gone without my help. I've merely removed a little of the nastiest dirt out of the way of her little feet. But her path, even so, is certainly a rough one. It must be. The world isn't kind to those who love. And in the end it leads into the darkness, for them and for all of us.

—Recke's been hard to get hold of recently, Markel said. I'm certain that rascal's up to something. I've heard it said he's after a little girl with a lot of money. Well, well, that's what will happen in the end, he has the debts of a crown prince. He's in the hands of the moneylenders.

—How do you know that? I asked, perhaps a shade more testily than there was any reason for.

—I don't, he replied insolently. I don't know it at all. But I perceive it. Vulgar minds have a way of assessing a man by his financial position. I go the other way about it: I assess the financial situation by the man. It's more logical. And I know Recke.

—You're not to drink any more whisky, Markel, Birck said.

Markel poured himself out another whisky, and one more for Birck, who sat staring into the empty air, pretending to see nothing. My drink was almost untouched, and Markel regarded it with a worried glance of disfavour.

Suddenly Birck turned to me:

—Tell me, he asked, are you looking for happiness?

—I suppose so, I replied. The only definition of happiness known to me is: what everyone in his own situation finds desirable. Therefore it must surely be self-evident that we are all trying to find it.

BIRCK: Of course. In that way it's self-evident. And your answer reminds me for the hundredth time that all philosophy lives by, and wholly feeds on, verbal ambiguities. Against the happiness-pancake so ardently desired by the mob, one person sets up his birthday-cake of salvation and another 'his work'; and both deny that they so much as know what is meant by trying to find happiness. An enviable gift this, of being able to deceive oneself with words. Haven't we all, always, a need to see ourselves and our efforts in the light of a certain ideality? Perhaps then in the last resort the deepest happiness lies in the illusion of not desiring happiness.

MARKEL: Man doesn't pursue happiness, only pleasure. "It's possible," said the Cyrenäics, "that there may be people who don't pursue pleasure; but, if so, the reason is that their intelligence is deformed and their judgment impaired."

—When philosophers, he went on, say that man seeks happiness, or 'salvation', or 'his work', they are only thinking of themselves, or at least of adults enjoying a certain degree of education. In one of his short stories Per Hallström relates how when he was small he used to pray: "The lantern comes, the lantern goes, whom God loves the lantern knows." [1]

Obviously at that tender age he didn't know the meaning of the word 'happiness' and therefore unconsciously replaced this unknown and uncomprehensible word with another, more familiar and easily understood. But the cells in our body know as little about 'happiness' or 'salvation' or a 'work' as infants do. And it's these cells that determine all our strivings. Everything on earth that goes under the name of organic life flees from pain and seeks pleasure. Philosophers are only thinking of their own conscious efforts, their *willed* efforts: that's to say, their imaginary efforts. But the unconscious part of our being is a thousandfold greater and mightier than the conscious, and it's the unconscious that tips the balance.

BIRCK: All you've just noted merely confirms my belief in what I said just now, that if we are to talk philosophy to any purpose, language must be re-made from the ground up.

MARKEL: Well, for God's sake, keep your happiness, I'll take the pleasure. Skål! But even if I agree to your way of using words, that doesn't mean it's true that everyone seeks happiness. There are people who haven't any gift for it at all and are painfully and ruthlessly aware of

[1] Swedish *'lyckan'*=happiness, *'lyktan'*=the lantern. An untranslatable verbal equivoce. "Happiness comes, happiness goes; whom God loves, happiness knows"—Swedish child's prayer. *Tr.*

the fact. Such people don't seek happiness, only to get a little form and style into their unhappiness.

And, suddenly without warning, he added:

—Glas is one of them.

This last astounded me. I just sat there, without a word to reply. Right up to the moment I heard my own name uttered I thought he was speaking of himself. And I still think so. It was simply in order to conceal it that he pounced upon me. An oppressive silence followed. I looked out over the glittering waters of The Stream. In the cloud-masses over Rosenbad the moonlight broke through, and a pale silvery light fell on the pillared façade of the old palace of the Bonde family. Over the Mälaren lakes a violet red cloud sailed on its solitary way, detached from the others.

July 25

Helga Gregorius: she is always before my eyes. I see her as I saw her in my dream: naked, holding out to me a bunch of dark flowers. Red perhaps, but very dark. Well, red is always dark in the twilight.

I never go to bed at night without wishing she would come to me again in my dreams.

But that ambiguous smile my imagination has gradually managed to erase; I see it no longer.

*   *   *

I wish the parson was back. Then she would be sure to come to me again. I want to see her and hear her voice. I want her close to me.

July 26

The clergyman: his face, too, persecutes me—with just that expression it wore at our last encounter, when I began to discuss sexual matters. How can I describe that expression? It was the expression of someone who smells something rotten and secretly finds the smell agreeable.

August 2

The moon is shining. All my windows are open. In my study the lamp burns. I have put it on my escritoire, in the lee of the night-breeze which with its gentle hush fills the curtain like a sail. I walk to and fro in the room, stopping now and then at my writing-desk and jotting down a line. For a long while I've been standing at one of the windows of the sitting-room, looking out and listening for all the strange sounds that belong to the night. But tonight silence reigns, down there beneath the dark trees. Only a solitary woman sits on a bench; she has been sitting there a long while. And the moon is shining.

* * *

When I came home at dinnertime a book was lying on my writing-desk. I opened it. A visiting card fell out: Eva Martens.

I remember she spoke of this book the other day, and I said, à propos of nothing, that it would be fun to read it. I said this out of politeness and in order not to be guilty of the indelicacy of scorning something in which she was interested. Since then I have not thought of the matter again.

But evidently she has.

Is it very stupid of me if I fancy she's just the littlest bit in love with me? I can see it written on her that she is in love. But if she loves someone else, how can she have so much interest over for me?

She has two bright, honest eyes and a wealth of brown hair. The nose is not perfectly modelled. The mouth—I don't remember her mouth. Oh yes, it's red and rather on the large side; but I don't see it clearly before me. And anyhow one is only really familiar with a mouth one has kissed, or longed very much to kiss. I know such a mouth.

I sit looking at the little simple, correct visiting-card, with the name in pale lithographic type. But I see more than the name. There's a sort of writing which only becomes visible under the influence of great warmth. Whether I possess such warmth, I don't know; but I can read the invisible writing even so: "Kiss me, be my husband, give me children, let me love. I am longing to be allowed to love."

"Here go many virgins, whom no man has yet touched, and who do not thrive by sleeping alone. Such shall have good men."

Thus, more or less, spake Zarathustra. The real one, the old one; not the chap with the whip.

Am I a 'good man'? Could I be her good man?

I wonder what image she can have formed of me. In her light heart, which contains only a few gentle and friendly thoughts about those close to her and perhaps a little rubbish besides, an image has formed, having certain outward features that are mine, but which is not me, and in that image, it seems, she is well pleased—God knows why, perhaps chiefly because I am unmarried. But if she really knew me, if by some chance for instance she happened to read what I write on these scraps of paper in the evenings, well then, I fancy she would shun the paths I walk in. I should think the gulf between our souls is a bit too broad. But who knows? When entering marriage it is fortunate, perhaps, if the gulf is as broad as this—if it were narrower, I should perhaps be tempted to try and fill it in, and that would never turn out well! But even so: to live side by side with her and never give her access to that which is truly me and mine—can one treat a woman so? Let her embrace another, believing it to be me—is it permissible to do such a thing?

Well, of course; of course one can! In reality, surely, this is what is always happening: we know so little about one another. We embrace a shadow and love a dream. And, anyway, what do I know about her?

But I'm alone and the moon is shining, and I long for a woman. I could be tempted to go over to the window and call her up, she who is sitting down there alone on the bench, waiting for someone who doesn't come. I have port wine and brandy and beer and good food and the bed has been made.

Wouldn't it be heaven for her?

*   *   *

I sit thinking of Markel's words the other evening, about myself and happiness. Verily, I might be tempted to marry and be as happy as a sandboy; just to annoy him.

August 3

Yes, the moon. There it is again.

I remember so many moons. Oldest of them all is the one that perched behind the windowpanes in my childhood's earliest winter evenings. Always it hovered over a white roof. Once my mother read Viktor Rydberg's *The Christmas Goblin* aloud to us children; I recognised it at once. But it still had none of the characteristics it was later to possess. It was neither wild nor sentimental, nor cold and horrible. It was just big and shiny. It belonged to the window, and the window belonged to the room. It lived in our home.

Later on, after they had noticed I was musical and let me take piano lessons and I'd got as far as being able to strum a little Chopin, then the moon became new for me. One night, I was about twelve then, I remember lying awake, unable to sleep because I had Chopin's Twelfth Nocturne running through my head, and because of the

moonlight. We were in the country. We had just moved
out there, the room where I lay was still without a blind.
The wild white moonlight flooded into my room, over bed
and pillow. I sat upright in bed and sang. I had to sing
that wonderful wordless melody that I couldn't get away
from. It melted into the moonlight and in both lay a
promise of something tremendous, something to be my lot
one day; I didn't exactly know what, an unhallowed happiness, or an unhappiness worth more than all the happiness in the world, something burning and delightful and
grand, awaiting me. And I sang until my father stood in
the doorway and yelled at me to go to sleep.

That was Chopin's moon. And it was the same moon
which afterwards shivered and burned over the water on
August evenings when Alice sang. I loved her.

Then, too, I remember my Uppsala moon. Never have
I seen a moon with so cold or averted a face. Uppsala
has quite another climate from Stockholm, an inland climate with air drier and clearer. One winter night I was
walking to and fro with an older friend on the white
snowy streets with their grey houses and black shadows.
We talked philosophy. With my seventeen years behind
me I scarcely believed in God; but I was being cussed
about Darwinism; it made everything seem meaningless,
stupid, squalid. We went in beneath a black vaulting and
up some stairs and stood close to the cathedral walls. The
builder's scaffolding made it seem like the skeleton of
some unheard-of monster from the depths of dead strata.
My friend spoke of our kinship with our brothers the animals; he talked and proved and shouted with a hoarse
uncultivated voice whose provincial accent echoed among
the walls. I did not say much in reply, but I thought to
myself: You're wrong, but I still haven't studied or
thought enough to be able to refute you. But wait—wait
just one year, and I'll come back to this same spot with

you, in the moonlight, just like it is now, and I'll prove
how wrong and stupid you are. For what you say cannot,
must not, on any terms whatever, be the truth; if it is
true, then I don't want to have any more part in things, I
have no business in such a world. But my comrade talked
and waved a little German volume he was holding in his
hand, and out of which he had got his arguments. Suddenly he stopped in the full light of the moon, opened the
book at a place where there were some illustrations to the
text and handed it to me. The moon shone so brightly I
could both see what it represented and read what was
written beneath. It was a picture of three craniums, rather
similar: the skulls of an ourangoutang, an Australian ab-
origine, and of Immanuel Kant. Seized with loathing, I
flung the book away from me. My comrade flew into a
rage and attacked me; we wrestled and fought in the
moonlight, but he was stronger and got me under him
and 'washed' my face in the snow, the way schoolboys
do.

One year passed, and others too, but I never felt equal
to refuting him; it was a job I found better left alone.
And though I do not really understand what business I
have in this world, still I have stayed in it.

And many moons I have seen since then. A mild and
sentimental moon between silver-birches by the lakeside.
. . . The moon scurrying through sea-mists . . . the
moon fleeing away through ragged autumn clouds . . .
the lovers' moon which shone on Gretchen's garden window and Juliet's balcony. . . . A girl no longer young
who wanted to get married told me once that she could
not help crying whenever she saw the moon shining over
a little wooden cottage in the forest . . . the moon is pas-
sionate and desirous, says a poet. Another tries to find a
tendentious ethical-religious meaning in moonbeams, lik-
ening them to threads the dear departed spin into a web

to catch errant souls in. For youth the moon is a promise
of all those tremendous things which await it, for older
people a memento that the promise was never kept, a reminder of all that broke and went to pieces. . . .

And what *is* moonshine?

Secondhand sunshine. Diluted, counterfeit.

The moon just now creeping out from behind the
church spire has a face of ill omen. Its features seem to
me distorted, dissolute, frayed by a nameless suffering.
Wretched man, why are you sitting up there? Are you
doomed, a counterfeiter—have you counterfeited the sunshine?

In truth, no mean crime. If one could only be certain
of never committing it.

August 7

Light!

. . . I sat up in bed and lit the lamp on my bedside
table. I had been lying in a cold sweat, my hair stuck to
my forehead. What was it I had been dreaming?

Always and always the same thing. That I killed the
clergyman. That he had to die because he already smelt
of the grave; and it was my duty to do it. . . . I found it
difficult, unpleasant. This was something unprecedented
in my practice—gladly would I have consulted a colleague, unwilling as I was to bear solitary responsibility in
so grave a matter. . . . But far off, Mrs Gregorius was
standing naked in a corner, in half-darkness, trying to
cover herself with a little black veil. And when she heard
me utter the word 'colleague' such a desperate and terrified look came into her eyes I realised it had to be done at
once. Otherwise, in some way I could not clearly understand, she was lost; and I must do it alone, in such a way
that no one would ever find out. So, my head averted, I

did it. How? I don't know. I only know I held my nose
and turned my head away, saying to myself: There, there,
now it's all over. Now he doesn't smell any more. And I
wanted to explain to Mrs Gregorius that it was a very rare
and strange case: most people, of course, only smell after
they are dead, and then they are buried; but if someone
smells while he's still alive, then he has to be killed, the
present state of science knows no other way out. . . . But
Mrs Gregorius had vanished and all round me was only a
great vacuum in which everything seemed to flee away and
avoid me. . . . The darkness lifted, giving way to an ashy
moonlight. And I was sitting bolt upright in my bed, wide
awake, listening to my own voice. . . .

I got up, put on a few clothes, and lit the lamps in all
the rooms. I walked to and fro with clocklike regularity, I
don't know how long. At length I stopped in front of the
sitting-room mirror and stared at my pale demented self,
as if at a stranger. But a fear of yielding to a sudden impulse and smashing to pieces that old mirror which has
seen my childhood, almost my whole life, together with
much that happened before I existed, assailed me; and I
went over and stood at an open window. The moon was
no longer shining. It was raining, and the rain blew full
into my face. It was a relief.

'Dreams run like streams.' . . . Hoary proverbial wisdom, I know you well. And in reality most of what one
dreams is not worth a second thought—loose fragments
of experience, often the silliest and most indifferent, fragments of those things consciousness has judged unworthy
of preservation but which, even so, go on living a shadow
life of their own in the attics and box-rooms of the mind.
But there are other dreams. As a lad I remember sitting a
whole afternoon pondering on a geometrical problem,
and in the end having to go to bed with it still unsolved:
asleep, my brain went on working of its own accord and

a dream gave me the solution. And it was correct. Dreams there are, too, like bubbles from the depths. And now I come to think of it more clearly—many a time has a dream taught me something about myself, often revealed to me wishes I did not *wish* to wish, desires of which I did not wish to take daylight cognizance. These wishes, these dreams, I've afterwards weighed and tested in bright sunshine. But rarely have they stood up to the daylight, and more often than not I've flung them back into the foul depths where they belong. In the night they might assail me anew, but I recognised them and, even in dreams, laughed them to scorn, until they relinquished all claim to arise and live in reality and the light of day.

But this is something else. And I want to know what it is, weigh it, assess it. One of the basic instincts of my being, it is, never to suffer in myself anything half-conscious, half-clear, whenever it lies in my power to bring it out into the light of day, hold it up, see what it is.

So, let's think:

A woman came to me in her hour of need and I promised to help her. Help, yes . . . neither of us, then, had realised or reflected on what this meant, or might come to mean. What she requested of me was, after all, so simple and easy. It cost me neither effort nor qualm of conscience, indeed it mostly amused me. I did this lovely woman a delicate service and at the same time played a nasty trick on that loathsome parson, the whole episode dropping into my dense black spleen like a rosy spark from a world closed to me. . . . And, for her, did it not mean life and happiness—as she saw it and got me to see it? I promised to help her, and so I did . . . what had to be done at the time.

But since then the whole thing has gradually come to wear quite another aspect, and this time I must take care to search out the heart of the matter before I proceed.

I promised to help her; but I don't like doing things by halves. And now, of course, I know and have known it a long while: she cannot be helped, short of being set free.

In a day or two the parson will be back—and the old tale begins all over again. I know him now. But not merely this; in the last resort she would anyway have had to get over it by herself, however hard it was, even if it tore her life to pieces and left her a shred. But there's something tells me, as if it had already come to pass, she will soon be bearing a child under her heart. Loving as she now does, there's little chance of her avoiding it. Per-. haps she doesn't even want to. And then: if this happens —when it happens—what then . . . ? Then the parson must be put away. Right away.

True: if this happens, then it's possible she will come to me and ask me to 'help' her with the same sort of help so many have begged for in vain—and if she does, well then, I suppose I shall have to accede, because I do not see how I can resist her in anything. But that's the end of the matter as far as I'm concerned. I've had enough.

But I feel, I feel and I know, it won't turn out like that. She isn't like the others, she'll never ask me for *that* sort of help.

And so the parson must go.

Turn and twist it as I will, I can see no other solution. Get him to see reason? Make him see he no longer has the right to foul her life, that he must set her free? Non-sense. She's his wife; he's her husband. Everything will be on his side: the world; God; his own conscience. Love, for him, is naturally the same as it was for Luther: a need of Nature, which his god once and for all has given him permission to satisfy with this particular woman. That she meets his desires with frigid distaste can never for a moment make him doubt his 'rights'. Anyway he as-sumes, I suppose, that at these moments she secretly feels

the same as he does, but as far as he's concerned it is perfectly in order that a Christian woman and a clergyman's
wife should not admit as much, even to herself. Even for
his own part he doesn't really like calling 'all that' a pleasure; he would rather it was called 'a duty' and 'God's
will'. . . . No, away with such a creature, away with him,
away!

Let me think: I was looking for a feat to perform,
wasn't I. Begging for it. Can this, then, be the feat, *my*
feat? The thing which has to be done, which I alone see
must be done, and which no one except myself can, or
dares, do?

One could say it looks a bit strange. But that's no reason, neither for nor against. An action's 'greatness' or
'beauty' is but the reflected light of its effect on the
public. But since it is my humble if natural intention to
keep the public in every sense out of this affair, this aspect needn't be considered. I am solely concerned with
myself. I want to inspect the seams of my action; see
what it looks like inside.

First and foremost: do I really seriously want to kill
the clergyman?

'Want to'—well, and what does that mean? A human
will is no unit; it's a synthesis of hundreds of conflicting
impulses. A synthesis is a fiction; the will is a fiction. But
we need fictions, and no fiction is more needful to us than
the will. Well then: *do you want to?*

I want to; and I don't want to.

I hear conflicting voices. I must interrogate them; I
must know *why* the one says: I want to, and the other: I
don't want to.

You first, who say 'I want to': Why do you want to?
Reply!

—I want to act. Life is action. When I see something
that makes me indignant, I want to intervene. If I don't

intervene every time I see a fly in a spider's web, this is because the world of flies and spiders is not mine, and I know one must limit oneself; and I don't like flies. But if I see a beautiful little insect with shimmering golden wings caught in a web, then I tear the web to pieces and kill the spider, if need be, for I do not believe it is forbidden to kill spiders. I go walking in the forest; I hear a cry of distress; I run towards the cry and find a man about to rape a woman. Naturally I do what I can to free her, and, if need be, kill the man. The law does not give me the right to do so. The law only gives me the right to kill another in self-defence, and by self-defence the law only means defence when in direct peril of my own life. The law does not let me kill someone else to save my father or my son or my best friend, or to protect my beloved from violence or rape. In a word, the law is absurd; and no self-respecting person allows his actions to be determined by it.

—But the unwritten law? Morality . . .?

—My good friend, the law, you know as well as I do, is in a state of flux. Even during those few fleeting moments the two of us have been living in this world, it has undergone visible changes. Morality, the proverbial line chalked round a hen, binds those who believe in it. Morality, that's others' views of what is right. But what was here in question was my view. True, in many cases, perhaps the vast majority, and in those that occur most often, my view of what is right is in tolerable agreement with others', with 'morality'; and in a multitude of other instances I even find the divergence of view arising between myself and morality is not worth the risks entailed in deviating from it; and therefore submit. Thus morality becomes consciously for me what it is in practice for each and every person, although all do not recognise it: not a fixed law, binding above all, but a *modus vivendi,* useful

for daily life in that unremitting state of war which exists
between oneself and the world. I know and I concede
that current morality in its broad and general outlines ex-
presses, like the bourgeois law, a concept of right and
wrong, the fruit of immemorial ages, handed down from
generation to generation slowly growing and changing,
concerning those conditions most necessary for mankind's
social existence. I recognise too that, if life here on earth
is to be at all liveable for such creatures as ourselves—
creatures not to be conceived within any other frame than
that of our social organisation and nurtured by all its
changing rights, libraries and museums, police and wa-
terworks, street lamps, nightly garbage disposal, changing
of the guard, sermons, opera, ballet, and so forth—these
laws, by and large, must be more or less generally re-
spected. But I know, too, that those individuals who have
had anything to them have never taken the law pedanti-
cally. Morality's place is among household chattels, not
among the gods. It is for our use, not our ruler. And it is
to be used with discrimination, 'with a little pinch of salt'.
For prudence sake we should always adopt the customs
of any place we come to, but to adopt them whole-heart-
edly or with conviction would merely be simple-minded.
I'm a traveller in this world; I look at mankind's customs
and adopt those I find useful. And morality is derived
from '*morales*', custom; it reposes entirely on custom,
habit; it knows no other ground. And I don't need to be
told that, by killing that parson, I'm committing an action
which is not customary. Morality—you're joking!

—I admit I raised the question largely as a matter of
form. Where morality is concerned I believe we see eye to
eye. But I'm not letting go of you, even so. Initially the
question we were discussing was not, in essence, how, flat
in the face of custom and morality, you dare to do what
we are talking of; it was a question *why* you want to. You

replied with a parable, the rapist who outrages a woman in the forest. What a comparison! On the one hand a crude criminal; on the other a blameless and respectable old clergyman!

—Yes, I admit my comparison limps a little. I referred to an unknown woman and an unknown man and to an imperfectly known relation between them. It isn't at all certain the unknown woman is worth my committing murder for her sake. Nor is it certain this unknown man who thus falls in with a young woman in the depths of the forest and is suddenly possessed and overwhelmed by Pan is, for that reason, worthy of death.

Finally, I cannot be sure such danger really threatens as would make such intervention necessary! The girl screams because she's frightened and because it hurts; but that's not to say the damage is to be measured by her screams. It may well turn out that these two people become friends before parting. Many a country marriage has begun with rape and yet turned out no worse than others and once upon a time the violent abduction of women was the normal form for engagement and marriage. If, therefore, in my chosen example, I kill the man to free the woman—the sort of action I fancy most people of moral views, jurists apart, would approve, and which, before a French or American jury, would even lead to my sensational acquittal, to public applause—I'm acting on pure impulse, without reflection; and it may well be I do something very stupid. But our affair is of quite a different order. Here is no question of an isolated case of rape, but of a relationship which is a matter of life and death and which, in essence, constitutes continuous, repeated rape. Here is no question of some man unknown, of value unknown, but of someone you know only too well! The Reverend Gregorius. Here it's a question of helping and saving, not a woman unknown, but your secret beloved. . . .

—No, no! That's enough! Not a word more!

—Can a man let the woman he loves be outraged, despoiled, trampled on, before his very eyes?

—Be quiet! She loves someone else. This is his business, not mine.

—You know you love her. Therefore it's your business.

—Be quiet! . . . I'm a doctor. And you want me hugger-mugger to murder an old man who comes to me for help!

—You're a doctor. How many times haven't you uttered that expression: Your duty as a doctor. Well, here it is now: perfectly clear, I think. Your duty as a doctor is to help the person who can and should be helped, and cut away the rotten flesh which is spoiling the healthy. Certainly, there's no glory to be reaped: you can't let anyone know of it, or you'll be sitting inside Långholmen or Konradsberg.

Afterwards I recall how a sudden gust of wind blew the curtain against the lamp, how its fringe caught fire and how I instantly stifled the little blue flame in my hand and shut the window. I did these things automatically, almost without being aware of it. The rain lashed the window-pane. The lights burned on, still and stiff. On one of them was a little fragile grey night-moth.

I sat staring at the stiff flames of the lamps, as if I wasn't there at all. I fancy I sank into a sort of coma. Maybe I slept a while. But suddenly I gave a start, as if from a violent shock, and remembered everything: the question that had to be solved, the decision to be taken, before I could go to rest.

Well, then, you *don't* want to: *why* don't you want to?

—I'm frightened. First and foremost, frightened of being found out and 'punished'. I don't underestimate your prudence and thoughtfulness on my behalf, and I can quite believe you will arrange everything so that it turns out satisfactorily. I deem it probable. But, even so, the risk is there. Chance. . . . One never knows what can happen.

—One has to risk something in this world. You wanted to act. Have you forgotten what you wrote here in your diary not so many weeks ago, before we knew anything of all that has happened since? Position, respectability, future, all these things you were ready to stow aboard the first ship to come sailing by laden with action. . . . Have you forgotten that? Shall I turn up the page?

—No. I haven't forgotten. But it wasn't true! I was bragging. I feel different, now I see the ship coming. Surely you can understand I never imagined it could be such a satanic ghost-ship? I was boasting. I tell you. Lying! No one can hear us; I can be honest. My life is empty, wretched, I see no sense in it; yet I cling to it; I like to walk in the sunshine and observe the crowd. I don't want to have something to hide and be frightened of. Leave me in peace!

—Peace, no—you won't have any peace, anyway. Do you want to see the woman you love drowning in a cess-pool, when by one bold swift action I can help her out? Will I have any peace then, can I ever be at peace, if I turn my back on her and go out into the sunshine and look at the crowd? Will that be peace?

—I'm frightened. Not so much that I'll be found out; I've always got my pills and can quit the game if people begin to smell a rat. But I'm scared of myself. What do I know about myself? I'm frightened of getting involved in something that binds and entangles me, never lets me go. What you require of me meets with no obstacle in my

views; it's an action of which, in anyone else, I should approve providing I knew what I know; but it's not my line
of country. It conflicts with my inclinations, habits, instincts, everything that's essentially me. I'm not made for
such things, I tell you. There are thousands of brisk, capital fellows who will as soon kill a man as a fly. Why can't
one of them do it? I'm afraid of having a bad conscience;
for that's what you get if you try to shuffle out of your
skin. To behave yourself means to know your limitations;
and I want to behave myself.

Every day people commit with the greatest ease and
pleasure actions which fly in the face of their deepest and
best-founded opinions, and their consciences thrive like
little fish in water. But try and act against your own in-
nermost structure, then you'll hear how your conscience
screams! Then you'll hear feline music! You say I've been
begging and pleading for an action to commit—it's impossible, it simply isn't true, there must be some misunder-
standing. It's unthinkable I ever had so insane a wish—I
who am a born looker-on, who want to sit comfortably in
my box and see how people on the stage murder each
other, while I myself have no business there. I want to stay
outside. Leave me in peace!

—Trash! You're just trash!

—I'm scared. This is a nightmare. What have I to do
with these people and their filthy affairs! The priest is so
loathsome to me I'm scared of him—I don't want his fate
mixed up with mine. What do I know about him? What I
loathe about him isn't 'him', himself, but the impression
he has made on me—he has certainly met hundreds and
thousands of people without affecting them as he does
me. The image he has deposited in my soul can't be
wiped out just because he disappears, least of all if he
disappears because of me. Already, alive, he has come to
obsess me more than I like; who knows what he can get

up to when he's dead? I know all about that. I've read Raskolnikov, I've read Thérèse Raquin. I don't believe in ghosts, but I don't want to bring things to such a pass that I shall begin to. What has all this got to do with me? I want to go away. I want to see woods and mountains and rivers. I want to stroll under big green trees with a finely bound little volume in my pocket and think beautiful, fine, benevolent, quiet thoughts, thoughts one can utter out loud and be famous for. Let me go, let me go away tomorrow.

—Trash!

Against the grey light of dawn the lamps burned with a dirty brown flame. On my writing-desk the night-moth lay with scorched wings.

I flung myself on my bed.

August 8

I've been riding and bathing. My morning surgery is over and I've paid my usual visits to my patients. Again evening falls. I am tired.

The brick tower of the church looks so red in the evening sun. The trees' greenery is so grand and dark just now, and the blueness beyond is so deep. It's Saturday evening: poor little children are playing hopscotch down on the gravel path. At an open window a man sits in his shirtsleeves, playing the flute. He plays the intermezzo from *Cavaleria Rusticana*. Strange, how melodies catch on! Scarcely ten years ago this tune arose out of chaos and crept over an impoverished Italian musician, perhaps one evening in the twilight, perhaps just such an evening as this. Inseminating his soul, it gave birth to other melodies, other rhythms and in consort with them instantly made him world-famous; gave him a new life, with new happiness, new sorrows, and a fortune to throw away at the tables at Monte Carlo. So the melody spreads out like

a disease all round the earth, doing its fated deed for
good or ill, bringing a blush to cheeks and making eyes
sparkle; is admired and loved by countless numbers, or in
others, often those who at first loved it most, awakens
only disgust and boredom. Ruthless, obstinate, it rings in
the ears of those who cannot sleep at nights; infuriates
the businessman who lies fretting because the shares he
sold last week have gone up; pains and disturbs the
thinker trying to collect his thoughts to formulate a new
law, or dances about in the empty spaces of an idiot's
brain. And all the while, as the man who 'created' it, perhaps more than any other, is sickened and plagued by it,
it calls forth salvoes of applause evening after evening
from the public in every place of entertainment on earth;
and the man over there plays it with feeling on his flute.

August 9

To will is to be able to choose. Oh, that it should be so
hard to choose!

Choice is self-denial. Oh, that self-denial should be so
hard!

A little prince was about to make an excursion. They
asked him: Will Your Highness go on horseback or by
boat? He answered: I want to ride on horseback and take
the boat.

We want to have everything, want to be everything.
We want to know all the pleasures of happiness, and
every depth of suffering. We want the pathos of action
and the peace of the onlooker. We desire both the desert's stillness and the uproar of the forum. At once we
wish to be the thoughts of the thinker and the voice of
the crowd; we want to be both melody and harmony. At
once! How can such a thing be possible!

"I want to ride on horseback and take the boat."

August 10

There's something flattened and empty about a watch without hands. It's reminiscent of a dead man's face. I am sitting looking at such a watch. In point of fact it isn't a watch at all, but an empty case with a beautiful old watch-face to it. Just now I saw it in the window of the hunchback watchmaker in the alley as I was coming home through the hot yellow twilight—a strange twilight; I've imagined such ends to days in the desert. . . . I went in and asked the watchmaker, who has mended my watch for me once, what sort of a watch it was, that had no hands. He threw me a coquettish hunchback's smile and showed me the lovely old silver case, a fine piece of work; he had bought the watch at an auction, but the works were worn out, useless, and his intention had been to put in some new ones. I bought the case as it was.

My intention is to put some of my pills inside it and carry it in my righthand waistcoat pocket as an appendage to my watch. A variant, only, to Demosthenes' idea of poison in a pen. There's nothing new under the sun!

* * *

Now night falls; already a star is winking through the foliage of the big chestnut tree. I have a feeling I shall sleep well tonight; it is cool and calm inside my head. Yet I find it hard to drag myself away from the tree and the star.

Night. Such a lovely word! Night is older than day, said the ancient Gauls. They believed the brief transient day was born of endless night.

The great, endless night.

Well, that's but a manner of speaking of course. . . . What is night, what is it we call the night? The slender conical shadow of our little planet. A little pointed cone of darkness in the midst of a sea of light. And this sea of light? what is it? A spark in space. The tiny effulgence around a little star: the sun.

Ah, what sort of a plague is this, that has seized on mankind, making them ask what everything is? What sort of a scourge is it, whipping them out of the family circle of their creeping and walking and running and climbing and flying brethren, here on earth; driving them out, to see their world and their life from above, from outside, with cold estranged eyes, and find it little, and nothing worth? Where are we going? Where will it all end? I must think of the woman's voice I heard complaining in my dream; I still hear it in my ears, the voice of an old woman, grown old with weeping: The world's on fire, the world's on fire!

Look at your world from your own point of view, not from some point in space. Modestly measure with your own yardstick, after your own status, your own predicament, the status and the predicament of man the earthdweller. Then life is large enough and a thing of consequence; and night endless, deep.

August 12

So gorgeously the sun shines on the weather-cock this evening!

I am fond of this lovely intelligent creature who always turns with the wind. To me he is a standing reminder of the cock who on a certain occasion crowed thrice, and an ingenious symbol of holy church, who is always denying her master.

In the churchyard the shepherd of the parish strolls slowly to and fro in the beautiful summer evening, supporting himself on the arm of a younger colleague. My window is open and outside it's so still that a word or two of what they are saying reaches up to me. They are talk-

ing of the imminent election of a new archbishop, and I
heard the rector mention the name Gregorius. He pro-
nounced the name without enthusiasm and with not entirely unmixed sympathies. Gregorius is one of those clergymen who have always had the laity on their side and
therefore their own colleagues against them. From his
tone of voice I gathered that the rector mentioned his
name more or less in passing, he did not regard him as
having any serious chances.

This is also my view. I do not think he has a chance. I
should be much surprised if he became Archbishop . . .

Today is the twelfth of August; he went to Porla on the
fourth or fifth of July and was to stay there for six weeks.
Therefore it will not be many days before we have him
here again, in health and spirits after his visit to the waters.

August 13

How is it to be done? I have known a long while now.
Chance has so arranged matters that the solution is as
good as given: my potassium cyanide pills which I once
made up without a thought to anyone but myself, must
be brought into service.

One thing is self-evident: there can be no question of
letting him swallow them at home. It must happen here,
at my place. It won't be nice, but I see no alternative, and
I want to bring this matter to a head. If he takes a pill at
home, on my prescription, and is promptly done for, it's
to be feared the police might tumble to a connection between these two facts. What is worse, she whom I wish to
save might easily be suspected and drawn into the affair,
her name sullied for life, perhaps condemned for
murder. . . .

Obviously nothing must occur which might arouse the
police. No one must know the parson has been given a

pill. He must die a perfectly natural death, from heart attack. Nor must *she* suspect anything else. For him to die
in my surgery is naturally rather bad for my reputation as
a doctor and will give my witty friends stuff for unpleasant comment: but that must make no odds.

One day he comes up to me, talks about his heart or
some other nonsense and wants me to certify that he is
better after his bathing cure. No one hears what we are
talking about; the big empty sitting-room lies between the
waiting-room and my surgery. I listen, tap, declare a remarkable improvement; but say there is, even so, one
thing which worries me a little. . . . I take out my pills,
explain they are a new drug against certain cardiac ail-
ments (I shall have to think up some name or other),
and advise him to take it at once. I offer him a glass of
port to wash it down with. Does he drink wine? Of
course, I have heard him cite the wedding at Cana. . . .
He shall have a nice little wine. Grönstedt's Grey Label. I
can see him in front of me; first he sips the wine, then he
puts the pill on his tongue, drains the glass and washes it
down. His spectacles reflect the window and hide his
glance . . . I turn away, go over to the window and look
out over the churchyard, stand drumming my fingers on
the window-pane . . . he says something, that it was a
nice wine, for example, but stops in mid-sentence . . . I
heard a thud . . . he's lying on the floor. . . .

But if he refuses to take his pill? Oh yes, he'll take it as
a delicacy, he's crazy about medicine . . . but *if?* Well, I
can't help it, the matter must drop. After all, I can't kill
him with an axe.

. . . He's lying on the floor. I remove the pill-box, the
bottle of wine, the glass. I ring for Kristin. The Vicar's ill,
a fainting attack, it'll soon pass over . . . I feel his pulse,
his heart:

—It's a stroke, I say at last. He's dead.

I ring up a colleague. Well now—who? Let me think. *He* won't do; seven years ago he wrote a thesis which I reviewed a bit sceptically in a medical journal. *Him;* too much sense. Him and him and him: gone away. *Him*— yes, we'll have to take him. Or else him; or, if need be, him.

I show myself in the doorway of my waiting-room, probably just about as pale as I ought to be, and declare in a low controlled voice that something has happened which obliges me to break off my surgery hour for today.

My colleague arrives. I explain what has happened. The Vicar had long been suffering from severe heart-trouble. In a friendly way he condoles with me on my wretched bad luck that the demise should have occurred just here, in my room, and at my request writes out a death certificate. . . . No, I won't give the clergyman any wine; he might spill it on himself, or the smell might give away the fact he has been drinking it, and that may be a troublesome thing to explain. . . . He'll have to be content with a glass of water. Anyway I'm of the opinion that wine is deleterious.

But what if it comes to an autopsy? Well, then I shall have to take a pill myself.

It is an illusion to suppose one can get embroiled in an undertaking of this sort without running a risk, so much I have known from the outset. I must be prepared for drastic developments.

Strictly, of course, the situation requires that I myself call for an autopsy. I don't see anyone else doing it— well, one can never be sure. . . . I tell my colleague I intend to ask for an autopsy; presumably he replies that it isn't really necessary, objectively speaking, the cause of death being obvious; but for form's sake it might be the right thing, after all. Afterwards I let the matter drop.

Here, anyway, is a flaw in my plan. I shall have to give it some closer thought.

Impossible, for the rest, to arrange every detail in advance. Chance will make its changes, even so. One must rely to some small degree on one's powers of improvisation.

Another thing—hell and damnation, what a fool I am! There isn't only myself to think of. Suppose it really does come to an autopsy and I swallow a pill and vanish through my trap-door to keep Gregorius company crossing the Styx, what explanation will be found for so rare a crime? Won't people turn for an explanation to the living —to *her?* Drag her before a court, examine her, bully her. . . . That she has a lover, will soon be sniffed out. That she must have desired the priest's death, longed for it to happen, would be almost self-evident. So much she might not even bother to deny. Everything turns black before my eyes. . . . And it would have been I who brought you to this pass, loveliest of blooms and of women!

I worry myself blind and grey over this.

But perhaps—perhaps I have an idea, even so. If I see an autopsy is necessary, then, in good time, before I take my pills, I must show clear symptoms of insanity. Still better—the one, indeed, does not exclude the other—I'll write a document which I shall leave lying open here on my desk in this room where I shall die; a paper scribbled all over with raving nonsense indicating persecution mania, religious *idées fixes,* and so forth. For years the priest has been persecuting me. He has poisoned my soul, therefore I have now poisoned his body. I have acted in self-defence, etc. Some biblical quotations can also be woven in, there are always a few that will suit. In this way light will be thrown on the affair. The murderer was crazy. That's explanation enough, no need to look for any other. I am given Christian burial and Kristin receives confirmation of what she has always secretly suspected— well, not always so secretly, either. She has told me a hundred times I am out of my mind. If need be, she can witness on my behalf.

August 14

I wish I had a friend to confide in. A friend to consult. But I have no one, and even if I did—after all there are limits to what one can ask of one's friends.

Always, I have been rather solitary. My loneliness I have borne about with me through the crowd as a snail his house. For some individuals solitude isn't a circumstance they've tumbled into by chance, but a trait, of character. And this, I suppose, can only deepen my solitude. Whatever happens, whether things turn out well or ill—for me the 'punishment' can only be solitary confinement for life.

August 17

Fool! Trash! Cretin!

But, what's the use of invective—no one can prevail over his nerves and stomach.

My surgery was over long ago. The last patient had just gone. I was standing at my sitting-room window, thinking of nothing, when suddenly I see Gregorius walking diagonally across the churchyard, straight for my doorway. Everything turned grey and misty. I hadn't expected him, didn't know he was back. I felt giddy, dizzy, sick, all the symptoms of sea-sickness. I had but one thought in my head: not now, not now! Another time, not now! He's coming up the stairs, he's standing outside my door, what am I to do. . . . Out to Kristin: If anyone asks for me, tell them I'm out. . . . From her wide eyes and gaping mouth I realised I looked strange. Rushing

into my bedroom, I locked the door. I only just reached
the handbasin in time: then I vomited.

*   *   *

So, my fear was right? I'm not up to it!

For it was just now it should have happened. He who
wants to act must seize his chance. No one knows
whether it will ever come back. I'm not up to it!

August 21

Today I've seen her and talked to her.

I walked out to Skeppsholmen in the afternoon. Just
across the bridge I met Recke: he was coming down from
the hill where the church is. He walked slowly, looking at
the ground, underlip thrust out, knocking pebbles out of
his way with his stick. He didn't seem exactly pleased
with his existence. I thought he wouldn't see me; but just
as we passed each other he looked up and nodded in a
gay and hearty manner there was no mistaking, his whole
face changing expression. I went on my way, but halted
after a few steps. She can't be far away, I thought. Perhaps she's still up there on the hill. They've had something to say to each other and have had a rendez-vous up
there where hardly anyone ever goes; and so as not to be
seen with him she has let him go down first. I sat down
on the bench which surrounds the poplar, and waited. I
should think it must be the biggest tree in Stockholm.
Many a spring evening in my childhood have I sat beneath this tree with my mother. Father never came; he
didn't like taking walks with us.

No, she didn't come. I thought I should see her coming
down from the hill, but perhaps she had gone down another way, or had never been there at all.

Anyway, I went up the hill by a roundabout path, past
the church—and there I saw her, sitting crouched on one

of the steps outside the church door, leaning forward, chin in hand. She sat looking straight into the sun, which was just then setting. That was why she did not immediately notice me.

The very first time I ever saw her it struck me how unlike all others she is. She isn't like a woman of the world, or a middle-class wife, or a woman of the people. Mostly the last, perhaps; particularly as she sat there, just then, on the church steps, with her fair hair free and bared to the sun, for she had taken off her hat and laid it beside her. But a woman from a primitive folk, or one that never existed, where class distinctions had not yet begun, where 'the people' still had not become the lower classes. A daughter of a free tribe.

Suddenly I saw she was weeping. Not with sobs, only tears. Crying like one who has wept much and hardly notices she is doing it.

I wanted to turn back and go away, but at the same moment I realised she had seen me. I saluted her a little stiffly, made to walk past. But at once she got up from the low step, as lightly and softly as from a chair, and coming forward put out her hand. Hastily she dried her tears, put her hat on and drew a grey veil over her face.

We stood silent awhile.

—It's lovely up here this evening, I said at last.

—Yes, she said, it's a lovely evening. And it has been a lovely summer. Now it will soon be over. The trees are already turning yellow. Look, a swallow!

A solitary swallow flitted past us, so close that I felt the air fanned cold on my eyelids. It curved sharply, its course seeming to the eye to make an angle acute as an arrowhead, and then vanished into the blue.

—The heat came so early this year, she said. That usually means an early autumn.

—How is the Vicar? I asked.

—Thank you, she replied. Quite well. He came home from Porla a couple of days ago.

—And is he at all better?

She averted her head a little, screwing up her eyes as she looked into the sunlight.

—Not from my point of view, he isn't, she replied in a low voice.

I understood. Just as I had expected. Well, it was not exactly hard to guess. . . .

An old woman was sweeping up withered leaves. She came closer and closer to us, and slowly we walked out of her way, further out on to the hillside. As I walked I thought of the clergyman. First I had scared him with his wife's health; that had worked for hardly two weeks. Then I had scared him with his own, and grim death; and that had worked for six. And, if it had worked for so long, then only because he had been separated from her. I begin to think Markel and his Cyrenäics are right: people care nothing for happiness, they look only for pleasure. They seek pleasure even flat in the face of their own interests, their own opinions, their faith, their happiness. . . . And the young woman who was walking beside me so straight and proud, though her neck with all its fair silken tresses was bowed deep beneath worries—she had done exactly the same: sought pleasure, caring nothing for happiness. And now it struck me for the first time how it was precisely the same behaviour which, while it filled me with disgust for the old clergyman, inspired in me an endless sympathy for the young woman, yes, with a shy awe as in the presence of the godhead.

Through the thick cloud of dust over the town the sun shone less brilliantly now.

—Tell me, Mrs Gregorius,—may I ask you a question?

—Please do.

—The man you love—I don't even know who he is—

what does he say about all this, and the whole business? What does he want to do? What does he want to come of it? Surely he can't be satisfied with things as they are—?

A long silence. I began to think I had asked something stupid and that she did not wish to answer.

—He wants to take me away, she said at length.

I started.

—And *can* he? I asked. I mean, is he a free man, well-to-do, independent of employment or profession, a man who can do as he likes?

—No. Or we should have done it long ago. He has his whole future here. But he wants to make a new way for himself in a foreign country, far away. Perhaps America.

I had to smile within myself. Klas Recke and America! But when I thought of her I felt cold. I thought: over there, thanks to precisely those same qualities that keep him afloat here, he'll go straight to the bottom. And then what will become of her?

I asked:

—And you yourself—do *you* want to go?

She shook her head. Her eyes filled with tears.

—I mostly want to die, she said.

Gradually the sun drowned in the grey mist. A chill breeze sighed through the trees.

—I don't want to ruin his life. Be a burden to him. Why should he go away? It would only be for my sake. His whole life is here, position, future, friends, everything.

There was nothing I could reply to this, she was only too right. And I thought of Recke. Such a suggestion, coming from him, seemed to me so strange. I should never have expected such a thing of him.

—Tell me, Mrs Gregorius—you regard me as your friend, don't you? Therefore I can be your friend. You don't dislike me talking to you about these things?

She smiled at me through her tears and veil, yes, she smiled!

—I'm very fond of you, she said. You've done something for me which no one else could or would have done. You may talk to me about anything you wish. I like it so much when you talk.

—Has he, your friend, has he wanted it for a long time, for you to go away together? Has he been talking about it long?

—Never before this evening. We met up here shortly before you came. He has never spoken to me about it before.

I began to understand. I asked:

—Does that mean something has happened just now . . . since he has hit on this idea? Something worrying?

She bowed her head:

—Perhaps.

Again the old woman with the broom was sweeping up her leaves close to us; we went back toward the church, slowly, in silence. We stopped by the steps where we had first met. She was tired: she sat down again on the step, and put her chin in her hand, gazing out into the grey falling dusk.

Neither of us spoke for a long while. Everything around us was still, but over our heads the wind soughed through the treetops with a sharper tone than before, and there was no more warmth in the air.

She shivered.

—I want to die, she said. I should so terribly like to die. I feel I have had everything that is mine, all I was meant to have. Never again can I be so happy as I've been these weeks. There has seldom been a day when I haven't wept; but I've been happy. I regret nothing, but I want to die. Yet it's so difficult. I think suicide is ugly, particularly for a woman. I do so loathe any violence to nature. And I don't want to bring him any sorrow, either.

I was silent and let her speak. She screwed up her eyes.

—Yes, suicide is ugly. But it can be even uglier to go on living. It's terrible how often one's only choice is between that which is more or less ugly. If I could only die!

—I'm not afraid of death. Even if I believed there was anything after death I wouldn't be frightened of it. Nothing I have done, either good or evil, could I have done otherwise; I've done what I had to do, in big things as in small. Do you remember how I once talked to you of my first love, and said I regretted not giving myself to him? I don't regret it any longer. I don't regret anything, not even my marriage. Nothing could have happened otherwise than it has.

—But I don't believe there is anything after death. As a child I always imagined the soul as a little bird. In an illustrated history of the world belonging to my father I saw how the Egyptians, also, depicted it as a bird. But a bird flies no higher than there is air, and that isn't far. It, too, belongs to earth. In school we had a natural history teacher who told us how nothing of what exists on earth can ever leave it.

—I'm afraid he got that a bit mixed up, I interposed.

—It's possible. Anyway, I gave up my bird-faith, and the soul became vaguer to me. Some years ago I read everything I could lay my hands on about religion, both for and against. Of course it helped me to clear my mind on a number of matters, but I never learned what I wanted to know. There are people who write so extraordinarily well, I believe they can prove anything. I always thought the one who wrote best and most beautifully was right. I worshipped Viktor Rydberg. But I felt and understood that, on the subject of life and death, no one knew anything.

A high warm colour came into her cheek in the dusk.

—But latterly I've come to know more about myself than in my whole life before. I've learned to feel and understand that my body is me. There is no joy, no sorrow, no life at all, except through it. And my body knows very well it must die. It feels it, as an animal can feel it. And that is how I now know there is nothing for me on the other side of death.

It has grown dark. The buzz of the city came up to us more strangely in the darkness, and down there at the corners of quays and bridges the lamps began to be lit.

—Yes, I said, your body knows it will one day have to die. But it doesn't *want* to die; it wants to live. It doesn't want to die until it's worn out and burdened with years. Consumed by suffering and burned up by pleasure. Then, and not until then, will it want to die. You think you want to die because everything looks so bleak just now. But you don't really want it, I know you can't want it. Let time go by. Take each day as it comes. Sooner than you realise, everything can change completely. You, too, can change. You are strong and healthy; you can be stronger still; you are one of those who can grow and be renewed.

A shiver passed through her form. She got up:

—It's late. I must go home. We can't go down from here together, it wouldn't do for anyone to see us. Go that way, and I'll go in the other direction. Good-night!

She gave me her hand. I said:

—I should so like to kiss your cheek? May I?

She lifted her veil and proffered her cheek. I kissed it. She said:

—I want to kiss your forehead. It is beautiful.

The wind tugged at my thinning hairs as I bared my head. And she took it between her warm soft hands and kissed my brow—ceremoniously, as if in a rite.

August 22

What a morning! A faint feeling of autumn in the glass-clear air. And still.

Met Miss Mertens on my morning ride and exchanged a few gay words with her as we passed. I like her eyes. I think there's more depth in them than one sees at first. And then her hair. . . . But after that there's not so much to add to the list of her merits. Oh yes, without question she has a good little character too.

I rode round Djurgården thinking all the while of her who had sat on the steps up there by the church and looked into the sun and wept, and who longed to die. And in truth: if no help comes, if nothing occurs—if that which I am thinking does not occur—then any attempt to help her with words is only silly chatter; this much I felt, even as I was speaking to her. Then she would be right, right a hundred times over, to seek death. She can neither go away nor stay. Go away—with Klas Recke? Be a burden to him, a ball chained to his leg? I bless her for not wanting to. They would both go under. He is nicely off here, so they say, with one foot in his department of the Civil Service and the other in finance. I have even heard people call him a man with a future, and if he has debts, well, things are no worse for him than they are for many other 'men with futures' before their position is made. He has just that amount of talent which usually helps a man on—in the right environment, of course; an elemental force he certainly is not. 'Make his own way' . . . no, that's not his line at all. No more can she go on living her old life. A prisoner in enemy territory. Bear her child under a strange man's roof and be obliged to play the hypocrite and lie to him and see his disgusting paternal joy—diluted, it may be, with suspicions he dare not voice but which he will make use of in order still further to poison her life. No, she quite simply *cannot do it;* if she tries, it will end with some catastrophe. . . . She must be free. She must be on her own, free to decide over herself and her child, as she may wish. Then everything will turn out well for her, life will become possible and good for her to live. I have sworn an oath on my soul: she shall be free.

During my surgery hour just now, I was in a horrible state of tension. I thought he would come today, I seemed to feel it in my bones. . . . He did not come, but that's all one; whenever he comes, he will not find me unprepared. What happened last Thursday is not to be repeated.

Now I am going out to have dinner. I should like to meet Markel, then I could invite him to dine with me at Hasselbacken. I want to talk, drink wine, see people.

Kristin has already got my dinner ready and she will be livid; but it's all one.

(Later)

It's over. It's done. I've done it.

So queerly it came about. So strangely did chance arrange it for me. I might almost be tempted to believe in providence.

I feel light, empty, like a blown egg. As I came in through the sitting-room door just now and saw myself in the mirror the expression on my face made me start. There was something empty, flat, about it; something, I don't know what, reminding me of the handless watch I carry about with me in my pocket. And I had to ask myself: What you've done today—is that all there has been inside you, is nothing left?

Foolishness. A feeling that will go over. I'm a little tired in my head. So much I may be allowed.

It's half-past seven; the sun has just set. It was a quarter-past four when I went out. Three hours, that is . . . three hours and a few minutes.

. . . Well, I went out to have dinner somewhere; I cut obliquely across the churchyard; walked through the alley; stopped a moment outside the watchmaker's window, was greeted with an ingratiating hunchback grin from the man inside, and replied to it, making, I remember, this reflection: Every time I see a hunchback, sympathy makes me feel something of a hunchback myself. Presumably a reflexual effect of that sympathy with misfortune drummed into us in childhood. . . . I came out into Drottninggatan; went into the Havana Store and bought two good Uppmanns; turned the corner into Fredsgatan. Entering Gustaf Adolf's Square I threw a glance into the window of Rydberg's, just in case Markel happened to be sitting there over his absinthe, as he sometimes does. But only Birck sat there in front of a glass of lemonade. A bore; I didn't feel the least inclination to have dinner with him tête à tête.

Outside the newspaper office I bought an *Aftonblad* and stuck it in my pocket. Maybe there's something new in it about the Dreyfus Affair, I thought . . . but all the while, as I went on walking, I was wondering how I could lay my hands on Markel. No use ringing up his office, he's never there at that time; and as I thought this I went into a tobacconist's and telephoned. He had just gone out. . . . On Jakob Square, then, far off, I saw the Rev. Gregorius coming towards me. I was making ready to salute him, when all of a sudden I discovered it was not him at all. There was not even any particular resemblance.

—So, I thought to myself, I'll meet him soon, then.

For according to popular belief, which I recalled my own experience had confirmed on some occasion, to mistake a person in this way is a sort of intimation. I even remembered having read in a pseudo-scientific journal 'for psychic research' a story about a man who, after such a 'warning', turned sharply into a sidestreet in order to avoid a disagreeable encounter—and ran straight into the arms of the very person he was seeking to avoid. . . . But I do not believe in such nonsense, and all the while my thoughts were still engaged in this razzia after Markel. It occurred to me I had once or twice met him at this time of day by the lemonade kiosk on the market-place. So I went there. Naturally, he was not to be seen, but anyway I sat down on one of the benches beneath the great trees by the church wall to drink a glass of Vichy water while I glanced through my *Aftonblad*. Hardly had I unfolded it and fastened my eyes on the standing bold-type headlines: The Dreyfus Affair—when I heard heavy crunching steps on the gravel, and the Rev. Gregorius stood before me.

—Well, now, if it isn't you, Doctor. How are you, how are you. May I sit down? I was just going to drink a glass of Vichy water before dinner. Surely that can't be bad for the heart, can it?

—Well, I replied, carbon dioxide isn't good, of course, but a little glass now and then can't do you much harm. How do you feel after your visit to the baths?

—Very fit. It was just what I needed, I think. I paid you a visit a few days ago, Doctor, Thursday I think it must have been, but I came too late. You'd gone out.

I replied that more often than not I am available for half-an-hour or so after my surgery hour is over; but that day I had unfortunately been obliged to go out a little earlier than usual. I asked him to come tomorrow. He was not sure he had time, but he would try.

—It's beautiful at Porla, he said.

(It is very ugly at Porla. But Gregorius, a townsman,

habitually finds 'the country' beautiful, whatever it looks like. What was more, he had paid for it and wanted to get the last drop of value for his money. So he found it beautiful.)

—Yes, I replied, it's quite nice at Porla. Though less beautiful than most other places.

—Perhaps Ronneby is more beautiful, he conceded. But it's such a long and expensive journey.

A half-grown girl served our Vichy water, two small quarter bottles.

Suddenly I had an inspiration. Since it has got to happen,—why not here? I looked about me. No one was near us just then. At a table far away sat three old gentlemen, one of whom, a retired cavalry captain, was known to me; but they were talking loudly together, telling tales and laughing, and so were not able to hear what we said or did.

A dirty little barefoot girl came padding up to us, proffering us flowers. We shook our heads and she silently vanished. Before us spread the gravel spaces of the square, almost empty at this late afternoon hour. Now and then, from the corner by the church, a pedestrian would take a short-cut down to the eastern avenue. A warm late summer sun gilded the Dramatic Theatre's old yellow façade between the linden trees. On the pavement the manager of the theatre was standing talking to the producer. The distance reduced them to miniatures, the play of their outlines only to be grasped and interpreted by an eye already familiar with them. The producer was betrayed by his red fez, which gleamed like a little spark in the sunshine, and the manager by those delicate movements of his hands which seemed to say: Well, damn it all, there are two sides to everything! I felt sure he was saying something of the sort. I saw the slight shrug of his shoulders, even seemed to hear his tone of voice. And I applied the words to my own affairs. Yes, there are two sides to everything. But no matter how wide you open your eyes to both of them, in the end you are obliged to choose only one. And I had long ago made my choice.

From my waistcoat pocket I took out the watchcase with the pills, selected a pill between my thumb and forefinger, turned aside slightly, and pretended to take it. Then I drank a gulp of water out of my glass, as if to wash it down. The clergyman was at once interested:

—I believe you're taking medicine, Doctor? he said.

—Yes, I replied. We've bad hearts, both of us. Mine isn't all it ought to be, either. Comes from smoking too much. If only I could give up smoking, I'd never need this rubbish; it's quite a new drug. I've seen it highly recommended in German medical journals, but I felt I ought to try it out myself before using it in my practice. I've been taking it for more than a month now, and find it excellent. You take one pill shortly before dinner; it hinders 'food fever', the distress and palpitations that immediately follow a meal. May I?

I proffered him the little box. Its lid was open, and turned in such a way he could not see it was a watch-face; that would only have given him stuff for unnecessary questions and chatter.

—Thank you, thank you, he said.

—I can write out a prescription for them tomorrow, I added.

Without further questions he took a pill, and swallowed it down with a draught of water. I thought my heart would stand still. I stared straight ahead of me. The square lay empty, dry as a desert. A majestic police constable walked slowly past, stopped, flicked a grain of dust off his well-brushed overcoat, and went on along his beat. The sun still shone as warm and yellow on the wall of the Dramatic Theatre, as before. Now the manager made a gesture he uses but rarely, the Jewish gesture of out-turned hands, the businessman's gesture meaning: I turn it inside out, I hide nothing, I put my cards on the table. And the red fez nodded twice.

—This lemonade stall is an old one, the clergyman said. It must be the oldest of its sort in Stockholm.

—Yes, I replied, without turning my head. It's old.

The clock on Jakob's Church struck thrice. A quarter to five.

Mechanically I took out my watch to see if it was keeping good time; but I fumbled, and my hand shook so that I dropped it on the ground, smashing the glass. Bending down to pick it up again I saw a pill lying on the ground; it was the one I had just pretended to take. As I crushed it beneath my foot, I heard the clergyman's tumbler fall over on the tray. I did not want to look, yet I saw his arm fall limply down and his head nod on his breast and the senseless eyes wide open. . . .

Ridiculous, but that was the third time since I came home I've got up and made sure my door is properly shut. What have I to fear? Nothing. Not the least thing! I have done my business, neatly and delicately, whatever else might be said about it. Chance, too, helped me. It was lucky I saw the pill lying on the ground and trod it to pieces. If I had not dropped my watch, I suppose I should never have seen it. So it was lucky I dropped my watch. . . .

The parson is dead, of a heart attack; I myself wrote out the death certificate. Hot and breathless from walking in the strong summer heat, and altogether too violently and without waiting for it to settle, he drank a big glass of vichy water. This I explained to the majestic police constable, who had turned and come back; to the terrified

little waitress; and to a few curious persons who had
gathered. I had advised the clergyman to wait a little, let
the fizziness go out of his vichy water before he drank it;
but he was thirsty and wouldn't listen. "Yes", said the
constable, "as I went by just now I saw how violently and
thirstily the old gentleman drank his water. And I
thought: that isn't good for him. . . ." Among the pas-
sers-by who stopped was a young curate, who knew the
deceased. He undertook to inform Mrs Gregorius, as
gently as possible.

"I've nothing to fear. Why, then, do I keep on feeling
my door? Because I sense the enormous atmospheric
pressure of others' opinions; the living, the dead, and the
still unborn, gathering out there, threatening to blow down
the door and crush me, pulverize me . . . that's why I try
the lock.

At last, when I got away, I climbed up on to a tram,
the first I could get hold of. It took me far out on to
Kungsholemen. I went on by road as far as the Traneberg
Bridge. We lived there once, one summer, when I was
four or five years old. It was there I caught my first perch
on a bent pin. I remembered the precise spot where I
stood. Again I stood there a long while, inhaling the familiar smell of stagnant water and sun-dried tar. Now, as
then, swift little perch darted hither and thither under the
water. I remembered how greedily I had looked at them,
and how hot my longing had been to catch them. And
when at last I succeeded, and a tiny, tiny perch, hardly
three inches long, was squirming on my hook, I screamed
with delight and ran straight home to Mamma with the
little fish hopping and shivering in my clutched hand.
. . . I wanted us to eat it for dinner; but Mamma gave it
to the cat. That was fun, too. To see how he played with

it and then to hear the bones crunching between his fierce teeth. . . .

On my way home I went into the Piperska Muren to have dinner. I did not expect to meet anyone I knew, but three doctors were sitting there and they waved to me to come and join them. I drank a glass of pilsner and left.

What am I to do with these pieces of paper? My habit hitherto has been to lay them in the secret drawer of my chiffonier; but this is no good. An eye of the least experience immediately perceives that such an old piece of furniture must have a secret drawer, and easily finds it out. If, in spite of all, something should happen, something not to have been foreseen, and anyone should hit on the idea of ransacking my home, they would soon be discovered.

But how am I to get rid of them? I know: I have a lot of cardboard boxes on my bookshelf, cases shaped like books, filled with scientific jottings and other old papers, carefully arranged in order and with labels on their backs. I'll have them in among my notes on gynaecology. And I can mingle them with sheets from my older diaries, for I have kept a diary before; never regularly, never for long, but periodically. . . . Anyhow, for the time being it's all one. I shall always have time to burn them, if need be.

*   *   *

It's over. I'm free. Now I shall shake this off, and think of something else.

Yes—but what?

I'm tired and empty. I feel absolutely empty. Like a punctured boil.

The simple fact is, I'm hungry. Kristin will have to heat up my dinner and bring it in.

August 23

All night it has been raining and blowing. Autumn's first storm. I lay awake listening to two boughs of the great chestnut tree outside my window creaking against each other. I remember I got up and sat by the window awhile, watching the ragged clouds chase one another across the sky. In the reflected gaslight they took on a dirty, fiery, brick-red glow. The church spire seemed to be bending to the storm. The clouds took on the shapes of dirty red devils blowing horns and whistling and screeching in wild pursuit as they whipped the rags off each other's bodies in all sorts of whoredom. And as I sat there I suddenly burst out laughing: I laughed at the storm. I thought I was taking the whole affair altogether too seriously. I was acting like the Jew when lightning struck just as he was eating a pork chop; he thought it was for the chop's sake. I was thinking of myself and my affairs; therefore I fancied the storm did the same. At length I dropped off to sleep in my chair. A cold shiver woke me. I went back to bed, but not to sleep. So at length a new day dawned.

A still grey morning, now; but it rains and rains. And I have a terrible cold in the nose. Already I've drenched three handkerchiefs.

Opening the newspaper over my morning coffee, I saw that the Rev. Gregorius was dead. Quite suddenly, a stroke. . . . by the lemonade stall in Kungsträdgården Park . . . one of the better-known doctors, who chanced to be in his company, could only confirm that death had occurred. The deceased was one of the capital's most popular preachers . . . had the ear of the public . . . an agreeable and open-hearted personality . . . fifty-eight years old . . . mourned by a wife, née Waller, and an aged mother.

Ah well, for God's sake, that's the way we must all go. And his heart had long been weak.

But he had an old mother, did he? I didn't know that. She must be frightfully old.

There's something grim and unpleasant, I see, about this room, particularly on these rainy days. Everything here is old and dark and moth-eaten. But I don't feel at home with new furniture. At all events I think I shall have to get some new curtains for the window, these are too dark and heavy and keep the light out. One of them is scorched along its edge since that night last summer when the lamp flickered and it caught fire.

"That night last summer. . . ." Let me think, how long ago can that be? Two weeks. And to me it seems a whole eternity.

Who could have guessed he had his mother still alive. . . .

How old would my mother have been now, if she had lived? Oh, not so terribly old, at that. Hardly sixty.

She would have had white hair. Perhaps she would find hills and stairs rather heavy going. Age would have made the blue eyes, lighter than everyone else's, still lighter now, and they would smile cheerfully under her white hair. She would have been happy that things have turned out so well for me, but even more would she have mourned for my brother Ernst, who is in Australia and never writes. She never had anything but sorrow and worry over Ernst. That's why she liked him best—But who knows, she might have changed into something else if she had lived.

She died too early, my mother.
But it's a good thing she's dead.

(Later)

Just now, as I came home in the twilight, I stood on
the threshold of the sitting-room, petrified. On the table
in front of the mirror stood a bunch of dark flowers in a
vase. It was dusk. They filled the room with their heavy
scent.

They were roses. Dark, red roses. Two were almost
black.

In my room, immense in the twilight, I stood stock
still, hardly daring to move, hardly breathing. I thought I
was walking in a dream. The flowers by the mirror—
surely they were the flowers from my dream?

For a moment I was afraid. I thought: this is a hallucination; I'm beginning to go to pieces, this is the beginning
of the end. I dared not go over and take the flowers in
my hand for fear of grasping empty air. Instead, I went
into my study. On the desk lay a letter. With trembling
fingers I broke the envelope, thinking it might have some
connection with the flowers; but it was only an invitation
to dinner. I read it and wrote a word in reply on a visiting card: 'Coming'. Then I went out into the sitting-room
again: the flowers were still there. I rang for Kristin; I
wanted to ask her who had brought these flowers. But no
one answered the bell. Kristin had gone out. No one was
in the flat except myself.

My life is beginning to merge into my dreams. To keep
life and dream apart is beginning to be too much for me. I
know all about that, I've read about it in big books: it's the
beginning of the end. But anyway the end must come one
day and there's nothing I'm afraid of. My life becomes
more and more a dream. And perhaps it has never been

anything else. Perhaps I've been dreaming the whole time, dreamt I'm a doctor and my name is Glas and that there was a parson who was called Gregorius. And at any moment I can wake up and find I'm a street-cleaner or a bishop or a schoolboy or a dog—how should I know. . . ?

What nonsense. When dreams and premonitions begin to come true and it isn't a question of servant-maids and old women but more highly organised individuals, then psychiatry says it is a sign of incipient psychic disintegration. But how explain it? The explanation is that in the great majority of cases one has never dreamed what 'comes true'; we *think* we have dreamed it or that we have gone through precisely the same thing before, even to the minutest detail. But my dream wth the dark flowers I have written down! And the flowers themselves they are no hallucination, they stand there, alive, I can smell them, and someone has come here with them.

But who? There's only one person I can guess at. Does this mean she has *understood*? Understood, approved, and sent me these flowers as a sign and an acknowledgment? But that's mad, it's impossible! Such a thing simply doesn't happen, can't be allowed to happen. It would be too awful. Such a thing simply cannot be allowed. There are limits to what a woman may be permitted to understand! If it is so, then I don't understand anything any more, I don't want any further part in this game. Yet they are lovely flowers.

Shall I put them on my writing-desk? No. They can stay where they are. I don't want to touch them. I'm afraid of them. I'm afraid.

August 24

My cold turned into quite a little bout of influenza. I've closed my doors to my patients, so as not to infect them, and I keep indoors. I've told Rubins I'm coming to dinner.

I can do nothing, not even read. Just now I was playing patience with an old pack of cards left by my father. I believe there are as many as a dozen old packs of cards in the drawer of the delightful mahogany card-table, a piece of furniture which alone could send me to perdition, if I had the least thirst for play.

As one opens it, the table-top is covered with green baize; it has long grooves along the edge of the markers, and the most delicate inlay.

Well, that was just about all he did leave me, my good father.

Rain, rain. . . . And it isn't raining water, but dirt. The atmosphere is no longer grey, it's brown. And when, sometimes, the rain falls less heavily awhile, it lightens to a dirty yellow.

On the top of the patience cards on my table lie the scattered leaves of a rose. Why have I been pulling off its petals? I cannot say. Perhaps because I happened to recall how, as children, we once used to throw rose petals into a mortar and roll them into beads, which we thereafter threaded on to bits of string and gave to Mamma as a necklace for her birthday. They smelt so nice, those beads. But after a few days they shrivelled up like raisins and had to be thrown away.

The roses—well, there was a tale, too! The first thing I saw when I went out into the sitting-room this morning was a visiting-card, lying on the mirror table beside the flower vase: Eva Mertens. To this very moment I do not understand how I could have failed to see it yesterday. And how at the very furthest corner of hell could it have entered the head of that nice pretty girl to send flowers to me, unworthy sinner? By straining my perspicacity, and overcoming my modesty, I can certainly make a guess at the deeper reason; but the immediate cause? Her pretext? However much I ponder the matter I can think of no other reason than this: She has read or heard tell how I happened to be present on the sad occasion of the clergyman's death; she supposes I am deeply shaken and therefore wishes to send me this evidence of her sympathy. She has acted suddenly, impulsively and as seemed most natural to her. That girl has a good heart. . . .

Supposing I let her love me? I am so lonely. Last winter I had a grey-striped cat, but he ran away at the first approach of spring. Now, as the glow of my first autumn fire dances on the flame-red mat, I remember him; just there, in front of the stove, he used to lie purring. In vain I strove to win his affection. He lapped up my milk and warmed himself by my fire, but his heart remained cold. What became of you, Puss? You had bad blood in you. I fear you'll have gone to pot—that's if you're alive at all. Last night I heard a cat screech in the churchyard, and I was sure I recognized your voice.

*   *   *

Who was it said: "Life is short, but hours are long." It should have been a mathematician like Pascal, but wasn't it Fénélon? Pity it wasn't me.

*   *   *

Why did I thirst for action? Most, perhaps, to cure my boredom. *"L'ennui commun à toute créature bien née,"* as Queen Margot of Navarre put it. But it's a long time now since tedium was the privilege of 'persons of birth'. Judging by myself and a few others known to me, it rather looks as though with the rise in enlightenment and welfare it's well on the way to spreading throughout the populace.

Action came to me as a great strange cloud, flung its lightning, and passed over. And tedium remained.

Anyway this is the most damnable influenza weather. On days like these a smell of old corpses seems to me to rise from the churchyard and force its way in through walls and windows. The rain drips on the window-sill. I feel as if it were dripping on my heart, to hollow it out. There's something wrong with my brain. I don't know whether it's too bad, or too good; but certainly it isn't what it ought to be. To make up for it, I feel my heart, at least, is in the right place. Drip—drip—drip. Why are the two little trees by Bellman's grave so thin and wretched? They must be diseased, I think. Perhaps poisoned by gas. He should be sleeping beneath great sighing trees, old Carl Michael. Sleep, yes—are we allowed to sleep? Soundly? If one only knew—two lines from a famous poem come into my head:

> *L'ombre d'un vieux poète erre dans la gouttière*
> *Avec la triste voix d'un fantôme frileux.*

"The shade of an old poet wanders in the roof-gutters, its voice sad as a frozen ghost's." Luckily for Baudelaire, he never had to hear what it sounds like in Swedish. Altogether, it is a damnable language we've got. The words trample on each other's toes and jostle one another in the gutter. And everything so crude and tangible! No half-tones, no airy allusions or soft transitions. A language which seems to have been created to suit the mob's ineradicable habit of blurting out the truth in all weathers.

It becomes darker and darker: December darkness in August. The black rose petals are already shrivelled. But in all this greyness the cards shine on my table, crude laughing colours to remind me how they were once invented to dissipate the melancholia of a sick and crazy prince. But the mere thought of the work involved in collecting them, turning them right side up and shuffling them into another game of patience, makes me mad, and I can only sit looking at them and hearing how "The Knave of Hearts and the Queen of Spades whisper grimly of their buried loves", as the same sonnet says:

> *Le beau valet de coeur et la dame de picque*
> *Causent sinistrement de leurs amours défunts*

I could wish to go over to the filthy old hovel, in the corner there, and drink stout with the girls. Smoke a sour pipe and take a spade with the madame and give her some good advice on her rheumatism. Fat and blooming, she was here last week, bewailing her lot. Under her double chin she wore a thick gold brooch, and paid cash with a five kronor note. A return visit would flatter her.

A ring at the hall door. Now Kristin opens. . . . What can it be? Haven't I said I'm not receiving anyone today . . . a detective? . . . pretending to be ill, in the guise of a patient. . . . Come in, my dear fellow, I'll put you to rights. . . .

Kristin half opened the door and flung a letter with black borders on to my table. Invitation to attend the funeral. . . .

*   *   *

—My deed, yes. . . . "If Monsieur wishes to have that History in heroic verse, it will cost him 8 skilling. . . ."

August 25

In a dream I saw figures from my youth. I saw her whom I kissed one midsummer night long ago, when I was young, and hadn't killed anyone. Other young girls I saw, too, who belonged to our circle in those days; one who was being prepared for confirmation the year I took my student exam and who was always wanting to talk to me about religion; another, older than I, who was only too willing to stand whispering with me in our garden in the twilight behind a jasmine hedge. And another who always made a fool of me, but who, when I made a fool of her for a change, became furiously angry and went into convulsions of weeping. . . . Pale, they walked in a pale twilight, their eyes wide open and terrified, making signs to each other when I approached. I wanted to speak to them, but they turned away and wouldn't answer me. In my dream I thought: It's quite natural. I've changed so, they don't recognise me. But at the same time I realised I was deceiving myself, and that they recognised me only too well.

Waking, I burst into tears.

August 26

Today was the funeral, in Jakob's Church.

I went; I wanted to see her. I wanted to see whether I could catch a spark from her starry eyes, through the veil. But she sat bowed deep beneath her widow's weeds, and didn't lift her eyelids.

The officiating clergyman spoke on Syrak's words: "From morning until evening the time changeth and all things are speedy before the Lord." He has the reputation of being a child of this world. And it's true I've often seen his pate gleaming in the stalls of theatres, and his white hands forming themselves into discreet applause. But he is a prominent rhetorician of the spirit, and it was clear that he, too, was deeply moved by the old words which through inconceivable generations have rung out on occasions of sudden death and hastily opened graves, and which so vividly express the terror felt by the children of men under the unknown hand that casts its shadow over their world, as enigmatically sending them day as night, and life and death. "Immobility, permanence are not given unto us," the clergyman was saying. "It would not be good for us, not possible for us, no, nor even bearable. The law of change belongs not only to death: first and foremost it is the law of life. Yet again we stand here, no less amazed, no less shuddering at change, when suddenly we see it accomplished, and in a way so different from anything we had ever expected. . . . It should not be so, my brethren. We should reflect: The Lord knew the fruit was ripe, although to us it did not seem so, and He has let it fall into His hand. . . ." I felt my eyes becoming moist, and hid my emotion in my hat. At that moment I almost forgot what I knew of the reasons why the fruit had so hastily ripened and fallen . . . or, to be more exact, I felt at root I knew no more about it than anyone else did. All I knew were a few of the most immediate reasons and circumstances, but behind these the long chain of causation lost itself in darkness. I felt my 'action' to be a link in a chain, a wave in a greater movement; a chain and a movement which had had their beginning long before my first thought, long before the day when my father first looked with desire upon my mother. I felt the law of *necessity:* felt it bodily, as a shiver passing through marrow and bone. I felt no guilt. There is no guilt. The shiver I felt was the same as I sometimes feel from great and serious music, or very solitary and elevated thoughts.

It was many years since I had been in a church. I recalled how, as a boy of fourteen or fifteen, I had sat in these same pews, grinding my teeth with fury at the fat scoundrel in his get-up at the altar, and thinking to myself how all this humbug perhaps might last yet another twenty, or at most thirty, years. Once during a long dreary sermon, I decided to become a clergyman myself. It seemed to me the clergy I had seen and heard were mere bunglers at their job, and that I could do all this far better myself. I should rise, become a bishop, archbishop. And, once an archbishop—by jove, then people would hear some funny sermons! Then there would be crowds in Uppsala Cathedral! But before the clergyman had got to his Amen my story was already over: I had a close friend at school with whom I used to discuss everything; I was in love with a girl; and then, too, I had my mother. To become a bishop I should have had to have lied and pretended to them, too; and that was impossible. A few people, there must always be, one can be honest with. . . . O Lord, that time, that innocent time. . . .

Strange it is to sit and let one's thoughts carry one back to a mood and a mental world of long ago. Thus one feels the flight of time. The law of change, the preacher was saying, (he's got that out of some play by Ibsen, by the bye). It is like seeing an old photograph of oneself. And I thought, too: how long a time can be left me still to wander about at random in this world of enigmas and dreams and phenomena that elude interpretation? Twenty years, maybe; maybe more . . .? If by some ghostly means I had been able at sixteen to see in a vision my life as it is now, how would I have felt?—Who am I in twenty years, in ten? What shall I think, then, of my life today? These days I have been expecting a visit from the Furies. They haven't put in an appearance. I don't believe such things exist. But, who knows—Perhaps they are in no hurry. Perhaps they think they have plenty of time. Who knows what, given a few years, they can do to me?—Who am I in ten years?

So, as the ceremony moved to an end, my thoughts like butterflies fluttered about me. The church doors were thrown open, people jostled at the exit under a din of

bells, and under the portals the coffin staggered and
swayed like a ship at sea, and a fresh autumn breeze
struck me. Outside, a greyish sky and thin pale sunshine.
I, too, felt greyish, thin, and pale, as one does after sitting
a long while squeezed inside a church, particularly at a
funeral or holy communion. I went to the bath house in
Malmtorgsgatan, to take a Finnish bath.

When I had undressed, and entered the *bastu*, I heard
a well-known voice:

—It's as hot and jolly in here as in a little departmental office of hell. Stina! Brushing in three minutes!

It was Markel. He sat crouched on a shelf, right up
under the ceiling, imperfectly hiding his gnawed-off bones
behind a fresh *Aftonblad*.

—Don't look at me, he said, as he caught sight of me.
Priests and journalists shalt thou not see naked, saith the
preacher.

I wound a wet towel round my head and stretched myself out on a shelf.

—A propos of priests, he went on, I see the Rev. Gregorius was buried today. You were at the church, perhaps?

—Yes, I've just come from there.

—I was on duty at the office when the news of his
death came in. The man who brought in the copy had
made up a long sensational story with your name all
mixed up in it. Which, I thought, was unnecessary. I
know you don't care much for publicity. I rewrote the lot
and crossed out most of it. As you know, our paper represents an enlightened sector of public opinion and we
don't make much fuss about a clergyman having a stroke.
Though, of course, a few kind words have to be said, and
they cost me no great pains. . . . 'Agreeable' came of its
own accord, naturally; but it wasn't enough. So it occurred to me he probably had a fatty heart or something

of that sort, since he died of a stroke. And my portrait was finished: an agreeable and open-hearted personality.

—My dear friend, I said, yours is a beautiful calling.

—Yes, and that's nothing for you to laugh at, he replied. Let me tell you something: there are three sorts of people—thinkers, scribblers, and cattle. It is true I secretly count almost all who are called thinkers and poets among the scribblers, and most of the scribblers belong among the cattle. But that's not the point. The business of thinkers is to search out the truth. There is, however, a secret about truth which, oddly enough, is but little known, although I should have thought it was clear as daylight—and it is this: truth is like the sun, its value depends wholly upon our being at a correct distance away from it. If the thinkers were allowed to have everything their own way they would steer our globe straight into the sun and burn us all to ashes. Small wonder, then, their activity sometimes causes the cattle to become restive and bellow: Put out the sun, in the name of Satan, put it out! It's the business of us scribblers to preserve a correct and satisfactory distance from the truth. A really good scribbler—and there aren't many!—*understands* with the thinker, and *feels* with the cattle. It's our job to protect the thinkers from the rage of the cattle and the cattle from too hefty doses of truth. But I admit the latter duty is the easier of the two, and the one we make the best job of in the ordinary way of things; and I admit, too, that in this we have the invaluable help of a mass of spurious thinkers, as well as of the more sensible among the cattle. . . .

—My dear Markel, I replied, you speak wise words, and quite apart from the suspicion, which dawns on me, that you reckon me neither among the thinkers nor the scribblers, but as one of the third species, it would be a real pleasure for me to dine with you. On that unfortunate day when I met the clergyman by the lemonade stall, I had been running all over town looking for you with just this in mind. Can you get free today? If so we'll drive out to Hasselbacken . . .?

—Excellent idea, replied Markel. An idea which alone suffices to class you among the ranks of the thinkers. There are thinkers, I forgot to mention, of such refinement that they hide themselves among the cattle. They are the genteelest sort of all, and I have always regarded you as being one of them. What time? All right, six o'clock, that's perfect.

I went home to free myself of my black trousers and white scarf. At home a pleasant surprise awaited me: my new dark grey suit which I ordered last week was ready and delivered. A blue waistcoat with white spots also forms part of it. It would be hard to achieve a more perfect confection for a Hasselbacken dinner on a fine day in late summer. On the other hand I was worried about Markel's appearance. For in this respect he is completely unpredictable, one day he can be turned out like a diplomat and the next like a tramp—after all, he knows all sorts of people and is as accustomed to move about in public as at home in his rooms. My anxiety was due neither to vanity nor to fear of others: I am a known man; I have my position; and I can dine at Hasselbacken with a hackney coachman if it amuses me; and as for Markel, I always feel honoured by his company without thinking of his clothes. But it wounds my sense of beauty to see a careless turn-out at a beautifully laid table in an elegant restaurant. It can take away at least half my pleasure. There are bigshots who like to underline their grandeur by going about dressed like junk merchants: this is indecent.

I had made my rendez-vous with Markel by Tornberg's clock. I felt pleasant and free, rejuvenated, renewed, as if

I had recovered from an illness. The fresh autumn air seemed spiced with the scent of my youthful years. Perhaps this could be traced to the cigarette I was smoking. I had got in a sort which used to delight me in times gone by, but which I had not smoked for many years. . . .

I found Markel in a sparkling good humour, with a scarf resembling a scaly green snakeskin and, in general, so rigged out that Solomon in all his glory was not nearly as chic as he. We got into a cab, the cabby cracked his whip, gave a flick to stimulate both himself and his horse, and drove off.

Markel had greater authority in the place than I, so I had asked him to telephone and make sure of a table for us near the rail of the verandah. While we made up our programme we dallied over an aquavit, a couple of sardines and some salted olives: Potage à la chasseur, fillet of plaice, quails, fruit. Chablis: Mumm extra dry; Manzanilla.

—So you didn't come out to Rubin's on Thursday? asked Markel. Our hostess certainly missed you. She said you have such a nice way of remaining silent.

—I had a cold. Quite impossible. Sat at home and played patience all the morning, and around dinnertime I went to bed. What sort of people were there?

—Oh, a whole menagerie. Birck, among others. He's managed to shed his tapeworm. Rubin told us how it happened: some while ago Birck reached a solemn decision to let his civil service job go to the devil, and devote himself wholly to literature. And when his tapeworm got wind of it, the wise beast also made a decision, and took itself off to another market.

—Well, and does he mean it seriously? I mean Birck?
—Not he! He's quite content to have made his decision, and stay in the Customs and Excise. And now he's trying to make out it was only a *ruse de guerre*. . . .

At a far-off table I fancied I glimpsed the face of Klas Recke. Yes, it was really he. In a *partie carrée* with another gentleman and two ladies. I knew none of them.

—Who are these people over there Recke is sitting with? I asked Markel.

He turned, but could not catch sight either of Recke or his company. The noise around us grew, competing with the orchestra, which was intoning the Boulanger March. Markels face darkened. He is an impassioned Dréyfusard and in this musical number he fancied he perceived an anti-Dreyfus demonstration, put on by a clique of lieutenants.

—Klas Recke? he resumed. I can't see him. But he must be out play-acting with his future in-laws. He'll soon sail into port, I should think. A girl with money has cast her really rather pretty eyes on him. But, à propos pretty eyes, I was sitting beside a certain young Miss Mertens at dinner at Rubin's. A nice girl, really charming. I've never seen her there before. I don't recall how it came about, but I happened to mention your name, and as soon as she realised we were close friends she couldn't talk about anything else and began asking me all sorts of things I didn't know the answers to. . . . Then, suddenly, she fell silent and the lobes of her ears turned scarlet. As far as I can see she's in love with you.

—You're a bit hasty in your conclusions, I objected.

But I reflected on his remarks about Recke, not knowing what to believe. Markel talks so much, without there being anything in it. It's his one weakness. And I didn't like to ask. But he was still talking about Miss Mertens, and spoke so heatedly I felt obliged to jest:

—Obviously you're in love with her yourself. It's burning a hole in your waistcoat! Take her, my dear Markel, I shan't be a dangerous rival. Me you can easily oust.

He shook his head. He was serious and pale.

—I'm out of the running, he replied.

I said nothing and we fell silent. The waiter served the champagne with the gravity of an acolyte. The orchestra began the Overture to Löhengrin. The rain clouds of the day now passing had blown over, massing themselves in rosy streaks along the horizon; but overhead the empyrean had deepened to infinite depths of blue, blue as this wonderful blue music. I listened to it, and forgot myself. The thoughts and ponderings of recent weeks and the deed in which they had culminated now seemed to me to be floating away into the blue distance, like something already gone, already unreal, something secreted and detached, never to trouble me any more. I knew I should never again wish or be able to do such a thing. Did this mean it had all been a mistake? After all, I had acted as best I knew how. I had weighed and tested, for and against. I had plumbed the matter to the bottom. Had I made a mistake? It was all one, now. At that moment the secret leit-motif broke through in the orchestra: "Thou shalt not ask!" And in this mystical sequence of notes, and these four words, I fancied I descried a sudden revelation of an ancient and secret wisdom. "Thou shalt not ask!" Not go to the bottom of things: or you yourself will go to the bottom. Not seek truth: you won't find it, only lose yourself. "Thou shalt not ask!" The little quantum of truth that is any use to you, you receive gratis and for nothing; and if it is mixed with lies and errors, this too is for your health's sake; undiluted, it would sear your entrails. Don't try to purge your soul of lies, so much else you didn't think of will follow in their wake; you'll only lose yourself, and all that's dear to you. "Thou shalt not ask!"

—When we want to get a subsidy for the Opera out of the Riksdag, said Markel, we have to dun it into their heads that music has an 'ennobling influence'. I wrote some such nonsense myself in a leader last year. Of course, it's true, in a way, although translated into a language comprehensible to our legislators. In the original it would read: Music excites and strengthens, it heightens and confirms. Confirms the pious in his innocuousness, the warrior in his courage, the debauchee in his vices. Bishop Ambrosius banned chromatic progressions in church music since, in his own experience, they gave rise to unchaste fantasies. In the 1730's there was a clergyman at Halle who saw in Handel's music a clear confirmation of the Augsburg Confession. I have the book myself. And out of a motif from Parsifal a good Wagnerian constructs a whole view of life.

We had reached the coffee. I offered Markel my cigarcase. He took a cigar, and gazed at it attentively.

—This cigar has a serious countenance, he said. It must be a good one. Otherwise, I was a bit worried over the cigar question. As a doctor you must know that the good cigars are the most poisonous. Therefore I was anxious you might give me some damned rubbish.

—My dear friend, I replied. From a hygienic point of view the whole of this dinner mocks common sense. In what concerns the cigar, it belongs to an esoteric strain in the tobacco industry. Its appeal is to the elect.

Around us the public had begun to thin out, the electric lighting was turned up and, outside, darkness began to fall.

—Yes, said Markel suddenly, now I see Recke. I can see him in the mirror. And sure enough he's in the company of the lady I surmised. I don't know the others.

—Well, and who is she?

—Miss Lewinson, daughter of the stockbroker who died last year . . . she has half a million.

—And you think he's going to marry for money?

—Why, certainly not! Klas Recke is a man of breeding

and sensibility. Calm yourself. You can be sure he will
first of all arrange to fall passionately in love with her,
and then marry for love. All this he will manage so well,
the money will come to him almost as a surprise.

—You know her?

—I've met her, once or twice. She looks very nice. The
nose is a shade too sharp, perhaps, and the intellect too.
A young woman who with an impeccable sense of probity
trims her sails between Spencer and Nietsche, and says
"There and there *he* is right, but there and there the other
one has hit the bullseye"—such a woman disturbs me,
but not in the right way. . . . What did you say?

I hadn't said anything. I sat lost in thought, but my
lips, it may be, had moved with my thoughts; perhaps
without knowing it I had mumbled something to myself. I
saw her before me, she who is ever in my thoughts. I saw
her walking to and fro in an empty street at dusk, waiting
for someone who did not come. And I mumbled to myself:—Dear one, this is your affair. All this you must go
through alone. No one can help you here, and even if I
could, I should not wish to. Here you must be strong.
And I thought further: It's a good thing you're free and
on your own, now. That way you will come through it
more easily.

—No, Glas, we can't go on like this, said Markel, dis-
tressed. How long do you imagine we're going to sit here
without a drop of whisky?

I rang for the waiter and ordered whisky and a pair of
rugs, for it was beginning to be chilly. Recke and his
party got up and passed our table without seeing us. Indeed he saw nothing at all. He walked with the purpose-
ful gait of a man who aims steadily at a goal. A chair lay
slightly in his path. Not noticing it, he knocked it over.
All around us the restaurant was empty. An autumn wind
sighed in the trees. The dusk grew greyer, denser. Draped

in our rugs like red mantles we sat on a long while, talking of matters both low and sublime; and Markel said things which are too true to be affixed with signs upon paper, and which I have forgotten.

August 27

Another day gone, and again it is night and I am sitting at my window.

Lonely one, beloved one!

Do you know already? Do you suffer? Do you stare with waking eyes into the night? Do you writhe in anxiety on your bed?

Do you weep? Or have you no more tears?

But perhaps he is fooling her up to the very end. He is considerate. He remembers she is in mourning for her husband. As yet he has not let her suspect anything. She sleeps soundly, knowing nothing.

Dearest, you must be strong when it comes. You must get over it. You will see how much life still has in store for you.

You must be strong.

September 4

The days come and go, one like another.

And immorality, that flourishes still, I note. Today, for a change, it was a man who wanted me to help his girl-friend out of a fix. He talked about old memories and headmaster Snuffe in Ladugårdslandet.

I was unshakable. I recited my doctor's oath to him. This impressed him to the extent of his offering me two hundred crowns cash, and a bill to the same amount, to-

gether with his lifelong friendship. It was almost touching;
he seemed to be rather badly off.

I threw him out.

September 7

From dark to dark.

Life, I do not understand you. Sometimes I feel a spiritual giddiness, whispering and warning and muttering that
I have gone astray. I felt like this just now. I took out my
procès verbal of the trial: the papers of my diary where I
cross-examine both my interior voices: the one that was
willing, and the one that was unwilling. I read it over and
over again, and couldn't come to any conclusion, other
than that the voice I finally obeyed was the one with the
right ring to it, and that it was the other which was hollow. The latter was perhaps the wiser, but I should have
lost my last ounce of self-respect if I had obeyed it.

And yet—and yet . . .

I have begun to dream of the priest. This of course was
to be expected, and therefore it does not surprise me. I
thought I should escape it precisely because I had foreseen it.

*   *   *

I understand King Herod's distaste for prophets who
went about waking up the dead. In other respects he held
them in high regard. But this branch of their activities
met with his disapproval. . . .

*   *   *

Life, I do not understand you. But I am not saying it is

your fault. I deem it more probable that I am an unnatural son, than that you are an unworthy mother.

And at long last the suspicion begins to dawn on me —perhaps we aren't intended to understand life? All this rage to explain and understand, all this chasing after truth, perhaps it's a wrong turning? We bless the sun because we are living exactly at that distance from it which is healthy for us. A few million miles nearer or further away, and we should burn up or freeze to death. What if it's the same with truth as with the sun?

The old Finnish myth says: He who sees God's face must die.

And Oedipus. He solved the enigma of the Sphinx, and became the unhappiest of mortals.

Not guess at riddles! Not ask! Not think! Thought is an acid, eating us away. At first we imagine it will only eat into that which is rotten and sick and must be removed. But thought thinks otherwise. It eats blindly. It begins with the prey you most gladly throw to it—but don't imagine it will be content with that! It doesn't stop until it has gnawed away the last thing you hold dear.

Perhaps I ought not to have thought so much; perhaps I should have gone on with my studies. 'The sciences are useful because they prevent men from thinking.' It was a scientist who said that. Perhaps I, too, should have lived out my life, as it is called, or 'lived it up', as it is also called. I ought to have gone skiing, kicked a football, lived healthily and gaily with women and friends. I should have married, put children into the world. I ought to have *done* my duty. Such things become footholds, supports. Perhaps, too, it has been stupid of me not to have thrown myself into politics or appeared at elections. The fatherland also makes its demands on us. Well, perhaps there will still be time for that. . . .

The first commandment: Thou shalt not understand too much.

But he who understands that commandment—has already understood too much.

I rave, everything goes round and round.

September 9

I never see her.

Often I go out awhile to Skeppsholmen, merely because it was there I last spoke with her. This evening I stood on the heights by the church and watched the sun set. It struck me how beautiful Stockholm is. I hadn't thought so much about it before. One is always reading in the newspapers that Stockholm is beautiful, so one attaches no importance to it.

September 20

At dinner at Mrs P's today Recke's imminent engagement was spoken of as a known thing.

I become steadily more impossible in company. I forget to answer when people speak to me. Often I don't even hear. I wonder if my sense of hearing is beginning to fail?

And then, these masks! They all wear masks. Worst of all, it is their chief merit. I shouldn't like to see them without. No, nor show myself without! Not to them!

To whom, then?

I left as early as I could. I walked homewards, becoming frozen; suddenly the nights have grown cold. I think a cold winter is on the way.

I walked on, thinking of her. I recalled the first time she came to me and asked for my help. How she suddenly bared herself and revealed her secret, quite unnec-

essarily. How warmly her cheek burned that day! I remember I said: such things must be kept secret. And she:
I *wanted* to say it. I wanted you to know who I am. Supposing I now go to her with my need, as she once came to
me? Go to her and say: It is more than I can stand,
alone, knowing who I am, wearing a mask, always, for
everyone! I must reveal myself to one other person; *one*
other must know who I am. . . .

Oh, we should both go out of our minds.

I wandered at random through the streets. I came to
the house where she lives. A light was shining in one of
her windows. No blind was drawn; she needs none, for on
the other side of the street there are only large unbuilt
sites with timber yards, and no one can look in. Nor did I
see anything, no dark figure, no arm or hand moving,
only yellow lamplight on the muslin curtains. I thought:
what is she doing now, what occupies her? Is she reading
a book, or sitting with her head in her hands, thinking; or
doing her hair for the night. . . . Oh, if I were there, if I
could be with her . . . lie there and look at her and wait,
while she does her hair in front of the mirror and slowly
undoes her clothes. . . . But not as at the beginning, a
first time, but as one time among many, in a good habit,
long enjoyed. Everything that has a beginning must also
have an end. This should have neither beginning nor end.

I do not know how long I stood there motionless as a
statue. A swollen cloudy sky, faintly iridescent with
moonlight, moved slowly above my head, like a remote
landscape. I was cold. The street was empty. I saw a
street-walker coming out of the darkness, approaching.
Halfway past me she stopped, turned, and looked at me
with hungry eyes. I shook my head: so she went away,
melting into the darkness.

Suddenly, in the lock of the door, I heard a key rattle.

It opened and a dark form glided out. Was it really she? Going out in the middle of the night, without snuffing her lamp? . . . What is this? I thought my heart would stop. I wanted to see where she was going. Slowly, I followed.

She only went to the letter-box at the corner, threw a letter into it and hurried quickly back. I saw her face under a street lamp: it was pale as wax.

I do not know whether she saw me.

*   *   *

Never will she be mine; never. I never brought a flush to her cheek, and it is not I who now have made it so chalk-white. And never will she slip across the street in the night, with anxiety in her heart and a letter to me.

Life has passed me by.

October 7

Autumn pillages my trees. Already the chestnut outside my window is naked and black. Clouds fly in thick droves over the rooftops, and I never see the sun.

I have got new curtains for my study; pure white. When I awoke this morning I thought at first it had been snowing. In my room the light was exactly as it is after a first fall of snow. I even fancied I caught the scent of snow freshly fallen. And soon it will come, the snow. One feels it in the air.

It will be welcome. Let it come. Let it fall.